PRAISE FOR C. J. WASHINGTON

"C. J. Washington's *Imperfect Lives* is an absorbing, cleverly plotted literary thriller that reveals a shocking connection between two strangers after an artist–cum–hit man's deathbed confession. Washington keeps masterful control of the psychological tension throughout the novel, twisting the narratives into a taut and unforgettable ending."

—Chris Cander, author of *A Gracious Neighbor*

"*The Intangible* is a fascinating story about a rare condition known as phantom pregnancy that had me spellbound from the start. Washington writes with great humanity, and I found myself rooting for his deftly crafted characters, who show just what it means to love and to long and to pick yourself up from the wreckage of a failed life to stagger on to something more. Inspirational and beautifully written, this is a story I will not soon forget."

—Suzanne Redfearn, #1 Amazon bestselling author of *In an Instant*

"In this excellent and emotional debut, C. J. Washington creates highly intriguing portraits of two grieving women: one dealing with a psychological condition that tricks her body into thinking she's pregnant and the other hoping her brilliant math can find the string in the universe that will allow her to talk to the dead. Well grounded in research and full of twists, *The Intangible* is like the beautiful math equation it works to solve—complex, fascinating, the answers to life's impossible mysteries within reach."

—Julia Heaberlin, bestselling author of *We Are All the Same in the Dark* and *Black-Eyed Susans*

"Washington's first novel is a brilliant portrait of human behavior, specifically how the mind evolves and devolves through time. This performance cements Washington as a powerful new force in fiction."

—*Booklist* (starred review), on *The Intangible*

IMPERFECT LIVES

ALSO BY C. J. WASHINGTON

The Intangible

IMPERFECT LIVES

A NOVEL

C.J. WASHINGTON

Little
a

Published by Little A, New York

www.apub.com

Amazon, the Amazon logo, and Little A are trademarks of Amazon.com, Inc., or its affiliates.

ISBN-13: 9781542034197 (hardcover)
ISBN-13: 9781662508066 (paperback)
ISBN-13: 9781542034180 (digital)

Cover design by Philip Pascuzzo
Cover image: © Kilito Chan / Getty

Printed in the United States of America
First edition

IMPERFECT LIVES

Prologue

This is Steve Easmon with your news on this day: Thursday, May 26, 2016. If you work with a killer for hire, what should keep you up at night? If that killer for hire is Cooper Franklin—

The screen split, and a mug shot of a man in his late forties materialized opposite Steve Easmon's likeness.

—your worst nightmare is that he will develop a terminal illness and refuse to leave the world without confessing to his many criminal acts. In Franklin's case, that's thirty-nine murders, spanning eighteen years and seven states. Franklin turned himself in to FBI agents in March, and since then, a slew of cold cases have been reopened. Thirteen arrests have been made, with authorities promising more. This man, Charles Johnson—

Cooper Franklin's image was replaced with that of a younger man wearing an orange jumpsuit.

—spent nine years in prison for a murder that Franklin confessed to. His conviction has been vacated, but many years too late: one of the numerous victims of this cold-blooded psychopath with a deathbed conscience.

~

Tamara Foster barely laughed. It was more of a titter. But her sister, Melinda, didn't let it go.

"You find that funny?" she asked. They were sitting in Tamara's living room drinking hot tea, a pastime they'd inherited from their mother: green for Melinda, white for Tamara.

Tamara turned from the news program and looked at her sister. "Kind of. Talk about bringing everyone down with you."

Melinda sniffed. "I wonder if Charles Johnson finds it funny."

"Charles Johnson probably doesn't find funny things funny. He just wishes the hit man got cancer sooner."

"You lack empathy," Melinda said.

"What?" Now, Tamara did laugh. "Excuse me for trying to stay upbeat. Sometimes you have to find nuggets of humor where you can."

"I wonder if the thirty-nine people he killed have found any nuggets of humor."

"I won't respond to that with a joke," Tamara said. "Drink your tea. I prepared it with a lot of love and empathy."

~

Cindy Fremont sat alone, so absorbed in the news segment that she didn't hear her children approach. She'd never accused either of them of being quiet, but she didn't know they were there until Cy said, "Gangsters have no honor anymore."

Cindy snapped up the remote and killed the television. She turned to find Amy, fourteen, standing next to her brother, Cy, twelve.

"What do you know about gangsters?" Amy asked Cy.

"I know the gangster code," Cy said.

"You've never met a gangster," Amy told him.

"Since when are you two interested in current events?" Cindy asked.

"We have a request," Amy said.

"Since when do you two join forces?"

"Since you read that book about sugar," Amy said. "You've been obsessed, and it's tearing the family apart. Cy has a birthday coming up."

Cindy nodded. "I'm aware. No one felt the day of Cy's birth like I did."

"I want cake and ice cream," Cy said. "The real thing. Not oatmeal cake and sugar-free ice cream."

"Cy, have you ever had oatmeal cake or sugar-free ice cream?"

Cy considered the question and shook his head.

"Go to your room and think about why I asked you that question." She turned to Amy. "Why are you here?"

"To support my brother. I want him to have a happy birthday."

"You don't even like him. You want cake for yourself. Go to your room and consider how and why you've lost your credibility."

"Can I have cake and ice cream, Mom?" Cy asked.

"If you go to your room now and do your homework, I'll consider it."

"Let's go," Amy said, turning to leave. "We can talk to Dad when he comes home."

Their father was as bad as they were when it came to junk food. Even so, Cindy had no plans to deprive Cy of cake on his birthday. She was just trying to get them to eat healthier day to day. "Your father doesn't plan birthday parties," she called to their backs. "If he ever does, it will be a month late. Minimum."

~

Cold-blooded psychopath with a deathbed conscience.

Cooper Franklin repeated those words as the news show paused for a commercial break. That had not been a good picture of him. He had no idea how many people watched Steve Easmon, but that unflattering photo annoyed him. He didn't know why. Did it matter? He was sitting in a cell, watching the tiny television from his cot. It was true that he wouldn't live long, but to say he was on his deathbed . . . well, no one watched Steve Easmon for the precision of his statements.

He was just glad the FBI hadn't leaked the conditions he'd set for his confessions. His plan required stealth. He had to ensure his family was taken care of.

Chapter 1

TAMARA

Tamara Foster surveyed the shop. It was cluttered, the aisles were too narrow, and everything was old. She couldn't turn without fear of knocking something delicate and irreplaceable to its ruin. She watched Melinda inspect a pale-pink Depression glass plate as if it were a meteorite from the heavens and not a mass-produced relic from the 1930s. It had a moderately interesting geometric pattern.

Not interesting enough.

"Are you hungry?" Tamara asked.

"I thought you ate before I picked you up?"

Tamara glanced at her watch. It wasn't that she didn't like shopping. A lack of materialism was not the problem. She liked new things, always had, the delight of being the first owner. Antiques were the problem.

"How many times," Melinda asked, "have you dragged me to the middle of nowhere to look at the sky?"

"You aren't comparing Depression glass to celestial bodies?"

"Actually, I am. There's history here." Melinda picked up a green pitcher with a leaf pattern. "People stopped buying expensive glassware during the Great Depression, so glassmakers shifted to inexpensive products. They would sell them to gas stations or movie theaters, and those businesses would gift them to customers. A piece might even come for free in a box of oatmeal."

"Like Cracker Jack prizes?"

Melinda sighed. "Sure. If that frame of reference works for you."

Tamara let the sarcasm slide because Melinda had a point about being dragged around to stargaze.

When Tamara was sixteen and Melinda twelve, Tamara couldn't have imagined they would be best friends one day. And yet, here they were.

She saw her sister most weekends, typically for an activity that included Tamara's son, Brian, and sometimes Melinda's husband, Jeff. It might be as mundane as lunch at Melinda's house, the two sisters catching up while Brian played games on Jeff's PlayStation, or an outing to the Museum of Life and Science, where Brian could sate his fascination with dinosaurs while Tamara and Melinda chatted.

Tamara changed her mind about letting the sarcasm slide. "When we observe the sky," she said, "we aren't taking our lives in our hands."

Melinda laughed. "What are you talking about?"

"Don't people get killed antiquing, violent arguments erupting over perfume bottles and cuckoo clocks?"

"Do those ladies frighten you?" Melinda asked sotto voce, nodding to a trio of white-haired women in pantsuits perusing kitchenware.

"That knife isn't insubstantial. Anyway, it's something to consider."

"No," Melinda replied, "it isn't." She held up an amber teacup with a matching saucer. "This is something to consider." She pulled out her phone to check, Tamara knew, a price guide.

They left the store forty-five minutes later, empty handed. Melinda was new to the hobby, still figuring out how to approach it. "Should I specialize or just buy whatever I like?"

The day was sunny and warm, and Tamara looked down at the sidewalk as her eyes adjusted. "Specialize," she said. "If you buy whatever you like, your collection will balloon, and soon you'll agonize over adding new pieces."

Melinda looped her arm through Tamara's. "I knew I brought you for a reason."

"No one else loves you enough to endure this," Tamara said.

They walked past a small furniture shop and a bakery before Tamara pulled her into a mom-and-pop coffee house. The moment they settled at a table with tea, Tamara's phone rang. She glanced at the screen and sent the call to voice mail.

"I assume that wasn't your neighbor," Melinda said.

"No," Tamara confirmed and sipped her tea. Brian was at her neighbor's house, playing with their son. She felt comfortable with the arrangement, as she knew they were well supervised, but things could and usually did go wrong when two eight-year-old boys played together. She kept her cell phone handy.

"A robocall? Or—" Melinda grinned. "I forgot to ask about your date. I'm sorry. I've been preoccupied. It was him, wasn't it?"

"Yes, and it wasn't a date."

"Right," Melinda teased. "Attractive guy who's clearly into you. How was your nondate dinner with a male stranger?"

"It was nice." And it had been. Mostly because it wasn't a date.

She'd initially met Kenneth a couple of weeks before at a roller-skating rink. She'd taken Brian and one of his friends, and Kenneth had been there with his daughter. They'd ended up sharing a table while the kids skated, and before they'd parted ways, he'd asked for her number.

She'd explained that she didn't date, busy widow that she was. Which was true. She hadn't been on a first date since she'd met her late husband in graduate school, a long time ago. *Instead of a date,* Kenneth had suggested, *how about two friendly people meet for dinner?* She'd agreed and, to her surprise, had a good time.

Had it been a date, it would've been stressful. She didn't know the rules for single mothers. What if she fell for a guy, only to learn that he wasn't a good fit for Brian? Perhaps she could send Brian out for first dates to screen potential partners for compatibility. It was a funny thought, and yet, she had to exist in the real world.

"So maybe," Melinda said, "the next time you meet, it will be a date."

"Or maybe not. Why have you been preoccupied?"

"Okay," Melinda said, "we're changing the subject." She hesitated. "Jeff got a job offer in Austin. A big pay increase."

Tamara felt a moment of panic. She covered it with a smile that had to be unconvincing. "That's great," she said, even as she imagined her sister moving halfway across the country. "That's huge for you two."

"He accepted the offer before he talked to me."

"Oh."

"That's what I said. He claimed it didn't make sense to pass up the opportunity. We had a big fight and agreed to table it for a few days."

"What are you going to do?" Tamara asked.

"I don't know. This all happened the night before last. I haven't really absorbed it yet."

"Do you want to talk about it?"

Melinda shook her head. "I need to think it through first."

"If you move," Tamara said, "I'm applying for an airline rewards card." The thought of it made her want to cry.

Melinda smiled. "Don't fill out an application yet. I just wanted you to know what's happening. Why do you search for extraterrestrial life?"

Tamara was taken aback by the question, by both the suddenness and the directness of it. It wasn't an unexpected question in certain social situations, especially since, in a previous life—before she'd moved to Durham, North Carolina, to enroll in a doctoral program in astrophysics—she'd been a quantitative analyst at a hedge fund. But it surprised her to realize that her sister had never asked.

"Why do I think intelligent life is out there, or why do I search for it?"

Melinda smiled, as if she knew Tamara was trying to dodge the question. "Why do you search for it?"

Tamara had pat answers for both questions, but the former was easy, dispassionate. The Milky Way, one of hundreds of billions if not trillions of galaxies, boasted a hundred billion stars and just as many planets. That immensity ensured, in Tamara's mind, that intelligent life was out there. Simple. No deflection. No deception.

Tamara found the latter question more difficult. *Why do you search for extraterrestrial life?* Typically, she began with deflection. *I study astrophysics because I find large numbers and immense scales comforting.* Sometimes, her interlocutor would respond with a familiar stab at humor: *Don't you finance folks deal in large numbers?* The easy answer was no. The manager of even the largest hedge fund would not in her professional life be required to think in septillions, the estimated number of stars in the universe. And perhaps, by now, Tamara was managing to turn the conversation in a new direction. But this was Melinda. She was asking a sincere question, and Tamara would give her a sincere answer.

"It gives me hope. When I can't find a scintilla of hope here on earth, I can imagine there's something out there that will help life make sense."

Melinda smiled. "I need a little hope right now. What do you think could be out there? What could help our lives make sense?"

Tamara shrugged. "I don't know. And that's the beauty of it. It's beyond my imagination."

"Mom thinks you're searching for extraterrestrials because you can't find Malik."

Tamara laughed. Malik was their brother, and true, Tamara couldn't find him, but that didn't make their mother's analysis any less ridiculous. "Mom is a psychologist now?"

"Mom is Mom. I take her with a grain of salt. But Malik did introduce you to astronomy. Does it make you feel closer to him?"

"Maybe," Tamara admitted. Melinda was a social worker. She'd majored in psychology and was well versed in the human condition, but still, Tamara didn't appreciate being psychoanalyzed.

She was patient with their mother, who, understandably, did not like big changes, especially in the lives of her children. Tamara's flight from her life in New York had undoubtedly been reminiscent of Malik's abrupt decision to drop out of college when he was twenty, a decision that would later be understood within the context of his burgeoning struggle with schizophrenia. Tamara had been sixteen then, Melinda twelve.

"Do you think about him often?" Melinda asked.

The question surprised Tamara, but perhaps it shouldn't have. They rarely talked about Malik. "Every day," she answered. "You?"

Melinda shook her head. "I couldn't do that. I try not to think about him."

Malik wasn't the first person with schizophrenia in their extended family, but his illness was their front-row seat to the unique ravages of delusions and paranoia. He'd upended everything, and then, four years ago, he'd disappeared. When the police had stopped looking, Tamara had hired a private investigator. She might as well have hired a psychic. Malik was gone.

"I think being an alien hunter suits you," Melinda said with a smile. "Even if it drives Mom and Dad crazy."

"I tend to refer to myself as an astrophysicist."

"You're so fancy."

~

"Please," Brian begged. It was the first official morning of his summer break, and he wanted cinnamon rolls for breakfast. "It was a hard school year."

Tamara didn't smile.

He'd used that line on Friday, the last day of school, when he'd wanted to stay up late to watch a movie. It had taken her by surprise, made her laugh, and she'd acquiesced. She didn't want to give in now. Cinnamon rolls were for the weekend. It was Monday, and the quip was old.

"Pleeeeeeease," he repeated.

She fortified her defenses. They were going bowling that afternoon, which ruled out a healthy lunch.

"Come on, Mom. Don't you ever just want to eat something that tastes good?"

Her will was eroding. She wasn't up for an argument. Besides, how much worse would it be than the cereal he normally ate? And, yes, sometimes she did just want to eat something that tasted good. "Fine, but you're eating vegetables at dinner. No complaints. You're going to ask for seconds."

He pumped his fist and retrieved a tube from the fridge. She should've known better than to buy more than two tubes at a time, but they'd been on sale.

She preheated the oven and greased a pan. She was looking forward to a week off with Brian. She had most of their days planned: strawberry picking, the trampoline park, the aquarium, and then next week he would be off to overnight camp, and she would return to the lab to work on her research. The deadline was tight, but if she could finish a paper while he was away, she could submit it to a planetary atmospheres conference meeting in Hawaii in the fall.

The oven beeped, and she put the cinnamon rolls in. She sat at the kitchen table and looked out the window at the pine trees that carpeted the backyard in needles every fall. She thought of Melinda and the likely prospect of her moving to Austin. She didn't know how heated Melinda and Jeff's argument had been or how large the pay increase was, but they would think about their lives with and without the extra money, and money, as it so often did, would win.

And Tamara would lose. Though Tamara had lived in Durham for four years, much of her social life revolved around Melinda. It was probably time to do something about that. Kenneth had called the day before and asked if she wanted to grab a friendly lunch. She'd begged off, as the week ahead was all about Brian. What would she say if he asked again next week while Brian was away at camp? Just thinking about it made her nervous.

The oven timer beeped, and she called Brian to ice the cinnamon rolls. He had a bizarre system that she chose to respect. He put all the icing on two rolls, leaving the other three bare. He gave one bare roll to Tamara, which she accepted without complaint, quickly ate the other two bare ones, and then savored the remaining rolls, sopped in icing.

When the doorbell rang, she wondered if it was Melinda. Not likely. Melinda was at work.

A man and woman dressed in dark business apparel stood on her porch. The woman introduced herself as Special Agent Smith and her partner as Special Agent Lewis. They both presented FBI badges. The man didn't speak. Neither did Tamara. Their names left Tamara's brain as quickly as they'd entered.

"Tamara Foster?" the female agent asked.

Tamara nodded.

"May we come in?"

Tamara thought immediately of Malik. Was he wanted for a crime? Was he dead?

"My son is inside," Tamara said. "He's eight years old."

"We understand," the man said. "Maybe we can speak somewhere private."

Tamara called to Brian. "I'm stepping outside. I'll be right back." He was four when Malik went missing. He knew nothing about his uncle.

She led the agents to the back of her house, to the screened-in rear patio.

It occurred to her that life could change in an instant. That's how it had happened with Malik's disappearance. There had been a moment when they'd realized he was missing. Life hadn't been the same since.

"Have a seat," she said, her voice tremulous. They did, and she did. Whatever this was, she didn't want to be alone for it. Her parents and Melinda should be here. But she'd always known it would be this way. Her parents would fall apart at the news. Melinda, the youngest, hadn't been as close to Malik as Tamara had. She alone had found and hired the private investigator. She alone would hear what the agents had to say.

"We're here about your late husband, Sam Foster," the female agent said.

Tamara sat silent, unable to process what the agent was telling her. *Sam? Why would they be here about Sam?*

The agents looked at each other, an exchange Tamara couldn't interpret. The male agent spoke carefully. "We understand that your late husband's death was ruled a suicide. But there have been developments. A killer for hire named Cooper Franklin has confessed to killing him."

Tamara gasped.

"Are you familiar with the name Jason Blakely?"

Tamara shook her head, unsure if she could speak. The name wasn't familiar.

The female agent handed her a tablet. "Do you know this man?"

It was a picture of a white male in his sixties. Tamara shook her head. "Who is he?" she asked, her voice a whisper.

The female agent answered. "Jason Blakely."

The male agent added: "We believe Blakely paid an associate of Cooper Franklin's to have your late husband murdered."

"Has he been arrested?" Tamara asked.

"We would like nothing better," the female agent said, "but he died of complications of COPD six weeks after your late husband's murder."

Chapter 2

CINDY

Cindy Fremont stepped onto the scale. "I'll wager my weight hasn't changed, plus or minus two pounds."

The nurse recorded the measurement. "Technically, two pounds would be a change."

Cindy followed the nurse to an examination room, where she dutifully submitted her arm for vitals. "Can't I just wear a watch to track this stuff?" Cindy asked as her blood pressure and oxygen saturation were measured.

"A watch can't laugh at your jokes," the nurse replied and efficiently removed the cuff and pulse oximeter. "Dr. Hughes will be with you shortly." The nurse exited and closed the door behind herself.

Cindy pulled out her phone, but before she could do anything interesting, Dr. Hughes entered. She smiled and sat on a stool in front of the computer screen. "How are you, Cindy?"

"I'm turning forty-two this year. I imagine you have new indignities in store for me."

"Nothing new," Dr. Hughes said, scanning the screen. "We'll be discussing a colonoscopy in a few years, but we aren't there yet."

"Of course," Cindy said, "because being closer to death than birth isn't insufferable enough."

Dr. Hughes turned to face Cindy and gave her a once-over. "You look great. Don't hold me to it, but I'd guess you're closer to birth. Your BMI is good. I don't get to say that often. How is your anxiety?"

"Manageable with exercise. I've been using the amitriptyline once or twice a week to help me sleep. I'm okay if I go to bed early. Bad things don't happen until after ten thirty."

"You aren't overdoing the exercise?" Dr. Hughes asked. They had this discussion every office visit. Dr. Hughes was concerned that she relied too heavily on exercise to manage her anxiety. Cindy couldn't conceive of another way.

"My body is holding up." She dreaded when it wouldn't. If she didn't fit in an hour to run or a couple of hours for a bike ride after dropping the kids off at school, she would spend the day battling all manner of negativity. Physical activity kept her sane.

"Have you considered talking to anyone?" Dr. Hughes asked. Again.

"I talk to someone every day," Cindy replied. "I've actually been thinking about talking less. One day a week when I talk to no one."

Dr. Hughes smiled. "Nothing wrong with your sense of humor."

"Thank this morning's run for that. Are you going to examine me, or are you in training to become a therapist now?"

~

The assorted ferns in Cindy's garden—navy star cloak, lady, resurrection, royal—were tucked beneath shade, but after forty-five minutes of weeding, her shirt was drenched, and she needed hydration. The pond, a perfect place to lounge with a glass of lemonade, beckoned, but the evergreens were growing disheveled, and she didn't trust herself to relax until they were tidied. Wielding clippers set her back another thirty minutes and left her weak with fatigue, done in by the Atlanta humidity. It was late May, already hot, and her body had yet to acclimatize to the change of seasons. She would be fine in a week or so, and until then, her dedication to her garden would get her through.

Ten years ago, when she and her husband, Ross, were house hunting, he'd been amused that she'd spent more time examining backyards than interiors. While he'd considered square footage, number of bathrooms, and kitchen counter space, she'd been preoccupied with prevailing winds, midday sun, and soil drainage. They'd lived in a two-bedroom apartment while Ross built up his law practice, and even when their second, Cy, was born, and they barely had space to accommodate toys, her fantasies had revolved around backyards. She'd visited native plant nurseries, strategizing the gardens she would landscape— woodlands, blooms, aquatic. In her reveries, she'd cultivated snakeroot and thistle for butterflies, honeysuckle and azaleas for hummingbirds, and black willow and buttonbush for wild bees.

Tired and hot now, she settled in the hammock beneath a chestnut oak she'd planted from an acorn when they'd bought the house. *Do you think we'll see it bloom?* Ross had asked a year later, his arm around her waist as they surveyed the seedling she'd just transplanted from a pot. The kids, unleashed with firm instructions about where they could and could not step, were playing with a ball. She'd looked at Ross, both of them young, a long future stretching before them. *I like it here,* she'd said. *My wish is to see it bloom.*

The oak was halfway to sexual maturity, and while Cindy didn't expect blooms for another ten years, it was generous with shade, and she was grateful for that as she settled with a book.

When the alarm on her phone rang, she was tempted to silence it and keep reading. But she didn't. She had errands to run and needed a shower before that.

~

"I thought you would be in court," Cindy said, surprised to find Ross in his office. The door had been closed, and she'd used her key to let herself in.

"The judge recessed early. Personal issue."

"Funny how that works. If you had a personal issue, the judge would threaten to hold you in contempt for inconveniencing the jury."

Ross laughed. "She's the judge." He hugged her before retrieving a folder from his desk drawer. "For you." He placed the papers in her hand, documents she needed to have notarized for their accountant. "Do you have a few moments?"

"Of course."

He closed the door, and the two of them sat on the couch.

"How did the morning go?" she asked.

He sighed.

"That bad. Maybe we should grab lunch. You can have a drink."

"Better not. I have a ton of prep. Honestly, I was relieved when the judge adjourned for the day. The psychologist is next on the stand, and I could use the extra time. If we make it through her testimony, Dorothy's sister will be up. That should be quick, probably no cross. We'll either rest our case, or Dorothy will take the stand. We've been back, forth, and around on that."

Dorothy Hurd, Ross's client and a former claims adjuster for an insurance company, was on trial for first-degree arson. After suffering stress in her personal life, she'd gotten so far behind at work that her days were consumed by covering up for what she hadn't done. Inevitably, her supervisor had noticed discrepancies. Dorothy had grown desperate, and one night, unable to sleep, she'd driven to the office and not so inevitably set it on fire. The flames had spread quickly, and though no one was hurt, millions of dollars in damage had been done. She faced twenty years in prison.

"I don't think the jurors like her," Ross said after recapping the morning's testimony.

Cindy was thoughtful. "She has to testify."

"That's dangerous."

"Your defense is that her abusive supervisor cultivated a toxic workplace, damaging her mental health and precipitating the arson."

Ross nodded.

"Ultimately, you want the jury to believe that her supervisor should be on trial with her and that if her supervisor can't be punished, she shouldn't be either."

"That's the subtle point," Ross agreed.

"Subtlety could land her in prison for a long time. You need to drive it home, and Dorothy is the only person who can do that."

Ross stroked his chin thoughtfully. "I've considered that. I'm worried what will happen to Dorothy under pressure. She feels very sorry for herself and has little perspective. James would—"

"Make her look bad?" Cindy asked. James Smith was the lead prosecutor. "It sounds like she already does."

Ross nodded his acquiescence. Before the prosecution had rested, he'd confided to Cindy that he was losing the case. "I'll need a sedative during her cross."

Cindy smiled. "I have plenty of those. But how about a stress ball instead?"

Now Ross smiled. "Can you imagine how that would look to the jury, me squeezing the hell out of a stress ball while James fillets my client on the stand?"

"You'll have to put on your game face," Cindy said.

"It's what I do." He sighed and stood. "I think you're right. I'll advise Dorothy to take the stand. If she agrees, we'll spend the day working on her testimony. Don't hold dinner."

"If she had just quit her job, she would be unemployed and so much better off than she is now. And you would be home for dinner."

"No one ever contacts me to ask if they should commit a crime. They always hire me after the fact. I would love to get paid to prevent crime."

"Maybe you should run an ad: 'Call me, and for a reasonable fee I'll tell you if you can get away with it.'" Ross laughed.

~

She delivered the notarized paperwork to the accountant, dropped off the dry cleaning, and stopped at the grocery store before picking up the kids.

"How was school?" Cindy asked once they were in the car, Amy in the front and Cy in the back.

"Fine," Amy said. Her vocabulary, or willingness to use it, seemed to be narrowing with age.

"Why didn't you go to college?" Cy asked.

"I didn't get the opportunity," Cindy answered, turning onto the congested road in front of the school. "Why would you ask that?"

"Everyone in class was talking about where their parents went for college. You're the only parent who didn't go."

"That settles it," Cindy said. "You're both going to public school next year."

"Great," Amy said. "I can wear Juicy Couture."

"Don't count on it," Cindy told her. "I paid too much for your school uniforms for you to stop wearing them now." Blazers with the school emblem on the breast were required year round, which meant they needed a set for cold weather and another for hot. The easiest way to meet the complex and exacting code for slacks, dress shirt, and loafers was to buy them from the officially sanctioned and exorbitantly priced uniform company.

"You'll turn us into outcasts," Amy complained.

"I'll make you trendsetters," Cindy replied.

"I am not going to public school," Cy protested. "Sixth grade is when things get good at Sembrook."

"He has a crush on Mrs. Anderson," Amy said.

"How would you know?" Cy shot back.

"Every boy does," Amy said with a knowing air. "There's nothing special about sixth grade at Sembrook. Except for Mrs. Anderson," she taunted.

"I don't have a crush on Mrs. Anderson," Cy insisted. "I just don't want to change schools."

Cindy glanced at him in the rearview mirror. "Middle school is the perfect time to switch. And there's nothing wrong with public school. I went to one."

"Is that why you didn't go to college?" Amy asked.

"What kind of question is that?" asked Cindy. "What did you two learn in school today?"

Neither child spoke.

"Just what I feared. All this money for private school, and my children aren't learning a thing. Aside from how to insult their mother."

Cy chuckled. Amy didn't respond, her eyes on the road, as if she were driving.

"What if I don't go to college?" Cy asked.

"Well," Cindy said, "I'll do a few things. First, I'll call our lawyer and have you written out of the will. Then, I'll convert your bedroom into the library I've always wanted. Third, I'll change the locks, so that you can't sneak in at night to sleep on the floor of my library. And finally, I'll change our phone numbers. That way we won't have to screen your increasingly desperate calls for money."

"You would disown your own kid?" Cy asked.

"Only if my kid didn't go to college."

"Dad would never disown us," Amy said to Cy. "Mom told me the exact same thing when I asked her what would happen if I got pregnant. I told Dad, and he said Mom has a perverted sense of humor."

"I'm sure your father said *perverse*," Cindy corrected. "He wouldn't disown you because you're his little girl and he thinks you can do no wrong. I know better. Cy, however, is not Daddy's little girl."

"Dad loves Amy more than me?"

"Of course not. Your father and I love you both equally."

"You say a lot of contradictory things, Mom," Amy said.

"That isn't true. Consider the context. I don't always speak literally."

"Whatever that means," Cy said.

"Dad said it's because of all the literature she reads," Amy said.

"It isn't easy to be the lone light in a family of philistines."

"I was born in Atlanta," Cy said.

Cindy shook her head as she turned onto their street. "True enough. And we've raised and educated you here. I'm going to talk to your principal about a partial refund on the cost of your tuition."

Cindy was startled to see a woman sitting on their front porch.

"Who is that?" Amy asked as Cindy pulled into the driveway.

"I don't know," Cindy said quietly.

The woman stood, and the shock of recognition was like a strong hand on Cindy's throat, squeezing. At once, her heart was racing impossibly fast, and her lungs couldn't pull in enough oxygen.

"Mom?" Amy said. "Are you okay?"

She concentrated on taking a deep breath. Perhaps she'd been mistaken. The woman was several yards away, stock still, just standing there. No, she wasn't mistaken. Cindy knew who it was. The face was older, gaunter, and unmistakable. How did she find me? Cindy wondered. She took another deep breath and forced calm into her voice.

"Amy, take your brother inside through the back door." She pointed in the direction away from the woman, so Amy would make no mistake about where she was to go.

"Who is that?" Cy asked.

Somehow, Cindy managed a grave but calm tone. "I swear, kids, go in the house. Watch television, play on your phones, eat cookies, do whatever you need to do. But don't ask me another question, and don't come outside until I say you can."

Cindy was grateful that her kids knew when she was joking and when she was serious. Amy and Cy got out of the car and hurried to the back of the house, as if they were performing an emergency drill. The woman, unmoving, watched Cindy warily. Cindy took a few moments and more deep breaths before waving the woman over. "Get in the car," Cindy said.

~

She backed slowly out of the driveway. She didn't feel fit to drive, and yet, to let the woman stand in front of her home for anyone to see felt even more dangerous.

"How did you find me?" she asked.

"Amelia, I—"

"Don't call me that," Cindy said. "Don't ever call me that."

"It's what I named you."

"Yeah, well, Amelia is gone."

"Right. You're going by Cindy now. Is that right?"

Cindy nodded, her eyes on the road. Another good thing about driving. She didn't have to look at her mother.

"What are you going by?" Cindy asked.

"Jessica. You can call me Mom."

Cindy snorted. "I don't know we'll be talking that long. What happened to Annalise?" Jessica was the name of the mother Cindy had known and loved. Annalise came later.

"That's a long story," her mother said. "I doubt you'll give me that long."

Cindy suppressed a wry smile. "Let's save the long stories. How did you find me?"

"Brittany gave me your address. Years ago."

"Of course," Cindy said, angry at the breach.

"She died. I thought you would want to know that."

Cindy turned right at a stop sign. She'd traveled this street many times, and yet, it felt foreign. Her mother's voice sounded foreign. Only the panic threatening to overcome her was familiar. Brittany was dead. The pain of that surprised Cindy.

"Why would I want to know that?" Cindy asked.

Her mother turned to look out the passenger window. She didn't respond. They drove in silence, and then: "She drowned. In a lake."

"Impossible. Brittany is the best swimmer I know."

"Some people say that anyone can drown. A cramp. Disorientation. Some people say she meant to drown."

Cindy didn't know what to do with that. "I guarantee you, none of those people know her." No one knew Brittany as Cindy had. No one knew Cindy as Brittany had. That had been undeniable once.

"I know things got complicated between the two of you."

Complicated? No. Sometimes hard truths were simple. She'd always thought she would see Brittany again one day. When she was ready. And now Brittany was dead. Nothing complicated about that either.

"I have a good life, Mom. I don't want you to ruin it." Her voice sounded childish to her own ears, like Amy on a bad day, but it was the sincerest thing she could say.

"Is that why you think I'm here? To ruin your life?"

"You were sitting on my porch. What if my husband found you? My kids saw you."

"They've never seen pictures of me?" her mother asked.

"They think you're dead."

"You tell people I'm dead?"

"You've been dead to me for . . ." Cindy paused to consider the passage of time.

"Nineteen years," her mother finished for her. "I didn't know what Evan was going to do to you. I didn't sanction that. He wanted to go after you, but I told him to let you go."

"And you stayed?" Cindy wiped away a lone tear. She'd worked hard to suppress the memories of her mother and the others she'd left behind.

There was a long hesitation before her mother answered, almost like a confession. "I stayed."

"Then you have no right to be here now."

"I don't have anywhere to go." Her mother's voice was plaintive. "I left my suitcase with the clerk at the extended-stay. I can't afford the room for another night, and I didn't want to show up at your house with everything I own."

Cindy's gut churned.

"I'm sorry, Amelia. I mean, Cindy. I'm sorry for everything. Don't you have regrets?"

Yes, Cindy had regrets. "I don't want you in my life. I don't want you near my children."

"Cindy." Plaintive again.

There was a time when it had been just the two of them. Surviving.

"Please, Cindy. I'm an old woman. You're the only thing I ever did right."

"You don't know anything about me," Cindy exclaimed.

"You're right. But I want to. I know you're a better woman than me. You've given your children better than I ever gave you."

"That's a low bar."

"Where do you want me to go?"

"I don't care."

"If I don't stay with you tonight, I'll sleep on a bench."

"I'll help you find a shelter."

"You don't mean that. Please, Cindy. I want to know you. I want to know my grandchildren."

Cindy tried not to remember the time before she'd left. She hadn't been angry with her mother then; they'd scarcely exchanged harsh words. Cindy's anger had built up in the intervening years. And honestly, Cindy didn't know if she was angry or scared. The past was threatening to intrude on her intricately built present. That terrified her.

"I can't believe this," Cindy said to no one in particular. Then to her mother: "You don't get three strikes. You get one. So, listen very carefully and understand how serious I am. You call me Cindy. If you call me Amelia in front of my children or my husband, you're gone. No hemming or hawing. You're just gone. Obviously, I can't bring you back from the dead, so you'll be my aunt Annalise. You shouldn't have problems remembering that name. I knew you when I was a child, but we lost touch and here you are. That's the story. Got it?"

"Thank you, Cindy. I—"

"I'm not finished. I spend most of my days in my garden. It's my sacred place, and you are not welcome there. Never set foot in my garden."

"That sounds like a commandment from the Bible."

"Take it seriously. You violate a rule, and I don't want to hear, 'I'm an old woman.' You're gone."

"What if I just tell your husband who I am and who you are?"

Cindy slammed on the brakes. Her mother cried out, her open palms striking the dashboard. Luckily, no cars were behind them.

"Maybe you should get out right here."

"I'm sorry. I don't know why I said that. The last thing I want is to cause you pain. I would never tell your family anything you haven't chosen to tell them. Any more rules?"

"That's all I can think of for now. The kids don't have much family to speak of. Ross's parents have passed away. His brother lives in Germany. They've never known a grandparent. But to be clear: You are not their grandparent. You are their aunt. Formerly estranged."

"Thank you, Cindy. I'm going to do right. You'll see."

~

Cindy felt a pang of regret the moment she walked into the living room and saw her children's faces. Cy, especially, looked traumatized as he watched the stranger standing behind Cindy. The television was on, but she doubted they'd been watching. She'd been gone for forty minutes, long enough to retrieve her mother's suitcase from the extended-stay motel, and she imagined that she'd left more than a little alarm in her wake.

"Cy," she said. "Amy. This is your great-aunt Annalise."

Cindy's mother offered a small wave and a half smile. Cy and Amy didn't move. Perhaps Cindy could've handled things better, but she didn't know how. The shock of seeing her mother after all those years—she couldn't imagine doing anything differently than she had. And she'd had no inkling that she would be introducing her mother to them forty minutes later. Awkwardness stretched as no one spoke.

"Aunt Annalise is my mother's sister. I haven't seen her since I was a child. I was in shock. That's all."

Still, the kids didn't speak. Amy sat on the sofa, and Cy sat on the floor, both of them looking up at Annalise. Cindy, in a display of hospitality, motioned for her to have a seat in a chair.

"Amy is fourteen. Cy is twelve. Amy does gymnastics and plays the flute. Cy is on the chess team."

"That's wonderful," Annalise said.

After a few moments of silence, Cindy added, "They both speak English. You'll have to take my word for it."

No one smiled.

Cindy considered taking the kids into another room and asking them not to tell their father how she'd reacted. But she'd already done enough harm. And they would want an explanation she didn't feel quite ready to give.

~

Amy and Cy were in their rooms, supposedly doing homework, when Ross came home a couple of hours after dinner. Cindy was talking to her mother at the kitchen table. The only safe subject was the kids, and she'd been prattling about Amy and Cy for a while. Ross looked exhausted.

"You won't believe who showed up on our porch," Cindy said with a smile.

Ross stared at her mother without recognition.

"My aunt Annalise."

Ross smiled. "It's great to meet you." He stepped forward and shook her hand as if he recognized the name. He couldn't, but he was being himself. Even during hostile cross-examinations, he was polite.

"Have you eaten?" she asked him.

"I ordered in at the office."

Cindy didn't comment. When he was stressed, he didn't find her cooking appealing, and he ordered in from the office. Tonight she'd made pasta and vegetables. When he was deep in a case and fretting over the jury, he preferred fried foods, and the only acceptable vegetable was a potato. "Aunt Annalise will be staying with us for a while. I already told her that you have a big day in court tomorrow. So go do what you need to do."

"Thanks, hon." He kissed Cindy on the cheek. "I just have another hour or so of prep. I'll be in my office. Welcome, Aunt Annalise."

"The case will last another two or three days," Cindy explained as Ross turned to leave. "Let me know if you want to go over anything," she called after him. He waved. He always rehearsed opening and closing statements with her, Cindy checking his performance for clarity, succinctness, and likability.

"You must be exhausted too," Cindy said to her mother. Cindy, herself, needed a moment to reflect on what she'd gotten herself into.

Once her mother was settled in the guest bedroom, Cindy wandered out to the backyard.

Night in the garden was a different world than it was in the day, especially since the cauldron of bats moved into the four wooden houses she'd had installed atop a pair of twenty-foot poles. To coax the bats to move into her backyard and for their striking white flowers, she'd planted goatsbeard, shooting star, and wild quinine. Bats had never held any appeal to Cindy, but neither had mosquito repellent. She'd taken a multifaceted approach to natural control of the pests, which included luring bats to her yard. She hadn't known it would take nearly a year for the bats to find her. Nor had she known that the efficacy of bats for mosquito control was such a hotly contested issue. But once they'd arrived, they'd become a pleasure in and of themselves. In low light, they could be mistaken for birds, but close observation of their flight revealed an unmatched grace. They were thrilling to watch. Cy enjoyed wearing an ultraviolet headlamp in the garden at night. The light would attract insects, and bats would swoop inches from his head to catch them. Cindy hadn't worked up the courage to try that.

Her love affair with bats was one she never could have anticipated. The desperate battle against mosquitoes had made bats palatable, and then their acrobatics had charmed her. Learning about the threats they faced, from destruction of their habitat to wind turbines to white-nose syndrome, had made her their champion.

In the nineteen years since Cindy had last seen her mother, she'd yearned for her only once: shortly after Amy's birth. Cindy's world had shrunk, and Amy had occupied nearly all of it. Only then had Cindy understood what it meant to be a mother. Presumably, Cindy had once been the center of her own mother's world, and she'd wanted to commune with the woman who had preceded her in the cycle. But ultimately, she'd been longing for an earlier version of her mother from a time that was done and past. Memories were just memories, and Cindy had allowed herself to be absorbed by the business of living and keeping an infant alive, and she'd chosen not to revisit the memories of her mother. She'd built a life.

And here her mother was.

Like the bats Cindy had never imagined welcoming, she'd invited her mother in. Now, she wondered if her mother would charm her as had the bats who flitted through the darkened sky over her gardens. Or would her mother destroy everything?

As if the universe were offering an answer, her mother called to her from the porch. "One minute," Cindy called back, annoyed. To her mother's credit, she hadn't entered Cindy's garden. Cindy joined her on the porch.

"There's something I didn't tell you," her mother whispered once they stood face to face. "I won't be able to sleep until I do."

Cindy glanced at the back door to make sure it was closed. "Will I be able to sleep after you tell me?"

"I don't know," her mother said.

Cindy held her breath.

"The FBI contacted me last week. They say your father paid a hit man to kill someone."

Chapter 3

COOPER

The FBI agents could sit for hours. They could maintain expressions of fascination as Cooper repeated the same detail dozens of times. They could ask a question in twenty different ways and pretend to have no clue how Cooper would answer. None of that impressed Cooper. They were doing their jobs. But he was delightfully surprised when he received the art supplies he'd requested and everything was correct down to the brands.

The agents had never heard of alizarin crimson, but here it was. The solvent was odorless, and the brushes were the style he preferred. The easel he'd used as a young man had been discontinued, but they'd found one that was close. The stool could have come from a box in his attic, where his artistic tools had been slowly degrading for the past eighteen years.

He set everything up, and though he was in a prison cell, it felt right. The lighting could be better, but he was in no position to demand perfection. It had been a long time since he'd painted and even longer since holding a brush had felt good.

As he focused on the canvas, his mind left the cell. Space and time lost their form, and he was young again, in love with art and all the possibilities it held.

~

It was the summer of 1997, and painting was Cooper's obsession. It was a singular experience, sending parts of his brain soaring while plunging others into hibernation. His body would fall away, continuing only the work essential to keep him upright at the easel as time lost its urgent qualities. On this evening, when his wife cleared her throat behind him, it might as well have been a gunshot for the jolt it sent through his nervous system.

Snatched back into the world, he turned, alarmed by Lisa's presence. He relaxed when he observed the amusement on her face. Her rounded belly pushed against her loose-fitting T-shirt as she stood, just inside the door, studying his latest, a half-finished landscape. She was a fan of his art, but she never came into the studio, not since Fernando. Six months after they'd adopted the gray-and-black tabby cat, Lisa had developed an allergy. Congestion and itchy eyes had severed her attachment to the cat, but Cooper and Fernando's bond had been unassailable. Lisa's doctor had prescribed an injectable medication, and Fernando had been banned from their bedroom. Since Cooper spent his mornings and evenings in the studio, he encouraged Fernando to make it his home. For the most part, Fernando complied. Now, he sat in his usual spot atop a bookshelf, watching Lisa with suspicion.

Cooper didn't notice the catalog tucked beneath Lisa's arm until she placed it on the table beside him. *Your Nursery Furniture Needs,* the cover proclaimed in big, bold red lettering.

"It's time," she intoned happily.

She was entering the third trimester. Five months before, they'd learned they were having twins, a boy and a girl. Lisa had been ecstatic at the news, convinced that a multiple birth was an auspicious omen. Cooper hadn't been so sure. She wanted four kids. *Want* was not a sentiment he associated with children. He saw progeny as something that came with age, like a mortgage or thinning hair, unavoidable and life altering. In the spirit of compromise, they'd settled on two. But he'd never agreed to two at one time.

He put down his paintbrush and made a show of looking at the catalog. "A nursery?" he asked. He'd thought he had plenty of time.

"Well, yeah. Our children will need a place to sleep."

"Won't they sleep in our room?"

"For a while." She squinted, despite the soft light. "Cooper." He recognized her expression. She'd had an epiphany. "You don't want to give up your studio."

"Of course I want to give up my studio," he replied, half playfully. "It has perfect light from five to seven in the summer. And close to perfect light every morning in the winter." The other half was self-pity. He didn't know these beings incubating in his wife's uterus. It was hard to believe they would just show up in three months and take his studio—the sacrosanct space where he did the only meaningful work he had. But that wasn't exactly right. They'd won even before showing up. Neither of them was even capable of surviving on their own, and Lisa was putting him on notice. She was asking him to help choose the changing table that would replace his easel.

"There's light in the basement," she told him. "It's the twentieth century. There's light everywhere."

He didn't respond. There was also space in the basement for a nursery. But Lisa might physically assault him if he suggested that. They had two bedrooms upstairs. One had served as his studio for the past three years. And he had to acknowledge that, despite the perfect lighting, he was no closer to quitting his day job.

Cooper worked at Upton Credit Union. He'd started in the mail room when he was nineteen, and eventually made a lateral move to the facilities department. On his first day, while Cooper was learning to sort mail into bins, his coworker had told him that things would get easier once he learned everyone's names. Cooper hadn't planned to learn anyone's name. He wouldn't have time. He'd met a gallery owner in Charleston, South

Carolina, the week before and wouldn't need more than two or three of the meager paychecks the credit union promised. He was glad he'd kept that thought to himself because ten years later, he still worked at the credit union. He knew everyone's name, and everyone knew him.

~

Lisa's enthusiasm carried them through the third trimester. Cooper dutifully packed his art supplies into boxes and moved them to the basement. She deluged him with catalog after catalog—furniture and accessories and clothing. Typically, she asked him to choose between two or three items she'd preselected. He would choose arbitrarily, knowing she'd be happy with any of them. She didn't offer choices she didn't like.

She encouraged him to paint some pieces for the nursery. Or a mural. He didn't tell her that he couldn't find the energy to unpack his art studio. He had several pieces in progress (dawn light filtering through a forest canopy, a curving tree-lined road, moonlight reflecting on a pond), but even the anticipation of completing them—well, it didn't feel like anticipation. His art sold for crumbs or not at all, but every time he picked up the brush, he held it with hope. But hope was feeling more and more like an illusion. Creating pieces for the nursery wouldn't offer even the illusion of the possibility of a sale, much less a break in his career.

Fernando, for his part, was protesting the conversion of Cooper's studio into a nursery. Now that Lisa's brothers, both employed in construction, were renovating, Fernando paced outside the closed door. Cooper would carry him to the basement, to the new studio, cluttered with unpacked boxes, but the cat seemed to understand that this room was no replacement. Fernando recognized a downgrade when he saw one.

~

Howard and Kathy, more often referred to as the twins, were a month old when Cooper unpacked his new art studio in the basement. He hadn't painted in four months, and during that time, beyond his awareness, a foundational shift had occurred. He wanted to blame the inferior lighting, but it wasn't that. Throughout his twenties, he'd painted near daily and felt anxiety when he didn't. He'd needed to paint. Now, the act of painting caused anxiety. Even when the house was quiet, Lisa and the twins engaged in fragile sleep, he couldn't shake the feeling as he sat at his easel that he should be doing something else. Anything else.

Maybe it was his refusal to paint pieces for the nursery. He hadn't refused, exactly; he just hadn't done it. Art required inspiration, and his inability to muster it for Lisa and the twins felt like a betrayal of their marriage. She was his fiercest champion, the only person—besides him—who believed in his dream. His mother and sister had been supportive in the beginning—as long as he held a real job. But they'd tired of asking if the promising connection he'd made with a gallery owner had borne fruit or if he'd had a good weekend at an art fair. Over time, art had fallen away as a topic of conversation. But Lisa. She believed even when his own faith faltered. She talked of Vincent van Gogh and the scant number of pieces he'd sold during his lifetime. *I've mastered failure,* Cooper would tease; *now I just need to die tragically.*

He lay on the couch in his studio and listened to talk radio. Without painting, he was bored. Even his boredom felt wrong. Lisa certainly wasn't bored. *I feel like a machine,* she'd lamented: *a milk-dispensing, comfort-giving, diaper-changing machine. And not a well-designed one.* She couldn't understand why applying her breasts to their God-given purpose made her nipples so sore. To Cooper, the twins were machines: eating, crying, waste-dispensing machines. He'd feigned rage at the credit union for not providing paternity leave. *They barely pay me,* he'd griped—all to conceal his relief. He couldn't imagine spending every waking hour on call for the twins. He changed diapers after work and did his best to calm a wailing twin, but neither of them ever seemed comforted by him. The feeling was mutual.

He considered going to look for Fernando. Though he hadn't been painting, Cooper had been spending his evenings in the basement. Fernando, meanwhile, had yet to accept their exile. Lisa had found him in the nursery a couple of times and, after chasing him out, had dictated that the door remain closed. Another room where Fernando wasn't welcome.

Cooper felt indignation on his behalf.

He also felt betrayed by Fernando.

During the time they'd occupied the upstairs studio, Cooper had been under the misconception that Fernando loved the space because he, Cooper, was so often there. Their banishment was enlightening, painfully so, because though Cooper had moved, Fernando showed no interest in following. Was their bond genuine? Cooper's feelings for Fernando no doubt were, but he had no evidence that Fernando felt anything for him at all.

He couldn't talk to Lisa about it.

"I feel betrayed by my cat," he said aloud to the empty space, just to see how the words sounded. In the best of times, Lisa would have struggled to empathize with that. The harried mother she'd become would likely scoff.

~

By six months, the twins had mastered sleeping through the night. Still, Lisa fretted about moving them into the nursery.

"The crib," Cooper pointed out, "is so much nicer than the pack and play." They'd yet to sleep in their crib. Even for naps, Lisa put them in the pack and play at the foot of his and Lisa's bed.

"Won't you miss having them close?" she asked.

He nodded, though he couldn't see what there was to miss. "They're growing up," he said.

On that night, their first in the nursery, Howard had an asthma attack. Lisa rushed him to the hospital, while Cooper paced the master bedroom, an inconsolable Kathy cradled in his arms. "Your brother will be okay," he whispered, pausing occasionally to sway gently. She didn't stop screaming. He could tell she didn't believe him.

～

"It's the cat," Lisa informed Cooper when she returned home. She put Howard down and picked Kathy up. She'd never been apart from Kathy for so long.

"How do you know?" Cooper asked.

Lisa didn't know. Not for certain. Allergies, the pediatrician on duty had told her, can precipitate an asthma attack. That it was their first night in the nursery was circumstantial evidence.

"Let's not speculate," Cooper said, "until we get the results of the allergy test."

When the allergy test results came back, they were positive for cat dander.

"What about medication?" Cooper asked.

"His lips were blue," Lisa said, horrified.

Yes, they had been. Cooper had seen.

Lisa glared at Cooper, and he couldn't meet her eyes.

～

As with any effective intervention, Cooper was trapped before he realized what was happening. The twins were upstairs and asleep in the pack and play in the master bedroom. Cooper sat in the recliner in the living room. His mother and sister sat together on the rarely used love seat. Lisa and her mother flanked him on the couch.

"Do you mind if I turn this off?" Lisa pointed the remote at the television.

Cooper did mind, but the *What's Happening!!* rerun was replaced by a black screen before he could respond.

"Do you understand what asthma is?" his mother began.

Cooper nodded.

"The airways narrow," his mother continued as if he didn't understand, "making breathing difficult."

"We all need to breathe," his sister added.

Cooper wouldn't argue with that.

His mother-in-law cut to the chase: "The cat has to go."

"We know you love Fernando," Lisa said quickly. "And we love you. But—"

~

The management and maintenance of paper records was Cooper's primary duty at Upton Credit Union. He maintained the storeroom on the eighteenth floor, accessible only by the building's freight elevator. It was a large windowless room packed with floor-to-ceiling shelves of steel and particleboard, straining beneath the weight of Bankers Boxes. It was home to records that were pulled often, such as mortgage applications and documents, as well as records with a short shelf life. Other documents were sent off site for storage, and Cooper maintained the paper trail for those.

Weekly, he destroyed documents past their retention date to make space for new paperwork that he collected from various departments. The storage room was gloomy and isolated. The bustling credit union offices were on the fourth through eighth floors, and Cooper, for the most part, was the sole visitor to the eighteenth floor. His supervisor, George Bides, had a key, but he never used it. When Cooper took vacation, he would invariably return to a pile of document requests. An emergency was required to get George to the eighteenth floor.

The idea had dawned slowly, and the more he'd thought about it, the less ridiculous it seemed. The storage room would be a safe place for Fernando to live until Cooper figured out other arrangements.

His mother had offered to take Fernando. *You can visit him whenever you like,* she'd said. But every time he thought about Fernando living with his mother, he remembered Oscar, his childhood chameleon, desiccated on the terrarium floor. When Cooper was twelve, he'd spent the week with his grandparents in Florida. All his mother had to do was spray the inner walls of the terrarium daily to keep them moist—marginally more difficult than caring for a houseplant. But she hadn't, and Oscar, not even a year old, had succumbed to dehydration.

Two days after the intervention, Cooper arrived at work an hour early with a scratching post and a litter box. The following day, an hour early again, he carried Fernando, tucked into his travel bag, and a few toys.

Fernando had to be coaxed out of the bag, possibly because, every time Fernando left the house, he was poked and prodded by the vet. But even when no vet appeared, Fernando didn't seem impressed. The rows were narrow, and the shelves, packed tight with boxes, weren't ideal for climbing. Cooper showed Fernando the litter box in a back corner and the scratching post hidden behind the third row. "It isn't our studio," Cooper said, "but it's only temporary. Just until I figure something out."

～

It felt like another intervention. Cooper sat in one of the two chairs facing Sheila Daniels's desk. George sat beside him. Following a long, uncomfortable silence, Sheila spoke first. She was the human resources manager at the credit union.

"I don't know where to start."

Cooper wasn't comforted by the remark. When he'd arrived at work that morning, he'd found a note from George on his desk asking him to report to Sheila's office. He'd considered a quick trip to the eighteenth floor to check on Fernando and give him fresh water, but Bethany, George's assistant, had told Cooper that George was with Sheila, waiting for him. *Why?* Cooper had asked. Bethany had looked at him like she'd known something. *That's what I want to ask you, Cooper. Why?*

Now in Sheila's office, George cleared his throat. "Cooper, I'm sure you've heard the rumors about the merger?"

Yes, Cooper had heard the rumors. States Credit Union, a larger institution, was in talks to swallow the smaller Upton Credit Union. Everyone was talking about it. Duplicate jobs would likely be cut. The larger credit union's leadership would likely decide who would go. The small guys were antsy.

"A few executives from States Credit Union visited this morning. I came in an hour early to give them a tour of the storage facilities."

Suddenly, Cooper's breakfast wasn't sitting well. "Our storage room?"

George nodded.

"On the eighteenth floor?" A bead of sweat rolled down Cooper's rib cage.

"The only one we have," George confirmed.

"Unfortunately," Sheila said, "their vice president of operations is severely allergic to cats."

~

"They were probably going to lay me off anyway after the merger." As Cooper drove, he spoke to Fernando, who sat quietly in the travel bag on the passenger seat. "This way, they don't have to pay me severance. Pricks."

Fernando was agitated. Probably because he thought he was going to the vet. Cooper was agitated too. He wouldn't qualify for unemployment.

"I've been in that job for too long anyway," he told Fernando. "This is a good thing. *Family comes first*," he said, mocking Upton Credit

Union's CEO. "What about my family? What about you?" he asked the cat. "Screw this. I'm an artist, Fernando, not a damn facilities gofer."

On the other hand, he'd really only made money as a facilities gofer.

He made an arbitrary right onto Camp Creek Parkway. He didn't know where he was going. He couldn't go home. Not with Fernando. Lisa thought Fernando was at a no-kill animal shelter. She thought that because, three weeks ago, he'd told her that Fernando was at a no-kill animal shelter. He couldn't tell her that he'd been fired for . . . Why had he been fired? He'd read the stupid handbook. There was nothing in there about cats not being allowed on the premises. And what was with all the people with cat allergies? Was there an evolutionary explanation, some environmental advantage, that explained cat allergies? Cooper couldn't think of one.

Beneath the rage and anxiety, a notion, like a point of illumination in the dark, percolated, unfolding into hope. "I'm an artist," Cooper repeated, even if his evidence consisted solely of unsold paintings. He would use this experience. He would take his newfound free time and create the realest art yet. He had children now. Two of them. He was finished playing at art, painting on the evenings and weekends after giving his best hours to the credit union. "This isn't over, Fernando." His voice was resolute, even to his own ears. "It's just the beginning."

~

It was a small, unfurnished room with an attached bathroom. There was no kitchen, but it had a private entrance. The neighborhood was sketchy, the house run down, but the woman only wanted $200 a month. "And a security deposit," she added. "Nonrefundable."

"How much?" Cooper asked.

The woman looked to the sky and bit her lip. "$273," she said.

Cooper agreed, though he suspected she'd invented the security deposit figure on the spot. She'd probably seen something she wanted to buy and was making him cover it to the dollar. But she let him move in immediately, and he was grateful for that.

"It's only temporary," he told Fernando. The cat refused to come out of his travel bag. "I know. It's been a lot."

Cooper had boarded Fernando for three days while he'd searched for an apartment. Fernando would live here, and Cooper would paint here. That was the plan.

He scattered treats on the shaggy orange carpet just outside the travel bag. Fernando didn't budge.

Still, Cooper felt optimistic. In this poorly lit room with dingy walls, Cooper would create the art he'd only managed to envision until now. Late one night, unable to sleep, he'd seen a documentary on F. Scott Fitzgerald. Poorly paid, abandoned by Zelda, he'd placed his hopes in writing. His triumph inspired Cooper, though Cooper would not follow his own triumph with alcohol dependency. Also, he and Lisa probably wouldn't travel to Europe as much as F. Scott and Zelda had, because honestly, who wanted to deal with intercontinental flights and unpronounceable food? He just needed to make enough money to buy a house with a detached room for Fernando. "Please come out," he begged the cat.

Fernando wouldn't look at him.

~

Fernando wasn't only ignoring Cooper. He was ignoring the litter box. When Cooper returned the following morning with new art supplies (new supplies for a new mentality), he found spots of urine on the orange carpet. The treats and Fernando's regular food were untouched. Cooper noticed, with chagrin, that the little bastard was still drinking water.

Because Fernando had always been a model cat, Cooper didn't know how to clean cat pee out of carpets. He went to a pet store and bought a special solution, and the morning was gone by the time he set up his new easel.

Lisa thought he was at work. He hadn't changed his morning routine. He regretted not being able to share his excitement with her. He was a full-time artist now. The credit union had paid him for his unused vacation time, and he had some savings. He would tell Lisa everything once he'd sold a painting for a shockingly large sum. They would celebrate and laugh. And laugh. And laugh.

~

Cooper sat alone in the exam room. There was a collage of dog photos on the wall, but none of cats. Cooper had worried about that the first time he'd brought Fernando here as a kitten. It wasn't universal, but pet owners seemed to divide into camps: dog people and cat people. Cooper was an unequivocal cat person, and he didn't want Fernando to see a vet who was biased toward dogs. It occurred to Cooper that Fernando might note the dog pictures and wonder why his kind didn't merit space on the wall, but he'd dismissed that concern, reluctantly, as anthropomorphizing. At any rate, Dr. Rottler had assuaged Cooper's concerns upon their first meeting. The vet had been thorough and concerned, and he'd taken time to answer Cooper's questions.

Dr. Rottler, tall and lean and wearing an impeccably white lab coat, entered the room and looked around. He smiled at Cooper. "Is Fernando hiding?"

"I didn't bring him."

"Oh," Dr. Rottler said. "The nurse didn't mention that." He sat on a stool and placed Fernando's chart in his lap. "How can I help today?"

Cooper had been going back and forth about how much to tell Dr. Rottler. He didn't want to jeopardize Fernando's care by concealing information.

"Are you and I covered by veterinarian-patient confidentiality?" Cooper asked.

Dr. Rottler smiled. "Technically, Fernando is my patient. But yes, his medical records are privileged and can only be released with your consent."

"If I tell you something in confidence that impacts Fernando, are you bound to confidentiality?"

Dr. Rottler was thoughtful. "No one has ever asked that before. And I field a lot of interesting questions."

"Let's narrow it down. If I share information that I don't want my wife to hear, are you bound by confidentiality not to tell her?"

Dr. Rottler nodded. "I see. I can keep a secret, if that's what you're asking. I've never met your wife, and I've been treating Fernando for"— he glanced through the chart—"three years. Will she be asking me to divulge anything from this conversation?"

Cooper shook his head. "She doesn't know I'm here."

"I should warn you. I am ethically bound to report animal abuse. So, if you share anything about an inappropriate relationship with Fernando . . ."

"What?"

"Well, I wouldn't contact your wife, but I'd be ethically bound to report—"

"Wait," Cooper interrupted, "we're getting afield."

He began with his and Fernando's eviction from the home art studio with perfect lighting. He told Dr. Rottler everything, ending in the dingy room with shaggy orange carpet. Dr. Rottler nodded sympathetically as Cooper spoke. "We've been there for two weeks, and he won't stop peeing on the carpet. He's started to eat again, a little, but he's living in the travel bag. That isn't like him."

"That's quite a story," Dr. Rottler said. "Cats often get attached to places and crave routine. You've both had a lot of disruption."

Cooper bit his lip. He didn't want to get emotional, but it was a relief to share, and Dr. Rottler's empathy was moving.

"This isn't at all uncommon," Dr. Rottler continued. "Well, aspects of your particular experience are uncommon, but Fernando's reaction is not surprising. I've had a lot of success treating this type of behavior with fluoxetine. You probably know it as Prozac."

"You think Fernando is depressed?"

"Depression. Anxiety. Something is amiss. Unfortunately, it can take a few weeks to see the full effects, but I've had good results in the past. Shall we try it?"

Cooper replied in the affirmative.

"I'll write a script. Is there anything else? You still seem troubled."

Cooper hesitated. "I'm an artist, but I haven't been able to paint. I felt so motivated when I rented the apartment, but I'm no F. Scott Fitzgerald."

"Zelda Fitzgerald," the veterinarian said.

"What?"

"F. Scott was a writer. Zelda Fitzgerald was a painter. I saw a documentary."

"I've spent the last two weeks staring at a blank canvas. I can't produce anything. I'd have better luck slitting my carotid and hoping for interesting splatter."

"Well," Dr. Rottler said, looking at his watch, "I'd better get that prescription. Best of luck to you." He smiled. "Scratch Fernando behind the ear for me."

~

"Are you okay?" Lisa asked.

Cooper was sitting on the edge of their bed, staring out the window, a view overlooking their front yard. He turned to her. She looked tired. As usual. Atypically, however, she wasn't holding one or both twins. It was midmorning on a Saturday. He needed to check on Fernando.

"Yeah." He stood. What did it mean to be okay, anyway? Did it mean that life had purpose? Did it require gainful employment? Did it mean being honest with your spouse about where you spent your days, how you spent your time?

"You don't seem like yourself lately. How is your painting coming?"

"It's coming." He pulled on a T-shirt. In truth, he hadn't painted a thing.

"How about work?"

He paused to look at her. Did she know something? "It's a job. Same as usual."

"You never talk about it," she said.

He sat on the chair to put on socks and shoes. "What?"

"Work. Art. Anything."

"I've been doing both for ten years. Nothing new to say about them."

~

What would he say to Lisa? *Oh, you thought I've been going to work?*

Telling the truth would make things easier. The only thing more depressing than spending his days in an empty apartment with a cat was pretending to come home from work in the evenings.

On the positive side, the Prozac seemed to be working. Fernando was using the litter box again, and he'd stopped sleeping in his travel bag. That was something.

For his part, Cooper spent too much time thinking.

As he merged onto the expressway now, headed toward Fernando's place, he was thinking. If he couldn't paint, he would have to get a job. But the thought of working another dead-end job—this time without even the prospect of being rescued by art—was unbearable. He might as well sell his soul to the devil while it still had value.

He missed talking to Lisa. She was his primary support system. He couldn't even talk to his friends because their wives were Lisa's friends.

Cooper knew that every secret (interesting ones, anyway) was shared with one other person, often a spouse. He couldn't trust anyone. And really, what was there to say? *I hate art.*

He settled into the fast lane and called Fernando's vet's office. Dr. Rottler was with a patient, but the receptionist promised that he would call back before the office closed, which would be early because it was Saturday.

His landlady had asked him not to park in the driveway, so he parked in the street in front of the house. If she'd noticed that he never spent the night, she hadn't mentioned it. She didn't show any interest in him beyond his ability to pay her. He appreciated that.

"Fernando," he called. "I'm home." He closed and locked the door behind himself. The cat didn't come out. It was just as well. Cooper was angrier than usual today and probably wouldn't make the best company.

He turned on the radio and sat on a beanbag he'd purchased from a thrift store once Fernando had stopped treating the place like a giant litter box. His phone rang, and he pulled it from his pocket.

"Dr. Rottler," Cooper answered.

"The one and only," the vet replied jovially. "How is Fernando?"

"Really good. Not a social butterfly today, but he's eating and using the litter box."

"Glad to hear it."

"I was wondering, would you like to grab a beer? Once you finish up. I'm just hanging here with Fernando, and I don't know how long I can keep this up. My wife is on to me. My savings are running out. I'm barely contributing to the household. We spend a fortune on day care while I do nothing all day. I help with the twins at night, but I'm the B team. Anyway, how about a beer?"

"A beer?"

"Yeah, we can catch up. I feel like I can talk to you."

"I'll have to pass."

"Too bad. Maybe next time."

"Cooper."

"Yeah."

"I once had to file a restraining order against a patient's owner. I never want to do that again. You understand what I'm telling you?"

Cooper was startled by banging on the door. Probably his landlady. "I've got to go." He hung up without a reply and stood to answer the door.

"Cooper! Open up. I know you're in there."

It was Lisa.

~

"I thought you were going to the hardware store," she yelled.

Cooper was still trying to understand what she was doing there. She held a twin in each arm. That wasn't unusual, but she was standing on the threshold of Fernando's apartment.

"Who's in there?" She tried to see around him into the apartment.

He stepped outside and closed the door. "You don't want to go in there."

"Don't you dare tell me what I want."

Kathy—distinguishable by her pink onesie—began to cry. Howard twisted up his face but remained silent.

"You're scaring the kids." He motioned to the small babe in her right arm.

"You want to lecture me about being a parent? What are you doing, Cooper? Who did you come here to see?"

Cooper tried to take Kathy from her arm. Lisa pulled her out of reach. Howard opened his mouth and joined his sister in a wailful harmony.

~

Cooper stared at the television, an old western, not absorbing any of it.

"My mother is here to watch the twins. Let's take a walk."

Cooper stood. Those were the first civil words Lisa had spoken since confronting him at Fernando's place that morning. After much screaming, she'd let him take the twins while she inspected the apartment. *It smells like cat pee in here!* she'd yelled. Cooper had stayed outside with the twins, keeping them safe from cat dander. He'd known what Lisa was seeing: a scratching post, a stool and easel, unused paint and brushes, a radio, a beanbag. She'd reappeared. *You aren't having an affair in there.* And still, she'd been furious.

Now they walked in silence. Cooper didn't know what to say. After confessing everything in the backyard of Fernando's place, both twins screaming, he'd apologized repeatedly and profusely until she'd told him to stop talking. He wasn't going to start talking now.

"It occurred to me," she finally said, "that I haven't been paying enough attention to you. I should have realized that you couldn't let go of Fernando so easily."

Cooper nodded. "You've been so busy with—"

She put up a hand. "Before you say anything, Cooper, you should know that was a fleeting thought. This is in no way my fault."

"You're right," he said, chastened.

"Why didn't you let your sister take Fernando? She told me she offered."

"Do you remember Sampson?" Cooper asked.

Lisa nodded. "Your sister's ex-boyfriend."

"I don't know if I told you this, but he was arrested at a dogfight."

"I think I remember something about that. She didn't know he was a dogfight enthusiast. Didn't she break up with him?"

"She should've been a better judge of character. I can't have her bringing men like him around Fernando."

Lisa sighed. "I will find a loving home for Fernando," she said. "Do you trust me to do that?"

Now, Cooper sighed. He nodded.

"I know that fatherhood has been an adjustment for you. Having twins doesn't make it easier. For either of us. I've tried to give you space." She glanced at him. "Too much, obviously. Because I know"— her voice cracked—"that you're going to be a wonderful father once you find your rhythm. You'll care for the twins just as you've cared for Fernando. While you search for your rhythm, I'll just have to accept that I have three kids." She smiled and took his hand. "You're going to find a new job, and you're going to paint again."

"For the first time since I picked up a paintbrush, I can't imagine painting again."

"If you don't, it will be okay. I believe you will, but it's okay if you don't. The only thing I expect of you is to be a husband and father."

"I can do that."

"But you do have to stop being an idiot."

~

Cooper painted until the pain in his back was too much. He stood and stretched, wondering if it was the cancer, the stool, the cumulative effects of sleeping on a prison cot, or a combination of them all. He was at a good stopping point, and he finally knew the name of this painting, the first he'd completed in nineteen years: *Losing a Friend*. He labeled it, and then he lay down to sleep.

Chapter 4

TAMARA

When Brian was three, Tamara had delighted in his predictability. When the two of them would arrive home, he would run through the house screaming *Daddy!* at the top of his lungs until he found Sam. Sam could be standing in the kitchen, clearly visible from the doorway, and Brian would fit in one shout before barreling into his father's legs.

On a Saturday afternoon, following a playdate in the park, Tamara and Brian were both puzzled when Brian's search stretched for a full minute. Tamara decided that Sam must have stepped out for a walk, which was odd because they had tickets to see *Winnie the Pooh* in forty-five minutes. It would be Brian's first movie in a theater, and Sam had been more excited than Brian. He would not have wanted Brian to miss the previews.

When she first glimpsed the brown of his skin against the white marble of the bathtub, she thought she was seeing things. Sam didn't take baths. He was a shower kind of guy.

What are you doing? she asked once she realized what she was seeing. But, still, she didn't really realize what she was seeing. Not at first. She'd managed to shut and lock the bathroom door moments after Brian ran into their bedroom but before he could reach the master bath.

Daddy!

Tamara frantically checked for a pulse while Brian banged on the bathroom door.

Brian, honey, Tamara called through the closed door as she pushed Sam's leg aside to pull the stopper from the drain. *Your daddy isn't here. I need you to get Bear for me. He's by the back door.* Bear was his favorite stuffed animal. Once snow white, now a shade of gray and growing darker, Bear went everywhere Brian went. Dropping him just inside the door upon arriving home was another predictable behavior.

She'd listened to the sound of Brian's receding feet before she opened the door. And just as she was closing it behind herself, she saw the bathroom mirror, the chilling scrawl in red lipstick: *I'm sorry.*

~

Tamara sat on the edge of her bed and stared into the blackness outside the window. She'd managed to fall asleep three and a half hours ago, but now she was awake and restless. The FBI visit, their words, as nonsensical as they'd been, seemed to float in front of her eyes in flickering fluorescence: *We believe Blakely paid an associate of Cooper Franklin's to have your late husband murdered.* She'd had more than twelve hours to process their visit, and still, she felt as if she were hearing the words for the first time.

For years, she'd been haunted by Sam's suicide, wondering what he'd felt in those moments before taking his own life. Now, she was haunted by his murder, wondering how it had happened. Postmortem toxicology had revealed barbiturate levels high enough to induce unconsciousness, but the cause of death was asphyxiation by drowning. How exactly did one stage that? The horror of the potential answers drove her from the bedroom to the kitchen to mop the floor. She needed distraction.

She'd googled a picture of Cooper Franklin shortly after the FBI left. She didn't know why, but she wanted to look into the eyes of the man who'd murdered her husband. The experience was anticlimactic. She found his mug shot, the photo she'd seen on the news broadcast, along with a more natural photo attached to an article about an art gallery. He had a face she'd seen many times before: brown skin, high-wattage smile encircled by a goatee, a face she could quickly forget.

Murder. The word still felt raw, so different in nature from *suicide. Murder-for-hire plot.* It didn't make sense.

Who would want Sam dead?

There was no list because Tamara couldn't think of a single person. Sam had been an anonymous quant who devised mathematical models to manage risk at an investment bank. If investors had made or lost money, they wouldn't have thanked or blamed Sam. They wouldn't have known Sam existed. He went to work before the sun rose and came home after it set. He and Tamara had a standing dinner date on Friday nights, and on weekends they did family stuff—playgrounds, children's museums, hikes. He liked to read novels and play video games.

Was he involved in something she wasn't aware of?

Or was it a case of mistaken identity?

Tamara couldn't imagine how Sam was connected to Jason Blakely, a retired car salesman who lived in Atlanta. Atlanta. Sam was born and raised there, but he'd only purchased one car in his life: a 2005 Prius. They were living in Connecticut at the time, still sharing the Ford that Tamara had been driving since graduate school. Why would he have ties to a car salesman in Atlanta?

She exchanged her mop for a duster and started in the living room. She moved quietly so as not to wake Brian, who was sleeping upstairs. There was no way she could explain why she was cleaning at this hour.

Brian knew his father had died—she'd had to tell him—but he didn't know anything of the circumstances. She didn't think so, anyway. One evening when Brian was five, they were watching a movie that ended with the cartoon villain trapped on a desolate world where he could never hurt anyone again. *Is he going to kill himself?* Brian had asked.

Tamara had lost her breath, the silence stretching for a long while before she could respond. *Where did you hear about people killing themselves?* She'd tried to say it nonchalantly, but her nervous system was raging.

I don't remember, Brian said. And they'd left it at that.

For days afterward, she'd probed, gently trying to tease out what the boy knew about his father's death. The answer, it seemed, was nothing.

She'd dreaded the day when she would have to tell Brian about his father's suicide.

Will it be easier, she wondered now, *to tell him that his father was murdered?*

Yes, Tamara decided. She would never have to answer the dreaded question: *How could my father choose to leave me?*

~

When Tamara awoke for a second time, the sun was up, and her father's lilting voice rose from downstairs. For a moment, she thought she was in her childhood bedroom. And then the memories rushed back: The FBI agents, showing themselves out, depositing their business cards on her glass-top table in case she remembered something. Calling Melinda at work and, half an hour later, her sister pulling into her driveway. The day had passed in a fog, and her sister was there for all of it, watching after Brian, making sure they all had food. Tamara didn't speak to her parents, but Melinda did. *They'll be here in the morning,* Melinda told her at some point the night before. And here they were, following a six-hour drive from Atlanta.

"I'm glad you're not waking too early," her father said when she made her way to the kitchen. It was nearly 10:00 a.m.

"I am," she told him. "You just wouldn't know it." She glanced at the floor, still shiny from her middle-of-the-night cleaning.

When she was growing up, her father had a rule against sleeping past 9:00 a.m. on weekends. She and Melinda and Malik had hated it. When Malik was sixteen, he'd threatened to find shift work over the summer. It would've worked. Above all, their father revered a strong work ethic.

"Have some juice," her mother said and then poured a glass. She set it at the kitchen table. From the looks of things and the lingering smell of toast, her mother had already served breakfast and cleaned the dishes. Tamara sat in front of the juice, across from her father. Brian wandered in, trailed by Melinda.

"It's like Grand Central," Tamara commented with a quick smile for Melinda.

Her father regarded her. "There was a time when I asked you useful questions," he said. "'Where is the economy headed? Should I put money in stocks or bonds?' Now, I guess I'll ask if you've spoken to any Martians lately?"

"Terry," her mother said sharply with a stern look at her father.

When Tamara quit her job in finance, she hadn't shared with her parents her interest in the search for extraterrestrial intelligence or her desire to one day work for the SETI Institute. For good reason. Melinda's husband had let that nugget slip over a family dinner.

"Actually," Tamara replied, "I spoke to an alien last week, though she wasn't from Mars. She told me her civilization has no concept of fatherhood and asked what a father is. I told her that I only had one, so my definition was anecdotal." Tamara paused.

"Yeah?" her father said gruffly.

"Yeah. I told her a father is someone who uses his children to right the disappointments of his own life."

"Stop it, you two," Tamara's mother admonished and then placed a plate of raisin toast in front of Tamara. "Brian is going to think you're serious."

"I am serious," Tamara said. "What do you think I tell Brian when he asks about his grandfather?" She winked at Brian, who was pouring himself a glass of orange juice.

"I'm serious too," her father said. "What do you think I tell my friends when they ask what my children are up to? One of my daughters is saving the world. The other is searching for life in space."

Tamara glanced at her mother, and then at Melinda, searching for the slightest hint of consternation. No one besides her seemed bothered by Malik's exclusion from her father's remark. But what did she expect her father to say? *My son is—actually, I have no idea. I can't even prove he's alive.* That would put a damper on things. And that was the opposite of what the banter between her and her father was meant to do. Her father wanted to know that she was okay, but he would never ask the question. You had to know him to identify his affection.

"Ignore them, Mom," Melinda said. "You're just encouraging it."

Their father had been strict in their youth, but he wasn't overly judgmental of his adult children. He wanted them to have opportunities he hadn't. The son of poor Black farmers in Mississippi, he'd been drafted to fight in Vietnam, a country he'd never heard of engaged in a conflict he didn't understand. He didn't learn about college deferments until he returned two years later, and he'd been bitter about them ever since. Not because he would've gone to college had he known, but because he hadn't finished high school, and college had never been an option for him.

He never spoke of his experience at war, but Tamara and her siblings had been raised on tales of American inequity. In high school, Tamara wrote a paper on the injustices of the Selective Service System during the Vietnam War. She learned that college deferments hadn't worked exactly as he'd thought—an automatic get-out-of-war-free card—at least not after 1965, but she'd never shared that with him. It was indisputable that poor men like her father had far fewer deferment options.

She admired her father. He'd earned his GED after returning from the war, only to learn that Vietnam vets didn't qualify for free college as World War II vets had—another point of bitterness for him. He got a job as a mail carrier for the post office and worked his way up to postmaster, a position he still held—would hold until his retirement in ten months. He'd done well for himself, but he'd always felt that he could've done better with more opportunity. Hence, he'd kept his teenagers on the straight and narrow. They, he was determined, would do better.

When Tamara switched careers, he wasn't disappointed so much as perplexed. She went from making a lot of money to making a little money. She was thirty-two and poised for career advancement. That meant a lot to a lifetime postal employee. Her mother, on the other hand, was beside herself, especially when she'd learned that her daughter meant to devote herself to the search for extraterrestrial life.

"We spoke to Brian this morning," her mother said, addressing Tamara. "We would like to take him back to Atlanta with us. We'll send him back by plane before camp starts."

Brian watched Tamara expectantly.

"If that's what you all want," Tamara said, not even annoyed that her mother had asked in front of Brian. She didn't feel fit to care for herself, much less an eight-year-old.

"Will you manage okay by yourself?" her mother asked with a pointed look that told Tamara she was masking her true concern for Brian's benefit.

She nodded. "I'll spend some time in the lab."

"Then it's settled," her father said as Brian beamed.

∼

Tamara's family had a way of handling things, effectively and efficiently, without talking about them. Her parents swooped in on the news of Sam's murder and departed three days later with Brian and his suitcase in the back seat of their car. Scarcely had Sam been mentioned. She imagined hushed conversations had occurred, her parents huddled with Melinda to discuss what was best for Brian. *To be far from his mother* had apparently been the answer.

Tamara was grateful. She needed the space and time, and she hadn't had to ask for it. Alone with Melinda, she could speak freely. "There were days," she said, the two of them in her living room, a bottle of red wine between them, "when I hated Sam for killing himself. And I felt shame. I found it humiliating that my husband committed suicide."

Melinda listened with sympathy.

"I felt like I failed him for not being enough to live for. Now, I think I failed him for not seeing who he truly was."

"How could you?" Melinda asked. "Everything pointed to suicide."

"Everything couldn't have pointed to suicide because it wasn't suicide. He left no note. He wouldn't have done that, left us with nothing. I should have recognized that, and I should've pushed the police to investigate foul play." She hadn't known then that police detectives could let her down. She hadn't learned that until Malik disappeared. In the wake of Sam's death, she hadn't pushed back on the narrative.

"You were told Sam committed suicide, so you found a way to make sense of it. No one can fault you for that."

Tamara nodded, though she was unconvinced. And there was something else. Sam's suicide made too much sense.

Three weeks before Sam's murder, he'd been hospitalized for depression. Whoever had him murdered must've known that. Staging it like a suicide was too much of a coincidence otherwise. But Tamara couldn't imagine that this was anything other than mistaken identity.

"Can we talk about something else? Anything else?"

"Okay," Melinda said. "Let's talk about antiquing."

"Let's talk about your marriage."

Melinda laughed, nearly spitting out a mouthful of wine. "Of course you'd bring that up."

"Did you tell Mom?"

"Of course not. I'm enjoying my current role as model child, the one who doesn't cause worry."

Now, Tamara laughed. "Things are never what they seem."

"No, they aren't," Melinda agreed. "You know what really pissed me off? I told Jeff that I didn't want to quit my job. He told me I can do social work anywhere."

There were times when Tamara wished she could coach her brother-in-law before he spoke. She liked him, but he needed help sometimes.

"I told him he can be an electrical engineer anywhere," Melinda continued. "But that's the crux of it. Because he makes more money than I do, even without a fifty percent pay increase, I should, without thought, pack up my life and follow him. He's always said he doesn't want to do managerial work. Guess what this is."

"Do you want him to turn down the offer?" Tamara asked.

Melinda smiled weakly, an expression devoid of mirth. "That's the thing. I don't. I don't want him to blame me for the missed opportunity. I just don't want to go with him."

"I see." But Tamara wasn't sure she did. Jeff had grown up in the house next door. Melinda and Jeff had played together since they were seven. She started referring to him as her boyfriend when they were twelve. Save a six-month breakup after college—during which they'd both been miserable—they'd never been apart.

Melinda looked into her wine. When her eyes returned to Tamara's, they were moist. "I don't know what it means not to love him. I don't know what it means to live without him."

"Part of you wants to find out," Tamara said.

Melinda nodded. "And part of me is terrified. But I have a life here. My job, everything is here. You moved here to . . ." Melinda didn't finish, but Tamara knew where she was going.

"I should not factor into this. I'll be fine." Tamara wasn't sure she believed that, especially now. Sometimes, it was hard to imagine ever being fine.

"What if I'm not fine?" Melinda said. "I want to watch Brian grow up."

"You don't think we'll visit?" Tamara smiled. "Brian will probably spend summers with you."

"I don't know," Melinda said. "There's this part of me that wants to know what it's like to be on my own."

Tamara didn't know what that was like. She'd lost Sam, but she'd still had Brian. No part of her wanted to know what it would be like to be on her own.

Chapter 5

CINDY

Cindy woke to find her mother in the kitchen making pancakes.

"You don't have to do that," she said. "I can handle breakfast."

"I know," Annalise said. "You've been doing fine without me for a long time. But I want to help."

It was her mother's third morning there.

"What is that wonderful smell?" Ross asked as he walked into the kitchen.

"Pancakes," Annalise answered with a self-satisfied smile.

He glanced questioningly at Cindy and then turned back to Annalise. "Perfect. That's just what I need this morning." He poured two cups of coffee, one for himself and one for Cindy, and settled at the table.

"Do you think the jury will return a verdict today?" Cindy asked.

"If I guess, I'll be wrong." He always provided some variation of that response, but Cindy kept asking. She didn't want him to think she didn't care.

She glanced up at her mother, who was focused on the pancakes. She leaned forward and whispered to Ross, "Have you heard of Cooper Franklin?"

He shook his head. "The name doesn't ring a bell. Should it?"

"He's been in the news."

"I haven't seen any news. Why are we whispering?"

"He was a killer for hire based here in Atlanta. He's dying, and now he's talking to authorities."

"Huh. Interesting," Ross said at normal volume. He sat back and turned his attention to his tablet, "Maybe he'll send some work my way."

She opened the browser on her phone and searched for Cooper Franklin. She skimmed a couple of articles, but there was nothing new. Cooper Franklin was married with two college-age children. He'd murdered a lot of people. He was dying of pancreatic cancer. She'd known all that.

"Mom!"

Cindy started. It was Cy.

"Mom!"

"Cy!" she yelled back. "Come into the kitchen and talk to me." She put her phone down and sipped her coffee while she waited. She was annoyed, though she told herself she should be grateful for the distraction. She wasn't finding any new news about Cooper Franklin.

Cy entered the kitchen wearing his uniform, the shirt untucked. "I need you to sign a permission slip. We're visiting a TV station. WXIA, I think."

"Fine. Where's the permission slip?" His hands were empty.

"I can't find it. Maybe Ms. Wright can email it to you."

"When is the field trip?" Cindy asked.

"Today."

Annoyed again, Cindy looked at Ross. His gaze remained focused on his tablet. "I'm not spending the morning waiting by the printer," she said. She would have to print the permission slip, sign it, and email it back. "I'll walk you to class this morning and talk to your teacher. I know how much you love that."

Cy groaned. "Okay." He said *okay* in the put-upon tone he'd used when he was five. She wasn't sure when that annoying habit had made a comeback.

"*Okay*," Cindy mocked him.

"We're having pancakes?" Cy asked excitedly.

"I'll bet you can eat four," Annalise said.

"Pancakes?" Amy asked, dressed but still groggy, as she joined them at the table. "That's awesome."

"I like your enthusiasm," Annalise said, sliding a plate in front of her. "You get the first one."

"Last to the table and first to eat," Cy complained. "How is that fair?"

"You'll have plenty of time to stuff your face," Cindy told him. "Should I cut some fruit?" she asked her mother.

"Sure," Annalise said. It clearly hadn't occurred to her mother to serve fruit.

Cindy pulled a cantaloupe and a honeydew from the fridge and sliced their flesh into green and orange cubes.

"Why don't you make pancakes?" Cy asked Cindy, his mouth full.

"Your mother doesn't make pancakes?" Annalise asked. "She used to eat them every morning."

"Mom ate pancakes?" Amy asked with disbelief. "No way. You never told us that."

Cindy typically served her family oatmeal, nuts, and fruit.

"When I was a child in the dark ages of the eighties, people didn't know better. Or they didn't care," she said with a pointed look at her mother. "Besides, I didn't eat them every morning."

"I'm pretty sure you ate them every morning," Annalise said.

"I don't know how you would know," Cindy snapped. "It's not like you're my mother." She had no idea why she'd said that. Did she want to give the secret away? She paused and took a deep breath. She was letting her emotions get the best of her. Her mother was here, under her roof, and Cindy could think of few things more dangerous than that.

Annalise looked away.

~

"I'll get the permission slip and bring it back to the car," Cy said as they pulled up to the school.

"Not a chance," Cindy said. "I'll walk in with you, sign the permission slip, and be on my way."

Amy laughed.

"What?" Cindy asked.

"There's zero chance of it going down like that," she told Cy with an unsympathetic grin. "I wouldn't want to be you."

Cy walked through the hall with his head down, Cindy at his side. "You need to remember to bring things home," she quietly admonished Cy as he walked into his homeroom ahead of her and took a seat at a desk. The class was half-full, a few students trickling in behind them.

Cy's teacher, Ms. Wright, exclaimed cheerfully when she saw Cindy.

"Hello, Ellen," Cindy said, "I'm here to sign Cy's permission slip. He seems to have lost it and then forgotten it until this morning."

"Of course," Ms. Wright said, retrieving a form from her desk drawer. "Cy, you should thank your mother for coming in to do this."

Cy didn't respond.

"Forgive my son's evil expression," Cindy said. "I think he prefers to have everyone think he's an orphan. It's as if he reads too much Dickens, but that most definitely is not the problem."

"He's a wonderful kid," Ellen said.

"I'm sure they all are," Cindy replied. "It's amazing you manage to keep them out of trouble despite their doing nothing all day."

Ellen Wright looked puzzled. "Doing nothing?" she asked.

"Every day, I ask Cy what he's learned. 'Nothing,' he tells me. I ask him, 'What was the best part of your day?' 'Lunch,' he says, if he bothers to say anything at all. I assume he comes to school and does nothing."

Ms. Wright smiled. "I can email you a link to some great conversation starters."

"It's no use. I've read up on the secret techniques of KGB interrogators. There's nothing more I can do. Anyway, I'll sign the form and leave. I promised Cy he would barely know I was here."

~

On the drive home, Cindy tried to figure out how to talk with her mother. They hadn't mentioned the FBI since their initial conversation three days before, but Cindy had barely thought about anything else. She was waiting for her mother to bring it up again, but that hadn't happened.

She pulled into her driveway, and as if conjured by her thoughts, her mother was sitting on the front porch.

"I hope you don't mind the pancakes," her mother said as soon as Cindy was out of the car.

Cindy was over the pancakes. Mostly. A sugary meal wouldn't kill her family. Not immediately, anyway. "I need to know why you're here," Cindy said.

"I don't have anywhere—"

"There's always somewhere," Cindy said, though she knew that wasn't true. Not for everyone. "What about this thing with the FBI? Have you told me everything? They didn't give you any indication of who my father allegedly paid to have killed?"

Her mother hesitated, and Cindy's mind raced. "What are you not telling me?"

"I've told you everything."

"Is the FBI going to talk to you again?"

"I don't know. They didn't say they would."

"I don't know my father. I barely remember the man. It just seems odd you would come here to tell me about that."

"I didn't only come because of that. We've been apart too long. I want us to reconnect."

Frustrated, Cindy shoved the front door open. "It's a little late for that," she said before walking through.

Chapter 6

TAMARA

We went to Six Flags," Brian told his mother breathlessly over the phone. "I wasn't tall enough to ride the Goliath or Batman, but I rode the Blue Hawk twice and Acrophobia three times."

"Three times," Tamara repeated. "Who rode with you?"

"Grandad."

"Grandad," Tamara said. "He rode Blue Hawk and Acrophobia?"

"Yup," Brian replied proudly.

"Did he enjoy it?" Her father was in good health, but he was in his sixties. She couldn't imagine it. Tamara, who had eagerly boarded Batman with Malik and Melinda when it was introduced in 1997, no longer had any desire to strap into a ride.

"He had to lie down when we got home," Brian said.

Tamara laughed, thinking he was lucky to have made it home.

"Are you okay, Mom?"

The question caught Tamara off guard. She stared at the television she'd muted when he called. The news was on, noise to keep her company. "I'm fine, honey. Why do you ask?"

"I don't know. I just wondered."

What did he wonder? "Well," she told him, "you don't have to wonder. I'm fine. I spent the day at the lab." She'd thought about it anyway. New atmospheric data from Triton had just been published, and she'd been looking forward to integrating it into her models. But she hadn't gone in. She'd spent the day thinking about Sam, searching her memory for something she'd missed. "I love you, and I miss you. Can I speak to Grandma?"

She listened as he ran through the house calling for his grandmother.

"How is he doing?" Tamara asked when her mother came on the line.

"Your father or your son?" her mother asked.

"Both."

"Well, your father insisted on riding everything. It was his idea to go to Six Flags. I thought we'd visit a museum. I didn't bother putting it to a vote."

"Smart. Is Dad feeling okay?"

"He'll be fine," her mother said dismissively. "He thinks he's still in his thirties."

"And Brian. Does he seem happy?"

"I watched the two of them ride everything Brian was tall enough to ride. I've never seen a happier boy."

Those words calmed Tamara's anxieties. Obsessing over Brian's happiness was a dangerous pastime for her. Tamara suffered from bouts of depression, as had Sam. They'd been drawn together in part by their shared struggle to find grace in a world viewed through the lenses of their instinctive pessimism. Her fear of passing that darkness along had made her reluctant to become a mother.

But she'd fallen in love with Sam, and maybe she'd believed the intensity of their passion would be enough to save them. Despite his tendency toward melancholy, Sam was capable of mustering optimism that could be infectious. *Our child will be perfect,* he'd told her. *I might be a goofy dad, but you'll be the perfect mother. And remember, darkness doesn't have only downsides.*

Life had happened fast. College, graduate school, internships, marriage, career. She'd been twenty-seven, almost twenty-eight, when they'd seriously discussed children for the first time. They still had time, but not forever, and the prospect of regret weighed on her. The decision would not affect only her, after all. Could she expect Sam to contentedly accept a life without children?

The day of Brian's birth had been the best and scariest of her life. As she'd felt his tiny chest expand for his first breaths, she'd known an unshakable love and a deep horror. The greatest pain imaginable, she realized, rested at her fingertips, and it left her overcome with a fierce compulsion to shield him from pain. She'd rebuked herself in those early days for being herself. Rocking him at night in the chair next to his crib, she'd felt sadness invade the pleasure of skin-to-skin contact as she'd considered the fast-moving division of cells within his body, the inevitability of the day when he would be too big to hold, too mature to comfort. Fearing that her darkness was contagious, she'd ordered her mind to cease with the negativity. There had to be mothers, she was sure, who could hold their children without despairing over the relentless passage of time. She herself recalled experiencing unadulterated joy in childhood. Where had it gone? Why couldn't she view beauty without encountering a twinge at its impermanence?

Sam's nervous breakdown when Brian was one only heightened her anxiety over Brian's future health. After Sam committed suicide, she'd grown obsessed with mitigating any depressive predispositions Brian might have. She'd ultimately realized that she had to start with herself. If she wanted him to grow up to be well adjusted and happy, she needed to become a model for well adjusted and happy. That was how she'd found the courage to uproot their lives.

She'd quit a lucrative job to pursue a career she found meaningful. She'd moved to Durham to be closer to her sister. She was fighting her own predispositions toward gloom in an effort to vanquish any nascent melancholy in Brian. She did it all for the son who would never have been born except that she'd been carried away by her love for Sam.

~

She'd met Sam in the fall of 2002. They were both in graduate school, in their first year of a quantitative finance program. She stood before a broad oak in front of the fitness center, trying to remember the last time she'd climbed a tree. The recesses of her mind offered up a generic memory, but she couldn't be sure it didn't belong to a picture book she'd read as a child or something she'd seen on television. She'd watched some boys climb this tree a week before. A low, sturdy branch jutted almost at a ninety-degree angle from its thick trunk, and the speed with which they'd propelled themselves up and over had made it look easy. At least, easy for them. She hoisted herself up and used both hands to grasp the branch above her head. So far, so good. She lodged the toe of her right foot into a hollow of the trunk, and with a bit of exertion and after a moment of panicked unbalance during which she imagined breaking a bone, the edge of the fitness center's roof was within range.

The garden rooftop was accessible by stairs, but it was after hours. Tamara wanted to be here now.

Slightly winded, she shrugged out of her backpack. She removed the blanket and spread it on the terrace. There were two chairs, one on each side of the small garden, but she chose to lie down.

The campus was quiet, the buildings around the fitness center closed for the night. When she heard a branch below her rustle, she assumed it was an animal. What kind of animal, she hadn't a clue. Something nocturnal. And she wondered if coming here at night was a good idea. She wasn't in a rainforest, but still, who knew what lurked in the darkness.

"Are you alone?" The whisper startled her, and she jumped. She sat up as a disembodied head peeked over the roof.

"No," she lied. "What do you want?"

"I don't want to disturb you. I saw you climb up here."

"Why are you here if you don't want to disturb me?" She fingered the pepper spray on her key chain. She'd always felt safe on campus. Until now.

The disembodied head didn't respond right away. "That's a really good question," he said as if he'd never in a hundred years expected it.

"Who are you?"

"We're in Numerical Methods in Finance together."

Right. She could see that now. He was the other Black person in the class.

"Are you studying for the test tomorrow?" he asked.

"Do you see any light?"

The question seemed to puzzle him. "Can I come up?"

"Sure." She held the pepper spray unobtrusively in her palm as he pulled himself onto the roof.

"I was wandering campus thinking about tomorrow's test. When I saw you climb up here, I thought maybe you know something I don't."

She smirked. "I probably know a lot of things you don't."

She didn't know him, not really. They sat on opposite ends of the classroom, she with a couple of friends. They nodded when they passed each other on campus. As an undergraduate, she'd known most of the Black students on campus. As a grad student, she wasn't active in any organizations. She'd done those things for her grad school application.

He turned one of the chairs to face her and sat. She resumed her supine position, her eyes locked once again on the moon.

"Let's start there. What do you know that I don't?"

"If we had binoculars, we could look right there"—she pointed with her finger—"and see Neptune."

He squinted up at the sky. "I'll have to take your word for it. And what can I do with that knowledge?"

"Oh, brother." She looked away from him. "You'll be a perfect quant."

"Thank you. I tell myself that every morning when I look in the mirror."

"You're lucky. Every morning, I tell myself that I didn't make a mistake, that there are worse things I could spend my days doing."

"Like what?"

"I once spent a summer making cold calls to sell photography sessions."

"Were you working for a photographer or just pranking people?"

Tamara laughed. "It was a portrait studio."

"You don't like quantitative finance?"

"It's fine. My roommate is getting a master's degree in medieval history. It's all she talks about."

"Check on her in ten years. See if she's still talking about medieval history."

"Spoken like a quant in training," Tamara said.

"You must have some reason for studying quantitative finance. Why are you here?"

"Here on this roof? Here at this university? Here on this planet?"

"One more question and you're going to lose me."

"Here in this universe?"

"Okay." He stood. "I'm leaving."

Tamara watched him.

"Just kidding." He sat. "I wanted to study creative writing."

"Why didn't you?"

"My aunt. She took me in when I was a teenager. I had no idea I was going to college until she told me. She's financing my education with money meant to send her on trips around the world. Creative writing to her is a hobby. Not a curriculum on which to spend your life's savings."

Tamara told Sam about Malik's illness, and Sam talked about his mother's death when he was sixteen. He'd been close to his father until he'd stopped being a father, and then there was only his aunt. They recognized a shared sense of duty, of financial responsibility, to their families.

When he leaned forward and kissed her, it seemed to astonish them both. To her further amazement, she found that she wanted him right here beneath the night sky. She appreciated that he didn't carry a condom in his wallet, but she felt utterly alone, waiting on her blanket while he trekked to the drugstore. What if he didn't return? The crowning glory of being stood up. Could she face him in class the next day?

It was a question she would never have to answer.

~

Tamara and Sam's compatibility felt heady and auspicious. Her desires and goals were vindicated in her mind because he shared them. They married in Atlanta the summer after graduation and moved to New York in the fall of 2004. Tamara found a job at Viltel Capital Management, a boutique hedge fund, and Sam was hired by Lehman Brothers. Neither felt qualified to construct models that dealt with sums of money larger than they'd ever contemplated, but they marched optimistically into the future. Talks of starting a family—the one topic on which they diverged—were on hold. They worked inhumanly long days and talked shop in the hours after work.

"Jana called me today," Tamara told Sam one evening over dinner. They dined nightly in a rotation of restaurants. Tonight was Chinese.

"What's she talking about?" Sam asked. Jana had been Tamara's roommate in graduate school.

"She met with a mortgage lender today."

"Yeah, where is she?"

"Sacramento. She's a beekeeper, does a lot of work with almond farmers."

Sam paused, a forkful of fried rice inches from his lips. "You're joking."

Tamara sipped her tea. "What?"

"Jana is a beekeeper? That's a job?"

"Have you been to a grocery store? Often, near the peanut butter, you'll see jars of an amber viscous fluid. It's called honey. Where do you think it comes from?"

"Yeah, I just—"

"Yeah, you're just being a snob," Tamara said. "Anyway, she met a mortgage lender, and he's offering her up to $750,000."

Sam put his fork down. "Does she have a partner?"

"Nope."

"And she makes?"

"What you would expect a beekeeper to make. The lender wasn't interested in her salary, didn't even require documentation. He's offering an interest-only, adjustable-rate mortgage fixed for two years at six percent."

"What did you tell her?"

"I told her to run and find herself a reputable bank. Turns out the lender is New Century Financial."

"Really?" Sam asked. "They're solid."

"I know. It's weird."

"Maybe she can afford it," Sam said. "She has two things going for her. Housing prices are rising like crazy. She gets some equity in, and she can refinance at a fixed rate later. Second, the president is pushing big time to expand homeownership. There's probably all sorts of federal incentives she can grab."

Tamara was skeptical. "I really hope she doesn't sign on for three-quarters of a million in debt."

~

At lunch with her boss the following day, Tamara mentioned her conversation with Jana. Ian Wilson, the manager of the fund, held the belief that human beings, including himself, were stupid. Compared to what? Tamara wondered but never asked. She was in the habit of asking Ian, whom she regarded as extremely intelligent, a lot of questions, but she didn't know him well enough yet to question his tenets.

"Something isn't right," he told her.

She started to repeat Sam's thoughts on rising home prices and a federal push to expand homeownership, but she didn't want Ian to think her husband was stupid.

"Look into it. If New Century is being run by idiots, we might want to short them," Ian said, suggesting they purchase positions betting that New Century stock would lose value.

～

Each time Tamara reported what she'd learned about mortgage lending to Ian, he told her, with increasing excitement, to dig deeper. By the time the fund moved into short positions on mortgage lenders and home-building companies, she was deep into trying to understand mortgage-backed securities and CDOs, two indecipherable types of bonds.

Mortgage lenders made loans to consumers. Many of those loans were then sold to investment banks, which packaged the loans into bonds. Investors could purchase the bonds, and when homeowners made payments, the investors made money. When homeowners defaulted, investors lost money. Ratings agencies rated these products based on their probability of default. US Treasury bonds, considered risk-free, enjoyed triple-A ratings. Like many concepts, it was simple until her fellow quants got involved. Tamara focused specifically on CDOs backed by subprime mortgage bonds, but as hard as she tried, she couldn't understand what was inside them. Sam introduced her to a quant at Lehman who did nothing but package these bonds, and a meeting with him left her even more confused.

Ian directed her to research credit default swaps, insurance policies against the default of CDOs. Soon, Viltel Capital held short positions on all manner of companies involved in the housing market as well as millions of dollars of credit default swaps.

"So basically," Sam said over dinner, an Italian restaurant, "you're betting the housing market will crash?"

Tamara sipped her wine. "Basically."

"All around the country, at the same time?"

Tamara nodded.

"When is the last time that happened?"

"1929."

Sam laughed. "I think we've become better stewards of the economy since then."

~

The fate of the housing market became a running argument between the two of them, and they maintained it through 2006. Tamara was doom and gloom, and she grew gloomier by the month. The words making up their debates were often novel, but their arguments varied only slightly. Tamara might say, *When you look at areas where home prices have risen less than five percent, you see all these defaults. What does that tell you? Forget falling prices. Stagnating prices mean death.*

At some point, tiring of the minuscule detail Tamara was increasingly mired in, Sam would throw his hands up and say, *You know, you have to ask yourself, Is everyone wrong, or am I?*

And she would reply, *Everyone is greedy. Mortgage lenders are making a killing selling these loans to investment banks. Investment banks are making a fortune packaging these things into something no one understands. Investors are reaping fat returns. The ratings agencies are being paid to rate them. Politicians are taking credit for expanded homeownership. Consumers, told they can afford big homes they'd never dreamed of, are buying them. Maybe I'm the only one thinking about consequences.*

Jana, her old roommate, had accepted the loan. With home prices rising, the house was an investment, she'd told Tamara. Tamara didn't know who'd given her that advice.

Still, although Tamara never admitted it to Sam, she struggled with doubt. No one else seemed to notice anything amiss in the housing market. On the contrary, it was a grand party that she and her colleagues at Viltel Capital refused to attend. And who were they to lecture anyone? The stocks they'd shorted were soaring. They were paying millions of dollars in insurance premiums that would only pay out if their selected subprime-mortgage-backed CDOs failed. All told, they were down 11 percent over the previous year. Ian's positions were based on her research, and what if she'd gotten it wrong? Sam was always quick to remind her: *You said yourself you don't understand these things. How can you be so certain they're bad?*

That was a good question. On the other side was a belief that complex black box models had eliminated risk where just last year it lurked. That wasn't believable to Tamara. Whenever she wondered aloud how exposed Lehman might be, Sam pointed out that they were knocking down record profits quarter after quarter. She couldn't say the same for Viltel.

Sam often worked late, and she would take the train home after dinner while he returned to the office. Alone in the apartment, she would fret over Viltel's bets against the housing market. The trades had been Ian's decisions, but she'd played a key role in leading him there. If she was wrong, Viltel and their clients would suffer deep losses. If she was right, millions of homeowners, like Jana, would default on their mortgages and lose their homes. She didn't want to be right, but she didn't want to be wrong. She could tell herself that she was betting against lending practices that shouldn't exist, but there were real people on the other side. Investing in a stock was an act of optimism, a vote of confidence in a business. A short position was something altogether different.

~

When home prices began to fall in the second half of 2006, Tamara didn't feel any less conflicted. By the time New Century Financial filed for bankruptcy in April 2007, Viltel's short positions were earning tens of millions of dollars.

"I have to admit," Sam told her that summer, "you weren't wrong." It was a Sunday, and they were walking in Central Park. Dozens of mortgage companies had filed for bankruptcy that year.

Tamara didn't feel that she'd been prescient. She'd just been fortunate enough not to have a stake in the game. No one was offering her a dream house she couldn't afford. She didn't work for a firm, as Sam did, that was making billions from those bad loans. Her boss and mentor liked to say that people believe what they want to believe. Ian would make that cliché his own by adding: *More often than not, the belief is stupid on its face.*

"Maybe," she told Sam cautiously, "you should shed some of your Lehman stock."

Sam laughed. "Did you see my last bonus? We're making money."

He was proud to work for Lehman Brothers. She didn't push it. And honestly, she didn't know how much exposure Lehman had. She knew they'd generated a lot of the subprime CDOs, but that didn't mean they owned them.

"I admitted you weren't wrong." He squeezed her hand. "Can you admit I'm right?"

"About what?" she asked.

"Having a child."

She wouldn't admit that.

"Life," he told her, "is beautiful. And, yes, there's inevitable pain and risk. But you and I can be great parents to our child. And I feel really fortunate to be in this place at this moment, taking this journey with you. Think about our ancestors in the Great Rift Valley two hundred thousand years ago. There was nothing great about it."

Tamara smirked.

"I'm serious," he said. "Parasites, predators, food that fights back. No dental care or plumbing or video games. But you and I are here together today because they chose to live and procreate. They didn't know the Pythagorean theorem or Einstein's theory of relativity, but they knew life was worthwhile despite the struggle and lack of soap. I can't think of anything more beautiful than creating a human being with you."

"I can't think of anything more beautiful than that either," she told him.

Chapter 7

Cindy

Cindy tuned into the interview late. *Jackie Perez, Cooper Franklin's former art teacher* was emblazoned across the screen. That stopped her flipping channels.

He was extremely talented, Jackie was saying. *One of my best students. I still remember him. I regretted that I couldn't do more for him, but he came of age in a tough market. Buyers were looking for pieces that went well with their sofa. Cooper wasn't that kind of artist.*

Were you surprised to learn that he became a killer for hire? the anchor asked.

Shocked. There was nothing in him, nothing in his art that—

"I want a truce."

Cindy hurriedly turned off the television. Her mother stood to the side, holding out a tray.

"Peanut butter oatmeal bars," her mother said, "with semisweet chocolate."

A big change from yesterday's pancakes. Cindy took one and tasted it. They were good. But they would be a hard sell for Ross and the kids.

"Thank you," Cindy said.

"Can I sit?" her mother asked.

"Sit," Cindy said.

Her mother sat on the love seat. Cindy turned the reclining chair to face her.

"I don't mean to pat myself on the back," her mother said, "but Amy and Cy really seem to like me. So does Ross."

"They don't know you, Mom." Even alone in the house, Cindy felt a pang of anxiety when she called her Mom. And still, she did it.

"They're getting to." Her mother studied her. "Do you think you know me?"

"I have some experience with you," Cindy said.

"I have some experience with you too. Why did you invent a new past for yourself? I can understand being ashamed of—" Her mother broke off as if she didn't know how to finish the thought. "None of it was your fault. None of it was so bad."

"You don't know as much about my past as you think you do," Cindy said.

"Then tell me. What happened after you left?"

"How about you tell me why you're here, the whole truth, and then I'll entertain your questions."

Mother and daughter locked eyes, neither of them breaking contact. It was a stare-off, and Annalise acquiesced by asking, "Are the bars good?"

Cindy took another bite. "Very. Thank you for making them."

"I'm glad you like them. I don't think I could eat one without frying it and rolling it in sugar."

Chapter 8

TAMARA

After a quick breakfast, Tamara drove to the lab. She'd lied to Brian the day before about spending the day in the lab, and she wanted to make that right. It was a slog. Just a week ago, she'd been excited about her research. Now, she couldn't read a paragraph of an astrophysics paper without losing her train of thought.

The lab was quiet, many of the graduate students off enjoying the first days of summer. That was fine with Tamara. She just wanted to try concentrating for thirty minutes without thoughts of Cooper Franklin or Sam.

Tamara was part of a team studying the habitability of planets outside our solar system. To be a good candidate for supporting life, an exoplanet couldn't be too close to its star, nor too far. It had to be the right distance to allow for the existence of liquid water. The size of the planet also mattered. Too small and the exoplanet might lack the gravitational force to maintain an atmosphere.

Atmosphere was Tamara's specialty. She built simulations of theoretical worlds inhabited by life. If a world contained oceans half the size of those on Earth, and those oceans supported plant life, what would the composition of the planet's atmosphere look like? Her job was to tell astronomers what to look for, and she loved her job. When she wasn't awake, she dreamed about this stuff.

Until Cooper Franklin.

Now she dreamed about Sam and searched their history for clues.

~

It was mid-March 2008, and Tamara held her breath, or maybe she just breathed more slowly, as she awaited the verdict of her home pregnancy test. She'd picked one up at a drugstore during lunch, fully intending to take it once she was home. But she couldn't wait. She wanted to know. So, she sat on the commode, locked in the restroom stall, comparing the number of lines in her results to the instructions. She closed her eyes for a few seconds and opened them just to be sure. She reached for her BlackBerry—she didn't know if she was going to call Sam or message him—and saw an alert that Lehman Brothers stock had plummeted 35 percent on news that JPMorgan Chase was purchasing Bear Stearns for two dollars a share. She put her phone and her pregnancy test back in her purse before leaving the restroom.

"Are we short Lehman?" she asked Ted, one of the traders, on her way back to her office.

He grinned. "Hell yeah! We're short all the investment banks."

Sam didn't leave the office to have dinner with her that night. She didn't ask him how things were going. The following day, Lehman released its quarterly earnings, exceeding expectations and driving their stock price up 46 percent. Sam looked exhausted but was in high spirits when they met for dinner, Mexican.

"You know," she said, "if you want to get out of investment banking, I know some hedge funds that are doing okay."

He scoffed. "We're doing okay. It's a rough patch, but honestly, if the media would stop predicting our demise and speculators would stop short selling our stock, we'd get over this thing."

Tamara busied herself with her enchilada. The media and short sellers were not the root of Lehman's problems, but she didn't want to be disagreeable tonight, even if their disagreements tended to be friendly, hovering above the realm of emotion.

"Don't be angry," she said. "I bought a home pregnancy test yesterday. I planned to wait until you were with me, but . . ." She paused.

"Are you going to tell me what it said?" he asked, beaming.

"I have a doctor's appointment Friday. We'll confirm it—"

Sam interrupted her with a celebratory fist in the air.

~

Tamara was seven months pregnant when Lehman Brothers, once an antebellum dry goods store and then the fourth-largest investment bank in the United States, collapsed. Sam called her, stunned. "It's over," he said. She couldn't tell if he was near tears or if their connection was bad.

She gathered her things and headed for the door.

"Are you okay?" Ian asked as she passed him in the hall.

"My husband," she said.

She watched Ian's face as confusion morphed into understanding. "Right," he said. "Go."

She went.

Sam sat on the couch in their living room, his face in his hands. Footage of men and women leaving 745 Seventh Avenue clutching boxes played on the television.

"I can't believe the Fed let this happen," he told her. He'd sat in that same spot all weekend, watching news coverage of Lehman, but he hadn't expected this.

Tamara hadn't either. The Fed had bailed out Bear Stearns, and she'd expected something similar for Lehman.

"Do they have any idea what this will mean?" Sam asked.

Tamara had some idea. Sam was just now grappling with realities she'd been struggling with for more than a year. Her phone rang, and she turned it off. Her father had called thirty minutes before, asking what this meant for the economy. A friend from high school had emailed her a similar question about his 401k.

"I turned mine off thirty minutes ago," he said and held up his BlackBerry.

She switched off the television. "Let's get out of here."

He looked at her, dazed.

"Let's get in our car and drive until we lose cellular service. We'll stay at a bed-and-breakfast that doesn't have a television. We won't read newspapers or check email."

"The economy is going to get really bad for a lot of people," he said.

She sat beside him. "I know. There isn't a thing we can do about it. Let's go."

~

They sat in lounge chairs, looking up at the night sky, drizzled with stars. They were on the back porch of a bed-and-breakfast in the Adirondacks. The temperature was cool, and their chairs were pulled close together. They held hands.

"Do you ever think about the beginning," Tamara asked, "and wonder if humans could have built something better?"

"As a matter of fact," Sam replied, "I've never had a single thought even remotely like that in my entire life." He laughed.

"So many accidents happened on the way here. If we calculated the probability of each of them happening again in succession, it would be practically zero. And this is what we ended up with. It feels like a waste."

Sam turned to look at her. "What scale are we talking here? Because if you're talking about you, me"—he placed a hand on her belly—"and this baby, I strongly disagree."

She smiled. She could barely make out his features after staring at the stars. "Human civilization," she said. "We can go back to our ancestors in the Rift Valley, the first life on Earth, or the big bang. Take your pick."

"Those are all mind-numbingly hard, so I'll take our ancestors in the Rift Valley."

"Fine. From the Rift Valley, we've created a global civilization glued together by greed. And here we are."

"That's cynical," Sam said. "Why are you so cynical? I'm the one out of a job. You're probably a million dollars richer today."

Tamara wouldn't tell him, at least not now, how wealthy she—and by extension, he—had grown betting against the housing market. The loss of his job and the few hundred thousand he owned in Lehman stock wouldn't hurt them.

"I'm scared," she told him. "When you and I came to Wall Street, I thought these were all brilliant people. Most of them don't know what they're doing."

"You seem to know what you're doing," he said.

"But I couldn't do anything about it." Except bet against it. And now, she needed to figure out where to put their money. Where would it be safe?

"People will look to Viltel for guidance. You'll be there."

She nodded.

"Lehman was my identity," Sam said. "I thought I would retire there."

"You're way too young to think about retirement." She considered her next words, perhaps taking advantage of being pregnant with his child, before saying, "Given that the Lehman brothers built their wealth on slavery, I can't say I'll mourn the demise of their namesake or the disappearance of their name."

"Don't think I haven't struggled with that," Sam said. "It's just, I got the internship there, and it was a great summer."

"You always want to belong to something," she added.

"That's true. I wanted to belong. And I did belong. In my day-dreams, I succeeded Dick Fuld as CEO. How powerful would that be? A descendant of slaves rises to sit atop the Lehman empire."

"The Lehman brothers would probably prefer to see the company collapse."

Sam laughed. "If so, they got their wish. It was a silly dream."

"It's time for new dreams," she said.

"Yeah." He touched her belly again. "Better dreams."

~

Portions of Lehman's businesses were acquired by the British bank Barclays, and Sam was waiting to see if that included him. No Lehman jobs were guaranteed.

"I'm not good at staying home all day," he told Tamara.

She agreed that he wasn't. He was watching a lot of news and responding to the broadcasts like a rabid sports fan. *Does no one understand what's happening?* he yelled at the television when the House failed to pass a financial rescue plan. Tamara didn't point out the number of times he'd brushed aside her own concerns about a housing bubble.

The stock market tumbled on Congress's inaction, erasing a trillion dollars of wealth in mere hours. Tamara was on her laptop purchasing undervalued stocks when Sam told her he wanted to get involved in local politics. "It has to be better than sitting around the house all day," he said. By the time the House passed TARP a few days later, Sam had already joined a local political organization.

The weeks passed in a flurry for Tamara. Sam told her they were dragging for him.

"I have a confession," he said one evening when she returned home from work. He sat on the couch looking sheepish. "Barclays offered me a job."

"That's great. We should celebrate."

He stared at her.

"Wait, what are you confessing?" she asked.

He looked miserable. "I don't want the job," he said quietly, and she understood. He felt guilty, tortured by his Puritan work ethic.

"If you don't want the job," she said, searching for a comfortable position in the recliner, "you don't want the job." Comfort was becoming a rare commodity as she moved deeper into the third trimester of pregnancy. "Why don't you want the job?"

"When I worked for Lehman, I thought I was serving the broader economy, creating liquidity that would allow businesses to grow and individuals to invest in that growth. I thought we all wanted that. I'm not sure anymore."

Tamara suppressed a smirk. "Really? You thought everyone wanted that?"

"Fine. I was naive. I just don't want to go back to that."

"What about politics?" Tamara asked. "Are you considering a career there?" She was only half joking. She couldn't imagine Sam running for office, and yet, she'd been surprised by his passion for financial reform.

"Politicians are worse than investment bankers. I'm done with local politics. Maybe teaching. I was thinking about looking for a lecturer position at a quant program."

"That's an interesting idea." She could see Sam teaching. "I think you'd be great at it. Just don't mention being naive in your interview."

~

A contact from Lehman helped Sam secure a lecturer position at a local quant program. His first class started in January, two months after Brian was born. He enjoyed teaching, as far as Tamara could tell, but she began to see hints of dissatisfaction by April.

"These kids don't care about how their skills can help society," he complained to Tamara. "They want to know how much money they can make."

"Well," Tamara said, "can you imagine how you and I would've felt if the financial crisis happened months before we were due to graduate?"

"They're not asking how they can improve things."

"You need to teach in the school of social work," she told him.

"Students in the school of social work don't need my encouragement to use their skills for good."

Chapter 9

COOPER

We've spent a lot of time together, Cooper," Special Agent Lewis, a guy out of the Atlanta field office, said. Cooper had met him after transferring to his new home, a medium-security federal facility in Georgia. "I've appreciated every minute of it."

Cooper nodded. He couldn't say the same.

"When a man who hasn't been caught confesses, it's usually because he's proud of what he's done. Maybe he hides his pride, maybe he doesn't, but you can tell he wants someone to know how smart he was or how tough he was. You got away with a lot for a long time, and yet, I sense no pride in you."

Cooper nodded again. He wasn't proud of anything he'd done.

"An intelligent guy like you. I just wonder. Why didn't you get a job?"

~

It was late fall in 1998, and Cooper couldn't remember the last time he'd worn a suit and tie. He could barely remember his interview at the credit union ten years before. But clearly, he'd done something right, and he would do it again. He had to believe that as he took a seat in front of the desk as Martha, his interviewer, settled behind it. Cooper took a deep breath.

"Thank you for taking the time to meet with me," he said.

Martha smiled and thanked him for coming. "I'm excited to meet you. We're very eager to fill the position."

"That's good," Cooper said. "I'm eager to fill it." He didn't know how much longer he could stay home with the twins. Even coming to this interview was a welcome break.

The job was a clerk position in the central supply department of a medical clinic.

"Tell me about yourself," Martha said.

It was a question Cooper expected, but he still found it awkward. And honestly, he didn't know who he was anymore. Husband—check. Father—with difficulty. Artist—not in a while. Cat owner—not anymore.

Martha, uncomfortable, it seemed, with even short silences, prompted, "What do you do in your spare time?"

"My wife and I are parents to eleven-month-old twins. A boy and girl. Pretty much, if I have spare time, I sleep." Cooper smiled. Really, he hadn't had spare time in years. In his previous life, when he hadn't been working, he'd been painting. When he hadn't been painting, he'd been networking in the art world. Now, between the two babies, he lived with perpetual wailing, without space even for thoughts. "When I manage to get away for a couple of hours, I enjoy volunteering at a local no-kill shelter." That was a lie, but he could imagine himself doing it.

"Nice. Do you have any pets?"

Cooper shook his head, a bit too morosely. A colleague of Lisa's had recently lost his cat of sixteen years. He'd been happy to take Fernando. After visiting the man's home and interviewing him, Cooper had reluctantly agreed.

Martha picked up a sheet of paper and read.

"You're not currently employed, but you worked at Upton Credit Union for ten years. Why did you leave?"

Lisa had a friend named Deborah who was the hiring manager at a real estate firm. Deborah had told Cooper frankly that given the circumstances of his firing, it would be too great a risk for her to hire him. But she'd offered advice. *Be honest. If you lie in an interview and get a job offer, you'll have to worry about the truth coming out.*

"It was a mutual decision," Cooper said.

"Mutual?" Martha asked with a frown. "Can you explain that?"

Cooper readjusted in his seat. The knot in his tie pushed into his throat.

Be honest.

"Well, they let me go. And I came to see they'd made the right decision."

"Okay," Martha said, waiting.

"My son has asthma and a bad allergy to dander. I couldn't keep my cat of three years, so I took him to work. Just until I could figure out what to do with him. My cat," Cooper hastened to add with a smile, "not my son."

Martha scrunched her face with confusion. "Was the cat in your cubicle? Or did you have an office?"

"I kept him in the storage room. I shouldn't have done that. I've reflected on it, and I'm better able now to separate my personal and work lives. And I no longer have a pet."

~

"Why do you want to work for Ted's Grocery?" the interviewer, a man wearing a white polo shirt and khakis, asked. Cooper felt overdressed in his dark suit.

I just want a job, Cooper thought. Watching the twins was nonstop toil except for the two-hour reprieve their daily nap granted him. Five days ago, he'd had trouble getting Kathy down for said nap. She'd wailed and wailed, keeping Howard awake. Finally, he'd left her in the baby-fence enclosure in the living room while he'd settled Howard for a nap in the nursery. That had been a win, but he'd still had Kathy, still wailing, to contend with. He was starving, so he put his lunch in the oven before retrieving Kathy from the enclosure. They'd rocked in the living room, and she'd quieted, and he'd been pretty certain she was on the precipice of sleep when the oven timer went off. Her eyes had gone wide, and she'd howled louder than ever as he'd hustled to the kitchen, Kathy in his arms. He'd been grumbling about not being able to properly enjoy his lunch when he'd opened the oven and grabbed the pan handle with his bare hand. A jolt had traveled through his arm and to his spinal cord, and he'd almost dropped Kathy. Overwhelmed by fear and pain, he'd clutched them both tighter. He could've sworn he'd heard the skin on his palm sizzle. He still couldn't touch a pan, even a cold one, without hesitation.

"I've shopped at Ted's," Cooper replied, flexing his right hand and feeling the stretch of healing skin. "The associates are all so helpful, and they just seem to have purpose." A lie. "I want to work in an environment that allows me to help people."

The position was stocking store shelves.

"Did you injure your hand?"

Cooper looked at his palm. "Oh, this. It was stupid. I grabbed a hot pan from the oven."

The interviewer, a judgmental look on his face, jotted a note. "Ouch. No oven mitts at home?"

"I do. I just wasn't thinking."

"In the course of your duties, you'll handle box cutters and may have to help in the bakery. Safety is of utmost importance here at Ted's."

"Of course." Sweat prickled on Cooper's chest. "I rarely have accidents. This wouldn't have been so bad. It's just I was afraid I was going to drop my daughter in the oven, so I held on to the pan longer than I would have otherwise."

The man raised an eyebrow. Cooper thought to expound but decided silence was his best course.

"You were holding your daughter over the oven?"

Cooper couldn't think of anything to say. He nodded. "I was."

The man put down his pen.

"Now is probably a good time to say that I spent years moving heavy boxes. I've never hurt my back once. I'm a very cautious guy."

"Okay." A beat passed before the interviewer picked up Cooper's résumé. "I see you worked for Upton Credit Union for ten years. That's good. We like stability at Ted's. Employee retention is important to us. Why did you leave?"

Just be honest.

"I managed the records storage room at the credit union. A stray cat found its way in and gave birth to kittens. The mother was stressed, and I didn't want to uproot the kittens prematurely, so I fed her. I didn't tell my supervisor. I planned to call animal control when the kittens got older."

Honest-ish.

Cooper couldn't read the interviewer's blank expression. "In case you're wondering about my strengths and weaknesses," he said, desperate to salvage the day, "for both, I would say, compassion and caution."

~

Cooper took the bus because he'd been told that parking was a nightmare. The walk from the bus stop to the warehouse, where he was interviewing for a warehouse associate position, was half a mile.

It was cold, low forties, and he wore a trench coat over his suit jacket. He'd had the foresight to wear athletic shoes, his dress shoes stashed in an empty laptop case slung over his shoulder. Unfortunately, he hadn't had the foresight to print directions from MapQuest. He'd thought he'd known where he was going, and he'd written down the street address, but now that he was here, it didn't seem to exist. He asked strangers for directions, but no one had heard of the IIV Packing Company.

They probably wouldn't hire him anyway. No one else would. He wondered again if he should just risk claiming that he'd been laid off.

If you lie in an interview and get a job offer, you'll have to worry about the truth coming out.

Cooper just wanted an offer.

He finally found a stranger who could tell him how to get to IIV Packing. That was the good news. The bad news was that he'd walked a half a mile in the wrong direction. His interview was in nine minutes.

Cooper ran.

He wasn't in running shape, but he kept a jump rope in the closet and pulled it out when he could.

He paused briefly at a red light and then ran some more.

He arrived with a minute to spare. The receptionist led him to a conference room and told him to have a seat. His interviewer, Greg, would join him in a moment.

He complied and realized he'd forgotten to change his shoes. He was tucking his athletic shoes into the laptop case just as a man in his early twenties entered. Cooper stood to shake Greg's hand, noticing as he did how damp his own hand was. He'd taken off his trench coat and draped it over a chair, but he was overheated from his eight-minute mile. He returned to his seat.

"It's good to meet you, Cooper. Why don't you tell me about yourself?"

Cooper gave his husband-and-father spiel. He wiped his brow with the back of his hand, sweat threatening to run into his eyes. He wished he had a tissue or something.

"Are you okay, man?" Greg asked.

Cooper fanned his face. "I'm great."

"Are you hot? Personally, I think they keep it a little chilly in here."

Cooper couldn't assess the air temperature, overheated from exertion as he was. "Nah, I'm not too picky about temperature." Cooper considered removing his jacket and using his shirtsleeve to wipe the sweat from his face. "My wife says I can adapt to anything. That's why I think I'll do well in warehouse work."

Greg nodded. "Good. It's a lot of pressure. The days can be long and stressful, with little downtime. You're dealing with all kinds of personalities."

"I'm made for pressure," Cooper said. His right hand was slick from his face sweat, so he switched to the left. "People tell me I have nerves of steel."

~

"Have you heard back from IIV Packing?" Lisa asked.

She was convinced he would get an offer on the warehouse job. He'd had eight interviews, and Greg had been the only interviewer who hadn't asked why he'd left the credit union. Cooper wasn't so sure.

"The man probably thought I was nervous," Cooper said. "He went on and on about the pressure of the job. They need someone who can stay cool under pressure. I couldn't stop sweating on a forty-degree day."

"I still don't understand why you didn't just explain. He probably would've been impressed that you'd sprinted a mile to get there on time."

"It wasn't really a sprint. But maybe you're right. I never know what to disclose in interviews. Innocent comments can just balloon. They're trying to figure out if I can do the job, and I don't think they even know what to ask. It's like having one meeting with someone before deciding if you'll marry them. What would you ask?"

"If he has a cat," Lisa said.

"Very funny."

~

Cooper hadn't been to Willie Ward's nightclub since it opened six years ago. He hadn't spoken to Willie in over a year. They'd been best friends in elementary and middle school but had grown apart in high school. Around the time Cooper took his first art class, Willie embarked on his first illegal enterprise: fencing stolen basketball shoes. Cooper had been a loyal customer but less and less of a friend as he gravitated toward the art crowd and Willie was drawn into the underground. Cooper had no idea how Willie, who had never held a job, managed to buy this club at twenty-four years of age. He didn't want to know.

The throbbing hip-hop reminded Cooper why he didn't care for nightlife. He'd never understood why everything had to be so loud. As he pushed through the crowd to the bar, he was already dreading the ringing that would fill his ears as he lay down for bed that night. The bartender leaned forward for his drink order.

"Willie is expecting me," Cooper yelled. "I'm Cooper."

The bartender nodded and turned to say something to a woman who was mixing drinks. She held up an index finger before picking up a phone behind the bar. A few moments later, a man wearing a navy sports jacket approached.

"Cooper?"

Cooper nodded.

"Follow me."

Thankfully, the club was built of solid soundproof walls, and the back office where Willie lounged on a plush sofa with a drink was relatively quiet. Willie stood.

"Cooper Franklin." They slapped hands, and Willie pulled him into an effusive embrace. "It's been a minute. Have a seat."

Willie returned to his spot, and Cooper swiveled the chair in front of the desk to face him.

"Empty handed?" Willie said. "You call on my fine establishment, and you're too cheap to purchase an adult beverage?"

Cooper smiled. "I have the twins at home."

"I'm joking. Paul," Willie called to the man in the navy sports jacket, who was at that moment easing out of the office, "bring Cooper a Red Bull and orange juice." Willie winked at Cooper. "I haven't forgotten."

Paul nodded and hurried out.

"Congratulations again on the twins. How is fatherhood treating you?"

"It's getting better," Cooper said. "They felt like strangers in the beginning, but I'm starting to see what Lisa sees."

"No offense, man, but I can't let you anywhere near Sheila. She's been talking about children for a minute." Sheila was Willie's wife. "I keep thinking, you want a child, but you're going to expect me to take care of it."

"It changes your life," Cooper said.

Willie sipped his drink. "I'm quite fond of my life. Sorry to hear about the job. Bad timing with the twins."

"You're telling me." He'd called Willie earlier in the week to inquire about work. "I just need something to keep me going for a while. Nothing illegal."

Willie grinned. "I thought you wanted to get paid."

"I have a competing priority of not going to prison."

"You've always been a different kind of cat, Cooper."

Paul returned and handed Cooper his drink. Cooper wondered briefly if he should tip Paul. He was serving Cooper, and yet, he didn't appear to be a waiter. Cooper didn't want to insult him. Paul was gone before Cooper could decide.

"Credit card fraud. Lucrative and foolproof. I need someone to—"

"Nothing illegal," Cooper repeated. "I've been applying to jobs, and I'm just not having any luck."

"Oh, you were serious? You want to sweep floors or something?"

"Anything. I'll sweep floors."

Willie considered him, and at that moment, Cooper felt nostalgia. He regretted that they'd taken such drastically different paths. "You still paint?" Willie asked.

"Nah. What's that Bible verse? When I grew up, I put away childish things."

Willie shook his head. "I've never been much of a reader. What were you making at the credit union?"

Cooper told him.

Willie coughed, as if suppressing laughter. "No wonder you don't mind sweeping floors. I can find some stuff for you to do around here."

"During the day?" He held his breath. If he worked nights, there would be no rationale for sending the kids back to day care. Lisa would care for them at night, and he would watch them during the day. He was growing fond of the twins, yes, but he couldn't bear many more days alone with them.

"Sure," Willie said. "You're a family man. Come in around noon tomorrow. I'll make sure you're home by dinner."

~

Cooper did whatever he was asked to do around the club. He might sweep floors or stock supplies or perform light handiwork—to the best of his limited abilities. Most of his job was listening to Willie talk. *Stop by my office when you finish that,* Willie would say, interrupting whatever task Cooper was engaged in. In the beginning, Cooper expected something to come of these summonses. The first time, he'd actually feared that he would be fired. But it was always nothing. Willie talked about his wife and sports and potential income-generating schemes. It was just two guys in Willie's office, one of them running off at the mouth.

More and more, Cooper found himself talking about the twins. Every week seemed to bring a funny story. There was a box in the basement, longer than it was high. Kathy would make the entire family sit on the box at the same time. Willie never found the stories funny. He would always say the same thing: *No offense, man, but I can't let you anywhere near Sheila. She's been talking about children for a minute. She wants a child, but I'm the one who will have to take care of it.* Cooper wondered if Willie realized that he repeated himself. No matter. Cooper kept telling his stories. To his surprise, he'd found himself in a not-unpleasant parenting role. Lisa was the taskmaster; he was the fun parent. The twins seemed to appreciate this, and Cooper's bond with them deepened. He couldn't pinpoint the moment, but somewhere along the way, he'd begun to feel like a father.

He typically arrived at the club at 11:00 a.m. and left at 5:00 p.m. On Wednesdays, he would try to leave at 2:00 p.m. to spring the twins from day care and take them to the children's museum or an indoor play gym. They could jump on inflatables for hours, and Cooper would picture the energy in their bodies, burning off and releasing into the atmosphere as heat, the promise of a relaxing evening for him and Lisa.

It was a leisurely life, and for his efforts, Willie matched his credit union salary. He worried that it wasn't sustainable, but for the time being, he decided to enjoy it. His dream of being an artist was an old one, and he still mourned its demise. Maybe he would find it in himself to paint again. Or maybe he wouldn't. For now, he would allow himself to heal. He kept his head down at work and ignored the evidence of criminal activity all around him.

~

Cooper didn't realize he was going seventy until he passed the fifty-five-mph-speed-limit sign. He lifted his foot from the gas and attempted to vanquish the familiar tension from his chest. He was late for work. When he was late, everything seemed to move too slowly—stoplights lasted too long, cars in front of him accelerated with needless deliberation. Ten years as an office laborer had ingrained in him a sense of urgency around being on time. The new reality was that Willie wouldn't care. It was 11:45 a.m., and Willie might not even be there.

He used his key to let himself into the club's back entrance and walked upstairs. He paused when he heard a groan, just before turning the corner to Willie's office. Was Willie having sex in there? An unknown object made noisy contact with flesh, and Cooper started to back away. Whoever was in there with Willie (doubtful it was his wife), it wasn't a scene Cooper wanted to walk into. Then Willie screamed. When Cooper listened closer, he could hear Willie pleading.

Cooper stepped forward and slowly approached the office. Willie, his face bloody, was on his knees. A large man stood over him, gripping a pistol. He cocked his arm. Willie put up a hand to protect his face, but the blow crashed through Willie's defenses, and the butt of the gun smashed into his cheek. He let out a cry.

Cooper considered creeping downstairs and using the phone behind the bar to call 911. How long would it take for the police to arrive? And what would happen when they did? Perhaps they'd stop the man from killing Willie. But Willie was a criminal. This gun-wielding man was clearly a criminal too. Cooper was not a criminal, but here he was, surrounded by criminals. He needed this job. He couldn't call the police.

He moved as quickly as he could without making inordinate noise. Willie kept a gun in the glove compartment of his car. Cooper would grab it and use the element of surprise to stop the beating.

He reached the car, breathing hard. The door was locked. He looked around for something and spotted a chunk of asphalt the size of his fist by the dumpster. He ran to pick it up and hurled it through the passenger-side window. He flinched at the crash and reached carefully through the broken window to retrieve the gun.

He took the stairs by threes, not worrying about noise this time. "Hey!" he said even before he'd turned the corner into the office. Willie was lying on the ground, pleading for his life. The stranger turned to Cooper. "Drop the gun!" Cooper screamed.

The man blinked, confused.

"Drop it," Cooper said, quieter now that he had the man's attention. Willie had stopped moving, and for all Cooper knew, he might've died.

Cooper and the stranger locked eyes. The man lifted his gun, and Cooper imagined himself taking a bullet in the chest. Would he feel it?

Lisa was under the impression that Willie was a legitimate businessman operating a legitimate nightclub. When the truth came out in the wake of Cooper's death, would she blame him for taking the job? Would the twins, barely older than a year, have any memories of him?

Cooper pulled the trigger. He hadn't checked to see if the gun was loaded, but the explosion and kickback were confirmation. The bullet entered the man's head just above his right eye. He dropped.

Ears ringing, Cooper kicked the gun out of the man's hand and ran to Willie, who was watching him, wide eyed. "You okay?"

"Do I look okay?" Willie wheezed. Then he laughed and spit out a tooth. "Damn," he said. "Is he dead?"

Cooper looked over his shoulder. The man looked dead.

Willie stood with difficulty, holding his ribs. His face was a bloody mess. "You saved me." He peered down at the dead man.

Cooper couldn't respond. He was shaking. He placed the gun on Willie's desk. The adrenaline had turned into something else now, inducing paralysis instead of action.

As Cooper felt himself shutting down, Willie seemed to be recovering. He patted Cooper on the back. "You're a stone-cold killer."

"I had no choice," Cooper said, his voice faint. "I had to do it."

"Yeah, you did. And you did it. Like a pro. He was going to kill me."

"Why?" Cooper asked.

Willie sat heavily on the couch. "I need a drink." He didn't seem concerned about the blood he was smearing on the expensive upholstery. "I slept with his wife."

"What?" Cooper's ears were still ringing, and he thought maybe he'd misheard.

"I slept with his wife," Willie repeated.

Cooper felt nauseous. "You slept with his wife, and I killed him."

"He definitely overreacted. He was my best friend. Can you imagine what he would've done to a stranger?"

The light in the office had a strange quality, as if Cooper had been drinking. "You slept with your best friend's wife?"

"It just happened. He was out of town, and a burglar broke into his house. It was the middle of the night. His wife and kids were freaking out. He asked me to check on them."

Cooper sat heavily in the chair. "I thought you were being robbed. Or that a drug deal had gone bad."

Willie laughed hoarsely. "Glenn was a youth minister. He wasn't into drugs. He wasn't into anything. He kind of reminded me of you."

Cooper's thoughts might have been traveling through molasses. He put his face in his hands. He'd killed the wrong man.

Willie staggered to his feet. He was still unsteady, but his strength seemed to be returning as he moved toward the bathroom attached to his office. "I should go to a hospital, but to hell with that. Nora must have told Glenn about the affair. When he doesn't come home tonight . . ." He turned to Cooper and splayed his hands. "Now is not an opportune time to be interviewed by the police." He resumed his trek to the bathroom. "I'm taking Sheila on vacation for a few weeks. If anyone asks, we left early this morning."

"What will you tell her?" Cooper asked.

"I don't know. I'll say I'm ready to make a baby. That will distract her."

Cooper heard water run in the bathroom. Then rummaging. He imagined a bag being hastily packed. He couldn't make sense of it. The day had felt so ordinary when he'd awakened that morning. Even in hindsight, there'd been no indication that he would kill a youth minister who happened to be having a really bad day.

Willie returned with a duffel bag and dropped it in Cooper's lap. "I owe you, Cooper." Cooper was surprised by the weight of it. Did Willie need him to carry his bag? "I'm a lot of things, brother, but I am not a murderer. To be honest, I'm feeling a bit out of my depth here. I'm going to leave you with"—he motioned to the dead man on the floor—"this."

Alone with the dead youth minister, Cooper unzipped the duffel bag. It held more cash than he'd ever seen.

～

"How did you sleep?" Lisa asked. She was sitting on the side of the bed.

"Surprisingly well. How about you?"

"Great," she said. "Both twins slept through the night. I'd better make sure they're still alive."

Cooper admired the silhouette beneath her sheer nightgown as she walked away. He hadn't expected to sleep at all. He'd killed a youth minister, had used the youth minister's car to transport the youth minister's corpse to a resting place near the Chattahoochee River, had cleaned the youth minister's car and left it, keys in the ignition, in a high-crime area—all the while too busy to absorb the implications of what he'd done.

He climbed from bed now, waiting for it to hit him. Guilt. Fear. Something. He walked quickly to his studio in the basement and locked the door behind himself. The duffel bag still sat on the top shelf of the closet. He pulled it down and placed it on a chair. He unzipped it and looked at the money. Nearly four times his annual salary at the credit union. Still there.

～

"I called my mother," Cooper told Lisa over breakfast. He was having oatmeal and coffee. Lisa was feeding the twins. "She's watching the kids this evening."

Lisa smiled. "I still find it ironic that you call your mother to watch our kids, but you wouldn't let her take your cat."

"Our kids have excellent survival instincts. You better believe my mother will get them water when they're thirsty. My point is you don't have to worry about anything. I'm taking you out tonight. What's that fancy restaurant you like? Samma Lacha?"

Lisa laughed. "Purple Sky. We can't afford it."

"I say I'm taking you out for a fine meal, and you're telling me what I can afford. I think you should pick out a dress, and be ready to leave at six p.m."

"I'm just making sure we can pay our mortgage. And after the twins, I don't think I can fit in my old dresses."

"Fine," Cooper said, "I'll watch the twins this afternoon. You go dress shopping. Whatever you want."

"What's the occasion, Daddy Warbucks?"

"Willie is taking a vacation. He'll be gone for a few weeks, and he asked me to manage the club. He gave me a really nice bonus."

She regarded him suspiciously. "That's great. It's just we don't do that kind of thing."

That was true. They didn't splurge. They never had money for splurging. And Cooper would be okay if he never dined at a fine restaurant. Lisa, on the other hand, loved it. She loved dressing up and drinking wine with tiny portions of artistically displayed food. When she'd met Cooper, she was dating a guy with rich parents. He'd taken her to fancy restaurants all the time. Cooper hadn't been intimidated, because he was an up-and-coming artist and would have money soon enough.

"That's why we're doing it. Buy yourself a fancy dress. We'll enjoy a fine meal with wine. And we'll put the rest of the money in savings."

The idea of putting money in savings seemed to free Lisa. He'd known it would. She'd complained they were behind on retirement. *The best thing we can do for the twins,* she'd say, *is fund our retirement. At least they won't have to take care of us.*

Now, she beamed, her grin childlike. He could see the wheels spinning in her head, her imagination soaring: dress shopping, a fine meal, wine. "I'll call Allison," she said. "See if she's free to go shopping this afternoon. What's my budget?"

Chapter 10

TAMARA

If you're not doing anything, would you like to have dinner tonight?

Tamara stared at the text message. Her finger hovered over the send icon. And then she deleted it. It was a little after 4:00 p.m., and the emptiness of the evening stretching ahead felt oppressive. Her excursion to the lab a few days before had been wholly unproductive, and she hadn't left the house since. Melinda had a networking event tonight, some society of professional social workers thing, and Tamara had almost considered asking to tag along. Before she'd moved to Durham, she hadn't considered how difficult it would be to make friends. She was a decade older than her peers in the doctoral program, and the younger professors who were near her in age didn't see her as a peer. She was friendly with a few of Brian's classmates' mothers, but she didn't know any of them well. It had been easier in Connecticut, when he was in preschool and she accompanied him for supervised playdates.

And today, she was tired of thinking about Sam, reliving moments from a life she would never have again. She had no idea who would want to kill Sam, and no amount of contemplation, she was coming to realize, would move her closer to an answer. She was reliant on the detective work of the FBI, which didn't feel great. The blend of helplessness and hope that came from relying on others was nothing new. She'd experienced it as she'd waited for the police to bring Malik home. When hope had faded into pure helplessness, she'd hired a private detective and repeated the cycle.

She retyped the text message, and before she could lose her nerve again, she hit send. She stared at her phone, awaiting Kenneth's reply. She didn't know what she feared more, a yes or a no. If he declined her invitation, she would eat alone, and the night would be long. If he accepted, they would share another meal, and he would have another opportunity to see how out of her depth she was. He'd asked her to dinner on Saturday, and she'd claimed to be busy, despite having nothing to do. She'd paid for that refusal, had sat in front of the television, unable to concentrate for more than fifteen minutes at a stretch. She didn't want a repeat.

Her phone buzzed, and she hesitated before looking at the message. *I'd love to.*

They went back and forth on restaurants before settling on something fancier than Tamara would have chosen. It had been so long since she'd dressed up that she wasn't even sure what was in her closet. She decided on a green dress and had to rummage beneath the bathroom sink to find her seldom-used makeup. Getting ready for a night out stirred familiar emotions that felt distant if not wholly unwelcome. Still, she worried that she was leading Kenneth on. Tonight was about distraction, not fun. She was seeking escape from solitude, not intimacy with another person. Or perhaps the two were not mutually exclusive. When it came to dating, she didn't know what she was doing, but when she appraised herself in the mirror, she liked what she saw.

~

"Where is Brian tonight?" Kenneth asked. They sat at a table by the window with white wine and Italian bread. Tamara was still considering the menu.

"In Atlanta with his grandparents. It was a spur-of-the-moment thing."

She asked Kenneth about his daughter, Ellie. She was thirteen, and Kenneth and his ex-wife shared custody, alternating weeks. It was hard for Tamara to imagine living separately from Brian.

Tamara settled on the risotto, and Kenneth ordered lasagna. They talked about her research, and Tamara sensed Kenneth wanted to ask what had spurred her career change. She gave him her pat answer. Most people had no idea what quants did or why they existed, but the association with Wall Street provided a readily understood narrative: too many hours in the office, not enough personal fulfillment. He knew Tamara was a widow, but she'd been sparing with details, and he could probably discern that probing would be unwelcome.

"I think it's fascinating," he told her. "You're a fascinating woman."

"Thank you," Tamara said, "but what I really want is to be boring." She meant it. She'd once been content with her life in Connecticut. Her work at the hedge fund had been challenging, even if she'd occasionally wondered about the true value of her contributions. Being Sam's wife and Brian's mother had given her all the purpose she needed.

"Why do you want to be boring?" Kenneth asked.

Tamara didn't know why she'd said it. She was backing herself into a conversational corner. "Less stress," she replied breezily. "Do you have any pets?"

Kenneth smiled. "Okay, I'll subtly ignore the sensitive spot I've inadvertently stumbled upon. I don't have any pets. I've thought about getting Ellie a dog, but it wouldn't really be her dog. And you? Any pets?"

The food was delicious, Kenneth was funny, and Tamara could almost believe for brief moments that her life was boring enough to enjoy the company of this man. She'd been so afraid of dating, especially the idea of a first date, but this, whatever it was, felt easy. She could imagine going out with Kenneth again. She could imagine him playing video games with Brian. And then, he asked her an innocent question that broke the spell.

"What is your all-time favorite novel?"

She drew a blank because the question made her think of Sam. She pushed thoughts of the past away. "*Snow Crash*, I think. I read it when I was thirteen, and I was transported. I'm still waiting for the Metaverse."

"Aah," Kenneth said, "a science fiction fan."

Tamara nodded, but she couldn't regain the earlier magic of the evening. Thoughts of Sam kept pushing their way into her consciousness.

Even after he'd dropped her off at home—she'd considered inviting him in, but the mood had been all wrong—she couldn't stop thinking of Sam.

What is your all-time favorite novel?

The question made her realize—and the realization was startling—that she'd never read Sam's novel, or what he'd completed of it.

～

Brian was eighteen months old when Sam told Tamara, "I've been haunted by this crazy idea I can't put away."

They were sitting at the kitchen table, eating the lasagna Sam had prepared.

Tamara waited for him to tell her. When he didn't, she said, "Don't make me guess. If you had a brilliant idea, I might have a chance. There aren't many of those. The possible number of crazy ideas is infinite."

"I want to write a novel."

That was one of the least surprising things he could've told Tamara. "What's crazy about that?"

"I don't want to teach anymore. I find it unfulfilling. I want to take the next year off and focus on writing."

Tamara inhaled. He was sounding a bit crazier now. She, too, had been infused with the Puritan work ethic. "Are you concerned about a gap in your résumé?"

Sam nodded. "I'm concerned about a lot of things. But I'm also excited. We can pull Brian out of day care. I can watch him and write while he naps."

Tamara smiled. "My husband, the stay-at-home dad."

"I've never seen myself that way."

"I've never seen you that way either," she said, feeling suddenly at odds with her Puritan work ethic.

"I'll adapt," he told her. "You already make so much more money than me that the loss of my salary will barely matter."

"What will you write about?"

"You're talking as if we're going to do this," he said.

"So are you."

"Coming of age," he told her. "Something based on my youth. I don't really know how to talk about it."

"Good thing you want to be a writer and not an inspirational speaker."

~

Tamara's awakening at four in the morning had a note of finality to it—the end of sleep, despite her exhaustion. Her first thought wasn't of the night before with Kenneth but was of Sam, a memory pulling at something—an old silver laptop. Hadn't Sam used it to write his novel? Hadn't she boxed it up at some point after his death? Had the box survived the move?

The light from the hallway did little to illuminate the stairwell that led to the attic. She couldn't remember the last time she'd climbed these stairs, and she used the flashlight on her phone to find her way. Fearing spiderwebs, she moved slowly, scanning first her path ahead and then the floor of each step. The attic was cluttered with boxes, stuff that didn't fit into her and Brian's new life. When they'd moved into the house, she'd unpacked everything they needed. Everything else was relegated to here, tangible representations of memories she hoped to pack away.

She located the pull string attached to a light and ceiling fan. The light came on, but the ceiling fan hadn't worked when she'd moved in. She'd never bothered to have it fixed.

She'd donated most of Sam's clothes to charity, saving a few of the items that had sentimental value: the sports jacket he'd looked so handsome in when they'd celebrated their seventh and last anniversary, the lavender shirt she'd bought him because it complemented his brown skin perfectly, the hideous tie she hadn't managed to talk Brian out of giving him for Father's Day. She'd also donated most of his books, but none of the ones he'd ever talked about, even in passing. If the book had meant anything to him, she'd held on to it, probably to give to Brian one day. She'd saved his jewelry and pictures, also for Brian. She'd saved the diploma he'd been granted in the same ceremony in which she'd received her own. She hadn't known what to do with the laptop, which meant she'd probably saved it. She remembered not wanting to see what was on it but also not wanting to lose whatever he'd left behind.

She meticulously unpacked and repacked boxes. She was sweating by the time she repacked the third box, and she wished she'd had the ceiling fan repaired. She soldiered on. She found the laptop in the fifth box. She opened several more boxes searching for the adapter but gave up a little after 5:30 a.m.

Back in her bedroom, she tried powering on the laptop. She hadn't expected it to work, and it didn't. She spent another thirty minutes googling on her phone trying to discern which power adapter she needed. Perhaps it was too early, maybe coffee could've helped, but she settled on buying a used version of the laptop that came with the power adapter.

She returned to bed despite feeling jittery, a jumble of anxiety and excitement and regret. She didn't know if Sam's unfinished novel was on the laptop. If it was, she didn't know what it would tell her. She'd never read a word of it, and over the year he'd worked on it, he'd spoken of it only in the vaguest of terms. When he'd put the incomplete manuscript away, all mention of it had stopped. That seemed sad to her now. For months, he'd focused solely on writing that book and caring for their infant son, and when he'd put it away, neither of them mentioned it again. The whole experience had been different from what she'd expected.

When they'd decided he would write a novel instead of finding a job, she'd imagined coming home from work each night and reading the day's pages, offering incisive commentary that would subtly shape his work. She'd also harbored a secret unease: What if his writing was bad? Would she lie to encourage him? As it turned out, he'd been one of those secretive writers unwilling to share anything until it was complete. And she'd turned out to be an exhausted working mother, struggling to find balance and easily distracted from her husband's internal life. Looking back on that period, she wouldn't have been surprised if he'd deleted his work. If so, she could only hope to recover the files. Though she didn't know what she hoped to find.

~

Tamara hadn't expected to fall asleep again, but the next thing she knew, her phone was ringing. Groggy, she answered without checking the caller ID.

"Good morning," Kenneth said. "Did I wake you?"

She sat up and glanced at the time: 11:00 a.m. "No," she lied, embarrassed. He was probably calling from work.

"I enjoyed dinner last night," he said.

"I did too."

There was a beat of silence before he asked, "Did I say something wrong last night? The mood seemed to shift, and I'm not sure why."

What is your all-time favorite novel?

"No. The evening was perfect." She paused, and then, before she could change her mind, she told him about Sam, and Cooper Franklin, and the FBI. The words spilled out, almost a relief. He didn't interrupt her once, and when she finished, she felt embarrassed, worried she'd said too much. "I'm sorry about telling you all of this. I don't even know if it's a good time for you to talk."

"I called you," he said.

"Right, but this isn't what you were expecting."

"No, this isn't what I was expecting. But thank you for telling me. Can I do anything to help you?"

~

Tamara texted Melinda to push lunch back by thirty minutes. She really hadn't expected to sleep so late.

Not a problem. Rough night? Melinda replied.

Interesting night, Tamara replied.

They met at a Thai restaurant a block from Melinda's office. They only had forty-five minutes, so Tamara launched into her story about Sam's computer and the manuscript she was searching for.

"What do you think you'll find?" Melinda asked.

Tamara shook her head. She had no idea. She just needed something from the past, some insight into how their lives had gone wrong. She told Melinda about her date with Kenneth before the conversation turned to Jeff.

"Mom thinks I'm overreacting," Melinda said.

"You told Mom? That was your big mistake. She probably thinks you're having a nervous breakdown."

Melinda laughed. "She's definitely worried."

"Overreacting?" Tamara asked.

"I guess. You think I'm doing the right thing?"

Tamara didn't know what was right. She liked Jeff. She'd always liked Melinda and Jeff together. Even more, she wanted Melinda to be happy. "I think you have the right to reconsider what you want."

Melinda nodded. "I told Jeff I'm not moving."

"What did he say?"

"He pouted for a day. Then he angrily told me he would decline the job. I told him not to bother, and he asked me if I wanted a long-distance marriage."

"What did you tell him?"

"I didn't tell him anything. That's where we left it. That was yesterday."

~

The laptop and power adapter arrived on Thursday. Tamara hesitated before powering on Sam's computer. She hadn't been able to look through it after his death, and even now, five years later, anxiety burned in her chest and tingled in her fingertips.

After his death was ruled a suicide, she'd been afraid of what she would find. He hadn't left a note, other than the scrawled *I'm sorry* on the bathroom mirror, and she could imagine a thousand ways in which it was her fault. But imagination was one thing. Finding proof of her shortcomings in his personal belongings was another. So, she'd packed his laptop away with the vague notion that she would look at it in a distant future when she was stronger. That future was today. She wasn't stronger, but she needed answers.

She powered the laptop on and was met with a password screen.

She guessed.

Access denied.

She guessed again.

Access denied.

She resisted the urge to smash the machine.

~

"Tamara Foster, old friend," Leonard Williams, an Atlanta-based private detective, enthused. "It's been a while."

"Yes, it has," she said, holding the phone to her ear. She'd hired him four years ago to find Malik. He'd searched for over a year until he'd had to admit that he didn't know where else to look.

"I still think about your brother."

Tamara squeezed her eyes shut. She didn't want to cry. "So do I." She sat on the porch in the same spot she'd occupied when she'd learned about Sam's murder. An awkward moment passed before she said, "I need help accessing my late husband's computer."

"What type of help?"

"I can't get past the Windows password. I might need help recovering deleted files, but for now, I just want to unlock it."

"You're in Connecticut? I can give you a name—"

"I'm actually in Durham now. If you can handle it, I'll overnight the machine to you."

He promised to have it back in a couple of days.

~

Melinda sat by Tamara's side as she powered on Sam's laptop. She unlocked her phone and pulled up the text message from Leonard Williams. He, or his person, however that worked, had reset the password. Fingers trembling, she typed the new password into the laptop.

"I know you're too young because I barely remember it," Tamara said, "but when we were little, Geraldo Rivera did a live TV broadcast of the excavation of a secret vault once used by Al Capone. There was all this hoopla, and it turned out the vault was empty. That's what I'm thinking about right now."

"And if we don't find anything here?" Melinda asked.

"It didn't seem to hurt Geraldo."

Melinda shoved her. "Seriously."

"Maybe it will be a relief."

"You haven't said," Melinda asked carefully. "Is it a relief that Sam didn't commit suicide?"

Tamara bit her lip. "I can't tell you how many sleepless nights I've spent pacing my bedroom, wondering if it was my fault or if I could have done something to stop it. I tried to train myself to stop thinking that way, but I couldn't. Maybe now I can stop."

"It isn't your job to find out why he was murdered," Melinda said.

"Whose job is it?"

"The FBI."

"I'll have to give Brian an accounting one day. The FBI won't be there to help with that."

Melinda squeezed her shoulder. "Okay. Let's open this vault."

Tamara pressed enter, and Sam's desktop loaded. Within moments, she located a folder called *Writing*. Inside were six files: *I, II, III, IV, V,* and *VI.*

Tamara stared at them.

Finally, Melinda said, "Should we open one, just to confirm the files aren't corrupted?"

Tamara didn't reply. She was absorbing the weight of the moment, sitting here, the unfinished novel that Sam had devoted so much of himself to at her fingertips. She couldn't bring herself to open a document. "What if I asked you to read it for me?"

"I think," Melinda said, "we should make a backup, just so nothing gets lost. When you're ready to read it, it will be here."

"We agree on something," Tamara said. She retrieved an external hard drive and began the process of copying Sam's files. And then she opened a bottle of wine. "Let's order in."

Chapter 11

CINDY

Aren't you glad we brought your aunt?" Ross asked and then sipped his wine. They were sharing a bottle of white, the two of them dining alone at a restaurant on Jekyll Island. They sat at a window table overlooking the beach. It was nice, their time without the kids, and besides, the live piano music and elegant ambiance would've been lost on them. Annalise had taken them for pizza, and Cindy didn't mind missing out on that.

"The kids love having her," Cindy conceded. They'd booked their family trip a month ago, three weeks prior to her mother's unexpected arrival. Ross had been the first to suggest including her. Cindy initially hadn't been sure. She'd watched apprehensively as her mother won over her wary children with sugary breakfasts and decadent desserts, video games with Cy, purse shopping with Amy. Even Ross seemed to be falling under her spell. He'd been exhausted at the conclusion of the arson trial and had spent a few days on the golf course, catching up with friends. He'd unwound in the evenings with television, old westerns that Annalise shared a love for.

Meanwhile, Cindy had existed in a state of constant vigilance, braced for disaster. Even more so than usual. For so long, she'd gotten away with so much. It hardly seemed possible. But that was under the best of circumstances—all connections to her past severed. With her mother here, living under her roof, how could her secrets possibly remain hidden?

She and her mother hadn't spoken about the FBI again, and Cindy found that maddening. If the FBI questioning had sparked her mother's visit, then why didn't she have more to say about it? Had the FBI sent her? Was her mother working for the FBI? That was just paranoia—why would her mother bring up the FBI if she was working for them?—but Cindy had trouble letting it go. Maybe her mother didn't know anything. No one seemed to know anything. Cindy couldn't even find a full list of Cooper Franklin's victims online. Ignorance seemed to be the prevailing state, and Cindy was practicing the art of being uncomfortable.

Ross had lost the arson case, and his client was facing twenty years. Cindy assumed he was disappointed, but she hadn't asked him how he felt. She never did. There was a part of him that was a mystery to her. Early in his career, she'd asked him if he thought one of his clients, an accused embezzler, was guilty. They'd talked at length then about the role of defense attorneys and the constitutional right to a fair trial. It was a personal rule of his not to form an opinion regarding his clients' factual innocence. He looked at the evidence and focused solely on legal guilt: the state's ability to prove its case.

Cindy understood. And yet, she didn't believe he could be rational to the point of dispassion. He found the law beautiful, but he had to see that once it was stripped of its sage, lofty ideals and exalted, tangled language, you were left with the crude purity of victims and perpetrators. Victims wanted—needed—perpetrators to pay, notwithstanding the legal guilt and circular arguments made by expensively clad lawyers. If perpetrators were set loose to reoffend without even a slap on the wrist, the future victims of their crimes wouldn't care a whit about the burden of proof. Real-life repercussions lay beneath the philosophy of criminal law, and Cindy couldn't believe that Ross was unaffected by them.

Cindy didn't engage him in such arguments because, skilled jurist that he was, he would take her back to the presumption of innocence and the sacred rights of the accused. It was an argument with no end. Eventually, you just had to pick a side.

He'd represented hundreds of clients. He'd lost some hard-fought battles and won many others. Given the numbers, Cindy thought it probable that some factually innocent clients he'd represented were sitting in prison, just as some factually guilty clients were walking the streets. He had to know that, too, and she wondered how he felt about it. Again, she didn't ask, because she knew she would receive a response enshrined in imposing language and rendered emotionless by legal doctrine.

She didn't push him because he didn't push her. It wasn't his way. For almost as long as he'd known her, he'd been aware of her anxiety and coping mechanisms, the hard exercise and sporadic use of medication. He'd asked her about it, and she'd told him it was biological, and he'd left it at that. He'd asked about her nightmares, and she'd talked about their unspecified nature, and he hadn't probed. It wasn't that he didn't care to know her, she believed. He was trusting. He took things at face value. And that was why she'd let her guard down with him. A man who wanted to fix her anxiety, root out a solution at its source, would have pushed her away.

She'd had to learn to be like him in that regard. She wasn't trusting and didn't take much at face value. Her way was to question, to delve, but she'd made a conscious decision early in their relationship not to do that with him. She chose to let him keep his interior life because safeguarding her own was imperative. She wondered if their mutual lack of pushing and probing made their marriage unusual.

"So before last week, you hadn't spoken to your aunt in twenty years?" Ross asked now as a server arranged vegetables on the table.

"That's right. Seeing her was a shock."

"What made her get in touch?"

"Hard times. There was nothing malicious in our separation. We just drifted apart. But she's family, and she meant a lot to me when I was younger. It seemed natural that she would seek me out when she had nowhere to go. We don't have much family."

Ross stuck his fork into his plate of spaghetti and twirled it. He smiled. "That's great." And she knew he meant it. He didn't have much family either. His mother died when he was in college. His father lived long enough to benefit from Ross's success before succumbing to the asbestos he'd been exposed to in his thirties. Ross had a brother, but they weren't close. "I'm sure you've enjoyed catching up with her."

Cindy sipped her own wine and nodded. "I'm glad she found me."

It was the only right answer. Was it the truth? In some ways, yes. For years, she'd resented her mother. She still resented her, but the resentment was a moving target. The night she'd run away had nothing to do with her mother. In fact, she hadn't thought of her mother on that night.

And now that her mother had found her, Cindy was experiencing emotions she didn't fully understand. Cy and Amy didn't call Annalise Grandma, but Cindy recognized the cliché: the grandparent who enjoyed her grandchildren in ways she hadn't enjoyed her own children. Annalise had giggled as she played with them in the ocean this morning. Annalise had never taken Cindy to the ocean or anyplace else memorable. That afternoon, they'd taken a dolphin tour, and Cindy hadn't realized, until she saw the delight on her mother's face, that Annalise had never been on a boat. Cindy saw herself then in her mother. Cindy had never experienced luxury of any kind until Ross's career took off. She and Ross had discovered the finer things in life together. Watching her mother experience this side of life for the first time was dredging up old memories that Cindy preferred to avoid.

Cindy rarely, for example, thought about her childhood. Occasionally, when her children picked at their food or complained about a piece of clothing's lack of designer status, she considered the labor, likely laced with suffering, that had brought the object of their apathy from raw materials to their fingertips. She didn't follow these momentary abstractions into the darkness of memory, but she knew where they came from, and the knowing itself was uncomfortable. Equally distressing as she got older was the length of her memory. She could look back so far, so much life lived, and most of it she would choose to forget. If only she could.

Her baby brother, Kevin, had died when she was four. That was a fact, but she didn't know which memories from that time were real and which were imagined details conjured up to make sense of what she'd been unable to understand. She distinctly remembered her confusion. Her father left her brother in his car seat, and he died. Her mother told her that Kevin wouldn't be coming home, even though they'd discussed his birthday a few days before. He was going to be one, and Cindy would still be four, and still, she would be four years older than her brother. Cindy asked her mother if she would die in her car seat, and her mother hugged her and sobbed, and before that, Cindy hadn't known that grown-ups cried.

Kevin was in heaven, high in the sky above the moon and the stars and everything. Her father had forgotten to drop her brother off at day care before driving to the automotive shop where he worked as a mechanic. Her mother didn't understand how her father could forget, but her aunt Linda, her father's sister, said that forgetting was passive. It was never something we meant to do. Her parents fought all the time, and her father never wanted to play anymore. He wouldn't make her stuffed animals talk or tickle her or even help her with her workbooks. He hired a lawyer, but he didn't go to jail, which was a relief. It scared Cindy to think of him living with burglars. Then he left. Or maybe she and her mother left. She had a memory of her mother telling her father that she would never forgive him. Cindy missed him until she didn't, until his absence didn't feel like a hole.

They moved from Atlanta to Savannah, where her mother's sister, her aunt Jean, lived. Her mother found work as a waitress at a hotel restaurant, and they slept on her aunt's pullout sofa for two years until something bad—Cindy didn't know what—happened with her aunt's new boyfriend. They moved a lot after that, her mother always working one or two jobs, a list of positions that Cindy probably couldn't recall if she tried: maid, cook, laundry attendant, convenience store clerk. For Cindy, the jobs were distinguishable by what her mother smelled like at the end of a shift: grease or detergent or sweat. She learned to read the word *eviction*, but her mother told her that it was like checkout time at a motel. She'd convinced Cindy that evictions were fun, serving only to usher in the new.

Looking back on it, Cindy couldn't fathom how her mother tolerated evictions with a smile. Even living in their car had been fun. When her mother was a motel maid, they would sneak into unoccupied rooms to shower. She wasn't certain, but she suspected her mother was fired for that. She'd shielded Cindy from the brutality of their lives, and for that, she considered her mother a hero. Cindy had never gotten the chance to tell her that.

Cindy developed her love for reading during her mother's evening shifts at the laundry service. She would burrow into a quiet spot in an unoccupied office while her mother cleaned linens. Her mother praised her ability to sit quietly for hours, but to Cindy it felt natural to enter new worlds and while away time there. Sometimes her mother would bring a sleeping bag, and Cindy would read until she fell asleep, slumbering until her mother woke her at unknown hours to go home.

As an adult, Cindy mourned her innocence, that time before she noticed the small indignities of her mother's life. When she was twelve, Cindy loved the pancakes at a restaurant where her mother was a waitress. It became their routine to have breakfast at the restaurant on Saturday mornings. Then, management made a rule that employees couldn't eat in the restaurant, something about being served extra food they weren't paying for. Cindy was welcome to eat pancakes during her mother's shifts, but Cindy no longer wanted them. She was insulted on her mother's behalf. And she felt something else that she never shared with her mother: if the restaurant deemed her mother unworthy of receiving service and her mother continued to work for them, maybe she was unworthy. And then there was the hotel that didn't allow her mother to use the front entrance when reporting for shifts.

What does it matter to me what door I use? her mother told her.

It mattered to Cindy, and she didn't fully understand why.

She saw her mother's exhaustion and worry and even learned to attribute her mother's flashes of temper to their rightful source. Once her mother's humanity was laid bare, Cindy wondered if it had always been there to see, masked only by the gullibility of youth, or if the years of hardship had worn her mother down, eroding her once-swashbuckling veneer.

Her mother injured her shoulder and for weeks winced at every wrong move, icing it and popping acetaminophen before shifts. A half a year later, her mother still favored the shoulder. It didn't occur to Cindy that her mother might see a doctor until Cindy had a sore throat that wouldn't go away. Wilma Prescott, a woman her mother worked with, had medical insurance through her husband's job, and they'd conspired to pretend that Cindy was Wilma's daughter. The doctor prescribed antibiotics, and the sore throat disappeared.

Cindy as a child was nothing like her own children. She didn't expect to get everything she saw on television. She didn't expect much at all. She was glad her children weren't like her in that regard. There had been times when she'd wanted and times when it hurt, and one particular memory could still bring tears to her eyes. She was fourteen, and her mother had taken her to a shoe store for a pair of boots. Almost instantly she'd fallen in love with a brown ankle boot with laces, a cute decorative strap, and a kitten heel. She'd tried them on, and they'd fit perfectly. *Can I wear them out of the store?* she'd asked her mother, hardly able to believe she would own them. They looked like something one of the popular girls would wear. At her mother's nod, she placed her old shoes in the boot box and carried them to the clerk, only to learn that the price on the display was wrong. Her mother had looked desperate, and that was the most painful part for Cindy.

Can you honor the price? her mother had pleaded.

The clerk had been apologetic, but a mistake was just that: a mistake.

Cindy had taken off the boots, despairing for herself and for her mother. She'd put on her old shoes, and neither of them mentioned looking at less expensive pairs. Neither of them mentioned the incident again.

As a teen, Cindy feared being a burden to her mother, adding to her stress and frustration and pain. Her mother did her best. She kept Cindy safe. Until she couldn't. Or wouldn't.

Cindy was fifteen when her mother came home from a shift—they were renting a trailer at the time—and told her that she'd met a man.

He's going to help us, her mother said. *Our lives, everything is going to be different.*

And it was.

Chapter 12

TAMARA

Tamara's hand trembled as she clicked on the file labeled *I*. She took in the title page, and then paused to catch her breath. It was late, and the stillness of the dark outside permeated the empty house. She should be asleep. Brian would be home the following day, and she would have two days with him before he left for camp. She should spend those days focused on him, making up for the bad start to summer. She could read Sam's manuscript later, while Brian was away. She could. But as she sat here in front of the laptop, not reading didn't feel like an option.

The manuscript had been calling to her. She wouldn't sleep until she'd read at least a little. She focused her eyes.

She read.

The Summer of Lorelai
by
Sam Foster
I

I didn't believe the far-fetched promise that my mother would live until I saw Lorelai, the only face I remember from that terrible first day. It was summer and school was out, and I was supposed to be preparing for my green belt test. But I understood that I wasn't going back to karate class. I understood that I wouldn't see Mitch and Jermaine, my best friends from the neighborhood, again. As we left our house for the last time, I'd turned in my seat to look at the for-sale sign in our front yard. Everything would be different now.

The house sold quickly, and my parents gifted the proceeds, along with the titles to our two cars, to Prophet Warren, a small price for what had been promised. We became prophets, and Marshall Warren named me Bahati.

"Fortune," he proclaimed. I knelt on the stage of an auditorium, Prophet Warren standing above me, the tips of his white robe brushing my legs when he moved. Presumably, he was speaking to me, but he projected his voice for the crowd. "You're fortunate to join us as a young man."

I was sixteen.

I caught Lorelai's eye, and she smiled, enigmatically, a bit of a smirk as if she didn't take Prophet Warren or my new name seriously. A rush of warmth filled my chest, and I smiled back. I couldn't help it. She was the most beautiful woman I'd ever seen. When she smiled at me, I could believe that the Prophets of the Torch was everything Marshall Warren promised. She quickly broke eye contact and, like everyone else in the auditorium, settled her gaze on Prophet Warren.

And now, not six months later, my mother is dead.

～

I await my father's rage, and even this anticipation, this small uplift of my spirit, feels wrong. My mother is dead. We came here because Prophet Warren promised she would live.

"We shouldn't have come," I say quietly to my father. I feel nerves at this small expression of defiance, even though it's just the three of us: my father, my dead mother, and me. He sits on the edge of their bed, holding her hand. I sit on the edge of my cot. We share a small bedroom that might have once been an office. My cot takes up most of the free space, so we store it underneath the bed during the day.

His eyes leave my mother and slowly turn to me. "This was the best shot she had." There's no anger in his words, just resignation. I'm disappointed in him.

We went to sleep last night, a night like any other. My father, a civil engineer, spent the day overseeing the reconstruction of the former high-school campus, now the home of the Prophets of the Torch. My mother, a former social studies instructor, spent the day teaching young prophets. I spent the day with Charley, a mechanic. I love cars, and Charley said the Prophets need more mechanics, so I've become his apprentice. Our first task is to rebuild the engine of an old school bus.

When we woke up, just a few minutes ago, my mother was dead.

~

Warren Marshall's face is red with anger. This fury is what I expected from my father, a rage that mirrors my own. Marshall has come alone to inspect my mother's body.

He checks for a pulse, first the wrist then the neck, as if there's been a mistake. My father and I stand to the side, in the empty space that my cot will occupy tonight.

"My faith," Prophet Warren states with his typical assurance, "has never wavered." He turns to us. "But I alone could not uphold her health. Only the full, unwavering faith of her loved ones could accomplish that." He looks accusingly at my father, but when his eyes reach mine, the blame seems to alight solely on me. "You were crying beneath the bleachers the other week." His eyes don't leave mine.

It's true. Pam, one of the women who works in the cafeteria, found me. It was embarrassing. She asked if I was okay, and I couldn't stop. I nodded mutely, and she assumed I was upset over my mother. I let her believe that. It was easier. In truth, I was homesick. I missed my neighborhood. Jesse, a six-year-old boy one block over, set up a lemonade stand every Saturday. The lemonade and cookies were so good and sweet, I would buy two of each and sit in their front yard downing it all and answering his mother's questions about girls, sports, and my plans for the future. I missed playing basketball with Mitch and Jermaine. I'd gotten my driver's license a month before, and I missed driving my father to the store, practice he required before I would be allowed to take the car out by myself. I was on my way to the shop to meet Charley and work on the bus, and it all hit me, and I had to duck beneath the bleachers to cry.

I don't answer Prophet Warren. I'm not sure it was a question anyway.

"Do you doubt my faith, Cliff?" Prophet Warren asks my father. It's as difficult for me to get used to hearing my father called Cliff as it is for me to answer to Bahati.

"Of course not," my father hurries to answer, and I turn away in disgust. I can't see Prophet Warren, but I feel him watching me.

"Do you doubt God?"

"No," my father says firmly but a bit less obsequiously. Perhaps he isn't oblivious to my feelings.

I expect Prophet Warren to ask me the same questions. He likes to do that, ask questions that have only one correct answer.

"I will have her moved to the auditorium," he says instead. "Bahati, you will spend the day and night with her, preparing her spirit. In the morning, I will resurrect her."

I look at my father, not bothering to hide my disbelief. His expression is puzzled, but I can't catch his eye, as if he's refusing to look at me.

"Bahati," Prophet Warren says solemnly, his eyes locked on mine in his aggressive way, "this will require faith."

~

My mother rests on her back on a green blanket on the stage. I don't know what I'm supposed to do. There is a folding chair beside the blanket, and I sit, facing away from her. I've been here for three hours, and I don't know if anyone will bring me food or where I'm supposed to sleep tonight. I leave the stage only to use the bathroom. The auditorium has several entrances, one of them ajar, but Marshall Warren does not need locks to keep me here. I know what happens to people who disobey.

My mother is not here. I know that. This is just her body, and I can no more take comfort from her than I can offer her comfort. My only instruction was to prepare her spirit for return. I don't know what that means.

I turn at the sound of footsteps as Lorelai walks through the open door. She wears a red halter top and blue jean shorts, and it feels wrong that I notice her legs.

My mother is dead.

I think Lorelai notices me notice her legs, but she just gives me that smile, the one that makes me wish that I could wake up every morning to her long dark hair and penetrating eyes, her feminine voice. It won't happen. She's twenty-two, and mostly, she treats me like a kid. When I arrived with my parents six months ago, she was assigned to show me around. She explained how life worked in the Prophets of the Torch and introduced me to others my age. In a candid moment she told me to be careful of what I say. *Assume your words will make their way to Prophet Warren's ears.* She smiled then. *Of course, I shouldn't have said that to you. I'm counting on you not to repeat it. To anyone.*

That smile.

I would never betray her.

She steps onto the stage and looks down at my mother. She shakes her head, and I see something I can't quite identify in her eyes. Sadness? Anger? She opens her mouth, and I think she's about to tell me, but the moment passes.

"Why did your family come here?" she asks.

"To save my mother."

I tell Lorelai about my mother's chronic kidney disease, and she sits in a chair in the front row to listen.

My mother was on the kidney transplant list until she developed irreversible heart disease. The doctors recommended that we focus on making her comfortable, the most useless piece of advice a family can receive. Of course we wanted her to be comfortable.

We moved our living room couch to the garage, and my father rented a hospital bed, and we just waited for her to . . . I glance at my mother. She's not here, but I wonder if she can hear me.

"A co-worker of my father introduced him to Prophet Warren. Prophet Warren visited us and—"

"He told you that he could save her?"

I nod.

"And your parents believed him?" Lorelai doesn't say it, but I know she thinks us ridiculous. She isn't like the others I've met here. She, like everyone, says the obligatory things, but I sense no reverence in her. The others speak of Prophet Warren almost as if he's a god.

"My mother felt better than she had in weeks after Prophet Warren's visit. We went for a walk in the neighborhood. Like we used to when I was a kid. We didn't go fast or far, but the sun seemed like a balm on my mother's skin. I couldn't remember the last time she'd left the house."

"You wanted to believe him," Lorelai says, almost offhandedly. She gives no indication that she's looking for a response.

"My parents both had dreams that night. My father dreamed we were walking through the woods. There was nothing special about it, just a family walk. And then, he realized I was an adult, and my mother was still alive. My mother dreamed the three of us were in a car. My father was driving. I sat in the back, and she turned to ask me where we were going. I told her we were going to pick up my daughter. They decided that they'd both had the same dream, and it was telling them to trust in Prophet Warren."

"I was fifteen when my mother brought me here," Lorelai says. She pulls a cigarette from her pocket and lights it. I look around. The auditorium is empty, but if anyone comes in, they'll smell the smoke. If Lorelai isn't here, they'll think it was me. But I don't say anything. I don't want her to leave. "My older brother drowned when I was a kid. He was on a boat with my father, and my mother hated him for that. It was just the two of us, me and my mother, for a long time. She worked waitressing jobs, and we moved a lot, following work or men she dated. And then she met Marshall Warren, and here we are."

She glances at my mother. "You're supposed to sit here all day and all night?" she asks.

"I guess."

"That's jacked up. She isn't coming back."

"I know."

"Marshall is going to blame you."

I suspected as much.

She offers me a cigarette. "What if Prophet Warren smells the smoke?" I ask.

"Blame her." She nods to my mother. "She woke up and asked for a cigarette. How could you refuse?"

I stare at Lorelai.

"I'm sorry," she says. "That wasn't funny."

I take the cigarette because she's talking to me like an equal. I don't want her to stop. She lights it for me, and I inhale deeply. My lungs feel violated, and I cough.

Lorelai laughs, and I'm just a kid again. "It's an acquired taste," she says.

We sit and smoke together. I could get used to this. And then she stands. "I'd better go." I'm not sure if she sees the disappointment on my face, but she adds: "Don't buy into his garbage. Your mother got sick, and she died. It happens every day, and if anyone could stop it, it wouldn't happen."

"How do you not buy into it?" I ask. Everyone else seems to. Even I had found a way to believe that my mother would be okay.

She's thoughtful. "I read books," she says. "It isn't encouraged around here, but my mom feels guilty, and she gets them for me. Most people here don't think about the world outside of this place."

I want to ask her what books she reads. I want to ask why she stays if she doesn't believe in Prophet Warren. But I can't. I've never seen her this way, open and vulnerable. I don't want to say anything that will remind her I'm sixteen.

Tamara didn't recognize a thing. Sam had told her that his mother died when he was sixteen. His father, unable to cope, had become less and less of a father until he was just a memory. Sam had rarely spoken of his father, but when he did, his words were drenched in undisguised resentment. Tamara had never met the man.

She wondered now if the cult was an invention meant to express some larger truth in Sam's life. She wanted to believe that because the alternative was that he'd hidden a huge part of himself from her. They'd had hours of conversations about anything and everything over the years. If he'd once belonged to a cult, a wacky one from the sound of it, how had that never come up?

The Summer of Lorelai
by
Sam Foster
II

My eyes are unfocused. It's morning, and I haven't eaten since dinner two days ago. I doubt I slept more than three hours last night. I couldn't bring myself to share my mother's blanket, and the auditorium chairs aren't good for more than thirty minutes at a stretch. I finally took off my shirt, balled it underneath my head, and stretched out on the stage, but that was only moderately more comfortable. I almost don't mind. My mother is gone, and though I've had a long time to prepare, I can't imagine the world without her. Suffering feels right.

Two men carry a table onto the stage and place my mother atop it. The auditorium is filling, and Prophet Warren, dressed in his ceremonial white robe, takes his place at the head of the table. He instructs me to stand at his side.

"Praise God," he begins. Everyone in the auditorium stands and as one, repeats: *Praise God.*

My father is in the front row, and we lock eyes. I see fatigue and sadness. I'm still waiting for the fury. I don't look for Lorelai, though I know she's here. Everyone is here. The auditorium is full.

"We say—" Prophet Warren calls.

The torch is bright, the crowd responds together. Somehow, standing next to Prophet Warren, I forget to speak.

"We know—"

The torch is hot. I move my lips but don't contribute to their voice.

"We will lead—"

Our people to the promised land by torchlight.

"We will destroy—"

Our enemies through the fire of the torch.

"You may be seated."

Praise God.

"The Lord gives," Prophet Warren begins, "and the devil takes. I am the Prophet of the Torch, and you, my torches, are prophets of God through me. The devil cannot take what you protect through faith. Janelle," he says, referring to the new name he's given my mother, "came to us a sick woman. I made her a torch and restored her spirit. But as much as it pains me, I cannot fight your battles for you. My faith cannot stand in the place of your faith."

My mind wanders. My parents claimed to enjoy Prophet Warren's meandering sermons, but I've never cared for them. At times, I believed in Prophet Warren, believed that my mother would be okay. How could she not be? My family gave up everything. Even now, despite Lorelai's warnings, I wonder if he can bring my mother back. If he couldn't, why would he attempt it so publicly? I want to sleep. I don't even want to go home anymore. I just want to lie on my cot and never wake up.

"Bahati has spent a day and night preparing his mother's spirit."

I still have no idea what that means.

"Satan"—Prophet Warren places a hand on my mother's forehead—"I command you to return this spirit. It was not yours to take, and I rebuke you."

I watch my mother, her closed eyelids. I search them for movement.

"Satan, you have no power here. I command you to return this spirit."

Prophet Warren steps back and rests his gaze on me. There's no anger, just pity. I look away, down at the stage. My mother hasn't moved.

He continues for an interminable time to rebuke Satan and to demand the return of my mother's spirit. It's hard to watch my mother, so I turn to the audience, where people are beginning to fidget in their seats. My mother doesn't move.

Prophet Warren grows frustrated. He's sweating profusely from his forehead and temples. He turns away from my mother and faces the crowd. "This is a lesson in faith," he roars. "Bahati loves his mother. I can see that love in him. I can also see the emptiness, the space where faith should be. We should not rebuke young Bahati. His lack of faith is not his fault. We should, each of us, hold our torches high in hopes that he may gain sight."

"Praise God."

Praise God.

Prophet Warren turns and leaves the stage. I wait for my father, but he leaves with the others. Soon the auditorium is empty. Not even Lorelai remains.

~

I'm afraid to leave the auditorium until hours later, when Lorelai retrieves me.

"I have news," she says. "I don't know if it will be good news to you. It would be great news to me."

I watch her as we walk, waiting. The day is unusually warm for December, the sunshine incongruous with the loss of my mother. We cut through the grass, toward the building full of offices that have been converted to living spaces.

"The Big Torch is giving you your own room."

I've never heard her or anyone else refer to Prophet Warren as the Big Torch. It sounds disrespectful, but Lorelai has a way with irreverence that clouds her true intentions.

"What about my father?" I ask.

"The last thing you need to worry about is your father. Not sure if you know it, but he's an important man around here. These idiots were having a hell of a time organizing a construction project before your father came. The Big Torch will take care of him. If you play your cards right, he'll take care of you too."

I don't know what Lorelai means. What cards? What game am I playing? I don't ask. I don't want to know. I want to sleep.

My room is smaller than the one I shared with my parents, but it has a bed. A duffel bag of clothes sits in the corner beside my basketball. The ball was the one non-clothing item my parents allowed me to bring. *We're trading all of this,* my father told me quietly, the two of us standing in my old bedroom in our old house, *to save your mother.*

I would've left the basketball behind had he pressed.

Lorelai checks her watch. "Lunch is in thirty minutes. Someone will bring it to your room. It won't be me. The Big Torch is meeting potential recruits, and he's taking me along." She starts to leave but then stops. "I hope you can read, Bahati, because I left a book under your bed. There's no rule against reading, but keep it low-key. These philistines will look at you funny."

I crouch to look under the bed.

"It's about death and immortality and anguish," she says as my hand grasps the hardcover book. *Interview with the Vampire.* "I hope it helps."

~

Two trays of food are next to my bed when I awaken. Lunch, I assume, and dinner. My room has no windows, and I have no idea what time it is. I fell asleep with the fluorescent ceiling light on. One tray holds lasagna and French fries. A sandwich and green beans are on the other. All of it is cold. I don't know which was lunch and which was dinner, but I sit on the edge of my bed and eat it all. I feel uncomfortably full afterward.

The bathroom is at the end of the hallway, and I'm glad to make it there and back without seeing anyone. I miss my father. I wonder if he came by my room while I was asleep. If so, he didn't leave a note.

I retrieve Lorelai's book from beneath my bed. My room doesn't have space for a chair or table, so I prop myself up on the bed and read.

My eyes tire, the words blur, and still, I read. Even halfway through, I don't want to stop. I don't want to think about my mother. And I don't want to think about Prophet Warren's accusations. I don't want to wonder where my father is and why he hasn't visited me. I'm in another world, and I feel close to Lorelai, being where she has been. I want to find Lorelai and talk to her about the book.

When I can't read another word, I return the book to its place beneath my mattress. I turn off the harsh fluorescent light and lie in bed imagining myself as a vampire, created by Lorelai, she instructing me in the ways of the immortal.

It was hard for Tamara not to conflate Bahati and Sam. Bahati's suffering was painful for her because she didn't know where the real-life Sam ended and the fictional Bahati began. She'd had to remind herself throughout the attempted resurrection that what she was reading wasn't real. But she wasn't convinced. There was a detail at the end that pierced her. *Interview with the Vampire.* That was the book that had opened the real-life Sam's heart and mind to the world of fiction. But he'd never told Tamara how he'd discovered it.

The Summer of Lorelai
by
Sam Foster
III

It's my father's wedding day. My mother has been dead for a month.

Charley and I finished restoring the bus engine last week. I guess he's attending the wedding because he isn't here. We've been working on an old motorcycle, and I just stare at it. The transmission is shot, and I just don't care. I don't want to work. I don't want to do anything.

"Here you are."

Her voice thrills me. I don't want to be thrilled.

"You have to go to the wedding," Lorelai says. She's wearing a simple yellow dress.

"I don't have to do nothing."

She sits on the bench beside me. I don't look at her.

"I'm a mechanic in training," I say. "What is your job?"

She laughs softly. I still don't look at her. "I don't have a title. I show new members around and help them adjust. Sometimes, I tag along with Marshall when he recruits. It suits me. It leaves a lot of free time."

"What if I don't want you to help me adjust?"

She laughs again. "Look at me."

I can't help it. And she's giving me that smile. She's looking into my eyes and our lips are so close.

"If I don't do my job," she says, "I get in trouble. This may surprise you, but I go out of my way to avoid trouble. What if we sit together at the wedding? Pretty please."

~

"You need to make friends here," Lorelai tells me. We're walking back to the auditorium, where my father will get married.

"I have friends."

"Who?" She knows everything about everyone in this place.

"Charley," I say. "You."

"Charley makes you dip your hands in motor oil and who knows what else. He can hardly be called a friend. I'm pressuring you to watch your father marry a woman you don't know. You need friends your age."

Her comment stings, but I hide the hurt.

"I wouldn't make it in this place without Stacey." Stacey, Lorelai's best friend, ignores me, so I don't really know her. "Words can be dangerous around here. You need people you can let your guard down with."

"You let your guard down with me," I point out.

She regards me. "Probably more than I should. But you don't know the half of it."

"So, tell me."

She smiles. "Another time." She checks her watch. "But I can show you something. Just a quick detour."

She turns to the right and leads me through the vegetable garden. "They grow turnip greens, broccoli, cabbage, and a ton of other things here. It was my first job," she explains. "I hated it. Actually, growing vegetables is one of those things I would like if it was my choice to do it. I was fifteen, and I think Vivian took pity on my rebellious spirit." Vivian was in charge of the garden. "She brought me to this clearing." Lorelai leads me through a dense copse of trees that opens onto a field. "She gave me wildflower seeds and told me how to plant them. I fell in love. I would show up at the garden, do the bare minimum, and then sneak back here. Vivian didn't seem to mind."

"You grow these?" I ask, examining pale-purple blooms.

"Yes. That's *Hepatica americana*. This"—she directs my attention to another shrub with white blossoms—"is winter honeysuckle. *Lonicera fragrantissima*. Smell it. This place isn't exactly a secret. Vivian knows about it. But it's mine. It helps to have something that belongs to you."

As we walked back through the vegetable garden, Lorelai asked, "Have you spoken to your father lately?"

"He asked me to be in the wedding."

"And clearly, you aren't."

"I'm not." There is so much I want to tell her, and we don't have many steps between us and the auditorium. She's probably right about me needing a friend. "He barely talks to me. I think he blames me for my mother's death."

Lorelai stops walking, buying us time. "I don't know your father, but I don't think he believes that. I told you words can be dangerous. Contradicting Marshall's words is especially dangerous. Your father is important here, but there are lines that can't be crossed. That goes for Marshall too. He's giving your father a wife, which tells me he wants to keep your father happy."

I didn't realize Prophet Warren is *giving* Jules to my father, like she's a piece of property. I should've known. Jules is barely thirty. "Why do you stay here?" I ask.

"Where would I go? Not to answer a question with a question, but what would I do? We all need food, shelter, and security."

~

A line forms to congratulate the bride and groom. Lorelai steps aside to speak with Stacey. I seize the moment. I hurry to my room and gather my clothes into the duffel bag. I leave the basketball.

I thought about this all through the wedding, Lorelai's words echoing around my brain. *We all need food, shelter, and security.* I will leave this place because I cannot stay. I will find food, shelter, and security. And then I will return for Lorelai.

Tamara stepped away from the manuscript to make herself a cup of tea. Sam's writing was dark, which wasn't a surprise. Sam had been dark. She'd thought she'd been acquainted with that part of him, but now she wondered if she'd misjudged its depth.

She wanted to stop reading, but she couldn't give up hope that an aha moment was a page away, that he'd written something that would make everything clear.

She settled in front of his laptop with tea and continued to read.

The Summer of Lorelai
by
Sam Foster
IV

I think I've gotten off lightly when Prophet Warren tells me I will have to kneel for two hours. He doesn't seem angry, just disappointed. He leads me to a classroom, where Jake, one of the security guards, sits behind a desk.

"I want you to think about why you left and why that was wrong," Prophet Warren says. "As a minor, your father is responsible for your physical welfare. If you leave here and get hurt, he must bear that responsibility. As your spiritual leader, I am responsible for the welfare of your soul. Outside of this community, you will find only corruption and sin and that will surely lead you to hell. It hurts me to mete out punishment but losing your soul would hurt me more. Jake"—he motions to the security guard—"will stay with you."

The floor is hard, thin carpet over what could be concrete. I kneel and it feels okay. Prophet Warren leaves. I look around for a clock. "What time is it?" I ask Jake.

"Silence." The word is curt, and I think he's joking. I haven't spoken to him much, but he's always been friendly. Not today. He doesn't tell me the time. He sits back in his chair and watches me.

If, as Prophet Warren said, I am my father's responsibility, where is my father? I haven't seen him since they brought me back here. Instead of thinking about why I was wrong to run, I think about what I can do better next time. I'll take a car, if only to get me to the nearest town. It's fifteen miles away, and I was halfway there on foot when they caught me. If I make it to town next time, they'll never find me.

I don't know how much time has passed, but pain is radiating from my knees and up my thighs.

"Keep your back straight," Jake says. I look up at him. He stares back at me, cold. "I won't say it again."

I straighten my back. My body trembles with pain and fatigue. I want to ask for the time, but I tried that already.

Jake reaches under the desk and comes up carrying a wooden staff. He walks slowly around the desk and, before I realize what's happening, he strikes me hard across the shoulder.

I scream as I fall forward.

"I told you to keep your back straight." He returns to his seat behind the desk, and I glare at him, the pain in my shoulder distracting me from the pain in my legs and lower back. I consider taking the stick from him and beating him with it. But then what? Prophet Warren could send me back here with two guards. Three guards. As many as it takes. "Do what you're supposed to do," Jake says, "and we'll get along just fine. Eyeball me again, and I'll kill you."

I'd like to crack his head open.

I banish thoughts of this place from my mind. I command myself not to think about my mother or my father or his new wife. When I think about those things, the physical pain feels unbearable. I feel like I can't go another moment. And I have no idea how many moments are left. I think about Sensei Tony. He would make us lie on our backs, lift our legs six inches, and hold. He wouldn't count. Not aloud, anyway. We'd relax when he told us to relax. *Knowing when the end will come,* he explains, *makes it too easy. In life, we don't know the outcome.*

But Sensei Tony didn't torture us. He trained us. I appreciate the difference, and I can't hold this position a moment longer. I think about Lorelai. I ran away for me but also for her. The idea of securing food, shelter, and security for her was intoxicating. I know I can do it. For us. I think about a future with her.

I've never felt this way about any girl. I had a crush on Lisa Turtle from *Saved by the Bell* when I was eleven. I used to rack my brain, wondering what I could do to meet her one day. I never really believed it would happen, but I spent enough time thinking about it. Then I had a crush on Mrs. Butler, my third-grade teacher. I never imagined anything would come of that either, but I thought about her all the time. I've had a couple of girlfriends, but they were just girls and not really all that different from friends. Lorelai is real and just barely out of reach. Food, shelter, and security away from this place is the pathway to our future.

I fall forward onto my hands and the relief is worth the risk of the staff. Jake rises, and this time strikes me on the buttocks. Pain explodes with the force of it. I'm breathing hard, but I don't cry out.

"Five," Jake says. "Four. Three."

I hurry back to my kneeling position. If I could just know how long I have left. Time eludes me. Has an hour passed? I think about standing. Sitting. Lying in my bed. I hold that future in my mind. If I just hold on.

My body is trembling, and I fear falling forward. I don't want to get hit again.

"Get up," Jake says.

I scrutinize his face to be sure I understand him correctly.

"Your time is up." He approaches me, without the stick this time, and extends a hand to help me up. I ignore it and stand on my own. My legs cramp, and I thought the suffering would end at the two-hour mark. He extends his hand for me to shake. "No hard feelings," he says. "You did wrong, and you paid the price."

I reluctantly shake his hand. I just want to go back to my room.

~

"Why did you run?" Lorelai asks me.

I'm alone on the basketball court with my personal basketball. I throw it to her, a bounce pass, and she catches it. Barely.

"Do you play?"

"Do I look like I play?" she asks, holding the ball.

"You look like me."

She scrunches her eyebrows.

"When I was five."

"Oh." She laughs. "You're funny, huh?" She turns to the basket. "Take this." She throws it up, no form, and shoots an air ball. She turns to me and laughs again.

"I was hitting the backboard when I was five," I say. I grab the ball and hit a layup. "I'll teach you how to play."

"You need friends your own age."

I throw the ball to her, easy, and again, she catches it. Barely.

"How many books have you given me?" I ask.

"Two."

"And I've read them both. Now, I'll teach you to play basketball."

"That doesn't sound like a fair trade," she says.

"You can throw in a massage for me," I say.

"You wish."

I do.

"Let's start with dribbling."

Gamely, she dribbles. I can tell she hasn't done it in a long time, if ever.

"There you go," I say. "Use the other hand."

Her left is useless, but she tries.

"Are you going to answer my question?" she asks.

"When I asked you why you haven't left," I say, "you told me food, shelter, and security."

She nods.

"You didn't tell me what happens when you get caught."

"I didn't think you would run away. Isn't food, shelter, and security enough?"

"I can't stay here."

"You can. I heard Warren went easy on you."

"Is that what they call it?" I ask.

"It can be worse. I've heard about people being burned with torches."

I show her how to shoot. She continues to shoot with no form.

"You have to find your niche," she tells me. "You like working with Charley?"

"It's all right. I miss karate. Does anyone here go to college?"

Lorelai shakes her head and shoots, hitting the backboard this time. "As aggressive as Marshall is about recruiting educated people, no one here goes to college."

"This isn't the life I was supposed to lead."

"If only life worked that way," she tells me. "We lead the lives we have."

We lead the lives we have.

Even after Tamara stopped reading to heat soup for her dinner, that line stuck with her. Had Sam believed that? She couldn't know for certain, but she didn't think he had.

On the first anniversary of Sam's death, Tamara had left Brian with a babysitter and driven to a campsite that she and Sam had frequented as newlyweds. Being there, on that night, had felt right.

Her telescope hadn't been out of its case in over a year, and she'd looked forward to getting reacquainted with it, but the sky had been so dark and full of stars that she'd wound up lying on her back and gazing upward with naked eyes. It boggled her mind to think that each star was orbited by a planetary system. One wouldn't know that by looking. Even aided by the most powerful telescopes on Earth, the planets beyond our solar system remained invisible, if not undetectable. Indirect methods could confirm the existence of these exoplanets: a slight dimming of the star as the exoplanet passes in front of its sight line to Earth; the minuscule variations in the star's movement caused by the gravitational pull of the orbiting exoplanet.

It was her and Sam's night, but thoughts of Malik had crept in. She and Malik had shared a gratitude for living in a time when so much was known. *Can you imagine how maddening it would be,* Malik had once asked, *to look up at the sky and not even know what the stars were made of, to have no clue how they'd gotten there?*

Do you realize, Tamara had replied, *that people living a hundred years from now might say the same about us? When they encounter intelligent life, they might pity us for never having known it?*

Such talk had always led to speculation about what such an encounter might bring: advanced technology, ultramodern social systems.

Shortly after Sam's death, Malik had visited her in Connecticut. *We never talked about that trip to Tearbritches,* he'd said.

For good reason, she'd told him.

She was teasing, but when he sighed, she saw a sadness that reached his eyes. *I was having a moment of crisis—*

You don't need to explain.

Tearbritches helped me. I can't explain that, so I won't try. I can get confused, but the stars are always true. Remember that. No matter how messed up things get here on Earth, or how confused you might be, the stars always remain true. They're beyond the reach of any problem humankind can create. I wanted you to know that at Tearbritches.

Malik and Sam. Sam and Malik. Those two loves of her life had encapsulated everything she'd lost. Only Brian had given her a reason to live.

But she hadn't been living. She'd been acting.

At home, she'd acted like a mother. At work, she'd acted like a quant. Brian had been a typical happy and giggly four-year-old. And Tamara had been consumed by the fear that she would transmit her depression to him. Brian had a father who killed himself. He had a mother who could barely cope. That added up to no chance at all for him.

She'd missed Sam. She'd missed Malik. And when she hadn't been careful, she'd catch herself mourning the depressed man Brian was destined to become.

That night, on the first anniversary of Sam's death, Tamara had felt emptier than ever, more alone than ever. Thoughts of the future had left her feeling cold.

But when she'd focused on the stars, let herself feel the sensations of floating, she'd felt somehow connected to Malik. As teens, they'd wanted nothing more than to encounter extraterrestrial life, to know the secrets of the universe. Even on that night, the thought of life somewhere out there had given her hope. Lying there, she'd been seized by a crazy thought: Why not take the energy she tossed daily into the black hole of finance and give it to the search for extraterrestrial intelligence?

The thought had been too crazy to entertain.

She'd heard Malik's voice. *The stars are always true.* And then she'd heard Sam's voice. *You should do it.* She'd felt Sam, as if he'd been beside her, the two of them having one of their thousand conversations. *You never know, maybe* that's *what you were meant to do.*

We lead the lives we have.

No, Tamara decided. Sam hadn't believed that.

The Summer of Lorelai
by
Sam Foster
V

I hear her voice, a whisper, and I think I'm dreaming.

"Bahati." She shakes my shoulder.

I awake to darkness and the urgency in her tone.
"Lorelai?" I ask, though I recognize her smell, the lotion only she wears.

"I'm leaving," she whispers. "Come with me."

I sit up.

"I'm turning on the light," she says a moment before my eyes are assaulted by brightness.

I squint until they adjust, and then recoil at the sight of her face. "What happened?" I ask. She has a black eye, and her lip is swollen.

Her lip quivers, but she doesn't answer.

"Who did this to you? I'll kill him."

That gets a response from her. "Don't be an idiot. If you want to leave this place, come with me. You won't get another chance."

When I don't respond immediately, she says, "Are you coming?"

"Where?"

"I don't know. Anywhere. Away from here. I have car keys. You need to decide now."

"I have to brush my teeth," I say, self-conscious.

"No time. I'm leaving." She makes a move toward the door. For the first time, I notice her bag. "Are you coming?"

I throw my toiletries into my duffel bag, which already holds the entirety of my wardrobe. I grab my basketball and follow her into the warm night.

～

She shushes me when I try to speak. I follow her in silence to the vegetable garden, where she stops at the shed to retrieve a garden trowel.

"Are we digging our way out?" I ask, an attempt at levity I don't feel.

She answers me with a shush and continues into the copse of trees. The darkness doesn't seem to impede her, and I follow as closely as I can without stepping on her heels. She doesn't pause in the clearing. She walks straight to a bush, drops to her knees, and begins to dig.

Ten minutes later, she's pulling plastic bags out of the ground.

"I've been collecting this money since I got here," she whispers.

By *collecting*, I assume she means *stealing*. A personal supply of money is forbidden here. All money belongs to the collective.

"I didn't know how well the freezer bags would work. I figured it was worth a shot. Isn't my money, anyway."

"I'd say it's your money." She hands me a bag, and its heft is impressive. "How much do you have?"

She shrugs. "I didn't keep count. In case it rotted in the ground. I didn't want to know."

She carefully refills the hole and uses her foot to scatter fallen pine needles over the ground.

"Let's go," she says, and I follow her back through the trees, past the vegetable garden, to the parking lot. She pauses at a Chrysler LeBaron and unlocks the door. We get in, and she brings the engine to life. The clock shows 2:36 a.m. She puts her foot on the gas, and we inch forward.

"Headlights," I say. From the passenger seat, I can't see three feet beyond the windshield. I can't imagine she is faring much better.

"Someone might see. No brakes either."

She drives slowly, leaning forward as if it helps her visibility.

"If we hit something," I say, "someone might hear that."

"I won't hit anything. Let me concentrate."

I lean back and, since I can't see anyway, close my eyes. I wonder if she can hear my heart pounding. It's been six months since I tried this. If we're caught, I'll get worse than I got before, but being in it with her helps. Some. I can't stop my hands from trembling.

"Headlights," she says. "Better?"

I open my eyes. We're on a dark road, but the headlights provide visibility.

"Yes," I say. "Better. What happened to you?"

She sighs. I think she's going to cry. Her voice trembles, but she manages to hold it together. "I was punished. But I guess you figured that out. Do you know Reginald Parker?"

"The doctor," I say. "I've met him."

"Warren told me—" Her voice breaks and she pauses. "Warren said I have to marry him."

I don't know what to say. Dr. Parker is like sixty years old. His hair is gray, and he has a big gut. He seems nice enough, but no one is that nice.

"I refused. Apparently, Reginald is pulling away. He has some concerns about the community, and Warren says it's my duty to show him the light. Whatever that means."

"Isn't Dr. Parker married?" I ask.

"That doesn't stop Warren. How many wives does he have?"

Three that I know of. I don't respond. There is nothing to say about the Prophets of the Torch that Lorelai doesn't know.

"I've dreaded this for years," Lorelai says. "That's what we do when we become women. We get married. And I don't know any women who choose their husbands. Warren says get married, and you get married. I was stupid enough to believe I could avoid it. Warren has always dangled me out as available. My value was being available, and I thought it could stay that way."

"So he beat you?" I ask.

She wipes a tear from her face, and then the floodgates open. She's sobbing, and I wonder if she can see the road. "Do you need me to drive?"

She doesn't answer. Finally, she says, "He forced Stacey to beat me."

Stacey. Lorelai's best friend. The one to whom she can confide anything. I consider that as Lorelai cries, her sobs downgraded now to soft weeping. Warren inflicted pain and deprived her of comfort in one stroke.

"We're never going back, right?" I ask.

"Right," she says, "we're never going back."

"Why did you take time to cover the hole?" I ask.

"Even when I stopped working in the garden, Vivian looked the other way while I used that space. I don't want that to blow back on her."

Already, I've come farther with Lorelai than I made it alone. I don't care where we go. Things are going to be better for us now.

~

Tamara couldn't read any more. Not at the moment. She had no idea what was going to happen next, but she didn't imagine things would be better for them.

Chapter 13

COOPER

Cooper's days and nights were spent in the past. Only his body lived in the present, his slow but steady weight loss a reminder that time was short. FBI interrogations, solitary time in his cell, even sleep: they all delivered him to the past.

He painted every day. Even when his mood was low and his body was weak, painting felt right. He worked with a sense of urgency and a clarity of purpose. He was recording his history on canvas, turning the story of his life into art.

In retrospect, each event of his life seemed like a logical extension of an event that had come before. Why, then, had life felt so unpredictable as he'd been living it? He reflected on the period when he'd worked in Willie's club and labeled the canvas *Bad Decisions*. His memories rose up as images.

~

"This guy is a piece of garbage," Willie had said. He and Cooper were in Willie's office at the club, speaking in hushed tones. "He molested this child for years, and now he's hired a high-powered attorney. Can you imagine a seven-year-old having to testify in open court about what that monster did to her?"

Cooper shook his head. He couldn't imagine it.

"Her father just wants him dead. No trial. Real justice."

"Why doesn't her father kill him?" Cooper asked.

"I would kill him myself."

"But you aren't a murderer," Cooper said, recalling Willie's words. He looked good—much better, at least, than he had after the beating three months ago. He had a scar above his left eye. Other than that, he wasn't the worse for wear.

"Where else can I turn?"

"Look," Cooper said, "I hate this. I have kids. If it were Kathy, I would strangle the guy with my bare hands. But it isn't my job to mete out justice. I don't know these people."

"It's your job because you're the only one who can do it," Willie said passionately. "That day, man. You just walked in. Didn't say a word. Pop! Dropped him."

"I told him to drop his gun," Cooper said. "Twice. He was aiming it at me."

"I don't remember that. I just saw a bad dude stroll in and do what needed to be done. You can do this. Do it for the little girl. Do it for her father. Do it for the next victims. The money won't hurt either."

Cooper bit his lip. He and Lisa hadn't taken a vacation in years. They used to talk about where they would go when he made his first big art sale. Her dream destination was New Zealand. He'd heard nice things about Hawaii. They could find a kid-friendly resort with super-vised playtime for the twins while he and Lisa enjoyed adult activities.

"No more cash," Cooper said.

"I'll pay you through the club," Willie told him. "A consulting fee. We'll do a Form 1099. Clean money."

~

Cooper didn't enjoy killing people. It was unpleasant, so he did it as quickly as possible and left the deed behind him. He was meticulous. He observed his target and moved only when the opportunity was right. A witness would mean a second needless killing. He made sure there were no witnesses.

He continued to work at the nightclub, drawing the small salary Willie paid. He cleaned when asked and listened to Willie's inane meanderings when summoned.

The twins were running around and talking, saying new and surprising things every day. Lisa wanted more time with them, at least until they started school, and they'd talked about her paring back to part-time work. Cooper's income was unpredictable, so they hadn't pulled the trigger. Saving money on childcare would be an upside, but losing Lisa's health insurance would be a bigger downside. Willie didn't offer medical.

Each job began with the target's transgression: rape, domestic abuse, theft. Willie provided Cooper with pertinent information: a name and picture at minimum. Cooper would take his time. He had no connection to these targets, and he was careful not to manufacture one.

~

"The case is cold," Willie told Cooper. They were in Willie's office at the club. More than a year had passed since Glenn, the youth minister, had died in this very room.

"How do you know?" Cooper asked.

Willie smiled slyly. "His widow requires comfort from time to time."

"Tell me you aren't sleeping with her."

"Someone has to. Her husband is gone. You don't expect her to take a vow of chastity."

Cooper usually just nodded and smiled at Willie's nonsense. Now, anger rose to his face. "I expect you to be a human being. Does it mean anything to you that he was your friend?"

Willie blinked. "Why are you so serious, Coop?"

"He was your best friend," Cooper yelled. "If you slept with Lisa—I'm serious because you deserved what he did to you, and I regret stopping him."

"Saint Cooper," Willie replied sarcastically, "you finally show your true face. You look down on me, but you're a murderer. I give you a job, and you hold me in contempt."

"You and I are nothing alike," Cooper said, unable to rein in his temper. "I kill people who deserve to die. I don't—"

Willie laughed uproariously. "You're clowning me, right?"

Cooper stared at him.

Willie put down his drink and laughed some more. "You didn't seriously believe those stories I told you?"

Why would Cooper not have believed them? "What are you saying?" He wasn't sure he wanted to know. "Wayne Malone wasn't a pedophile?"

Willie shrugged. "I have no reason to believe he was. But you never know. He was alive, and now, thanks to you, he isn't. That's all I know about Wayne Malone. That's all I need to know. I collected the money and didn't ask questions. Do I look like a social worker to you?"

Cooper couldn't respond.

Willie sipped his drink and watched Cooper. "I said those things to make it easier. I didn't think you were stupid enough to believe them. We don't live in a comic book. You aren't Luke Cage."

Cooper stood, either to kill Willie or to leave. He didn't know in that moment. He could reach forward, grab Willie's head, and snap his neck where he sat. Or he could bludgeon him with the whiskey glass. He walked away instead.

"You can't walk away from me," Willie said. "What are you going to do without me?"

Cooper stopped and turned to him. "Let me tell you something, you imbecile. I'm not John Gotti. I didn't make Glenn disappear.

If—when—they find him, it won't look good if you're screwing his widow. Stay away from her."

~

Willie was right about one thing: Cooper couldn't walk away from him.

It was a little after 3:00 a.m., and he sat in a child-size chair in the twins' bedroom. Kathy and Howard were the portrait of peace. Cooper hadn't slept soundly since his argument with Willie.

He couldn't stop thinking of the men he'd killed. He'd thought they were bad men, deserving of death. He'd thought he was making a better world by removing them from it. But had he really thought that? Had he really been so naive? Or had it just made it easier for him to take the money?

Did it matter?

He couldn't decide.

Lisa had cut her hours back to part time, and she'd been so much happier since doing so. They'd lost her health insurance, and replacing it was expensive, a small price to pay for the extra time she had with the twins. They did something fun as a family every weekend, and that wasn't cheap either. The money he could drop on lunch and a movie for the four of them would've made him sweat on his credit union salary. Watching the twins sleep, he thought about the plans he and Lisa had for them. They'd talked about starting them in private school next year.

No, Cooper could not walk away from Willie.

Even once he'd admitted that to himself, and accepted it, he still couldn't fall asleep. He lay beside Lisa, listening to her breathe. On their wedding night, he'd told her he would take care of her. They hadn't been able to afford a honeymoon because of the cost of the ceremony, but he'd promised her a good life. She'd believed in him.

He'd never imagined that he would find himself where he was right now.

~

"Good to see you," Willie said. He sat behind the desk in his office. A week had passed since their argument.

"I won't stay long."

Willie motioned for him to sit. Cooper remained on his feet.

"I won't be coming here again," Cooper told him. "It isn't a good idea."

Willie nodded.

Cooper dropped the package he was holding on Willie's desk. "It's a disposable cell phone."

"Huh," Willie said. He picked up the package and studied it with curiosity. "What will they think of next?"

"When you have a job for me, call on this. I'll tell you where to meet. You'll pay me in cash. From now on, you and I don't have a relationship on paper. We'll only talk when we absolutely must to conduct our business. Can you do that?"

Willie nodded. "I'll talk to you soon, Cooper."

Chapter 14

TAMARA

Sam's manuscript, what Tamara had read of it, lived inside her. She'd managed to suppress thoughts of it while she was on the miniature golf course with Brian, but over dinner, as he'd talked with excitement about horseback riding, canoeing, and archery, all camp activities that would be new to him, her mind had pulled up the darkest passages from the novel. Thoughts of Sam sitting watch over his mother's corpse or being punished for trying to escape made her shudder. And his infatuation with Lorelai . . . reading it had felt like she was being bludgeoned.

She drove Brian to the camp where he would spend the next two weeks. That seemed like a long time to her (she'd never attended overnight camp as a child), and she'd considered letting him go for only one. But his friend Phillip had been signed up for two, so she couldn't really say no. He was quiet on the drive, filling the two hours with games on his tablet (electronic devices, to her delight, were not allowed at camp), and she spent more time trapped in her head with Sam's novel.

Halfway through the return trip and sick of the rumination, she called Melinda. Instead of thinking about the manuscript, she talked about it.

"Sam wasn't my first crush," Tamara said, "and I've always assumed I wasn't his either."

"I see where you're going with this," Melinda told her. "I just want to remind you that Lorelai might not be real."

"The infatuation doesn't bother me. I can handle that. What really gets me is that darn reference to *Interview with the Vampire*. He once told me the Vampire Chronicles was his gateway to a deep, lifelong love of fiction. He didn't say a word about the woman who introduced him to it. But what would he have said? 'Reading fiction is an integral part of my life, introduced to me by my first love, who, by the way, isn't you.'"

"Oh, Tamara," Melinda said, "don't cry."

"I'm sorry. I don't want to cry. It's just frustrating. I wish I hadn't read the book."

"He should've shared it with you while he was writing it," Melinda said. "That way you two could've discussed it."

"But he didn't. And I think I see why."

"We all have a past," Melinda said. "We usually just don't share every detail with our partners. Why are you laughing?"

Tamara wiped her eyes. "Because you're right. Except that you're the rare exception. You and Jeff are each other's past."

"Maybe that's my problem," she said. "I don't have a past."

"Do you think that's it?" Tamara asked. "Curiosity."

"I don't think so. But I don't know. I just know what I feel, like we've reached a crossroad. If I take his path, I'll resent him for it. If he takes my path, I'm afraid he'll resent me. And we can't go back."

"Where does that leave you?"

"Well, he starts the new job in two weeks. He's looking for a furnished apartment in Austin. I'll stay in the house for the time being." Tamara could tell that Melinda was struggling to maintain a neutral tone, to conceal the magnitude of her pain. "And you think you're sneaky, changing the subject. Back to Lorelai. She might not even be based on a real person."

Melinda was right. Tamara had even tried this logic on herself. Truthfully, she just wanted to wallow for a bit longer. She didn't want to deal with the bigger question, the potential holes in her knowledge about Sam.

She knew a list of things about his childhood that she'd once believed composed a narrative. His mother died when he was a teenager. His father, unable to cope with his mother's death and single parenthood, had sent Sam to live with his aunt. He played a lot of basketball and video games. That's what he'd told her. There'd been no mention of a crazy cult. He'd never spoken of abuse, physical or mental. Sam had missed his father in those early days, and to his astonishment, he'd never stopped missing him. Those were the things Tamara knew. So where in the hell had this book come from?

Perhaps Marshall Warren and the Prophets of the Torch and even Lorelai were symbols for some emotional truth Sam saw in his childhood. He'd never told her a bestselling-novel-worthy story from his past, and he often said he wanted to write a *big* book. Perhaps he was taking a painful, if humdrum, childhood and adding entertainment.

"I wonder how he was going to present this to me," Tamara said. "I never understood why he was secretive about it. I took him at his word that he didn't want anything to influence his process until he was finished. But he had to know the book would bother me."

"I imagine that's something writers and their families have to deal with," Melinda said. "I'm sure a lot of books cause discomfort. Maybe that's why he didn't finish."

"Maybe," Tamara said, though she knew why he hadn't finished. She hadn't shared the reason with Melinda or anyone else, mostly because she thought it was Sam's prerogative to share or not share. "He used to tell me about this writer he admired—I can't remember the name—but the author's family hated him because he aired their dirty laundry."

"I don't even want to think about Jeff writing a book about our marriage. Especially if it's fiction. I wouldn't know how to take any of it. Have you finished Sam's manuscript?"

"I have a chapter to go. I read until I couldn't anymore. I have a bad feeling about what's coming next."

"Why?"

Tamara didn't know how to answer. She hadn't told Melinda about the Prophets of the Torch and Bahati and Lorelai's escape. She would, but she wasn't ready to talk about that part yet. And honestly, she didn't know why she had a bad feeling about the next and final chapter. Sam had told her the novel was dark. And, yes, it was dark. But she'd left it on an upbeat note. She sensed something bad was coming. And she didn't want to read it.

When she arrived home late that night, exhausted from driving, instead of returning to the manuscript, she turned to the past. She tried to picture the man who'd written those words. He'd laid down the novel by day and lain in her bed by night, and all the while, she'd missed something. Had she known him at all? She searched her memory for an answer.

〜

A variety of emotions pulled Tamara's mood in an assortment of directions as she returned to work after New Year's 2009. She missed Brian, despite having only been apart from him for a couple of hours. She'd hidden her jealousy of Sam as she dressed for work that morning, pulling on a business suit for the first time in six weeks. In his new position as lecturer, he wasn't required on campus until noon, allowing him a leisurely morning with Brian. She should be happy, she knew, that Brian was spending less time in day care, and still, she wrestled with jealousy. She was nervous about being in the office, though in some respects she'd never left. She'd attended meetings virtually, chatted here and there with

Ian. Between feedings and naps, she'd kept abreast of financial news. She was excited about a new year. Barack Obama would be sworn in as the forty-fourth president of the United States in fifteen days, and she felt the collective hope of the nation. The state of the economy, domestic and global, caused her anxiety, and she wasn't alone. Worry was palpable in the office. Her fund had thrived during the early days of the crisis, but the ban on short selling was hurting their bottom line. She had to learn to be a working mother under the worst of conditions, and she wasn't certain she was up to it. Finally, she was glad to be back on the job. After weeks of wearisome chores, the gratifying labor of keeping a small human alive and quiet, her mind needed to be stretched. She needed the puzzle of mathematical models.

~

So much changed so fast that Tamara couldn't always identify cause and effect. After work, instead of meeting Sam in the city for dinner, she would hurry home, the breast milk she'd pumped during the day on ice in a bag slung over her shoulder. She would settle in the living room with Brian, he perhaps on his tummy time mat, while Sam cooked magnificent dinners, a skill neither of them had known he possessed. They would talk about Brian over dinner, the latest thing he'd done, followed by prognostications on his budding personality. And then, as if time hadn't passed, their conversation would turn to finance and the economy.

Sam kept a wary eye on Main Street, fixating on unemployment numbers: 7.6 percent in January, 8.1 percent in February, 8.5 percent in March. *We're going to ten,* he predicted darkly. Tamara didn't dispute it.

"How is your writing coming?" she asked him one evening.

"It's going well," he said, his typical response. And then he steered the conversation to the automotive bailout. He saw the bailouts as necessary, if unpalatable. *But the bailouts plus the current disparity in wealth,* he complained, *is a recipe for social disaster.*

Tamara didn't want to talk about the bailouts. "Are you writing about the economy in your novel?" she asked, wondering at her own flash of annoyance. She hadn't realized until then that she'd been looking forward to being married to an artist. She'd expected—reasonably, it seemed to her—that writing would change him in interesting ways. Not that he wasn't interesting before; she'd just been anticipating something new. She'd thought he would discuss literature over dinner, if not his own writing. She'd expected their conversations to skew away from the practical and into the philosophical. And she realized that she needed that. Finance was so dark these days. She needed to think of something else when she wasn't working.

"What?" he said, as if thrown by her change in subject. "No. My novel takes place in the late nineties. During the dot-com bubble. But I'm not writing about that."

"What are you writing about? All you talk about is the economy."

"I don't know how to talk about my writing," he said quietly.

She'd heard this before. And she'd always let it go. Not tonight. "How do you find time to read so much economic news? Doesn't that take time from your writing?"

"I turn the radio on when I'm hanging with Bri."

Even this, Tamara found unsatisfactory. "Are you talking to him?" she asked. "He needs to hear language. From the people caring for him." Sam regarded her, just now seeming to notice her irritation. He looked so taken aback that she felt guilty. Why was she attacking him, suggesting he was derelict as a father? "I'm sorry," she said. "I'm just tired. Please, let's just talk about something besides the economy."

They talked about Brian.

～

Tamara's hedge fund made money, but it was a trying year. Sam continued to obsess over the Great Recession and to write. Tamara presumed he wrote. She experienced moments of doubt, but her apprehensions were too weird to entertain. Husband leaves career to pretend to write a novel. She'd heard of stranger things. But that wasn't Sam. He told white lies now and again, like everyone, but he wasn't a liar.

Late in 2010, she saw the first evidence that her husband was indeed an aspiring novelist. He was quiet over dinner, agitated. He responded to questions with two-word answers. "Did something awful happen?" she finally asked him.

He sighed. "My writing hasn't been going well," he said.

"What's wrong?" Neither of them had mentioned his writing in weeks, as if it didn't exist.

"Writer's block, I guess."

"Oh."

"I was thinking." He paused. She wondered what he was thinking. "Maybe I can go away for a few weeks, jump-start things."

"Are you close to finishing?" she asked.

"I'm stuck. I wouldn't say I'm close to finishing, but I'm at a tough part. If I can get through this scene, the writing will flow again. But I need time to think. Maybe we can hire someone to help with Brian while you're at work."

"How long do you need?" she asked. "Where will you go?"

~

"Could the cult have something to do with Sam's murder?" Melinda asked.

They were at Tamara's house, drinking tea. Melinda was eating the sandwiches she'd brought to go with the tea. Tamara had no appetite.

"I don't even know that the cult is real. Can you imagine that he experienced something like that as a teenager and never mentioned it to me?"

Melinda sighed. "I don't know. It is hard to imagine. But maybe he couldn't talk about it."

"I've considered that. It just doesn't make sense. How would I not know that about my husband? Did I know him at all?"

"If he couldn't talk about it, that might explain why he wouldn't let you read the novel. Why didn't he finish it?"

Tamara paused before responding. "He became suicidal."

Melinda looked as if she'd been handed a complex math problem. She seemed to be puzzling something out before she asked, "When?"

"Shortly after Brian turned three. His writing was blocked, so we hired a nanny, and he went to stay at a friend's empty beach house. The friend had helped to drive Lehman into the ground, but a placement with Barclays had saved his vacation home in Cape Cod. Anyway, Sam and I spoke every night on the phone, and things seemed to be going well. He was supposed to stay for three weeks, but on the seventeenth day, he confessed that he hadn't written anything in nearly a week. I asked what he'd been doing: sunbathing, swimming in the ocean? I was teasing because it was so cold.

"I'll never forget how matter of fact he sounded when he said, 'I've been imagining ways to kill myself.' He said it as if he were admitting to spending his days in antique shops looking at Depression glass."

Tamara paused. Melinda didn't acknowledge her attempt at humor.

"The first few days there, he told me, watching the sun rise over the Atlantic inspired his creativity. Then, he found himself fantasizing about small sea creatures consuming his flesh and returning his matter to the ocean for reuse. The idea held such appeal that he researched small-craft rentals. First, he liked the idea of tying a heavy rock to his ankle and sinking to the bottom. The thought of being without oxygen, even for a short time, terrified him, so he turned his thoughts to sleeping pills. He could drive a boat far from shore, take the pills, and then float on his back in the water until sleep took him."

"What did you do?" Melinda asked.

"I booked him on a red-eye flight home that night. I made him stay on the phone while he packed and while he was en route to the airport. I told him to find a charging station for his phone while he waited at the gate. We didn't hang up until the pilot ordered all electronic devices off. Even then, I made him give the phone to a flight attendant, who assured me they were on a plane that would land at JFK in one hour. I have no idea what she must've thought. I was at the airport when he arrived, and I got him an appointment with a psychiatrist the next day. He was hospitalized for a week."

"Why didn't you tell me? You shouldn't have dealt with that alone."

"If Sam had a heart attack," Tamara told her, "I would've called you and Mom and Dad immediately. But it wasn't a heart attack, and I didn't want Sam to feel embarrassed in front of you guys. But nor did I want to ask him, 'Is it okay if I tell my family that you wanted to drown yourself?' It's delicate."

"Yeah, because your family doesn't know anything about mental health issues," Melinda said sarcastically.

"I never told people about Malik's schizophrenia for the same reason," Tamara said. "I didn't want it to be the thing he was known for."

"I always warned new friends before they met him," Melinda said. "I never knew what he would do or say."

"I stopped bringing new friends home. Anyway, we're both familiar with mental health issues. But I never fully understood Sam's depression. He was really bothered by the financial crisis. He seemed to hate himself for it."

"Why?"

"He chose to become a quantitative analyst. In the best of times, one can question what good we contribute to society."

"He felt responsible for the crisis?" Melinda asked.

"I wouldn't say that. But he understood the role greed played. And he came to hate that greed in himself. Even after he left finance, he followed economic news closely. I didn't think that was good for him. It wasn't good for me, but I didn't have a choice.

"Before his release from the hospital, I met with Sam and his doctor. The doctor advised Sam to stop writing. He explained that every generation uses their most advanced technology as an analogy for the brain. In Freud's day, it was the steam engine. They had the idea that negative emotions needed to be released like steam. Holding in anger or sadness could lead to an explosion. Now, the advanced technology analogy is the computer. The doctor believed that negative emotions could be like a computer virus. If you don't execute the program slash negative emotion, it's harmless. But if you execute it, it can spread to the rest of the brain. This is what he thought was happening with Sam's writing. Sam was ruminating on past traumas, leading to depression. He advised Sam to put the manuscript away forever.

"I was skeptical. As I said, I thought the economic crash caused Sam's depression. But Sam followed the doctor's advice, and he seemed to get better."

"Until . . . ," Melinda said.

"Right. But he didn't commit suicide."

"Jason Blakely, whoever he was, must've known about Sam's depression. What was the name of the cult in Sam's novel?"

"The Prophets of the Torch."

Melinda pulled out her phone and typed. After a few moments, she said, "Nothing. Let's try *cult torch*." Tamara waited expectantly. "Strike two," Melinda said. "How about *cult torch Georgia*. Aha." She paused to read. "According to this 2014 article, there was a commune in middle Georgia called People of the Torch." Melinda read the article aloud.

> Evan Kent, the son of a small-town pastor in north Georgia, dropped out of college at twenty and returned home to work for his father. When he was caught stealing from the church (over a thousand

dollars), his father pressed charges and insisted on jail time.

"Do you think Dad would have done that to us?" Melinda asked. Tamara shook her head. "Dad could be hard. But not that hard."

Because it was a first offense, Evan was given probation. He spent the next few years working landscaping jobs until he stumbled upon an easier way to get by: finding women to support him.

"Jesus," Melinda editorialized.

He posed as a successful entrepreneur and targeted single women. Brenda (who asked that her real name not be used) met Evan at a nightclub in Atlanta in 1977. He told her that he owned an import/export business. He was cute and had a good sense of humor. "He took me to nice restaurants and paid for everything. He drove an expensive car and dressed well. And then, one day, he needed to borrow my car because his was in the shop. So, I gave him my car, and I borrowed my mother's. Shortly after that, a pipe burst in his condo, so he needed to stay with me. I thought he was just having a run of bad luck. He lost some money on a deal, he told me, so we curtailed going out. I didn't think much of it until my mother pointed out that I was supporting him. I was like, 'Oh, crap, I thought I was just helping my boyfriend.' But my mother was right."

"You think?" Melinda said as an aside.

"Overnight, he didn't have anything. I was loaning him money, but he promised to pay me back once a big deal he was working on came through, something about Persian rugs. Big surprise, I never saw the money, and the scary thing is I don't know how long things would've continued if my mother hadn't jarred me out of it. I broke up with him, and he begged me for one week. If I gave him one week, he would pay back the money he owed me and move out. And, you know, looking back on it, I suspect he used that time to find another woman. He had use of my car, and he probably told her he owned it. He had my cash to wine and dine her. After ten days, my brothers came over and told him he had to leave. I never saw him again."

In 1982, Evan, 37, purchased an abandoned high school and moved in with 53 members of what would become the People of the Torch. The group grew as Evan recruited new members. He was aggressive about recruitment, Dale, a former member, said, especially people with means. "When you joined, you sold your possessions and gave the money to Evan. It was a big source of income."

Having returned to his roots as a pastor's son, Evan acted as a spiritual leader for the group. He held services, but it wasn't a typical church. "You couldn't question him," said Kendra, a former member. "He convinced us that he was the only way to salvation. He demanded we believe that, and once we did, it was easy for him to control us. We would do anything to please him."

The group persisted until 2014, when a former member, Daniel Stills, 53, returned to the commune and shot Evan. Evan's bodyguards responded quickly and killed Daniel. On Evan's orders, Daniel was buried on the property, and Evan's wounds were treated by a physician who belonged to the group. When Evan's condition deteriorated and he lost consciousness, he was taken to a hospital. He survived his injuries, but local authorities were alerted and quickly grew suspicious. An investigation ensued, leading to the discovery of Daniel Stills's body. Group members were interviewed, and evidence of child abuse was uncovered. Evan Kent, and many in his circle, are currently imprisoned, awaiting trial.

"Does that sound like the cult in Sam's book?"

"I don't know." The article didn't answer a single question for Tamara. She needed a roster of past members, a list she could scan for Sam's name. "The cult in his book was housed in an abandoned high school. That's the most striking similarity I see. Even so, Sam could've based the Prophets of the Torch on research he'd done on the People of the Torch."

Melinda typed on her phone. "I can't find any information about the People of the Torch prior to 2014. I guess that doesn't prove anything."

And his novel, Tamara thought, did not prove that he'd ever had any connection to the People of the Torch.

"I think you should pass this info along to the FBI agents," Melinda said.

Tamara nodded agreement. But she needed to finish reading first. Maybe there was something else there.

Chapter 15

CINDY

When Cindy offered to make her mother a sandwich along with her own, she hadn't meant it as an invitation to have lunch together. But her mother looked bereft as Cindy, a book in hand, packed her sandwich and lemonade to carry out to the garden.

"When will you be back?" her mother asked, forlorn.

They'd been home from Jekyll Island for three days, and Cindy was still catching up on the week away from her garden. The house was empty, save the two of them, and the quiet seemed to augment her mother's frailty, tugging at Cindy's conscience. She sighed. "Would you like to have lunch with me?"

Her mother's face lit up, so Cindy joined her at the kitchen table. Neither of them spoke. Without the distraction of chitchat, the anger, always beneath the surface of Cindy's consciousness, bubbled up. "Why did you take me there?" Cindy finally asked, the agitation in her voice revealing more than she'd intended.

Her mother hesitated, but Cindy knew she understood. "I moved there as well," her mother replied.

"Fine," Cindy said. "Why did you move *us* there?"

"I always did my best to take care of you."

"I'm not asking you to defend yourself," Cindy said impatiently. It was infuriating, and yet, Cindy recognized the truth of what her mother said. For Cindy, motherhood was challenging, and she didn't face a tenth of her mother's difficulties. Her mother had been dealt a bad hand, and her life had been hard. By extension, Cindy's childhood had been hard. Those were facts, but they didn't absolve her mother of everything. "Just tell me why you joined."

Her mother's face was contemplative.

"Have you never thought about this?" Cindy snapped. Her anger was growing, and she couldn't rein it in. Why had she brought it up? It was the last thing Cindy wanted to talk about.

"I try not to," her mother answered meekly.

"Well, it's time you did. I was fifteen when you took me there. Why did you do it?"

"I was so tired when I met Evan," her mother said. "I was scared all the time. I worried about losing a job or losing hours or losing the place we lived. Nothing was mine. Except for you."

"And I was a mouth to feed," Cindy said.

"You were my responsibility. And you were a good kid."

Cindy rolled her eyes.

"Evan was like a light in the darkness. He was hope in hopelessness."

"Oh, jeez," Cindy said, "you sound like him."

"You asked me to explain."

Cindy waited.

"He listened to me. I know that doesn't sound like much, but when I talked about the difficulties I was having with a boss, he listened. No one really did that. Me and the others complained to each other, but it felt like we were competing for the Most Miserable Award. He listened. And he seemed so smart. He talked about the failures of capitalism, how a rising tide left so many underwater. He said it wasn't sustainable and that there was a different way. It was exciting, but more than anything else, it was his promise of a better life, one without worry. He promised to take care of us."

"Do you know what a cult is, Mom?"

Her mother smiled and looked around. "You'd better be careful. You don't want anyone to hear you say that."

Cindy felt her mood lighten, just a bit, at the humor, but she withheld a smile. She wouldn't give her mother that. "No one is here."

"I believed Evan was a prophet," her mother admitted. "At least, I wanted to believe it. Things were so hard, and honestly, I felt like they couldn't get worse. So, it was like, I can give this man a chance, and he can make everything better. Or he won't, and I can just find another job and another place to live. I had everything to gain and nothing to lose. And over time, believing became easier. When he first said that he was the key to heaven, I could believe it. I was wrong, but I truly believed it."

Cindy stared hard into her mother's eyes. "Did we truly have nothing to lose?"

When her mother didn't answer, Cindy looked away. She didn't know what she wanted from her mother. Cindy knew, in broad strokes, why people joined cults. She also knew there was a mystery to human gullibility that she would never understand. Humans had the ability to imagine new and amazing things. They also had the ability to believe anything they could imagine.

"Why did you leave?" Cindy asked.

Her mother looked surprised. "You don't know?"

"I wouldn't ask if I knew."

"Evan is in prison."

Cindy nodded. "That's a good place for him."

"Things started to go downhill after Brittany died. She wasn't the same after you left."

"And you? Were you the same after I left?"

"Brittany and I had long conversations. She couldn't make sense of what she did to you. She felt awful about it."

Cindy felt tears threatening and fought them back with everything she had. "That made two of us."

"She thought about leaving after that, finding you. But she was afraid she would go to hell if she left."

"She was as stupid as the rest of you," Cindy sneered.

Her mother regarded her before saying, "You've always been skeptical. I don't know if that makes you smarter, but you saw things others couldn't."

"I saw things others wouldn't," Cindy corrected. "That makes me smarter."

"Brittany couldn't believe she hurt you."

"Well, she did." When she'd bumped into Brittany six years ago—at the grocery store, of all places—she'd felt simultaneous urges to embrace her and to flee. Her oldest, closest friend's face had sparked both nostalgia and fear. She'd once begged Brittany, armed with an extension cord, to stop beating her, a memory Cindy had relived as she'd looked into Brittany's eyes. They'd spoken awkwardly in aisle four next to the pasta sauce, long enough for Brittany to confess that their meeting hadn't been accidental. Brittany had gotten Cindy's address from Daniel Stills. *As soon as I realized you left,* Brittany had told her, *I knew you went to him.* She'd watched Cindy's house and had followed Cindy to the grocery store to engineer this meeting. And there they were. *Did you leave the People of the Torch?* Cindy had asked, the permutation of words strange in her mouth. She hadn't said *the People of the Torch* in a long time. If Brittany had answered yes, their conversation might've continued. Or maybe if Brittany's face and voice hadn't elicited traumatic memories, their conversation might've continued. But Brittany said something about her little sister and not being able to leave. And Brittany's little sister wasn't Cindy's problem. And neither was Brittany's need to make amends. *I'm going to finish my shopping,* Cindy had told her, *and then I'm going home, and I think you should do the same.* Cindy hadn't finished her shopping. She'd left her half-filled cart behind and fled the store.

Cindy looked up at her mother. "Why did you stay after Evan made Brittany do that to me?" She didn't want to cry, but a tear escaped her right eye. Then one from her left. She wiped them away.

"I was scared."

"I was scared, Mom."

The two women stared at each other. Cindy still didn't know what she wanted. An apology would just infuriate her. Her mother seemed to understand that.

"A lot of people didn't agree with what Evan made Brittany do to you."

"Wonderful, enlightened people," Cindy said sarcastically.

"After Brittany drowned, it stirred everything up again. People began to question Evan, and that really hadn't happened before. His sermons became more extreme, until he was claiming to be the son of God. Zack Lee criticized him openly, and a faction began to form around Zack. Evan established a band of armed security guards he called soldiers. Things quieted after Evan married Zack to a fifteen-year-old girl, but then he tried to marry Vicky Stills to one of Zack's cronies."

"Vicky?" Cindy asked, fully attentive now. Vicky was nine the last time Cindy had seen her.

"She was a sweet girl, pliable enough, but Daniel showed up out of nowhere to get her out." Daniel was Vicky's father.

"What happened?" Cindy asked, her heart rate accelerating.

Her mother shook her head. "Daniel shot Evan."

"And Daniel?" Cindy asked.

"One of Evan's men killed him."

Cindy put her face in her hands.

Her mother touched her shoulder. "Are you okay?"

Cindy didn't remove her mother's hand as she said, "Daniel gave me a place to stay when I left."

"Oh," her mother said. "I didn't know that."

"How would you?"

When her mother didn't respond, Cindy looked at her. Her face held anguish, a mirror, perhaps of Cindy's own. Daniel had done so much for Cindy. He'd helped her get her first job. At a waterskiing school. And eventually, as Cindy had built her new life, she'd lost touch with Daniel. "You're right to blame me," her mother said. "And I accept your blame. But you didn't come to me before you left. You didn't give me a chance to help you."

"I didn't think I could count on you. Was I wrong?"

Her mother shrugged. An acknowledgment? She continued her story. "Dr. Richards tried to treat Evan's gunshot wound, but they had to take him to a hospital. The police showed up the next day, and, in time, everything came out. Evan will never get out of prison."

"What do you think of Evan now?" Cindy asked.

"It's taken me a while," her mother said, "but I think he's a sick man who has ruined many lives."

Chapter 16

COOPER

I'm sorry," Special Agent Lewis said. He liked to apologize, but Cooper doubted he ever meant it. "You just seem strangely incurious about why you were committing these murders."

"I was committing them for money," Cooper said.

"Right, but I think you know what I'm getting at. Why were these people being targeted? Why was someone paying you? You weren't curious about that?"

"If I'd allowed myself to be curious about that, I couldn't have done the job. How would it help me to know? How many life insurance policies would I hear about?"

"Did you ever kill anyone for personal reasons?"

~

In the summer of 2000, Cooper opened an art gallery. The venture was purely practical. He had little interest in business, and art for him had become, more than anything, a painful reminder of fallen dreams.

He'd been picking out bananas at the grocery store when he bumped into Heather Walker, an associate from his starving artist days. Having recently been laid off, she needed a job, and Cooper needed a cash business. Heather was smart, hardworking, and passionate about art and the business of art. The twins were nearing their third birthday, and eventually they would want to know what their father did for a living. They would want to tell their friends. Art gallery owner suited Cooper. He put up the capital, and Heather did the work. Dirty money from Willie flowed through the business and came out clean.

"Are you ready to start painting again?" Lisa had asked with enthusiasm when Cooper broached the idea.

"I don't think so," he said. "I won't say never, but for now, just working in the business is enough for me."

Lisa had found that odd, given that their personal finances would be utterly neglected if she didn't manage their money.

She didn't realize that the art gallery would be utterly neglected if Heather didn't manage everything.

Cooper's biggest challenge was filling the free hours in his day. He had an office at the gallery, but he was assiduous in leaving the work to Heather. He signed up for an unlimited subscription to Netflix's DVD service, but his appetite for movies on his computer was finite. He played strategy video games, and they were interesting until they weren't. He picked up a paintbrush but felt none of the old fire. Occasionally, he even missed Willie. He called Heather into his office to chat once, but he realized, as she glanced covertly at her watch, that someone had to keep the gallery running.

In time, restlessness pushed him to venture out of the office. He tried half a dozen coffee shops before he landed on one with a reclining chair that seemed custom fitted to his back and the best cinnamon-powdered doughnuts ever to come out of a kitchen. He ate lunch in a new restaurant every day until the most beautiful woman he'd ever met served him an exquisite portobello mushroom sandwich with a side of perfectly seasoned roasted potatoes. He was finding his spots.

The server's name was Talitha, and through observation, he learned which section she served and was able to request a table accordingly. Eventually, if she saw him walk in, she would meet him at the host stand and seat him herself. She was friendly, and he enjoyed talking to her.

In time, the barista at the coffee shop recognized Cooper and started his order before he reached the counter. He began to pick out familiar faces in the other patrons—nothing necessitating more than a casual nod. He developed a comfortable level of familiarity, a sense of belonging. As he settled into a routine and his days homogenized, time seemed to speed up, months passing in what felt like weeks. And then a familiar face became too familiar.

"I admire your powers of concentration. My mind is always going." The man sat at a table near Cooper's recliner, a mug and doughnut in front of him.

Cooper was reading the newspaper. "You sound like my son." Cooper didn't tell the man that his son was six years old. It went without saying. A man should be able to sit down and read the news. Without interruption from another man who should be on a low-dose stimulant.

"I'm always thinking about multiple streams of income. Do you think about that?"

On occasion, Cooper did think about multiple streams of income. Mostly, how to make multiple streams look like one stream. Heather Walker was exceedingly good at what she did, and the art gallery managed—even without Cooper's cash infusions— to turn a healthy profit. Coming from this stranger, however, the mention of multiple streams of income brought pyramid schemes to Cooper's mind.

"When I'm here," Cooper replied, "I like to think about the paper."

"That focus." The man smiled, undeterred. "I sell a weight-loss product engineered for men. It's amazing. Ask me for testimonials."

"I'm not much of a salesman." And that was probably true. Ten years of painting had resulted in enough sales to buy himself a few cups of coffee.

"I think you're selling yourself short." The man laughed. "Is that a pun?"

Cooper shook his head. "I think puns are supposed to be funny."

"High comedic standards. I appreciate that. And I get that sales isn't for everyone. I'm Tim, by the way."

Cooper nodded, declining to share his own name. He glanced at the paper.

"I can get you a good price on a three-week supply. If the pounds don't melt away, I'll give you a full refund."

Heat rushed to Cooper's face. He'd turned thirty-five the month before. The month before that, he'd bought new pants with a more expansive waistline. He'd been loath to do it, but for quite a while, he'd been unbuttoning his pants before getting into the car.

Why did you unbutton your pants? Kathy had asked one day after he'd picked her and Howard up from school. He hadn't known how she'd seen that from her booster seat. Humiliated, he'd lied: *I didn't unbutton my pants.* After that, whenever the twins were with him, he'd drive around with his pants buttoned, the waistline digging into his gut. Buying new pants felt like giving up, but Cooper chose to think of it as a temporary retreat.

So, he knew that he'd gained weight, but he didn't know it was noticeable with his clothes on. He still saw himself as young and fit. Was he in denial?

"I'll get back to my paper," Cooper said, allowing an edge into his voice.

"I won't keep you. Just think about it. You'll be lean and mean in no time."

Cooper couldn't stop thinking about it. Half of his doughnut remained, and suddenly, he had no appetite for it. Without the doughnut, his unsweetened black coffee was unappetizing. He tried to read, but his hand kept going to his belly. It felt soft and squishy. After a few minutes, he threw the doughnut and coffee in the trash.

"Take care," Tim called. "Think about it."

Cooper didn't reply.

~

Lisa rented a beach house on Tybee Island for their annual vacation. The balcony off the master bedroom overlooked the Atlantic, and Cooper didn't want to leave it. It wasn't only the view—which was sublime; Cooper was having trouble getting into the spirit of vacation. As soon as they'd arrived, the twins had wanted to play in the ocean. He'd taken them while Lisa made a grocery run.

Why are you wearing a shirt? Howard had asked. He'd been in the ocean with them, tossing them into the air by turns.

UV protection, he lied.

Do we need UV protection? Kathy asked.

Cooper felt like sticking his head under the water and hiding there.

The shirt was bright yellow, and when he emerged from the water, his back strained from tossing the twins, the cotton fabric clung to his stomach, round and bulging like a giant sun. He wasn't the most out of shape man on the beach, but he found little comfort in observing the less robust.

That afternoon, after lunch, Lisa spotted a fudge shop, and the three of them lined up enthusiastically to order: chocolate for Lisa, cookies and cream for Kathy, peanut butter for Howard, and chocolate mocha for Cooper. Lisa and the kids enjoyed their fudge with the unbothered joy reserved for the young and effortlessly thin. Cooper could taste every single calorie in his chocolate mocha confection. He didn't finish it.

That night, at dinner, he opted for a salad that left him hungry and in a foul mood.

"Are you feeling okay?" Lisa asked.

He wasn't feeling okay. And he couldn't talk to her about it. Before the trip, she'd modeled her bathing suits for him, and she'd looked better in each one than she had the last.

"I'm just a little bloated," he told her.

~

The barista was pulling a cinnamon-powdered doughnut out of the case for Cooper when he stopped her.

"I'm trying something different," he said. "There. The bran muffin."

She wrinkled her nose but retrieved the muffin and prepared his usual coffee.

With each bite of the muffin, he told himself he would eat it until he liked it. He was already irritated because the reclining chair was taken. He focused on the paper. When he looked up, he glimpsed Tim standing in line.

"Long time no see," Tim said, making his way toward Cooper, a mug in one hand, a doughnut in the other. He was rail thin, probably still in his twenties. "I was worried about you."

Cooper had been gone for a week. What did the guy think, he'd had a coronary? He wasn't that overweight. Was he?

"That's nice." Cooper returned to the paper.

Without asking, as if they were old friends, Tim joined him at the table. "Are you ready to take control of your health?" he asked. His smile was reminiscent of a used car salesman's. "I can offer you a great deal." He leaned in. "Your wife will like it too. You'll be like a teenager. If you know what I mean." He winked.

Cooper could guess what he meant. "My teenage years weren't the most productive," he said curtly. He looked at his watch. "I have a meeting."

There was no meeting. Cooper finished the coffee and bran muffin while cramped in his car. He lacked space to unfold the paper, so he was forced to focus on the taste and texture of the muffin.

~

Sex. He couldn't stop thinking about it. He and Lisa didn't do it as much as they once had. They'd been married a long time. And they were both busy and tired. The twins still wandered into their bedroom following nightmares.

Or was his libido failing?

Or was Lisa repulsed by his squishy body?

How many years of sex did he have left? Thirty-five? He considered looking up how often the average seventy-year-old male had sex, but he didn't want to know. Some indignities of aging were better left unanticipated. He chose to assume that he had thirty-five years of sex left. If he and Lisa had sex three times a week, that would be about fifty-five hundred times. That didn't seem like much. Twice a week (more realistic) would amount to less than four thousand times. So little?

He resolved to have more sex with Lisa. But when he tried, he couldn't shake the feeling that his belly was getting in the way. Ridiculous, he knew, because (a) Lisa seemed (pretended?) to enjoy it, and (b) his belly hadn't gotten in the way before. He only managed to finish by closing his eyes and blotting out all thoughts of himself.

A few nights later, lying in bed beside her, determined to try, he felt on the verge of panic as he touched her hip through her nightgown. She turned over to face him, her signal that she was open to more.

"How are the investments going?" he asked. She'd recently done something with real estate.

She blinked, momentarily confused.

"I think it's time to rebalance our retirement portfolio," he said when she didn't respond.

"I think you're right," she said. "Let's talk in the morning. I'm tired."

That was fine with him.

~

"Hey, boss," Tim said, taking the table near Cooper's chair. Cooper still hadn't told Tim his name.

Cooper pretended he didn't hear him.

"Boss. Boss." Tim snapped his fingers.

Not looking up felt awkward.

Tim grinned. "You've taken that concentration of yours to the next level."

Cooper nodded.

"You ready to turn the clock back ten years?"

Cooper imagined himself strangling Tim. Enough was enough. Every time Tim saw him, Tim spouted some catchy phrase that amounted to calling Cooper fat. Cooper didn't know how much more he could take.

When enough really was enough, Cooper waited outside the coffee shop. He parked at the edge of the lot, where he could see the entrance but no one was likely to notice him. He watched Tim enter the shop. He followed Tim once he left the shop. He learned where Tim worked, where he lived. When the opportunity presented itself, Cooper killed him.

Chapter 17

CINDY

Cindy didn't want to be angry with her mother. She wanted to create a clean slate for the two of them to build upon. But elements of their past were like an insidious weed with roots both deep and wide and impossible to eradicate. Her mother was part of a history that had to stay buried. Her mere presence complicated that.

Caring for your offspring shouldn't be complicated, Cindy thought as she walked through her wooded garden. Even plants had strategies for ensuring that their progeny thrived. Those strategies didn't always work. They usually didn't work. But the plants tried. Cindy had pulled the short straw when it came to parents. Maybe she had a right to be angry.

~

Cindy's father was a sick man when he'd contacted her out of the blue in 2011.

"Your aunt Jean gave me your number. I hope that's okay." His voice was weak and sheepish and completely unfamiliar. That his voice sounded alien was not a surprise. She hadn't heard it since she was four.

She was in her garden when she took the call, and she was grateful for the privacy. She'd never spoken in more than vague generalities about her father to Ross or the children. They understood, given that she'd never really known him.

"It's fine," she said, a multitude of thoughts traversing her mind, one especially suspicious and maybe even outlandish: *How do I know it's you?* "I haven't spoken to Aunt Jean in years. How is she?" After being released from jail, Cindy had stayed with her aunt Jean for a few weeks. Cindy had been as helpful to her aunt as she could, cleaning and cooking, but Cindy hadn't felt welcome. It was a surprise that her aunt still had her phone number. It seemed strange, once the question was out, to ask a stranger about another stranger. But that probably wasn't the strangest thing happening at the moment. And why would someone call her pretending to be her father?

The following morning, after dropping Amy and Cy off at school, she drove to the hospital. It felt curious in many ways, but one of the more peculiar thoughts that occupied her mind as she walked the hospital corridors searching for his room was that he'd been so close. For all these years, she'd been living her life, never thinking of him, and he'd been living his own life a single county away.

He lay in bed watching television, a nasal cannula feeding him oxygen while an IV drip emptied into his arm. She stood just outside the open door, looking for a hint of familiarity in his skeletal face. Nothing. She could've passed him on the street without an inkling of the DNA they shared. As she mentally prepared herself to meet him, she wondered if he would experience the same lack of recognition. Unlikely. The older she got, the more she resembled her mother. Her mother was twenty-four the last time he'd seen her, twelve years younger than Cindy was now. Still, he had an advantage in recognizing her.

She stepped forward and tried to force a smile. It felt more like a grimace. "Jason," she said. She hadn't known what she would call him. *Dad* would've felt too weird.

"Amelia?"

She nodded, and his face lit up. She hadn't corrected him on the phone, and she didn't correct him now. Amelia belonged to the world where he'd once been her father. She existed in that world for this moment, and it would never meet the world in which she was Cindy, a wife and mother.

She paused a few feet from his bed, relieved not to have to experience the awkwardness of hugging him or not, of shaking his hand or not. He didn't look to be up for either of those things. She smiled weakly, and he said, "You're as beautiful as your mother."

He was in end-stage COPD, and he wanted to know if she smoked. "I quit years ago," she told him.

He smiled. "I wasn't going to lecture you. I was hoping you could slip me one."

She retrieved a stool from the corner of his room and rolled it to his bedside. She sat, and neither of them spoke. It required effort on his part, every sentence followed by a pull of breath. There was a certain cruelty in this, Cindy thought. To be absent from her life for all these years, and then to reenter in this state, near death. She hadn't wanted a father in a long time, but if she had, finding him this way would've been heartbreaking.

She listened as he tried to make her understand his absence. He thought of her and her brother every day. Even now, the guilt was crushing. He carried the suffering that her brother must have experienced in that car. As a younger man, he'd wanted to die; the smoking, the drinking, it was all in service of an early death. "It's easier to want to die," he told her, pausing to catch his breath, "when you're young and healthy." He held her eyes. "All I want now is more time."

He'd probably been headed toward an early death, he explained, when he'd been arrested for identity theft in the late eighties. He'd turned into a career criminal, working with a crew. All of that had changed while he was on the inside. He'd had to go to prison to meet Maxine, his future wife.

She must be a prize, Cindy thought but did not say.

Maxine had changed his life, given him something to live for. He opened an auto shop, and they had a daughter, Christine, who was now a sophomore in college.

A college girl, Cindy thought. Christine's life has been much different from my own.

He'd always thought about getting in touch with Cindy. It had been a New Year's resolution for decades. But he'd been a coward. Her mother blamed him for Cindy's brother's death. Rightly so. He blamed himself, and he just couldn't invite more blame into his life.

"I was four when it happened," Cindy told him. "I didn't blame you." She didn't care why he hadn't gotten in touch. They'd all lived their lives. He'd walked his path. Cindy had walked hers. Christine was walking her privileged path.

He talked about getting sick and medical bills. He'd had to sell the auto shop, and he was concerned that they would have to pull Christine out of college.

Cindy braced herself for it. If he asked her for financial help, she would stand and leave without another word. It would be easy. She would never look back.

But he didn't ask her for money. He was just talking about the things that preoccupied him. He asked Cindy about her life, and she gave him the barest of outlines. She pulled out her cell phone and showed him pictures of Amy and Cy, nine and seven at the time. His grandest wish was to meet them. "They'd probably be scared of all the tubes," he said with a smile and a labored breath. He didn't force Cindy to tell him that she wouldn't entertain the idea of introducing her young children to a long-lost dying relative, even their grandfather.

She felt much heavier leaving the hospital than she had walking in. She didn't know why she'd come. It had all happened so fast. He'd called her the day before and told her that he wanted to see her before he died. Saying no had felt riskier, more permanent, than saying yes. And she'd been curious. She hadn't been angry at her father, as she was her mother. Maybe she should've been. He just hadn't been a part of her life. Now, she felt weighted down by the lost years.

She'd thought that seeing him would be emotionless. He was her father strictly by biology, after all, and that meant little without a social construct behind it. But something was there that she hadn't anticipated. Some part of her that was attached to the father she hadn't seen in thirty-three years.

~

And still, three weeks passed and Cindy didn't return to visit him. Every day was a day of indecision. Every morning, she awoke in fear of the phone call: *Your father passed away in his sleep.* She wanted to visit, and yet, she wasn't sure there was anything to say. She wanted to get to know him, and yet, she didn't want to grow attached.

Her ringtone became a source of anxiety. When her phone rang at 2:30 p.m. on a Wednesday afternoon, her pulse quickened. It wasn't the news she'd been dreading. It was something much scarier.

"Amelia, this is Sam. Sam Foster."

She nearly dropped the phone. The voice was familiar. She would've known it was him even without the name.

"Sam?" Her voice was strained. She wasn't sure what she was asking. *How did you get my number? Why are you calling me?*

"It's been a long time," he said. Fourteen years.

"How have you been?" she asked.

"Not so great."

She held her breath, waiting for him to elaborate. Who says "not so great" when asked how they're doing? she thought. Someone bearing bad news. He didn't elaborate.

"We need to talk."

"Okay," she said cautiously. "About what?"

The silence stretched so long that she almost asked if he was still there. "Do you remember the last words I said to you?"

She did. *I'm going to write a novel for you.* "That was all a very long time ago," she said. "I don't remember much."

"I tried to write the novel," he told her. "About that summer."

"Sam?" Again, she didn't know what she was asking. "You can't write about that. We agreed to never speak—"

"I know. I wanted to turn what we experienced into art, and I learned some things . . ." He trailed off, and her vision blurred as she contemplated what he was telling her. That summer was off limits, buried deep, and they'd sworn to never unearth it. Did he not realize how dangerous this was, not only to him but to her and her family? She wanted to scream, but she forced calm into her voice. "Sam, listen to me—"

"I'm in Atlanta," he told her. "I need to see you, and we need—" He didn't finish the thought.

"That's fine, Sam. We'll meet. How about coffee?"

"No. We'll meet at Beecham Water Tower."

Cindy gasped.

Chapter 18

TAMARA

Tamara was sitting in front of Sam's laptop when her phone rang. She'd opened the final document, labeled *VI*, but she hadn't allowed her eyes to focus on the words. She was scared—not only of what the pages would contain but also of what they wouldn't. This was it. As difficult as reading his work had been, she felt hollow at the thought of finishing it. This manuscript was a connection to him. Her last.

She answered the call before it rolled over to voice mail. It was Melinda, and Tamara was happy for the distraction.

"You busy?" Melinda asked.

"No, just spacing out." Tamara didn't want to talk about Sam's novel. The courage she'd worked up to open the concluding document was tenuous. Anything could push her the other way.

"I agreed to fly to Austin with Jeff tomorrow."

"Okay," Tamara said neutrally. The last time they'd spoken, Melinda had told her that Jeff would be moving to Austin without her.

"He's looking at apartments, and he doesn't want to do it alone. He guilted me into it."

"It's good that you two are still speaking," Tamara offered. "Is he trying to convince you to move with him?"

"He wants me to see Austin before I rule it out."

"You've already ruled it out."

"Exactly," Melinda said. "He made a reservation at a fancy restaurant. I drew the line there. It isn't only about Austin, and he refuses to see that."

"What else is it about?" Tamara asked.

Melinda didn't respond for a long while. "I'm not sure," she finally said. "Anyway, I just wanted to let you know I'm flying out in the morning. I'll be back on Thursday."

Tamara returned to her staring contest with Sam's illuminated laptop screen. Still, she didn't allow her eyes to focus. When her phone rang again, she answered without checking caller ID. Hearing Brian's voice was a nice surprise.

"Hey, stranger," she said. Campers were allowed to call home every evening after dinner, which had been a big selling point to Tamara. It hadn't occurred to her that Brian wouldn't take advantage of it. Some nights he called her. Often, he didn't. She hid her disappointment from him.

"Hey, Mom. I slid down a waterfall today. It was crazy high."

"On purpose?" Tamara asked.

"What?"

"Did you fall down the waterfall, or did you intentionally slide?"

"Intentionally. We all did it. Except for this guy named Stephen. He was scared."

Was it safe? She wanted to ask but didn't. She'd done her research and had decided to trust Camp Lawl and its counselors. "Was it fun?"

"So much fun. I was really scared at first, but I closed my eyes and did it."

"That's great. I'm proud of you. What did you have for dinner?"

"Spaghetti."

"Are you making new friends?"

"I need to go, Mom. I just wanted to tell you about the waterfall. It was really high, and I felt like I was sliding forever."

"Okay. You be careful."

"Thanks, Mom. Bye."

"I love you," Tamara said before she realized she was talking to the dial tone.

Her baby was away at camp, and he didn't need her. She was pretty sure she should be happy about that. She wasn't.

Fortified by knowing all was well with Brian—though she wouldn't have minded a tiny bit of homesickness—she returned to the manuscript. And still, she hesitated. When she'd left off, Lorelai and Bahati were in a car together heading for . . .

Tamara truly did not want to know.

The Summer of Lorelai

by

Sam Foster

VI

Lorelai tells me about Richard Hunt as she drives. Richard is in his early forties and left the cult two years ago, a move that cost him his wife and nine-year-old daughter Vicky. He gave Lorelai a number to call before he left, and the two of them kept in touch. Occasionally, under the guise of taking Vicky into the city to sell fruit, Lorelai would secretly take her to visit Richard. Each time, Richard would send them back with so much money that, blinded by greed, Prophet Warren would praise Vicky's gift for sales.

"He'll help us," Lorelai says. "Unfortunately, he's a long-haul trucker. He could be out of town."

"We're going to his house?" I ask.

"I don't know where else to go."

"I have an aunt," I say. "My father's sister."

"What if she calls the police? You're a minor. Technically, I've abducted you."

"Right."

"Also, I'm taking you across state lines. He lives just on the other side of the South Carolina border. That makes it federal."

I keep checking the rearview mirror, and finally, Lorelai asks what I'm looking for.

"To see if someone is following us."

"No one followed us," she assures me.

She exits the freeway and makes several turns before entering a subdivision. She parks on a curb in front of a small home with an overgrown yard. It's nearly four a.m.

"We can sleep in the car until morning or ring the doorbell and wake him up. If he's home." The house is dark, as are the others on the street.

"If a morning jogger sees us sleeping in the car," I say, "they might call the police."

"Good point." Lorelai smiles and it looks painful with her split lip. "I knew I brought you for a reason. Stay here."

She climbs from the car, and I watch her walk up the driveway to the front porch. She rings the doorbell, and I wait, holding my breath. We need this. If he isn't home, I don't know where we will go. She rings the bell a second time. The porchlight comes on and I exhale. Lorelai speaks to someone and then turns and motions for me to join her.

Richard Hunt is wearing a bathrobe. He invites us in. The living room is bare. An old couch is positioned in front of an old television set. The off-white walls are blank. Lorelai sits on the couch, and I sit beside her.

"What happened?" Richard asks.

Lorelai shares the full story without hesitation. Richard continues to stand—maybe because there's nowhere to sit—and listens attentively. He looks distressed, and I wonder if he's concerned about Lorelai or if he's considering the prospect of never seeing his daughter again. Either way, he agrees to let us stay. He leads us to a guest room with a mattress on the floor.

"Your timing is fortunate," he tells us. "I'm hauling a load to Seattle the day after tomorrow."

Lorelai takes the mattress, and I sleep on the floor.

~

The sun is just peeking over the horizon when Richard wakes us in the morning. I feel like I haven't slept.

"I presume the car is stolen?" he says to Lorelai, who slept in the clothes she wore the night before.

She nods. "We need to get rid of it."

"Or at least move it," Richard says. "Do you think Warren will report it stolen?"

"Depends on if he wants us back. He doesn't like interacting with police, but he will. Can we just leave it somewhere with the keys in the ignition?"

Richard drives his car. Lorelai and I follow in the stolen LeBaron. An hour passes before Richard pulls into an empty mall parking lot. Lorelai parks on the periphery, far from the nearest store.

"What about fingerprints?" I ask as we exit, the keys still in the ignition.

"You watch too many movies." Lorelai smiles and, again, I think it must be painful. "If Warren reports the car stolen, there won't be any dispute as to who stole it. We just don't want the car to lead to Richard's house."

"Right."

Lorelai climbs into the front of Richard's car. I get into the back.

"This doesn't look like a bad part of town," Lorelai observes.

"It isn't," Richard says. "I like the pancakes across the street."

"How do we know someone will steal the car?" Lorelai asks.

Richard shrugs. "Does it matter?"

"I guess it doesn't."

"What if one of your neighbors steals it and brings it back to your neighborhood?" I ask.

Richard and Lorelai look at each other. "Is this guy for real?" Richard asks.

"I think so," Lorelai says.

Richard treats us to pancakes. He seems glad that Lorelai is out. He also seems concerned about how he'll see his daughter again. "If I hire a lawyer," he asks Lorelai, "will you share what happened to you?"

Lorelai doesn't hesitate. "Yes," she tells him.

He looks visibly relieved. "I'd love to get Vicky out. But I'll need a new job."

We brainstorm career changes for Richard. Party clown, Lorelai suggests. Not wanting to be left out, I say: exotic dancer.

"The family court judge will love me," Richard jokes.

On the drive back, Richard tells us we can stay at his house for as long as we need to. He even agrees to let Lorelai use his car if she drops him off at the terminal. She'll just need to pick him up when he returns in six weeks. I can't believe our good fortune.

~

Lorelai leaves me at Richard's house while she drops him off at the terminal, and that evening, we go for a walk. We wander aimlessly, and after an hour or so, find ourselves in a small downtown district. We buy two jumbo cookies and eat them on the sidewalk before sauntering into a bookstore.

"He's finally done it," Lorelai exclaims, pulling a thick hardcover from the shelf. "This book was supposed to come out years ago." She scans the inside cover and then looks at the price. She sighs before replacing it on the shelf. "We need to save our cash." She moves along the aisle, continuing to browse.

"I'll meet you outside," I call. I don't think about what I'm doing because thought will cost me my nerve. I grab the book, tuck it beneath my arm, and walk out as if I already paid for it. I wait for someone to come after me. No one does. I sit on a bench across the street and wait for Lorelai.

"You bought it?" she asks when I hold it up for her to see.

"I borrowed it." I have no cash of my own. "We'll be careful with it and return it once we're done."

She takes the book from me and smiles. "Poor, naive Bahati." She says it with affection. She still calls me

Bahati, and I still call her Lorelai, but it's almost mocking now. "You might become the first thief to be caught sneaking stolen goods back into a store."

That night, Lorelai lies on Richard's bed while I lie on his floor. We take turns reading the stolen book to each other, alternating chapters. She pauses midsentence and says: "His use of language is beautiful." She continues to read, her voice beautiful to me, and I've never felt so good about stealing anything in my life. I begin to nod off at 2 a.m., but I pretend to be fully alert when she hands the book to me. I read most of the chapter before falling asleep and dropping the book on my chin.

Lorelai laughs with uncontrolled mirth as I probe the inside of my lower lip with my tongue, tasting blood. "We can't return the book now," I say. "I've bled all over it." This causes Lorelai to erupt in fresh waves of laughter.

"Everything seemed fine," she says, struggling through laughter to get the words out, "and then your voice slurred, and then bam! You should've heard your scream."

"It hurt," I say. Mostly, I was startled.

"You didn't really bleed on the book," she says and grabs it from my hand.

No. I didn't. She's still laughing as I walk down the hall to sleep in the guest room. It feels nice to sleep on a mattress.

~

When Lorelai and I tire of being indoors, we take long walks. When we tire of walking, we read or watch television. On Friday night, we walk to Blockbuster and treat ourselves to three movies, anything not in the more expensive New Releases section. It doesn't matter which section we shop. Where movies are concerned, we might as well have been living under rocks. We haven't seen anything. She chooses a drama. I choose a comedy. We compromise on a thriller. We stay up late watching movies and talking, and I realize that I never think about the future. We never talk about it. We're living in Richard's house, and we have no plan, but I don't care. As long as I know we'll be together tomorrow, I'm okay.

~

Lorelai's face is nearly healed, some lingering discoloration around her eye, when we meet John Ray, a cashier at the grocery store. I don't like John from the start. He's Lorelai's age, and he flirts with her as if I'm not there, and then purposely forgets to scan a few of our items before bagging them. I don't think Lorelai is interested in him romantically, but she likes the free groceries, and he never disappoints. One morning, we go to the store, and Lorelai refuses to *buy* the frozen pizzas and French fries we'd come for because John isn't there. "Do you think money grows on trees?" she asks me.

On our second Friday in Richard's house, John invites us to a party. I was hoping for a Blockbuster Video night, but Lorelai wants to go. She's never been to a party, which I find hilarious. Even I've been to parties.

We haven't used Richard's car much, to save money on gas, but the party is in Anderson, a fifteen-minute drive. We meet John Ray in front of an apartment building, and he takes us up. Lorelai wears jeans and a red blouse. I wear jeans and an Atlanta Falcons T-shirt.

The party is nothing like the few house parties I've attended. Everyone is older, Lorelai's age, the music—Usher—is quieter, and the mood is mellower. John Ray introduces us around, and after a few people ask how old I am, and regard Lorelai dubiously after she answers twenty-one for me, I settle on a beanbag in the corner of the living room with a beer. There's more mingling than dancing, the living room and kitchen crowded with people. A lot of drinking. I try to keep an eye on Lorelai, but she's in constant motion. If one were to observe the two of us, they would probably assume that I was the one who'd never been to a party.

I'm still on my first beer when Lorelai finds me. "Are you okay?" she asks, her voice raised over the music. She bends toward me and almost loses her balance. She's had too much to drink.

I nod and hold up my beer. "Just relaxing."

She disappears, and I don't see her again until she's ready to leave. I'm annoyed, but she takes my hand and holds it while we walk to the car, and the night, everything, is perfect again. "I'll drive," I say. "You're drunk." She hands me the keys.

John Ray calls Richard's house to invite us to another party the following night. I don't want to go. Lorelai suggests she go alone, just for an hour or two. I find that scenario even more disagreeable. I wind up in another corner, this time in an uncomfortable chair, sipping a beer.

~

"I'm going to talk to Richard about getting a job," Lorelai says during one of our walks. "The problem is that I have no experience. I'm twenty-three, and I've never had a real job. I didn't finish high school. What do I say I've been doing for the past eight years?"

"I need a job too," I say.

"You're a high school dropout," she says, not unkindly. "We're a sad pair. But we'll be fine until Richard gets back."

I don't know how much cash exactly Lorelai managed to steal, and I don't know how much is left. Richard is due home in three weeks.

~

"Should we go back to the bookstore?" I ask. We've read the one book in our possession front to back a couple of times and many sections more than that. Richard doesn't have books in the house.

Lorelai shakes her head and smiles. "I'm fond of you, Bahati. I don't want to see you go to jail."

"I was thinking we could buy a paperback."

She considers and relents. That night, we stay up late taking turns reading to each other from *Sophie's Choice*.

~

The first party I halfway enjoy has a game of gin rummy going in the kitchen. Lorelai doesn't play, but I take a seat at the table as cards are dealt. The other players know each other and gossip casually, but as we play

205

hand after hand, and I imbibe drink after drink, I begin to feel like one of them. I'm drunk when the party winds down. I can't assess Lorelai's state, and I don't offer to drive. We make it home and stumble to our separate bedrooms.

The next party doesn't have a card game, but I've learned that alcohol makes its own fun. I talk basketball with a guy named Quentin. "I don't meet many Pistons fans in South Carolina," he tells me. He lived in Detroit during the Bad Boys era, and his father took him to the championships in 1989.

"I grew up watching Pistons games with my father," I tell Quentin. I feel a pang at the memory, but more alcohol helps.

"You're learning how to party," Lorelai says when she finds me. She's ready to go home, even though it's early.

"No thanks to you," I say, a rare hint of bitterness escaping my lips.

"That's not fair," she pouts and entwines her arm with mine.

Some random guy blocks our path and says to Lorelai: "You can't leave. The party hasn't started."

"That might be true," Lorelai says, "but you've already had too much to drink." Everyone has. Lorelai promises to see him again soon, and we walk outside to the car. I climb into the passenger seat.

We're on the expressway when Lorelai turns off the radio. The clock reads 10:30. I groan because I know what's coming. She grins at me. She presses play on the tape deck, and the one tape Richard has in his car plays: "Aquarius / Let the Sunshine In."

She sings along, loudly, partly because she loves the song and partly because she knows I hate it. Her singing voice is the only thing about her that isn't beautiful. I cover my ears.

"Can we play something from this decade?"

She sings louder, shouting the words as she exits the freeway at the Beecham Water Tower. I turn to look at her.

Everything seems to go wrong at once. She screams. Something slams into the windshield, cracking it. She slams on the brakes and cuts the wheel to the right. The car skids, out of control. But I can't be sure of that because I was never controlling the car. We stop, the force of it snapping my neck.

Lorelai is silent but "Age of Aquarius" plays.

"What happened?" I ask.

She doesn't answer. She gets out of the car, unsteady on her feet. I join her, the night dark and quiet. I follow her gaze to the form, lying on the ground, unmoving. She approaches, and I stay close to her. A man lies on his back, his face bloodied. I startle when he groans. His eyes open, but it looks like one of them is gone.

"Get help," I say. "I'll stay with him."

Lorelai is crying. I'm not sure if she heard me. She's staring at the man, her eyes glazed. And then, she seems to snap out of it. "Get in the car," she orders. She turns without awaiting a reply.

I sit in the passenger seat. The engine is running, music blaring. Her hand trembles as she turns the key in the ignition. The starter grinds against the flywheel, making an ugly noise that startles us both. Without my having to ask, she turns off the music.

"I should stay with him," I say.

"I'm drunk," she says as she pulls onto the road. I don't immediately understand the significance of that. Neither of us have fastened our seat belts. "We can't get help."

"We'll say I was driving."

"That's worse. You're a drunk Black man," she says. It takes me a moment to understand the significance of this also. She's thinking ahead of me, but she isn't thinking of the man lying on the road. "We'll call for help," she says. "It was right off the exit. We'll send help for him."

Neither of us speaks as she drives. If she feels any urgency to send help for him, it doesn't show. She drives slowly, cautiously. She stops at red lights and stop signs. Otherwise, she doesn't stop until she has pulled into Richard's garage.

My thinking is catching up with hers. "We can't use Richard's phone," I say as she unlocks the door attached to the garage.

She looks at me and shakes her head. I'm telling her things she already knows.

I don't say anything else.

She takes my hand and leads me to Richard's bedroom. We lie on the bed, my mind reeling with alcohol and the memory of the man's eye. Was it covered by dirt or blood or was it just gone? She's shivering as she reaches for me. My body responds instantly and with a totality that can only be explained by thousands of years of evolution. She kisses me, and electricity grips my entire being. I have no thoughts of the man or the eye as she guides me inside of her. The fit, exquisitely perfect, is like nothing I've imagined, as if she were designed for me and I for her, both of us intended for this one purpose. I wonder briefly if I'm doing it right, but even my insecurity can't find space beside the all-engulfing pleasure.

"Pull out," she whispers, and though my body is telling me not to, I follow her instructions. I don't realize I'm having an orgasm until it's over, and I've released into the sheets.

I lay beside her. In shock. It happened so fast. Almost as fast as the accident, and I know my life will never be the same. I know that I will do anything for this woman. I start to ask if it was her first time, but I don't want to know. We hold each other close.

~

In the morning, we hazard a look at Richard's car. The front bumper looks okay, but the windshield is cracked.

"Get it fixed or get rid of it?" she says. I'm not sure if she's talking to me or herself. "Someone might've seen the car."

I already know what she's decided.

We walk to a package store that afternoon and buy a large bottle of the cheapest vodka they sell. We drink shots for lunch, and we don't talk about the man or the car. She's thinking. I can tell. We make love again in the early evening, and then she tells me her plan.

~

We wait for nightfall, a couple of hours before we're slated to meet John Ray at a diner within walking distance of Lake Hartwell. We're looking for a scenic spot Lorelai visited with her mother and one of her mother's boyfriends years before the Prophets of the Torch. "If memory serves," she tells me, "there's a dock we can drive onto." She knows this, she explains, because she remembered seeing a car parked on the dock and wondering darkly if its owner intended to drive into the lake.

We arrive at the lake to find that Lorelai's memory was correct.

"Are you sure we want to do this?" I ask.

"I'm not sure of anything."

She puts the car in neutral, and I push it into the lake. We walk to the diner, and John Ray drives us home.

~

Lorelai reports the car stolen before she calls the number Richard left for her. She reaches dispatch, and Richard returns her call an hour and a half later. I don't listen to her end of the conversation. When she finishes, she finds me on the back porch.

"Are we okay?" I ask.

"He wanted to know if there's something I'm not telling him. I told him there wasn't. I left the garage door open, and the car was stolen."

I nod. We make love in Richard's bed, and afterward, Lorelai turns on the news. We wait, snuggled together, not speaking. She turns the television off after we see what we were looking for. Police have no leads in the hit-and-run death of a local father of two.

~

Straight vodka with lunch. That becomes our thing. We wait until noon to start drinking. It isn't difficult because we typically wake after eleven. We don't watch the news. We don't talk about the local father of two. *Two what?* I ask myself occasionally, usually after many drinks. *Rabbits? Abstract designs on T-shirts?* I really want to be that dense, but I know. I think about him a lot, that one eye—covered or missing? Vodka blurs the image. I want to talk to Lorelai about him, but I don't want to uncover her pain. We watch television and read from our two books. John Ray invites us to parties, even offers to pick us up and give us rides, but Lorelai always declines.

"Let's go for a walk," I suggest.

"I've had a lot to drink," she says.

"So have I."

We hold hands, and I think about how much she and I have been through together. The time with the Prophets of the Torch was the worst of my life, but it's led me here. Lorelai and I are taking care of each other, and that feels right to me.

I hear the police officer before I see him. Monumental things happen fast.

"Have you two been drinking?"

Chapter 19

TAMARA

Even as her eyes burned with exhaustion, Tamara opened documents on Sam's laptop, looking for manuscript notes or anything that would tell her what happened next.

Have you two been drinking?

Was that really the last thing he'd written?

She clicked on everything from obscurely named documents like *ps375* to clearly labeled files that likely had nothing to do with his book: *Retirement, Training, Old Resume*. His computer held many documents, but only six that pertained to Bahati and Lorelai, and she'd read every word of each of them.

She was close to giving up for the night when she came across a letter he'd written to his aunt Evelyn. There was nothing special about it, just a note inquiring about her plantar fasciitis, along with some tips he'd found on sleeping in a boot.

Tamara was almost too tired to make the connection, but then it hit her. His aunt Evelyn, his father's sister, had taken Sam in after his mother's death. If Lorelai and the cult existed outside of Sam's imagination, his aunt Evelyn would know about it. If Tamara wasn't so tired, she would've pumped her fist.

~

Want to do lunch or dinner this weekend? Kenneth texted. It was shortly after noon on a Thursday.

Can't. I'm going to Atlanta, she replied.

Her phone rang almost immediately. Kenneth.

"I just hung up with a friend from Atlanta," he said. "He's going through a divorce. Having a hard time."

"Seems to be a lot of that going around," Tamara said, thinking of Melinda, though Melinda hadn't made it to divorce. Yet.

"Always, it seems. Anyway, why are you going?"

"I need to visit my late husband's aunt."

"Are you searching for answers?" Kenneth asked.

"I don't know what else to do."

"Let me drive you."

"You really don't have to do that." She wouldn't mind his company for the drive, but as much as she was coming to like him, she still barely knew him.

"You'd be doing me a favor," he said. "I was just thinking that I would love to visit my friend. How long do you plan to stay? I can drop you off at your aunt's house, spend a night or two with my friend, and then pick you up for the return trip."

"I can't accept that," she said.

"What's to accept? I'm happy to do it. You don't have to decide now. Just let me know tomorrow."

She had no intention of taking him up on his offer until she considered the long drive ahead. With only billboards and fleeting radio signals to distract her, what would she think about for five and a half hours? The answer to that was obvious and even more unwelcome. She called Kenneth back that night, and they made plans for their road trip.

~

They hadn't planned for the downpour that plagued motorists on I-85 South all the way into Charlotte. They rode in silence for much of that stretch, Kenneth clutching the steering wheel and leaning forward slightly to follow the red glow from the lights of a truck in front of them. Occasionally, a car would blow past, and Kenneth would mutter, "How can they see anything?"

Tamara was tense, but mostly because of the silence, and the question she couldn't push away. Was the hit-and-run fact or fiction? It had to be fiction. She couldn't believe that Sam, the man she'd known well enough to marry and have a child with, had harbored such dark secrets. Or maybe she hadn't known him at all.

"You doing okay over there?" Kenneth asked, not moving his eyes from the road.

"I'm good," she said. "I'm not the one driving in almost zero visibility."

Kenneth grunted, and they continued their journey through the storm.

They stopped in Charlotte for coffee, and by the time they reached Spartanburg, the sun was shining. After filling the tank, Tamara took the wheel for the next leg.

"Of course, the weather is beautiful while you drive," Kenneth said. "Do you mind if we stop in Anderson for lunch? I want you to meet someone."

"Who?" Tamara asked. She wasn't really in the mood to meet people. She wanted to get to Atlanta and find answers.

"Diane and her son, Ben. They're old friends."

"Okay." She didn't want to be rude. And, either way, they had to eat lunch. "Why do you want me to meet them?"

"I have my reasons," Kenneth said. "But I want you to meet them before I tell you."

He made a phone call, and Tamara listened to his end of the conversation. He explained that he was passing through Anderson with a friend and confirmed lunch.

"Diane is making stew," Kenneth said once he'd hung up.

"We're going to her home?" Tamara asked. She'd assumed they would meet at a restaurant. Restaurants were less intimate. And they came with a timer. Once the food was done and the dishes cleared, you only had so long to sit and talk.

"You'll thank me. Her stew is magnificent."

"She makes stew when you're passing through," Tamara said. "How do you know her?"

"I'll answer all of your questions in time," he promised. "Just be patient and meet them first."

Tamara sighed. "Just what I need. Another mystery."

Kenneth directed Tamara to pull into the driveway of a small white home in a neighborhood filled with other small, well-kept homes. The front porch was accessible by stairs as well as a paved ramp. Before Kenneth could ring the doorbell, a young man in a wheelchair answered the door. When he saw Kenneth, he slammed it. Kenneth turned to Tamara, who watched, stunned. She heard the dead bolt turn. Kenneth shook his head.

She was about to ask if they should leave when the door opened again. The man in the wheelchair laughed and gave Kenneth a fist bump. "This is Ben," Kenneth told Tamara, "the juvenile delinquent I warned you about."

Ben smiled at Tamara. "Yeah, but I'm not a juvenile anymore."

"He's an old man now," Kenneth told Tamara. "He turned eighteen last month."

"This guy gave me baseball cards. He thinks it's the 1980s."

"Some baseball cards are still valuable," Kenneth said. "I hope this knucklehead has the sense to keep them."

Diane appeared behind Ben. "Are you going to invite our guests in?" she asked her son.

Ben backed up his wheelchair. "I was trying to get rid of this loser, but his friend seems nice."

Diane, a middle-aged woman with silver-streaked hair, stepped forward and shook Tamara's hand. She gave Kenneth a hug. Tamara was no closer to guessing who these people were.

"Are you hungry?" Diane asked, once she'd settled Kenneth and Tamara in the living room. "Lunch will be ready soon."

"It smells wonderful," Tamara said. It really did.

"I put it on as soon as Kenneth called."

Diane disappeared into the kitchen before calling them all to the table. The stew tasted as good as it smelled. Ben and Kenneth seemed to be engaged in a competition to outeat each other.

"My money is always on Ben," Diane said. "You should see him put away pancakes."

"She'll only make them once a week. Hey, are you staying the night?" Ben asked Kenneth. "She'll make them tomorrow if you're here."

"I hate to disappoint," Kenneth told Ben, "but we're headed to Atlanta after lunch."

"I tried," Ben said.

Diane asked Tamara questions about her research as Kenneth and Ben traded affectionate barbs.

"Are you okay to drive?" Tamara asked Kenneth when they finally stood up from the table.

"Sure," he said. "I'll just loosen my belt." He winked at Diane.

To Tamara's surprise, she'd enjoyed lunch. She didn't think about Sam once while she was with Diane and Ben.

"Are you going to tell me who they are to you?" Tamara said once they were back in the car, Kenneth behind the wheel.

"Yes," Kenneth said. "I will. Let's get back on the highway first. It's a long story."

"Delays, delays," Tamara said with a sigh.

~

Nine years ago, Kenneth was on the eve of his thirtieth birthday. He was driving home from a business trip in Anderson because he'd recently, and inexplicably, developed a fear of flying. His work required three to four business trips a year, and travel had never been a problem until a premonition prevented him from booking flight 673: Durham to Orlando. The flight took off and landed without incident and without Kenneth aboard, but his fear had nothing to do with reason. His practice of avoiding flying had begun, and it felt like the least of his worries. His marriage, by any objective standard, was coming undone. The harder he fought to save it, the further it seemed to slip away, but he couldn't stop himself from fighting because the thought of sleeping in an empty apartment, without his wife and four-year-old daughter, was unfathomable. Even his work as a project manager, his reliable companion, had turned sour. He'd worked at the same chemical company for ten years. He'd loved every moment of it until his boss retired and was replaced by an external hire named Ted. Ted took an immediate dislike to Kenneth, probably because Ted wanted to hire his own person to do Kenneth's job. He couldn't fire Kenneth, but he was perfecting the art of making Kenneth's work life difficult.

None of that was on Kenneth's mind as he focused on navigating an unfamiliar side street through a thunderstorm that was as bad as any he'd ever seen. *Turn left,* the GPS system advised in its robotic voice. He hadn't caught the street name, but it didn't matter. The sheets of rain splashing over the windshield rendered street signs undecipherable. Having already missed three turns, he decided to pull over to wait out the rain. He put on his emergency lights, and almost immediately, the worries of his life began to flicker through his mind. He considered pulling back onto the road for the distraction.

Instead, he turned on the radio and startled when a thunderous crack filled the air. He reflexively turned down the volume before he realized that the clap, followed by a crash, had come from outside the car. The earth seemed to shake, and a terror-infused scream cut through the cacophony of the storm. The oak tree next to his car had fallen.

It could have fallen on him, but it had fallen the other way, on what he believed to be a corner store.

Kenneth got out of the car, and the rain, which drenched him within seconds, was cold. Lightning pierced the sky, and he thought he could feel the crackle of electricity across his scalp. A second scream emanated from the ruins of the store, and he ran toward it. A boy lay on the ground, half inside the destroyed building, half out, his pant legs soaked with rain.

"I'm losing the pulse!" a woman screamed.

Kenneth saw her then. She was trapped behind rubble and a massive branch, but her fingers, outstretched, felt the boy's neck. "I'll call 911," Kenneth said, fumbling for the phone in his pocket.

"The clerk is on the line with them now," the woman said. "Help my son."

Kenneth knelt and checked the other side of the boy's throat. "I can't feel a pulse."

"Do you know CPR?" the woman asked.

"I think so. Maybe not." He'd taken a CPR class years before and had learned the technique on an inauthentic mannequin. He'd barely had confidence in his skills as he'd received the certificate. Now, he couldn't know what he'd forgotten.

"I'll talk you through it," the woman told him. "Quick."

And she did. She told him how to position himself above the body. She talked him through chest compressions and mouth-to-mouth. He performed CPR until he felt a pulse. "He's breathing," Kenneth said, his voice breaking with emotion.

"Thank God!" the woman exclaimed.

They'd been focused on restoring function to the boy's heart and lungs. They'd had no inkling in those moments of the damage that had been done to his spine.

~

"You saved his life?" Tamara asked quietly, in awe.

"His mother and I," Kenneth said.

"Wow."

"I didn't introduce you to them or tell you that story to pat myself on the back."

"It's a pretty big pat on the back," Tamara teased. "Why then?"

"Even though I don't know what it means," Kenneth said, "I thought it might help you. This incredible, terrible thing happened to us. It impacted us in different ways and taught all of us drastically different lessons. Diane was a religious child, but she lost God as a teenager when her father died. When I told her how I happened to be on that road, her faith was restored. A few years ago, Ben told me that, for a long time after the accident, he'd wished I'd found the courage to take a plane. He hadn't seen me as a savior but as a jailer, damning him to his chair. Even now, he can't believe in a God that would take the use of his legs, but he's grateful that he didn't lose more. He's found peace."

"What about you?" Tamara asked. "What did you learn?"

"I'm still working it out. I want to believe I was meant to be there. Sometimes I do. It's hard to dismiss it as coincidence. But then I think of the senseless tragedies that happen every day. I don't want to believe they're meant to happen. So, I don't know. I do know—and Diane and Ben are all the proof I need—that life has the power to astonish me. For whatever reason, a long string of ordinary days can be followed by something extraordinary. I recognize that understanding in you. When life on Earth underwhelms you, you set your sights on the cosmos."

A tear rolled down Tamara's cheek before it could even occur to her to guard her composure.

~

"I'm making a peanut curry for dinner," Evelyn said after hugging Tamara at the front door.

"It smells good." They paused in the living room, and Evelyn told her to have a seat. Tamara wanted to hurl her first question, but she took a deep breath and sat on the couch while Evelyn went to the kitchen. She hadn't been to Evelyn's home since before Sam's death, but little had changed. The freshly vacuumed mauve carpet was a bit more worn, but still in good condition. The cream-colored furniture hinted at an owner who appreciated familiarity. "It's been a long time," Tamara called, wondering how long she'd have to wait to get down to business.

"Too long," Evelyn said. "I was thrilled to see Brian last week. He's growing up so fast."

"Too fast. If you have any secrets for slowing time, please share them with me."

Evelyn appeared and beckoned Tamara into the kitchen. "If I figure that out, I'll sell it to the highest bidder."

Tamara was patient over lunch. Evelyn reminisced about Sam, but nothing she shared hinted at the darkness in his writing. Just things Tamara knew. Sam had taken up chess at the late age of seventeen, and Evelyn had driven him around the state to play in tournaments.

"It's so good to see you," Evelyn interrupted herself to say.

Tamara smiled. "It's good to see you too." It really was, even if Tamara was distracted. Their eyes met over empty bowls, and Tamara saw what she thought were new wrinkles. Evelyn had let her hair go gray and was wearing it short now. She was sixty and vibrant.

"How have you been? How is your research going?"

"It's good," Tamara said, but she had no more patience. "I should've reached out to you sooner. Has the FBI contacted you?"

Evelyn tensed. She shook her head. No one, Tamara thought, wants to be contacted by the FBI.

"Sam was murdered." She didn't want to leave Evelyn in suspense.

"What?"

Tamara told Evelyn about Cooper Franklin. Evelyn had heard the name but hadn't been following the story. "He murdered Sam. He was told to make it look like a suicide."

"Why?"

"I don't know. A man named Jason Blakely paid him. Do you know the name?"

Evelyn shook her head. "I never believed that Sam would kill himself."

"I believed it," Tamara said, "because he'd been depressed before."

Evelyn shook her head. "I've been depressed before. I'm sure you have also."

"Sam was hospitalized three weeks before his murder."

"Oh," Evelyn said.

"He didn't want to worry you."

"No, he wouldn't. That's why he wouldn't kill himself," Evelyn said sharply, as if adding another point to her scoreboard.

"He tried to write a novel. Did you read any of it?"

Evelyn shook her head but smiled. "He told me he was going to write a novel. I think he was seventeen then. I told him to focus on school."

"I read it for the first time last week. I have questions that I hope you can answer."

Evelyn waited.

"Did Sam's parents join a cult when he was a teenager?"

Evelyn didn't respond immediately. "Do you mind if we take a walk?" she asked. "It's a nice day out." Which was true. Tamara had left the rain two hours outside of Atlanta. But she wanted answers now. Evelyn must've seen her consternation because she added, "I'll tell you everything. I can't do it cooped up here."

~

Evelyn changed into a forest-green tracksuit and sneakers. Tamara's flats weren't the most comfortable for walking, but she didn't want to waste time retrieving her bag from the trunk and then checking to see if she'd packed shoes with more support. She'd left the house in a daze that morning with little thought of what she would need for the trip. She would spend the weekend at her parents' house, and she just had to hope she'd packed enough underwear.

"I was going through a bad divorce when Cynthia got sick."

Cynthia, Sam's mother, died from lung disease when Sam was sixteen. Tamara knew this and wanted to interrupt to repeat her question. *Did they join a cult?* But she listened instead as they walked through Evelyn's neighborhood.

"I was emotionally unavailable, and I blame myself for that. I'll always blame myself for that. Looking back, my marriage wasn't that great to begin with, but at the time, I felt like my world was coming to an end. Even when Cynthia got sick, I couldn't see past my little world."

"I've heard people say that divorce can be like losing someone to death."

Evelyn's smile was small. "Even if my ex-husband had died, he wasn't worth being emotionally unavailable for my family."

"Ouch," Tamara said.

"He wasn't a good man. It took me some years to realize that."

Tamara wondered why Evelyn hadn't remarried. But even if she didn't have more urgent questions, she wasn't sure she would feel comfortable asking.

"Cynthia got sick, and they joined a cult."

There it was. She'd been racking her brain for any hint Sam had given about the cult. Nothing. She'd just assumed that he hadn't talked about his father because there was nothing to say. The man had abandoned him after his mother's death. The man hadn't been able to handle his grief. Not much more to say about it.

"I don't know how it happened because I wasn't around. She was sick, and then she was dying, and then the next thing I knew, they'd sold their house and moved into an abandoned school. I tried to talk to Cliff, but he was always too busy. He wouldn't let me visit, so I never saw where they were living. Tense, brief phone conversations were all we had. Eventually, I let them go. Way too easily. I was in a bad way myself. But as I recovered, and rebuilt my life, it haunted me. I didn't know what was going on, but I knew it wasn't right. And I wondered if I could've prevented it had I been more available. The opportunity to take Sam in felt like a second chance."

"How did that happen?" Tamara asked. "How did he come to live with you?"

"He escaped from the People of the Torch." Evelyn shuddered. "The name alone gives me the creeps. He was arrested for underage drinking. The authorities got in touch with me. I'm more grateful for that than anything else in my life."

"Underage drinking?" Tamara asked. "That was all?"

"I don't remember the technical legal stuff. He was in public, so I think there could've been a charge for that. In the end, he wasn't charged with anything. He was a good boy." She smiled at Tamara. "But you know that."

Tamara didn't know anything anymore. "Was he arrested alone?" She held her breath. She wanted the answer to be yes.

"No, he was with a woman. She was charged with buying Sam alcohol or something. She'd helped him escape from the cult, and I was grateful to her for that, so I spoke to the prosecutor, but I don't know if it helped. I never met her."

And even though Tamara had known it was coming, she felt like her entire world was imploding. Again.

Chapter 20

CINDY

Do you ever wonder if you truly know me?" Cindy asked Ross. It was date night at Purple Sky, one of their favorite restaurants.

Ross sipped his wine and grinned. "As in, can anyone truly know anyone? What are you reading these days?"

"A fascinating novel set among the Cherokees before de Soto arrived. But it has nothing to do with that. I'm just wondering if you ever wonder if you truly know me."

"I don't know why you're asking me this. That could be an argument that I don't truly know you."

Cindy sighed. "You're hilarious, darling."

"Your aunt popping up out of nowhere was definitely unexpected. But that's been good."

"Are you finished mocking me?" Cindy asked.

He reached across the table and took her hand. "To be honest, I felt like I truly knew you the first time you gave me a waterskiing lesson."

Cindy smirked. "You haven't lost your charm."

~

On an overcast summer day in 2001, Cindy started an old towboat and steered toward a quiet spot on the private lake. She liked days like these, the sun blunted by whitish stratus clouds that offered little threat of rain. She wore a two-piece swimsuit and didn't feel the need for anything more, save sunscreen. She carried a cover-up tunic for those cloudless days when the sun was high in the sky, its rays punishing her skin. Edward, her boss, encouraged her not to cover up, but she ignored him and the implications of what he thought she was selling. He rarely provided spotters for instructors. He never mentioned instructors wearing life vests, but he wanted to ensure that she always had cleavage showing. Not a great guy to work for, but she felt lucky to have the job. She was twenty-seven, and it was her first real job. That was hard enough to explain. And then there was the misdemeanor conviction for furnishing alcohol to a minor.

"How long have you been skiing?" her pupil, Ross Fremont, asked.

Cindy hesitated. She didn't like the question. Or rather, the answer. Three years didn't seem like a long time. But she'd packed a lot of hours into those years. She'd gotten her instructor certification a month before. It was Ross's first lesson, and he was her third student. "A few years," Cindy said and quickly changed the subject. "What got you interested in skiing?"

A mischievous twinkle flashed in his eyes. "Emma Faulk."

Cindy smiled. "Sounds like there's a story there."

Ross looked to be her age, midtwenties. "Our first date is this Friday." It was Sunday. "She does a lot of waterskiing. Her parents live on a lake and own a boat. I told her I know how."

"Aah," Cindy said. "And you've never skied a day in your life."

"I panicked. I wanted to take it back the moment I said it. But how do you take that back?"

"Sorry. I lied," Cindy offered.

Ross laughed. "This is easier."

~

Russ looked apprehensive as he waited in the deepwater start position. She repeated each of her instructions before climbing behind the wheel. She watched him in the rearview mirror as she pressed the gas, accelerating smoothly. He lost his balance just as he was trying to stand. Not unexpected. Cindy had seen only a few people stand successfully on their first try. She circled back, and he resumed the start position.

She accelerated and he stood, a wide grin on his face. She kept the speed steady, and he gave her a thumbs-up, the signal to go faster. She was at twenty-five miles per hour. She inched up to twenty-seven. He was still grinning when he fell backward. Again, not unexpected. But instead of letting go of the line as she'd instructed, he held on. "Let go," she muttered, watching him in the mirror. The rope snapped him forward, out of his skis, and flipped him onto his back. Finally, he let go as he hit the surface and dipped below. Thank goodness he was wearing a life vest.

He came up coughing, and she circled back. Teaching beat the miscellaneous tasks she'd previously done for Edward—cleaning the boats, cleaning the shop, cashiering on occasion—but was it too much to ask that grown men follow instructions? Especially when she'd repeated them several times.

"I'm okay," he said, once she was within hearing distance. "I'm ready to go again."

Cindy hoped Emma Faulk was as pretty on the inside as she was on the outside.

~

Cindy was sitting inside the shade of the shop reading *Another Country* when a man said, "Interesting book. Good choice."

She looked up to see Ross. He wore jeans and a gray shirt. She rolled her eyes.

"I know what you're thinking," he said, taking a seat beside her on the couch. "This guy will say anything to a beautiful woman. But I really did read *Another Country*."

She wondered what he was doing here. She hadn't seen him since his lesson a few weeks before. His performance had been solid. He wouldn't be doing tricks or jumps anytime soon, but he could stand and ski at a steady speed.

"Prove it," she said.

"The main character is Rufus Scott."

"Okay." She nodded, surprised. "How did it end?"

"You haven't finished."

"I've read it twice."

He told her what he could remember.

She smiled. "Did you enjoy it?"

"Moderately. Maybe not at all. It was my mother's favorite book. She read it like once a year. When she was dying, I wanted something to talk to her about."

"I'm sorry," Cindy said. "About your mother."

He looked stricken for a moment. Then he said, "It sucks, but it's okay."

She'd never heard anything so touching in real life, a man reading a book to discuss with his dying mother.

"Isn't it crazy," he asked, "that you happen to be reading the one novel I've read since middle school?"

"I read a lot of books."

"Not at the same time. On this couch."

She conceded the point with a nod. "Are you here for another lesson?"

He sighed. "My waterskiing days are behind me, I'm afraid."

"What happened with . . . ?"

"Emma."

"Right. Emma."

"I took her out to dinner, and I was too honest, unfortunately."

"You seem to swing between too deceitful and too honest."

"It's a personal failing. We're both third-year law students at Emory. She asked why I chose law, and I told her the truth."

"Which is?"

"To make a lot of money."

"Emma doesn't like money?"

Ross smiled. "I'm sure she does. She was born with it. Otherwise, she wouldn't find the pursuit of it crass. I grew up poor. Hell, I'm still poor. All I have is this degree I'm earning. That's why I was afraid to tell her that I'd never water-skied. For all I know, all rich kids water-ski."

"Plenty of rich people come here who can't ski worth a dime."

"I wouldn't know that," Ross said. "She got bent out of shape over the money answer. She wants to work in child advocacy. Whatever that means. It's for the best. I want my children to be privileged enough to have her attitude. I don't want to marry it."

"You have children?" Cindy asked, teasing.

"Oh, no, no, no." He waved his arms as if she'd asked if he wanted to sample blowfish. "I'm speaking of hypothetical children."

"So why are you here?"

"I was hoping I could take you to dinner tonight?"

Cindy raised her eyebrows. "You can't be serious."

"We both have to eat."

"Yes, but not together. I gave you lessons to impress a girl you lied to."

"You helped me to amend a lie. Now that I can ski, it's no longer a lie. Let's call it an anachronism. And before you go thinking I'm a liar, keep in mind that I could've milked *Another Country* for something. I didn't claim to like it or suggest that I'm a literary scholar or even an avid reader. Though I do read a lot of case law."

"Sounds fascinating. What would we talk about? I read novels. You read case law."

"You can tell me about your favorite novels," Ross said. "I'm actually a good listener. And I make case law interesting."

"Tempting."

"Say yes," he said. "What time do you get off?"

~

Cindy was regretting saying yes—about nine months too late—as Ross's cell phone rang. *Pick up,* she muttered, the cordless phone pressed to her ear.

You have reached Ross Fremont, the voice mail recording announced. She moaned and waited for the beep to leave a message. "Ross, I expected you home an hour ago. Anyway, I think I'm in labor. I need you to call me or come home or do something."

She sat heavily in the recliner and placed the phone on the coffee table beside her. It was a little after 6:00 p.m., already dark outside. Her due date was yesterday, and she'd been having Braxton Hicks contractions on and off for the past three days. This was different. They didn't stop when she stood and walked around, and more telling, they hurt. She could feel them in her back.

She grimaced as a contraction took hold and focused her attention on the second hand of her watch. *10 seconds. 25 seconds. 40 seconds. 53 seconds.* She exhaled slowly. The longest contraction yet. She noted the time when it subsided: *6:18, 15 seconds.* She watched the ceiling and waited. She thought about turning on the television, but there was nothing she wanted to watch. She wanted to escape her body. She wanted the baby to come while her spirit was off . . . doing anything else. She closed her eyes and centered her attention on the tingling in her forearms. It radiated to her fingers. You're okay, she told herself. Anxiety can't hurt you.

The baby's large head can.

She had to silence that voice. She called Ross again. *You have reached Ross Fremont.*

She hung up. Another contraction came, and she checked her watch: *6:23, 8 seconds.* Less than five minutes since the last one. The contraction lasted for sixty-three seconds, and she called Ross again. When the call went to voice mail, she had to resist throwing the phone across the room. Where is he? she wondered.

She couldn't figure out what bothered her more: waiting for the next contraction, being alone, or knowing that she could be in labor soon. She sat in the recliner for an hour, standing to walk around every fifteen minutes or so. She was growing more and more uncomfortable, her anxiety blossoming despite her attempts at relaxing self-talk. She left Ross two more messages, and then she started hanging up before the beep.

They'd spoken at three that afternoon. She'd told him that tonight could be the night, and he'd told her he would be home at five. He'd rushed off the phone because he was on his way into a client meeting, but he'd promised her Chinese food.

She couldn't think about eating now.

A particularly painful contraction seized her, and she squeezed the soft armrest. Just three minutes since the last.

She called Daniel Stills, and her mood lifted when he answered. The connection was full of static, and she could barely hear his hello.

"Daniel," she said, "I think I'm in labor, and I'm all alone."

"Hold on!" he yelled. In a few moments, he said, "Sorry, had to turn down the radio. It sounded like you asked me to do you a favor and throw you a bone."

"No," she said, louder this time, "I think the baby is coming. Ross isn't answering his phone."

"The baby is coming?" His voice rose with excitement.

"Maybe. I'm all alone here."

"Do you need me to turn this truck around?"

She smiled. Of course, he couldn't. He was who knew where, hauling who knew what. "Where are you?" she asked.

"Just outside of Akron, Ohio."

"Yes, please," she teased, "turn the truck around."

"I wish I could be there. Are you okay?"

"I think I need to go to the hospital."

"Where is Ross?"

"Who knows. Maybe he's in a bar. If I knew where, I would call and have the bartender send him home."

"In a bar? Does he know you're in labor?" Daniel asked.

"I'm joking. Ross doesn't go to bars that I know of. I don't know where he is."

"Do you have someone to take you to the hospital?"

That's why Cindy was calling him. "Yeah, I do," she said. "I was just checking to see if you were home first."

"I wish. I hate that I can't be there. Keep me posted, okay? I'll be driving on pins and needles until I hear from you."

Cindy didn't have anyone else to call. The people she worked with were just people she worked with. She considered 911, but she had no idea how much an ambulance ride would cost. More money than she or Ross had. The next contraction sent panic through her body. She couldn't give birth here. Alone.

She was in Ross's apartment surrounded by his stuff because baby arrivals were unpredictable, and he wanted to be with her when the contractions started. So much for that. After another fruitless call to Ross, she staggered through the front door into the hallway. She'd been living here for the past few weeks, but she hadn't gotten to know any of his neighbors. She should've insisted that Ross sleep at her place, but that only made sense in hindsight. Her place was a trash dump. His was moderately better. She knocked on the door directly across the hall, unit 257. A man in his early twenties answered. He squinted into the light of the hallway.

"I live with my boyfriend across the hall," Cindy said, still recovering from the last contraction. "I think I'm having a baby."

He glanced down at her belly, mouth open. "I'm pretty sure you're having a baby."

Cindy closed her eyes to center herself. The man was still gaping when she opened them. "Yes, I'm having a baby. Like, right now. I think I'm in labor."

"Holy . . ." The man trailed off as if catching himself before swearing. "Congratulations."

"Thank you. Is there any way you can give me a ride to the hospital?"

"Oh." He drew out the word. "I would, but I just ate like five brownies. They have more than chocolate in them, if you know what I mean."

"I know what you mean," Cindy said, bracing for the next contraction. They were coming regularly, and she didn't have long.

"I can get my mom to drive you. She's at home, but she can be here in like ten minutes."

Cindy forced a smile. "That's okay. Thanks."

"You sure?" the man called as she made her way to the apartment next door.

Cindy didn't have the mental energy to respond. She knocked on the door. When no one answered, she said a silent prayer and knocked again. She inhaled when she heard the lock disengage. The door opened slowly, just a crack. It was dark in the apartment, and she couldn't see who was peering out.

"I'm in labor," she said quickly.

The door opened, and a shirtless man stood on the threshold. Cindy noticed his chiseled physique before her eyes settled on the handgun he was holding nonchalantly, pointed at the floor. He must've seen something in her expression because he said, "I have a permit for this."

"Right, of course," Cindy said, backing away. "I'm sorry to bother you."

"You banged on my door to let me know you're in labor?" He sounded annoyed.

Cindy didn't want to annoy him. "I had the wrong door. I'm sorry. I thought you were my boyfriend's friend."

"Whatever." He closed the door, and Cindy was relieved.

She knocked on unit 257 again. "Would you mind calling your mom?"

~

"Oh, sweetie, it's so good to meet you. I'm Janet." Janet walked quickly toward Cindy, who stood on the sidewalk in front of the apartment building with the bag she'd packed for the hospital. She still hadn't gotten the neighbor's name, but his mother was short and round with a kind face. Cindy offered the woman a smile and introduced herself.

"Are you wearing that to the hospital?" Janet asked her son. He stood beside Cindy in gym shorts and an old Kurt Cobain T-shirt that was coming apart at the neck seam.

"I'm home, Mom," he whined. "The game is on. I can't go to the hospital."

Janet pursed her lips and glanced at Cindy. She forced a polite smile. To her son, she said, "I think you should put some clothes on and come with us."

"It's been a long day, Mom."

"Nick, please—"

"Oh," Cindy said, clenched by another contraction. "Can we go?"

Nick took her arm to help her to the car.

"You aren't coming?" his mother asked a final time, incredulous, once Cindy was settled in the front, the seat pushed back to its limits and reclined for her comfort.

"I'm settled in for the night," he said before closing Cindy's door.

"It really is nice to meet you," Janet said as she pulled away from the curb. "Not the ideal circumstances, but . . ." She trailed off.

Cindy focused on her breathing. Where was Ross?

Janet sighed. "Nick was born on the opening day of deer season. His father never missed the opening day, and Nick's birth wasn't an exception. While I was giving birth, he was killing deer." She sounded bitter. "But he isn't a bad man."

Cindy didn't know if Janet was defending him for missing his son's birth or killing deer. "You're more forgiving than I," Cindy said. "I want to kill—whoa!" This contraction was really something.

Janet patted her shoulder. "Just breathe, dear. I'm sorry Nick isn't here. He's high. I could tell. He'll grow out of it. And I think he'll be more responsible when he does."

Cindy laughed despite the pain. "You think Nick is the father?"

The woman glanced away from the road to look at Cindy. "Isn't he?"

"I just met him tonight. My boyfriend lives across the hall."

Janet laughed. "Whoo," she said. "That's a relief. Sorry. You seem like a perfectly nice girl, and I'm sure you'd make a wonderful mother to my first grandchild. But I've never heard of you until tonight. Nick called me and said, 'Cindy is at my place, and she's in labor. Can you pick her up and take her to the hospital?' I just assumed . . ."

"Understandable," Cindy said between deep breaths.

"Don't get me wrong, Nick is a good boy, but I could already imagine being responsible for this baby. That's what would happen. I've been there and done that."

"Ross asked me to marry him, and I couldn't say yes," Cindy blurted out. She had no idea why she was confiding in this woman. If Cindy was good at anything, it was keeping her own counsel.

"Ross is the father?"

Cindy nodded. "I didn't think he would abandon me like this." She was close to tears, and she didn't care. She didn't know if it was the pain from the contractions or the fear of what was to come or . . . hormones. She didn't know what it was.

"Does he know you're in labor?" Janet asked.

"I've lost count of the number of messages I've left. He always returns my calls."

"Oh, sweetie," she said.

~

When Ross had taken her to a fancy restaurant out of the blue, she'd asked, "Did you land a big client?"

He smiled and shook his head. "Can't I take my pregnant girl-friend someplace special just because?" She was eight weeks pregnant, the pregnancy confirmed just the week before.

"You can. Will your pregnant girlfriend have to help you wash dishes?"

"Good one." He held up his glass of wine. She sipped ice water. She'd ordered an entrée on the lower end of the restaurant's price range. He'd apparently come to splurge. The small criminal law practice he worked for paid decently, but his bills—rent, car loan, student loans, credit cards—swallowed most of each check.

She ordered tiramisu for dessert, and the server brought her an empty plate with an engagement ring in the center.

"You bought this?" she asked, incredulous.

~

"Are you her mother?" the nurse asked as he helped Cindy into the bed.

"No," Janet said but didn't elaborate.

"You can go," Cindy told her. "Thank you so much for getting me here. You don't know how relieved I am."

Janet squeezed her hand. "You shouldn't do this alone."

And Cindy felt another wave of gratitude. She knew this woman barely better than she knew the maternity nurse, and yet, she did feel a little less alone.

She'd been shocked by Ross's proposal. Before she'd glimpsed the ring, the possibility of marrying him had never occurred to her. She'd hit a man with a car and left him to die. She didn't deserve the life Ross was proposing. Even if, somehow, she could get past the guilt, she couldn't expect to walk away unscathed. Her secret stalked her, a deadly predator. She lived on borrowed time. She could never tell Ross what she'd done, and the idea of marrying him was a fantasy.

You haven't given me one good reason why we shouldn't get married, he'd said a couple of months after she'd turned down his proposal. She knew he was disappointed, but she'd never imagined he would abandon her like this.

"Do you have a cell phone?" she asked Janet, desperate. She'd just realized that Ross had no way of getting in touch with her.

Janet nodded.

"Can you call my boyfriend and tell him where we are? Ask him to call on your phone." While Janet made the call, Cindy asked the nurse for pain medication.

～

Amy Leigh Foster—eight pounds, two ounces—was born three minutes after midnight. Using her strong lungs, she emitted boisterous cries and passed the Apgar test with flying colors. Cindy had thought a lot about Ross during labor, her fury a tool used to push Amy along. Everything shifted the moment she held Amy to her breast. She felt a love she couldn't doubt, a feeling she hadn't experienced since cuddling with her own mother—a feeling that had long been absent in her life. She had to do everything she could to ensure the well-being of this little soul in her arms. She had to live for this baby.

Sometimes, she felt so guilty, so afraid of the police knocking on her door that she considered turning herself in—anything to relieve the agitation. Now, holding Amy, she understood that she no longer had the luxury of guilt or anxiety. This little girl needed a mother, and Cindy would be her mother. And Ross . . . Why had she let him get away?

She was very fond of him. Maybe, even—she wasn't sure how to tell she loved him. She didn't play love songs in her room and think of him as she had her grade-school crushes. She didn't feel that she couldn't breathe without him, but on any given day, given a choice, he was the person she would want to spend time with. They never ran out of things to talk about. The sex was spectacular. Did all that amount to love? At the moment, she wished she had a mother or even a friend to ask. She didn't even have Ms. Florence, her probation officer, now that her probation was over. Ms. Florence had seemed to really like her, and Cindy wondered how the woman would react if Cindy called to ask her for advice about marriage.

"She's beautiful," Janet said again. Cindy could see the fatigue in her eyes, and she knew Janet wanted to leave.

"Thank you so much," Cindy told her. "We'll be fine. We probably all need to sleep."

Before Janet left, Cindy considered asking her if she'd made a mistake by not marrying Ross.

~

Nurses periodically woke Cindy to feed Amy, and Cindy was so tired that she would fall right back to sleep. Even after the sun rose, she would wake for just long enough to nurse. It was early afternoon when she woke to find Ross sitting at her bedside.

"I came as soon as I could."

The fury rushed back. As soon as he could? If this was his best, he'd come up short. But she also felt relief. Maybe it wasn't too late to build the life Amy deserved. "Where were you?"

"I was in a car accident."

She looked him over. His eyes had a haggard look to them, but, other than that, he seemed perfectly fine. Her mind flashed back to their first meeting. *She does a lot of waterskiing. I told her I know how.* "A car accident?" She didn't hide her disbelief.

"I'm pretty banged up," he said, lifting his right arm as if to test it out.

"Do you have a bruise? Or a scrape?"

"I know what you're thinking. Hear me out. I had a meeting with a client at a prison. I was driving back on some country road, and I guess I fell asleep. When I woke up or came to or whatever, the car was flipping, I think. It happened so quickly. I ended up in a shallow creek. The car was so bent out of shape that I couldn't get the seat belt off. The CD player was stuck on a loop of 'My Name Is.' My cell phone was on the passenger floor, and I could hear it ringing, but I couldn't reach it. It was the worst feeling I've had in my life. I was just stuck out there in the middle of nowhere with no one to help."

Cindy wasn't convinced, but she asked, "How did you get out?"

He smiled. "A dog found me."

"Like Lassie? The dog found you and told rescuers where you were?"

"Almost. I was able to reach the notepad and a pen in my briefcase. I coaxed the dog to the window. It was broken, and he was skittish, and I was so worried he'd step on a shard of glass and bolt. But he didn't. I managed to tuck a note in his collar. It worked. His owner found me the next morning and called 911."

"How long were you in the car?"

"About sixteen hours. Long enough to hear 'My Name Is' two hundred times. Sometimes I stopped praying for rescue and just pleaded for the battery to die. Or my hearing to give out."

～

When Cindy and Amy were released from the hospital, Ross took them to a fire station in the middle of nowhere to meet the firefighters who had rescued him.

As they drove home, he asked, "Now do you believe me?"

Sitting in the back with Amy, she smiled. "I guess even you wouldn't go so far as to corrupt first responders."

"I'm driving a rental car," he said, as if that should have been sufficient evidence.

"Are you ever going to ask me to marry you?" she said.

He grinned. "I've asked you a hundred times."

"That's an exaggeration. I think we should get married, but I have a condition."

He groaned. "Of course you do."

"We can't live in your apartment."

"Why not?" It only had one bedroom, but they'd already converted the dining room to a makeshift nursery.

"One of your neighbors pulled a gun on me."

His eyes left the road for the rearview mirror. "What?"

"Okay, I'm exaggerating. I'll tell you that story another time. Right now, I just want you to agree to my demands so we can tie the knot."

Chapter 21

TAMARA

You hired a private investigator?" Melinda asked Tamara.

They sat in lounge chairs on the shore of the private lake in Melinda's neighborhood.

"The same investigator who looked for Malik," Tamara said.

"Why don't you just tell the FBI what you've learned?"

"I haven't learned anything. I feel like I know less than the first time they spoke to me. How crazy would I sound? 'I know I told you my husband had no enemies, but it turns out he belonged to a bizarre religious cult as a teenager, and he was arrested with a mysterious woman before I met him.' They'll think I've cracked under the pressure."

"No, they won't. You've told me all of this, and I don't think you've cracked under the pressure."

Tamara lifted her sunglasses and looked hard at her sister. "Not even a little?"

Melinda smiled. "Maybe a little. Your adventure with Kenneth is a little out there."

"That's the crazy part to you," Tamara asked, "Diane and Ben?"

"A little."

Tamara acquiesced with a nod. "It's a little crazy to me too. Whenever I think about Diane, I wonder if I could survive what she did. I certainly couldn't do it with her grace."

"You survived the death of your husband," Melinda said. "What you thought was a suicide. You survived it, and you built a new life on top of it."

"I did that for Brian. I survived so that he could grow up and have a life."

"You think it's any different for Diane? Her son is here, and she's making sure he can have a life."

"She's a hero."

"You're a hero." Melinda smiled teasingly. "What's the deal with Kenneth, anyway? Is he your boyfriend now?"

"No," Tamara said, "not even close."

"Do you want him to be?"

"No," she said more emphatically than intended. "Honestly, I like spending time with him. I think about him when we're not together. But I'm not ready for a relationship. I don't know what I want from him."

"That sounds like a start."

"I don't want to lead him on. That isn't fair to him."

"Don't lead him on. Be honest. Let him decide for himself."

"What if he decides to have nothing to do with me?"

"It'll be his loss. You'll move on. We've been through so much. We always keep going."

"It's hard," Tamara said.

"I know." Melinda paused and set her jaw in that way she'd had since they were children. It could mean a number of things and was always difficult to interpret, but it always preceded Melinda saying something uncomfortable. "What happened that year when Malik dropped out of college?"

Tamara was surprised. "You never heard the story?"

"No one would tell me. Eventually I stopped asking. Am I old enough to hear it now?"

Tamara detected what might have been resentment in Melinda's tone. She sighed. "It probably wasn't right for Mom and Dad to keep things from you. They were trying to protect you." Melinda was eleven when Malik had his first breakdown. Their parents had responded, in part, by sending Melinda to stay with cousins.

"Maybe they did protect me, somewhat. But it left me to imagine the worst. Who was protecting you?"

"I was helping Mom and Dad." It wasn't Tamara's idea to send Melinda away or to shield her from what was happening, but she'd been a participant.

"That must've been difficult for you," Melinda said, and Tamara imagined her sister, the social worker, speaking to a client. "It was scary for me. You were missing, and then Malik was missing. And then Dad told me I was going to Aunt Sharon's house for a week. I came home while Malik was in the hospital, only to be sent away again when he was released. None of it made sense to me."

"It didn't make much sense to me either. I can't believe you don't know the story."

"We've established that our family is good at keeping secrets," Melinda said, annoyance edging into her voice. "Will you tell me already?"

"I was fifteen, so you would've been eleven. Malik was a first-year student at Stanford, so it was"—Tamara paused for some quick arithmetic—"1995. I hadn't seen Malik in months when he woke me, a finger to his lips . . ."

~

"Malik?" Tamara asked. The En Vogue CD was still playing, the next to the last song, so she knew she hadn't been sleeping long. "What are you doing here?" Summer was a month away.

"Get dressed. I have something to show you." He turned and left her room before she could respond.

She pulled on the denim shorts and khaki shirt she'd worn that day and turned off the stereo. She found Malik at the kitchen table eating the spaghetti her father had made for dinner. He was shoveling it into his mouth, as if he hadn't eaten for days.

Tamara laughed. "Did you heat it?" Congealed oil clung to the pasta.

"So good," he answered, his mouth full.

She sat across from him. "Is college food that bad?"

"I've gained fifteen pounds." Most of that had been during his first semester. She'd noticed it when he was home for winter break.

"Are you trying to put on another pound tonight?"

He ignored her, as if mesmerized by the spaghetti.

"Or maybe you wanted to show me how they eat at Stanford."

He smiled but didn't slow the pace of his ingestion.

"Do Mom and Dad know you're here?"

He shook his head. When the last of the spaghetti was gone, he put his plate in the sink and drank from the faucet. Classic Malik. Their mother found that disgusting. He wiped his mouth with a dishcloth. Even Tamara disapproved of that.

"You ready?" he asked.

"Ready for what?"

His smile showed teeth this time, the charming smile she associated with her brother. "I got a new telescope."

"Sweet." Her grin matched his.

She followed him outside to his car. The night was cool and clear, good weather for stargazing. She stood by the front bumper while he climbed behind the wheel.

"You getting in?" he called.

"Where are we going?" She'd expected him to pull his telescope from the trunk. Perhaps they'd take it up to the roof, if the scope was small enough.

"You'll see."

"It's almost one a.m. Dad will kill me."

"Dad won't know. If he finds out, I'll handle it."

Tamara considered it. This was Malik, after all. Firstborn son. High school track star. Recipient of a full-ride academic scholarship to Stanford. Model human being. The boy who did no wrong—besides the occasional drink from the faucet.

"I'll get my purse."

"Don't wake anyone."

~

They traveled north on I-75, and Malik listened as Tamara chattered about school. Chad had a crush on her, but she liked Tom. Tom liked Tamara's best friend, Lynne, but thankfully, Lynne was more interested in Mario. No one was hooking up because no one could pair up. This seemed to please Malik. Or maybe she just imagined that it pleased him, because he wasn't saying much. He wasn't reacting at all.

"How is school?" she asked. They'd been driving for a while, and she was still waiting for him to exit the freeway. Where are we going? she wondered.

"I quit," he said, matter of fact, as if he were talking about intramural lacrosse.

"Like dropped out? Do Mom and Dad know?" He was a straight-A student. Malik quitting school was beyond Tamara's imagination.

"I don't know what they know. Mom and Dad," he said, "have been controlling me since I got there."

"Controlling you?"

"I didn't notice at first. They were shaping the curriculum. The textbooks, everything. My professors' words were coming straight from Mom and Dad."

Tamara felt a flutter in her stomach. Is he joking? she wondered. Is he on drugs? "I don't understand."

"I didn't understand either. I spent a whole night trying to make sense of Fourier transforms." Malik was a physics major. "And then it hit me, just as the sun was rising. My whole curriculum was written by Mom and Dad, and the more I integrated it into my intellect, the more they were able to control my thoughts."

Tamara thought about Malik sitting at the kitchen table, cramming cold spaghetti into his mouth. She'd sensed then that something was off, but she'd dismissed it. He was Malik.

She hesitated. She didn't want to offend him. "Are you using drugs?" She watched the road, wondering if he was safe to drive. They passed a lone car now and again, but mostly, the interstate was empty. Maybe that was a good thing.

"What? No. My mind is clear. Clearer than ever."

"We need to turn around." She wasn't panicked, but she felt fear rising from her stomach, expanding in her chest.

"We're almost there," he said, nonchalant.

They fell into silence, just the hum of the engine and wheels on asphalt. She'd been in a car with him, just like this, just the two of them, dozens of times. She'd never felt alarm. This was different. She'd never sneaked out of the house to go anywhere with him. But it hadn't felt like sneaking thirty minutes ago. He'd wanted her to come, and everyone had been asleep. Was she supposed to wake her parents to ask permission? Malik was an adult, old enough to live on his own. Old enough to go to war.

"Tell me where we're going."

"Tearbritches."

She had no idea what that was. "If you quit school, what's next?" She wanted him to talk more, to assure her he was okay. Maybe she just hadn't understood what he was trying to tell her.

"I have options." He was pure confidence, pure Malik. "I've been getting messages. I'll explain everything."

And with that, she lost all desire to probe further. She wanted to go home. She wanted to tell their parents she was worried about Malik.

~

Malik and Tamara were alike in ways that simultaneously bonded them while setting them apart from the rest of the family. Malik got his first telescope when he was thirteen. Tamara was nine, Melinda five. At the dinner table, he would talk excitedly about Io, Callisto, Ganymede, and Europa—the Galilean moons of Jupiter. His parents listened with the same feigned interest they'd shown a year earlier as Tamara was learning to recite the names and characteristics of various dinosaurs. They all listened to Malik, but Tamara alone absorbed his knowledge. The two of them spent hours in the backyard, poring over sky maps, stalking celestial bodies, and perfecting their dexterity with a telescope. They watched alien films together: *Aliens*, *2010*, *Close Encounters of the Third Kind*, *They Live*. They pondered the evidence of alien encounters and agreed it had yet to happen. They speculated on how the first encounter would go down. Growing up, Tamara played mostly with Melinda, but she idolized Malik. She, in turn, was his favorite.

~

Her anxiety was ratcheting up. Nearly an hour had passed since Malik told her they were almost there. They'd been on US 411 for a while. Whatever she asked, however she asked it, he'd assured her they would be home soon. "Snug in your bed," he'd told her.

They passed through a small town, and Malik navigated the roads as if he'd done it before. He probably had. That was better than believing he was making random turns. They stopped for gas, and she considered using the pay phone to call her parents. But what would she tell them? She was in the middle of nowhere with Malik, and he was saying strange things?

Back on their way, he turned onto a gravel road engulfed in darkness. Nothing outside the beam of his headlights was visible. A new worry twisted Tamara's insides: What if his car broke down?

She clung to the image of herself at home, snug in her bed.

∽

Tearbritches was a trailhead, and the path seemed to lead straight up. Navigating by flashlight, Malik carried the telescope, and Tamara, carrying nothing, huffed upward.

"It's really late," she told him. "I'm tired. I need to sleep."

"It's early," Malik said. It was nearly 4:00 a.m.

"What?"

"You said it's late. I'm telling you it's early. It's all about how you frame it."

"Screw you." She could no longer suppress her irritation. "Once you show me whatever it is, I want to go home."

"Snug in your bed," he repeated with a grin.

∽

They stopped at a clearing on Grassy Mountain, and Malik set up the new telescope while Tamara rested on a rock. Malik deftly located Proxima Centauri, the closest star to the solar system.

"And?" Tamara said, gazing through the lens. Either of them could find the Centaurus constellation in their sleep. Without a telescope, Alpha Centauri A and Alpha Centauri B looked like one star. As kids, they'd been blown away the first time they saw them shining distinctly.

"I received a message from C," he said, referring to Alpha Centauri C, another name for Proxima Centauri.

"A message?" Tamara asked. "C is four light years away. How old are these messages?"

"They told me to drop out of school. I'll never be my own man if I don't get away from Mom and Dad."

He wasn't making sense. "You brought me here to see Proxima Centauri?"

"I'm expecting another message. I dropped out of school. I need to know what's next."

"I want to go home."

"We will. I just need a nap. Give me an hour. Then we'll leave."

Tamara didn't want to give him a minute. "I'll drive."

"No," he said, "you won't." He pulled a camping pillow from his pack and handed it to her. He balled up a pair of pants to tuck beneath his own head. "You've always loved sleeping beneath the stars."

She lay down on the packed dirt, the pillow beneath her head. As she listened to his soft snores, she tried to convince herself that they would go home once he'd had his nap. Missing curfew was irrelevant at this point. She would have to tell her parents everything. She would tell them that Malik offered her a short ride and extended it into a trek against her will. She would tell them that Malik claimed to be receiving messages from Proxima Centauri. She would tell them that something was wrong, and they would fix it. She had to believe that. Without notice or her consent, the unexpected happened: she fell asleep.

∼

The light of dawn brought a rush of fear.

Tamara sat up. Something was wrong.

"Malik!" she called, her voice echoing through the wilderness. His telescope and pack were still here, but he was gone. She listened. Nothing.

She waited.

She was thirsty.

She checked his pack. No water. No filter. Malik knew the woods. The brother she knew wouldn't come to a place like this without water. He might neglect food but never water. His car keys weren't in his pack.

Cold, she pulled on the pants he'd used for a pillow. They were long and baggy on her. It didn't matter. She waited. She sat on a rock, her knees pulled into her chest until she couldn't put the bathroom off any longer. She took off his pants and walked into the woods. When she finished, she shouted his name again. Only her echo responded.

~

An hour later, when she decided to leave, she couldn't remember which way they'd come. It had been dark, and she was exhausted from both the arduous climb and the lack of sleep.

Which way did we turn to enter the campsite? she wondered. Left or right? She had a fifty-fifty chance. The odds weren't comforting.

She turned right and walked downhill, leaving his telescope and pack behind. Most of their hike in had been a climb, but it had been a rolling climb, like a graph from calculus class. She didn't bother looking for landmarks, as everything looked completely different in the morning light. Her best-case scenario was finding Malik.

The temperature rose as she pressed forward on sore feet. She was no longer cold, but the incipient heat didn't bode well for her growing thirst. She walked for miles, eyes peeled for Malik. She saw no one, not even a stranger. She wasn't a survivalist. She'd camped and hiked with Malik, but they'd never been this lost, never been without water. If she stayed on the trail, she reasoned, she would hit a trailhead, either

Tearbritches or another. But a trailhead wouldn't necessarily bring salvation. She didn't remember seeing a visitors' center at the Tearbritches trailhead. She might've missed it in the darkness, but that was doubtful. The Tearbritches trailhead was located off ten miles of unpaved road, probably too remote for a visitors' center. If she made it to Tearbritches and Malik wasn't there waiting for her, she would have the gravel road to contend with.

Why hadn't she left a note for her parents? It hadn't occurred to her. But even if it had, she wouldn't have known what to tell them. *Malik is showing me something. Be right back.* That wouldn't have helped them find her. Perhaps Malik had told someone he was bringing her here. She could only hope.

~

As her legs grew heavy, she distracted herself with a silent chant, stepping to the rhythm of the incantation, forcing each foot in front of the other. *Why,* left foot, *Did,* right foot, *You,* left foot, *Leave,* right foot, *Me,* left foot, *Malik,* right foot. Her thirst had subsided an hour ago, overtaken by hunger. She was furious with her brother but also worried about him. She wondered if she should've waited longer at the campsite. Probably not. If she didn't find him or anyone else, she had to make it to a town before nightfall. She walked.

The blister on her left toe was forcing a limp by the time she reached the Tearbritches trailhead. The parking lot was empty, Malik's car gone. She sat heavily against a tree stump, her body convulsing with sobs. She was so tired. She was hungry and thirsty, and town was ten miles away. She'd convinced herself somehow that Malik would be sitting on the hood of his car, grinning and waiting for her. She would scream at him, but her anger would subside as she rested in the passenger seat, his car pointed toward home. Now, she had to contend with reality. She needed to keep walking. Daylight was finite, after all. But she'd lost all momentum.

She was still sobbing when she heard a car approach. She held her breath, hoping to glimpse Malik's red Toyota. The mud-splattered white pickup truck knocked her mood to a new low. It moved slowly, bumping noisily, and she considered standing to wave it down. The white men inside were bearded, and the rifle mounted in the rear window made up her mind to stay put. She watched the ground, hoping the truck would pass. Fear pulsed from her fingertips to her chest when the truck stopped.

"You alone, gal?" the passenger called, his mountain accent thick, menacing to her ears.

Tamara considered bolting into the woods. She was exhausted, but the fresh wave of adrenaline might be enough to carry her away. She met his eyes and tried to make her voice strong. "My brother is right behind me." Despite her efforts, her voice wavered, carrying fear and traces of the tears she was crying.

The passenger door opened, and the man stepped out of the truck. He was big, dressed in camo and brown boots. He regarded her, and Tamara again considered bolting.

"I don't see him."

"He'll be here. My father too."

The man looked unimpressed.

"Let her alone," the driver called.

Yes, Tamara pleaded to God or whatever else could hear her thoughts, *let me alone.*

"Do you see a car?" the passenger asked the driver. "She's here by herself, bawling."

Tamara stood. Her legs and feet ached despite the adrenaline. Instead of bolting into the woods, she walked at a fast clip down the gravel road, away from the pickup's rear bumper.

The passenger laughed. "What I tell you?"

Tamara picked up her pace. If she needed to, she could still dash into the woods.

"Eton is ten miles," the passenger called. "You can't walk. There's wild boar out here."

Tamara felt a jolt, her fear ratcheted up that much more.

"They don't come out until night," the driver said.

Tamara was in a race against the sun.

"They come out when they want to come out," the passenger replied. They were talking to each other, voices raised, presumably for her benefit.

She kept walking.

"If a wild boar attacks you," the driver said, "stay on your feet. Don't let it knock you down."

She heard a door close, and she hoped the men would continue on their way. That hope met the same death that every hope before it had. The truck turned around and pulled up alongside her.

"I can't let you walk," the passenger said.

"I'm fine," Tamara told him, still crying. She'd watched *Deliverance* with her father, and it was all she could think of now. That, and being raped and murdered by these men in the bed of the truck.

"We're not gonna hurt you," the passenger said.

"Thank you," Tamara said and meant it. But she kept walking. She didn't know what else to do.

"Get in the truck." It was a command, not an offer.

Tamara bolted. The woods were thick, and she headed straight for them. She'd barely started running when she was off her feet, her shoulder slamming hard to the ground.

"Aw, heck," one of the men said. He was on her in an instant. "You didn't see that rock?" It was the passenger. He grabbed her beneath her arms and lifted her as if she weighed nothing. Fighting seemed pointless. He placed her on her feet before the passenger door. Her ankle throbbed despite the terror flooding her nervous system. "Go on. Get in. We're not gonna hurt you."

She got in.

The two men didn't talk as they drove. Have they done this before? she wondered. Tamara stayed silent. Look for an opportunity, she told herself. She used her peripheral vision to search for landmarks. All she saw was trees.

She startled when the passenger spoke. "Are you gonna tell us what you were running from back there?"

You, Tamara thought. She didn't want to antagonize these men. "My father and brother will be looking for—" Sobs broke through her words. No one would be looking for her. By now, her parents must have realized she was missing. But they wouldn't look here. She wondered if she would ever see them again.

"Don't cry. We gonna help you."

"I told you to let her alone," the driver said.

"It isn't too late," Tamara said, her voice soft. "You can let me out here." She didn't care if she had to hobble a hundred miles on her ankle. She wanted out of the truck.

"It ain't safe," the passenger said with a finality that brooked no discussion.

The truck lumbered along, the three of them bumping down the unpaved road. Tamara prayed for a passing car. If she could just signal for help. Her prayers went unanswered. Even in Eton, the streets were abandoned. They turned onto US 411, and Tamara watched unobtrusively. This might be the best chance she had before they arrived at their destination.

Tamara thought of horror films, teenage girls kept chained in basements. How had this happened to her? Just last night, she'd been snug in her bed. Why had Malik done this?

When she saw a parked police vehicle, she perked up. When she saw that the vehicle was parked in front of the Eton City Police

Department, she prepared to scream. She considered grabbing the wheel and crashing the truck. Her left forearm tensed. *Do it!* Her heart rate accelerated. She didn't do it.

The driver put on the blinker and turned into the police department parking lot. Tamara wondered if this was some kind of trick. Did Eton police traffic in teenage girls?

The truck stopped, and the passenger climbed out.

"I'd rather not talk to the boys in blue," the driver said as the passenger helped Tamara out of the truck. She tested her ankle, and pain shot up her thigh.

The passenger helped her through the front door of the police station.

"Guess I'll be on my way," he said to Tamara. He left without another word. She didn't even get to thank him.

~

Tamara wasn't in trouble. There was too much confusion at home for that. Malik was missing for a week until he was arrested in Stanford at his ex-girlfriend's place of work and charged with stalking. Their father flew to California and brought him back to Atlanta. Malik grudgingly allowed himself to be committed to Grady Hospital's thirteenth floor, the psychiatric ward. He stayed there for eight days.

When her parents brought him home, she was in the living room in front of the television, too nervous to watch it.

"Thanks for visiting me?" Malik said to her with a grin.

"Thanks for ditching me in the woods," she replied.

"Tamara," their mother scolded.

She was teasing. Kind of. Really, she just wanted to put it behind them. She probably should've visited him at the hospital. But she was still wary. Even as the medication stabilized his mood and time healed her ankle, she remained wary.

~

"I can't believe I've never heard that story," Melinda said with astonishment when Tamara finished talking.

"It's not a memory I revisit often. I had no idea it was only the beginning."

Tamara's parents had remained optimistic in the face of Malik's illness. They hadn't accepted it as an illness at first. *He's had a time of it,* her mother had said. *He's young and sensitive, and the breakup with his girlfriend and being away at school was just too much. A perfect storm.*

Tamara hadn't disagreed. Why would she? She hadn't known anything about schizophrenia or its chronic thrall. There had been family members on her father's side who hadn't been quite right. But that's all Tamara had known about them. Not quite right. It hadn't been discussed. Even after everything had settled down, the Tearbritches fiasco behind them, and Tamara had come home to find that Malik had moved most of the downstairs furniture outside to the backyard, she hadn't grasped the new reality of her family. The furniture had been damaged by heavy rains, and Malik had been returned to the hospital. Tamara was still innocent then, unaware of the tribulations awaiting her family.

Malik would be hospitalized nineteen times over the next fifteen years. He would live many of those years at their parents' home, though there would be stints of living on his own. He would be arrested four times but never for anything violent. Tamara would never again feel as afraid as she had in that pickup truck bumping along the unpaved road. Until, perhaps, when Malik disappeared.

Once or twice a year, Malik would call Tamara and say: *I want to see you, sis.* She would hang up the phone and book him a plane ticket, and he would fly in to LaGuardia. He loved the energy of New York. To visit, not to live, he would tell Tamara. They would go to Rockefeller Center and Central Park and the Metropolitan Museum of Art. He had his favorite breakfast, lunch, and dinner spots, and every evening they would eat chocolate chunk cookies from his favorite bakery. *I think you come here for the food,* Tamara would tell him at least once every visit. *Sister,* Malik would reply, *I'd visit if you fed me beans and rice for every meal.* She believed him.

"I'm happy for you, Tamara," he told her during one visit as she'd dropped him off at the airport.

"Why?" she asked.

"I'm always searching," he said. "Searching the skies, searching the ground. You've found happiness right where you are."

"Thank you," she said because she *was* happy. She couldn't know it then, but Sam would be dead three months later. Six months after that, Malik would disappear.

Chapter 22

COOPER

I spoke with a woman here in Atlanta," Special Agent Lewis told Cooper. "She's in her early twenties, extremely close to her father. Well, she was. See, when she was fifteen, her mother was murdered. Her mother was a doctor, volunteered at this homeless clinic, actually ran the thing. One night, when she was closing up, bang! She never knew what hit her. The only clue was some missing narcotics."

Cooper closed his eyes. He hated having his murders described to him.

"Case was cold. The local police thought it was a junkie. The daughter thought it was a junkie."

"I was told to make it look like a robbery," Cooper repeated. He'd already confessed to killing the doctor.

"Willie pointed us to the girl's father, the victim's husband. It wasn't hard to convince me, but you wouldn't believe how hard it was for me to convince the girl. You can have all the evidence in the world, but sometimes, people just don't have the imagination for it."

Those words stuck with Cooper.

Cooper, for a long time, despite all the killing, hadn't seen himself as a murderer. He hadn't had the imagination for that.

Back in his cell, he settled at the easel and labeled the canvas: *Failure of Imagination.*

~

On a cold day in December 2003, Cooper entered Piney's on Piedmont as Talitha exited the kitchen. She'd caught his eye, smiled, and signaled for him to wait while she served a table.

He skimmed a menu on the wall, not really attending to what he was seeing. He was there for the portobella sandwich and roasted potatoes.

"Have you been working out, Cooper?" Talitha asked by way of greeting.

Cooper, pleased she'd noticed, shrugged, nonchalant. "Been playing some ball here and there." He didn't know why he'd lied. He hadn't played ball in years. Perhaps it was his sensitivity to weight gain and his wish to avoid the topic even retrospectively. What he'd done was join the gym and spend every morning lifting weights instead of drinking coffee and eating doughnuts. He'd also cut the late-night snacking. He climbed into bed every night hungry, and he wondered if he would ever get used to that.

"It agrees with you," Talitha said and smiled, and Cooper's pulse accelerated. She led him to a table and, once he was seated, said, "I'm going to guess your order. Are you ready?"

"My behavior can be difficult to predict."

"A mushroom sandwich and roasted potatoes."

Cooper beamed. "Your powers of divination never disappoint."

He watched her walk away, his appreciation matching the experience of seeing her coming. Then he retrieved his phone and pulled up his favorite picture of Lisa and the kids: the twins, five years old, flanking Lisa at Niagara Falls, grins across all three faces. He needed a reminder of what was at stake. He could still vividly recall the image of Lisa standing outside Fernando's apartment, a twin in each arm, ready to confront him over an imagined affair. He didn't want to find himself on the wrong side of that rage. Also, Talitha was married. Cooper had never met her husband and had no grasp of the man's capacity for violence, but it didn't take much for him to envision the youth minister administering a beating that Willie wouldn't soon forget.

He read a book while he waited for lunch.

"Have you solved world hunger?" Talitha asked as he moved his book to the side. She placed the plate in front of him. "Or maybe you're working on world peace?"

Cooper shrugged. "I'm just trying to understand what it means to be a good person. To live a good life."

A few weeks after he'd joined the gym, he'd found a book abandoned behind the incline bench press: *A History of Great Thinkers*. He'd taken it to the art gallery and found himself entranced by the chapters on Socrates, Plato, Aristotle, Confucius, Lao-tzu, and Gautama. When he wasn't reading the book, he was thinking about it. When he reached the end, he'd gone to the bookstore and left with a stack of books that covered each of the great thinkers in more depth.

His greatest fear became running out of books.

Before joining the gym, he'd been fixated on Tim. Killing him had been easy, like the others. But it was different in one disturbing respect: the guilt. After killing the youth minister, Cooper had waited for the guilt. It hadn't come. The youth minister had left Cooper no choice. Cooper had understood that. The others, Cooper had believed, had been terrible men. By the time Cooper had learned the truth, killing had become his job. Tim was different.

The morning after he'd killed Tim, Cooper awakened in a panic. He had to face what he'd become: a killer.

"You're living a good life," Talitha told him. "Art gallery owner. Budding philosopher. A sandwich and potatoes every day for lunch."

"I'm living *the* good life," Cooper said, holding up his sandwich for emphasis. "Living *a* good life is more complicated."

~

"Where on earth will you find the time?" Lisa asked Cooper.

It was a Friday night, and they were dining at a Mexican restaurant, their biweekly date. The twins were home with their favorite sitter—the neighbors' teenage daughter—who played video games with Howard and hosted tea parties with Kathy. They'd recently moved into a new home with more space and a bedroom for each twin. The neighborhood was a step up the socioeconomic ladder. *We live next door to an engineer,* Lisa had told her mother with pride.

"I'll do what I can," Cooper said. "See how it goes."

He'd just told Lisa that he wanted to take a philosophy course at the local community college. Finding time would not be a problem. He was already spending his days studying philosophy.

"Where is this coming from?" Lisa asked.

"Philosophy means *love of wisdom,*" he told her. He'd tried on occasion to talk to her about philosophy, but she had zero interest. No one he knew had any interest. Kathy would listen when he talked about the Ring of Gyges or Pascal's wager, but inevitably, often while he was mid-sentence, she would cut his musings short: *Thanks for the talk, Dad.* She would be halfway out of the room before he realized the chat was over. He'd asked his mother why she'd never introduced him to philosophy, and she told him that she hadn't wanted to waste his time. He desired to meet others who loved philosophy. "I want to acquire wisdom. That's where it's coming from."

~

Cooper enjoyed the routine of being a student. He started with a single Introduction to Philosophy course that met on Mondays, Wednesdays, and Fridays from 11:05 to 11:55 a.m. After his fourth philosophy course, Contemporary Moral Issues, he decided to go for a bachelor's degree and began to sign up for electives. His office at the art gallery became his library and study room. The evenings and weekends were set aside for family time, and he took jobs as they came in. It was a life he'd never imagined for himself, and over time, he couldn't imagine it being any other way.

Chapter 23

TAMARA

Tamara wanted so badly to call the woman—better yet, email her. But she didn't have an email address for Amelia Taylor, who now went by Cindy Fremont, according to Leonard Williams, the private investigator she'd hired. It had taken him three days to produce a home address and cell phone number. And a phone call was so easy to brush aside. Tamara knew, as terrified as she was, that she had to meet the woman in person. She had to show up unannounced at her home.

And here Tamara was, parked in front of a large house in an upscale neighborhood in Buckhead. She considered driving away. She knew more than enough now to go to the FBI. If they thought Amelia Taylor knew something, they could interview her themselves. And yet, that wasn't why she remained parked. She needed to see this woman who arguably knew Tamara's late husband better than Tamara did, this woman who had set Sam on the course of trying to write a novel that would nearly kill him.

She shut off the thinking part of her brain and climbed out of the car. She focused on the sensations of her breath, shallow and ragged, as, on automatic, she stepped along the pathway of flat stones that wound through the spacious lawn to the front porch. Thoughts entered her mind. What will you say? You can still turn back. No harm in starting with a phone call.

She let them pass in and out of her consciousness as she focused on her breath. She rang the doorbell, refusing to really consider what she was doing.

A woman with short gray hair, too old to be Amelia Taylor, answered the door.

"I'm looking for Cindy Fremont," Tamara said, her voice stronger than she'd expected.

"Wait here," the woman said and turned. She left the door cracked behind her.

Time seemed to pass slowly, and yet, all too soon, the woman stood before her, pretty and fit, with long dark hair. One word echoed through Tamara's mind: *Lorelai*. Something—recognition?—flashed in the woman's eyes, but it passed too quickly for Tamara to discern. Cindy held the door open, not really inviting, more a show that she could shut it at any moment. Tamara considered addressing her as Amelia, just to show Cindy that she wasn't completely in the dark, but decided against it out of respect. "Cindy Fremont?" she asked.

The woman smiled. "And you are?"

"My name is Tamara. I think you knew my late husband, Sam Foster."

"Late?" Cindy asked. "Sam is dead?"

Tamara studied her, noting the familiar use of his name. She looked shocked. Not bereft, but certainly perturbed. "For five years now."

"What happened?" Cindy asked.

"He was murdered. It could've had something to do with the People of the Torch."

"Murdered," she repeated softly. She looked as if she'd been punched in the stomach.

Tamara waited a beat for her to say something more, and then finally asked, "Can we sit and talk?"

Cindy stepped onto the porch and closed the door behind herself. "My children are inside, and my husband will be home soon. They've never heard of the People of the Torch, and I want to keep it that way."

"I'll only take a second of—"

"You need to leave," Cindy said forcefully enough that Tamara took a step back. "I'll meet you later, and we can talk. But not here. Do you have a number I can call?"

Tamara gave the woman her number. "One more thing," Tamara said before Cindy turned to go back inside. Cindy waited. "Do you know Jason Blakely?"

"Jason Blakely?" Cindy repeated. "I don't. Should I?"

Chapter 24

CINDY

Cindy hadn't known where to go. Her father's hospital room didn't seem the place, but that was where her ruminations pulled her.

"How is he?" she asked a nurse who was leaving his room as Cindy arrived.

"He's having a good morning," the nurse said. "Good appetite at breakfast. Are you family?"

"I'm a friend of the family," Cindy said.

Her father was asleep, so Cindy settled in the chair beside his bed. Her mind returned to her meeting with Sam the night before. As requested, she'd met him at the Beecham Water Tower at 10:30 p.m.

The time and place were proof of his instability, but what options did she have? Ignoring his demand to meet wasn't one of them.

I haven't been here since that night, he'd told her.

Why would either of us come here? she asked.

The man who died here—who we left to die here—had a family. Did you know that?

Cindy shook her head. *I didn't. I have a family. Do you have a family, Sam?*

He nodded, and Cindy pulled out her phone. *This is Cy.* She stood beside Sam so he could see her phone. *He's seven. And this is Amy. She's thirty.*

Sam raised an eyebrow.

Actually, she's nine, but she thinks she's thirty.

Sam didn't laugh. He didn't even smile. But he looked at the pictures. At her prodding, he shared pictures of his wife and son, Brian, three years old.

We have to take care of them, Sam.

You want to hear something funny? he asked.

I want to hear what's on your mind.

I never forgot those nights when you and I stayed up reading to each other. I saw the impact stories had on you, and I never lost my desire to do that.

Cindy nodded encouragingly.

So, I finally did. I wrote about you and us and all of these things I hadn't thought about in years. I just let it pour out. At some point, I realized that the man who died here was an essential character in our story, and I didn't know a thing about him. So, I did what novelists do. Research. His name was Allan Kline. He had two daughters, fourteen and thirteen years old. His sick grandfather lived with him and his family. He worked as a paralegal, representing low-income clients facing eviction. Maybe for the first time, I realized that we left a human being out here to die.

Sam, we—

Let me finish.

Cindy nodded.

I went back and read what I wrote about you. I'd made you a hero of sorts, and I wondered why. Why didn't I show you as the manipulative, callous person you were.

Sam—

I think it's because I was in love with you then, and I wanted to be in love with the character I was writing.

I'm not a character, Sam. I'm a human being with a family. This happened a long time ago. Fourteen years. But, Cindy knew, there was no statute of limitation on criminal offenses in South Carolina.

You might think we got away with something, but we didn't. Trying to write that novel almost killed me. I was this close to suicide. Sam demonstrated with his thumb and forefinger. *My wife had to hospitalize me. I'm going to make this right. I'm going to turn myself in, and you should do the same. If there's any decency in you, you'll do the same.*

That wasn't the end of their conversation, but everything after had been noise to Cindy. She tried to make Sam understand that there was no such thing as making it right. What had happened was horrible for Allan Kline and his family, and there was no way of taking that horror away. Turning themselves in wouldn't change anything. They had to live good lives now, for their families.

All her words were lost on Sam, and Sam's words were lost on her. He gave her two weeks to prepare her family because he intended to turn himself in and confess everything.

When it came to preparing her family, Cindy didn't know where to start.

Her father awoke slowly, and he smiled when his eyes focused on her.

"Amelia." His voice was hoarse. He seemed weaker than when she'd seen him last. "I'm glad you're back. I wanted to call you, but—I can't seem to avoid old traps."

She smiled and squeezed his hand. "It's okay." Coming back hadn't been easy for her. She'd worried about running into his family, especially his daughter. But she needed to talk to someone, and there was no one else. He would be gone soon, so at the least, she could count on him to take her secrets to the grave. "You asked me about my life," she began, looking for a way into the story. "There were things I didn't tell you because—" She paused again, and he reached out and touched her forearm reassuringly.

She told him about life with her mother, no sugarcoating, no embellishments. She spoke about the People of the Torch, sparing him nothing. The catharsis of the moment, her vulnerability, his sympathy, caught her off guard. She'd never spoken of these things, and she hadn't realized how badly she'd needed to. Now she understood why her doctor harped on therapy. Talking was an exquisite release.

She cried and he cried as she described the hit-and-run, the full truth of it. She told him about Sam's ultimatum.

"I don't deserve the life I have."

"No." He reached to touch her hand, but she was rambling now.

"I know that. But I also know with certainty that Amy and Cy deserve everything they have. My husband is a good person. He represents dubious clients occasionally, but that's his job. He deserves everything he has. None of them deserve me and what I've done.

"I wish more than anything that I could go back and talk to my twenty-three-year-old self. If I couldn't stop her from driving drunk, I would demand that she call for help and wait at the scene of the accident. Nineteen years later, it's clear to me what I should've done. I might've gone to prison for a few years, maybe five, but I would've survived. If nothing else, I'm a survivor. Who knows? I might've still ended up with the same beautiful family."

"I wasn't there for you through any of this," her father said once Cindy had stopped talking long enough for him to interject. "Maybe if I'd been there, this wouldn't have happened."

"No one can help me," Cindy said.

"Maybe I can help," her father said. Cindy couldn't imagine how. Who could even know how much longer he would live? "I'm not proud of the life I've lived. I've changed, but I was who I was. When I faced my charges, I didn't talk. I could've gotten a lighter sentence, and there are people who owe me for that. I know a guy. Willie—ah, you don't need details. These guys. They can make sure Sam doesn't talk."

Chapter 25

COOPER

Special Agent Lewis leaned back in his chair. "Let's talk about Sam Foster."

"We've talked a lot about him," Cooper said.

"And yet, I think you still might be able to help us with it. You killed him and staged it to look like a suicide."

Cooper nodded. "That's what I was told to do."

"And you had no idea who was hiring you to do that?"

"None."

"Willie fingered Jason Blakely. You've never heard the name?"

"Not until you mentioned it to me last time," Cooper said.

"Jason Blakely paid Willie to have Sam murdered. And then six weeks after that, he conveniently died. The puzzling thing is that we can't find any connection between Jason Blakely and Sam Foster. It's doubtful they'd ever met."

Cooper nodded, waiting for a question.

"Did you do any research on Sam Foster? Can you remember anything about him?"

Cooper feigned thoughtfulness, mostly for Special Agent Lewis's benefit. "These aren't memories I nurtured," Cooper finally said. "If

I found myself thinking about a guy I killed, I forced myself to think about something else. None of those memories were pleasant."

~

It was 2011, and Cooper had just settled at his favorite table at Piney's when Willie called and asked to meet ASAP. Cooper hesitated before inviting Willie to join him. Cooper was a regular here, and he didn't like to mix his two worlds. But it wasn't like Willie was a stalker. Willie would order a drink, maybe some fries, Willie would leave, and Cooper would have details for his next job.

"What is all this?" Willie asked when he arrived. Books and class notes were splayed on the table.

"This is called a book," Cooper said, holding one up for Willie to see. "If you open it, and you're literate, you may or may not learn something useful." He put the book in his backpack and cleared space for Willie to sit.

"You've always been a different kind of cat, Cooper."

"So you say."

Cooper was opening his mouth to ask about the job when Talitha appeared.

"Will you be having the steak today, Cooper?" she teased with a smile, her dark hair pulled into a bun today.

"Not manly enough, Talitha. Make it a mushroom sandwich."

She laughed at the running joke between them. To Cooper's chagrin, Willie ordered the shepherd's pie. Cooper had hoped Willie would provide the job details and leave.

Willie watched Talitha walk away. "I think you could hit that," he said to Cooper.

"I'm married."

Willie snickered. "So am I."

"And that's where the similarities between you and me end."

"You're a man," Willie said. "At least you used to be. Everyone I know is married. None of them wear monk's robes. You telling me you wouldn't like to hit that?"

"I wouldn't like the stress of looking over my shoulder. Lisa doesn't play."

Willie leaned forward. "You kill people for money. You're worried about your wife getting mad at you?"

"If Lisa worked for the FBI, I wouldn't kill people for money."

Willie leaned back. "Fair enough. You've always been—"

"A different kind of cat," Cooper finished for him.

"About this job." Willie leaned forward again. "It's in Connecticut. Time is of the essence. Can you leave tonight?"

Cooper shook his head. "I have finals. I can leave Friday afternoon." It was Tuesday.

Willie swore. "I told him you're a professional. You have finals? You in med school or something?"

"Philosophy major."

"Philosophy? You're kidding me. The philosopher killer."

"I could do it on Wednesday, but I'd have to be back Thursday afternoon. I'd rather not rush it."

Cooper smiled when Talitha returned with their food. She smiled back with something in her eyes that seemed to be just for him. "Let me know if I can get you anything else."

"I'd let her know what she can get me," Willie said once she was gone. "Rushing leads to mistakes. Just leave on Friday. As early as possible. The client is an old associate. A stand-up guy. He's dying and he wants to see this happen before he goes." He pulled a picture from his pocket and handed it to Cooper. "Make it look like a suicide."

"Huh," Cooper said and studied the photo. He'd never been told to make a murder look like a suicide. He wondered why. Wouldn't it be better if they all looked like suicides? Even if a hit was meant to send a message. If you're a crime boss and your associates start killing themselves, that's a pretty strong message. "Got it. Any details about this guy?"

Willie gave him the usual: address, known hobbies. "He's unemployed, a former stock trader or something. The client would prefer you didn't, but if the wife gets caught up in it, a murder-suicide is okay. He has a three-year-old son. Do not kill the kid."

"Jesus," Cooper said, "why would anyone think I would kill a kid?"

Willie shrugged. "They don't know you like I do, Coop."

~

"Good luck with your studying," Talitha said when she stopped to pick up Cooper's check. He met her eyes, and he saw an opportunity he didn't want to let pass. He'd imagined sleeping with her even before a few months ago, when she'd told him about her pending divorce. Actually, he'd thought about it plenty of times but never seriously. Not until Willie fertilized the seed that was germinating now with alarming speed.

"Thanks, Talitha. I have a business trip after finals. When I'm back, would you like to have lunch?"

She smiled. "I'd love to. Anyplace but here."

She wrote her number on the back of his receipt.

Chapter 26

CINDY

Cindy had recognized Sam's widow the moment she'd seen her standing on the porch. Not exactly *recognized*. If she'd passed Tamara Foster in a grocery store aisle, Cindy would not have taken a second look. But she'd spent a lot of time dreading the day when her past would knock at her front door, and when Tamara did, even before she'd spoken, Cindy had known. Sam had shown her a picture of Tamara when they'd met at the Beecham Water Tower, but that was a long time ago. Cindy had been distracted, and the flash of the picture was brief. Still, Cindy had put it all together before Tamara opened her mouth.

Now, she walked circles around her pond, thinking, trying not to panic. Sam was murdered five years ago. The timing was right. Or all wrong. Wrong because Sam had threatened her five years ago. Five years ago, her father had promised her that Sam wouldn't talk.

Why hadn't Sam just left the past buried?

Another question haunted her as if the widow were standing behind her, whispering in her ear:

Do you know Jason Blakely?

How much digging would it take to learn that Jason Blakely was her father?

She hadn't known that Sam would be murdered. But if she was honest, she hadn't known that he wouldn't. She hadn't had the courage to ask. She'd just wanted Sam quiet. Maybe her father had tried less extreme measures to obtain Sam's silence. Maybe Sam had refused and brought it on himself.

If she'd known, would she have stopped her father from having Sam murdered? She thought of Amy and Cy, of losing them. The question was academic. She hadn't known.

Even when her mother had shown up, Cindy couldn't know that the FBI visit had anything to do with Sam. Her father was a criminal. She didn't know the extent of the things he'd done.

But now she knew.

Now, she had to do something.

Her father wasn't around to help. He could only hurt her now. She was the only link between her father and Sam.

In Cindy's nightmares, it was the hit-and-run that stalked her.

In this reality, it was the widow.

She had to do something about the widow.

Chapter 27

COOPER

Sometimes Cooper felt guilty about Willie. Other times, he didn't. Willie was the second arrest after Cooper himself. From what Cooper understood, Willie was cooperating with the FBI, to a degree. He was providing information in dribs and drabs, blaming a hazy memory, and exacting a price for every piece of information.

Cooper had made shameful choices, and he didn't blame Willie for them. Nor did he forgive Willie for tricking him into those early murders. Even those, however, Cooper didn't absolve himself of. Willie was right when he'd pointed out the absurdity of his lies. They didn't, after all, live in a comic book. But it wasn't lost on Cooper that he never would've traveled this road had he not been acquainted with Willie. Willie hadn't made Cooper do anything, but Willie had been a major influence in Cooper's life. The only thing Cooper could say with certainty was that he wouldn't know today that he was capable of murder if he hadn't sought Willie out for a job.

~

For Cooper's forty-third birthday, Lisa gave him a new sports watch. He'd started jogging last year, and it was much appreciated. Howard gave him a book on Indigenous American philosophy. Books on philosophy made for simple gifts and were always welcome. Kathy's present to him was a bit more complicated. He tried not to give anything away, but when he opened the envelope and found two passes for a dough nut-making class, he hoped it was a mistake. When he didn't respond immediately, Kathy, a big grin on her face, filled the silence. "You love doughnuts. And we can do it together."

"Give a man a doughnut," Lisa said and patted Cooper's stomach, "and you feed him for a day."

Cooper wasn't sure how the proverb was relevant. He could buy a dozen doughnuts for less than ten dollars. When the value of his time was factored in, he couldn't hope to make them at a competitive rate. Even so, it didn't address the coercive nature of Kathy's gift. She was literally forcing him to do work. Of course, the use of *literal* was questionable. She wasn't employing violence, only love. And he'd been searching for something they could do together, just the two of them. He coached Howard's baseball team and couldn't see himself doing the same for Kathy's competitive dance. What could he add to the choreography? He could barely stomach the music. Everything from the twenty-first century sounded like noise to him.

He smiled and hugged her. "I can't wait, honey."

Why hadn't she just made him a platter of doughnuts?

~

Cooper's experience in the kitchen was limited. When he had to cook, he maintained a healthy respect for the trade-off between time and quality, invariably opting for the quick and easy, preferably a single tin can that held the entire meal.

The doughnut-making instructor, a petite and perky middle-aged woman, began with an overview of the tools they would use. Most were familiar and self-explanatory. A pot was a pot, after all. He was familiar with the concept of a stand mixer but couldn't recall ever having used one. The class lasted for two and a half hours, and Cooper silently committed to giving it his best effort.

The ingredients, as well, were all familiar to Cooper. Except cardamom. That was a new one for him. He didn't know instant yeast from eternal yeast, but as a rule in the kitchen, *instant* appealed to him.

Kathy baked occasionally with Lisa's mother, and she watched Cooper closely, lending a hand, even as she mixed her own ingredients. He watched her knead the dough and did his best to mimic her.

"Ho, ho, you *can* teach an old dog new tricks," he said when his risen dough looked identical to Kathy's.

"Are you surprised, Dad?"

"I'm not surprised by yours," he said. "I'm surprised by mine."

"I know the feeling," she said. "Sometimes it's hard to believe when things turn out right."

They used doughnut cutters to shape the dough and checked the heat of their frying oil with thermometers.

"Beautiful child," he said, addressing Kathy, as he dipped a fried doughnut in glaze, "I never would've believed I could do this."

She beamed. "Are you having fun?"

"The time of my life," he said sincerely.

Kathy tasted her doughnut and moaned. "So good."

Cooper tasted his doughnut. "Oh my!"

"Are you okay, Dad?"

The offensive taste still clinging to his tongue, he turned on the faucet at his station, bent his head, and rinsed his mouth in the sink.

"Dad?"

He picked up his tray of doughnuts and dumped them in the trash.

Chapter 28

TAMARA

"Can I spend the night at Phillip's?" Brian asked without a hello or any other form of greeting when Tamara answered the phone. "They have a toothbrush I can use," he continued before she could answer. "It's still in the box." Tamara was in the kitchen, making dinner. For two.

"Don't you want to hear what you'll be missing for dinner?" she asked. Brian had been home from camp for less than a week. Clearly, he hadn't missed home.

"I'm sure it's great. Ms. Joy said we could order pizza."

"Let me talk to her."

"So, yes, I can stay?"

"I didn't say that. Let me talk to Ms. Joy, please."

Tamara checked the water for the pasta while she waited. Still not boiling. Phillip's mother sounded exuberant when she came on the line, which made Tamara glad that Brian was with her. Tamara did her best to fake normalcy. Exuberance, even pretend, was out of her reach.

"I just wanted to make sure Brian didn't invite himself over," Tamara said after exchanging pleasantries.

"Brian is a perfect gentleman," Phillip's mother answered. "He's no trouble at all. Honestly, I think he's a good influence on Phillip."

"Great to hear." And it was. Phillip and pizza. Tamara couldn't compete with that. She hadn't wanted to say no.

~

Tamara's phone rang as she was putting away the leftover butternut squash and swiss chard pasta. She thought it might be Brian, calling to request that she drop off one of his video games or something. She kind of hoped it was. It would give her something to do. Otherwise, she would spend the evening looking for a movie she could lose herself in. The caller number was unavailable, but she answered anyway.

"Tamara?"

"Yes."

"This is Cindy Fremont. Can you meet now?"

"Now?" She glanced at her watch. It was a little after 8:00 p.m. Yes, she could meet now, but this felt overwhelmingly sudden. She needed time to mentally prepare. Knocking on Cindy's door had taken a tremendous amount of energy. "It's late. Can we do it—"

"My husband is out with the kids, which is rare. I was really hoping we could talk now."

"Okay." Tamara's heart was racing. "Maybe we can meet somewhere for coffee."

"Not in public. The People of the Torch is a sensitive subject. If you know something about them, I can't be seen with you."

"So, you were a member?"

"Something like that. There's a lot I can tell you. How about your house? Sorry for inviting myself. I don't even know if you live alone."

"I live with my son," Tamara said. "But he won't be home tonight."

"Great. What is your address? I'll head over now."

Tamara hesitated. She wasn't sure why. This woman might have answers. She recited her address.

"I'm close," Cindy said. "I'll be there in fifteen minutes."

Tamara rehearsed her questions while she waited. Fifteen minutes came and went.

Chapter 29

COOPER

Sometimes, Cooper believed, the agents shared details about his victims to torture him. Typically, they used the details to spark connections in Cooper's mind that might lead to a break in the case, but occasionally, they would tell Cooper a story that ended with a theoretical question that had no pragmatic bearing on solving anything.

Once upon a time, Special Agent Lewis began, *a boy named Eric fell in love with a girl named Julie. It could've been a beautiful love story, but there was a hitch. Julie was engaged to Eric's best friend. Eric knew it was wrong, but he couldn't let it go, so he paid a hit man (technically Willie) to kill his best friend. It was a terrible thing, but it worked out for Eric. He married Julie, and their life was like a Disney storybook.*

And then, the unexpected happened. The hit man confessed to killing the best friend. It was all downhill from there. Willie was arrested, and he provided enough information for a couple of hardworking agents to put things together. The moral of the story is obvious. If you fall in love with your best friend's fiancée, you go off and find yourself a different girl. My question is this: After all that's happened, do you think Julie will ever be able to fall in love again?

Cooper had no idea. He wondered—not aloud—if Eric had ever loved Julie to begin with. If so, he had an odd way of showing it. For Cooper, the true moral of the story was that, sometimes, it was difficult, yet crucial, to differentiate between love and infatuation.

That night, at his easel, he labeled the canvas *Infatuation*.

~

"Cooper," Talitha had said with surprise, "I didn't expect to hear from you."

"Honestly," Cooper had said, "I didn't expect to call."

It was well past sunset, and Cooper was in his office at the art gallery. Heather had locked up and left an hour before.

"But you aren't calling to ask me out again?"

Cooper shook his head, though he knew she couldn't see him.

"I'm giving you a hard time," she said. "It really is okay."

"Our picnic was wonderful—"

"You don't have to explain."

They'd met for lunch in the park. The weather had been warm and sunny, and Talitha had worn her hair up, casually beautiful in a white sundress. She'd brought the food, an avocado pine nut salad to start, followed by burritos and then chocolate-covered strawberries for dessert. Everything was delicious. They talked and laughed and walked in the park after their meal.

"I have PNS."

"PNS?" she repeated.

"Pine nut syndrome."

"You're making a joke," she said, a smile in her voice.

"I wish I were. There's nothing funny about PNS. My daughter and I took a doughnut-making class together. I'm not much of a cook. I was so proud of the look and smell of my doughnuts. They were indistinguishable from everyone else's. And then I tasted one."

"What happened?" she asked.

"It tasted like arsenic."

"Arsenic?"

"It was sad. When we got home, I cut a Sugar Kiss melon."

"What is that?"

"Imagine a cantaloupe," Cooper said. He paused. "Seriously. Are you imagining it?"

"Sure."

"It tastes good, right?"

"Is that a rhetorical question? Because I'm really trying here. I can see the color and even feel the heft in my palm. But I can't taste it."

"What do you taste?"

"Pistachios. I ate a handful before you called."

"Okay. Let's move on. Cantaloupe is delicious. But imagine it softer and sweeter. When you bite into it, your mouth fills with juice. Are you with me?"

"I'm not sure."

"It's a beautiful thing. As I said, I cut a Sugar Kiss melon open when I got home. I placed it in a bowl, but I didn't start eating until I found the right television show. I wanted to laugh. I wanted heavenly sweetness. And it tasted like arsenic."

"Arsenic again?" Talitha asked.

"It fits. Arsenic, beryllium, mercury—take your pick."

"I'll pass on all."

"I want to convey that the greatest fruit ever picked from a vine tastes like arsenic to me."

"I wasn't going to say anything, but you're still on this arsenic. Arsenic doesn't have a taste. Have you never read a murder mystery?"

"Forgive me. I'm not hip on the latest poisons," he said. "I run an art gallery."

"You're a philosopher," she said.

"Yes," he agreed. "A philosopher first."

"How does one contract pine nut syndrome? Is it contagious? We hugged after our date."

Cooper felt embarrassment at the memory. He'd thought about kissing her. He'd wanted to kiss her. But there was the weight of twenty years of unblemished marriage.

"Eating pine nuts. It was the salad."

"Oh."

"It isn't your fault," he hurried to say. "You hadn't even heard of it."

"No," she agreed. "And I certainly didn't intend to give you PNS. I'm glad you have a sense of humor about it."

Cooper smiled. He had to. He deserved PNS, maybe worse. He was grateful for PNS. It was a sign. He wouldn't share the metaphor with Talitha: a casual meal with a beautiful woman ending with a bitter taste in his mouth. It could have been far worse.

"Does it go away?" she asked.

"Two to four weeks."

"You're funny, Cooper. But you're also earnest. I mean that in a good way. I had fun on our picnic, but I realized that neither of us is cut out for this sort of thing."

Cooper agreed. "I was trying to be something I'm not."

"I've been lonely."

"Your husband is an idiot."

"Thank you for saying that."

"Do you want me to make him disappear?"

She laughed. "That won't be necessary."

"Okay. It's a standing offer."

"Thank you. I'll see you at Piney's? Once your PNS clears?"

"I don't think so," Cooper said. "That's why I called. I didn't want to just disappear. You're a special woman."

And so is my wife, Cooper thought.

Chapter 30

CINDY

Cindy felt like she was going to throw up. She'd planned meticulously to reduce her risk, but she hadn't planned for nausea. She'd purchased a prepaid mobile phone and driven to a crowded shopping plaza to call Tamara, possibly the last call Tamara would ever receive. She'd removed the battery from the phone and placed it in the trunk of her car, to be disposed of later. Her own cell phone was at home.

She'd parked a quarter mile from Tamara's house, guided by a new GPS device that she would later destroy. The walk through this neighborhood was the riskiest part. The sun had set. She wore a hat and dark clothing, but it could be problematic if an unfortunately placed home security camera captured a clear shot of her.

But there was little she could do about that. She was left with the risk of doing nothing versus the risk of doing . . . this. Doing nothing, she'd decided, was riskier.

She walked nonchalantly, feeling anything but calm. Could she actually kill someone? She could live with the guilt of it—and there would be guilt. That wouldn't be the problem. It was the act itself. Could she actually go through with it?

The need to look as if she belonged was the sole force that drove her to put one foot in front of the other—versus stopping to retch in one of Tamara's neighbors' shrubs. She thought of her children. If she didn't do this, their lives would be destroyed. They deserved to have happy, normal lives. She had to keep Amy and Cy top of mind.

Chapter 31

COOPER

Cooper wanted his family to remember him the way he'd been in the days when they'd taken each other for granted, when every moment together hadn't been precious. He'd told Lisa they didn't have to visit him in prison, but they did, weekly. He welcomed them because he wanted to support their agency in choosing how to deal with his death.

No one said much. Mostly, they sat together, Cooper absorbing the hostility that radiated off the three of them despite their best efforts to conceal it. Kathy and Howard had both decided to take the semester off from college. Cooper hoped they would get back to school soon, but he was in no position to offer advice.

Back in his cell, he arranged his art supplies and picked up where he'd left off. He labeled the fresh canvas: *Imperfect Lives*.

∼

When the damage from the pine nuts wore off and Cooper's sense of taste returned to normal, he told Lisa to make a dinner reservation. *Anywhere you want to go.* Predictably, she chose Purple Sky.

"I think we should renew our vows, throw a big party," Cooper said over wine and appetizers.

Lisa frowned. "That doesn't seem like a Cooperish thing to do."

It was true. For Cooper, the only thing worse than attending a party was being the center of attention at one. "It isn't," he agreed. "It's a Lisa thing to do. I want you and everyone to know that I'm all in on us. Do you want to renew your commitment to this thing we have?"

She smiled. "I do."

~

Portobello mushroom caps lined the countertops. Ten different types of sandwich buns sat beside them. What Cooper thought would be a team effort turned out to be a lonely task.

"Do you know what today is?" he'd asked his family at breakfast. The four of them were at the kitchen table enjoying Lisa's pancakes.

"Saturday," Howard said.

"Right, but do you know what is happening today?"

"I'm going to the mall with Laura and Stephanie," Kathy said.

"Wrong. It's Portobello Sandwich Challenge Day. I'm going to buy more portobello mushrooms than all of us can eat, and we're going to try every recipe we can find until we've found the best."

"Mom already said I can go to the mall," Kathy said.

"Fine." He turned to Howard. "You like portobello mushrooms, right?"

"Not really, Dad."

Cooper smiled reassuringly at him. "You will after today."

Howard looked to his mother. "Do I have to?"

"What is this about?" Lisa asked Cooper. "Since when do you cook?"

"This isn't about cooking," Cooper said. "This is a search for truth."

"I have a hair appointment," Lisa told him. "Maybe you can bribe your son into embarking on this journey for truth with you."

Alas, no bribes were adequate to keep Howard in the kitchen. Cooper worked alone, consulting recipes and instructional videos on his phone. He employed various techniques, mixed a multitude of sauces, and sampled a host of breads. In the end, none of the sandwiches quite compared to those from Piney's. "Oh, Talitha," Cooper whispered after tasting his final failed attempt.

Chapter 32

TAMARA

When Tamara's phone rang, she expected Cindy. It was Phillip's mother.

"I'm sorry," she said. "The boys had an argument. I don't think it was anything big, but Brian wants to come home. I tried to get them to hang out in different rooms for a few minutes, but it's a no go."

"I'm sorry," Tamara said. "They'll probably be best friends again tomorrow. I'll come get him."

"No, you stay put. I already have my car keys in hand. We'll see you in about fifteen minutes."

Now, Tamara had an excuse. She navigated to her recent calls to let Cindy know she couldn't meet tonight. But the number was unavailable. She had no way to call Cindy back.

The doorbell rang just as Tamara placed the phone down. Cindy. Tamara's stomach clenched. This woman terrified her. Every new thing Tamara learned led her down a darker path. Who knew where Cindy would lead her.

She opened the door, and Cindy stood before her, wearing black jeans, a dark-gray blouse, and a tweed newsboy hat. She carried a big black purse, and when she smiled, Tamara felt like she was being greeted by an old friend. "Thanks for meeting on short notice."

"Thank you," Tamara said and invited her in.

"You have a lovely home."

Tamara studied her. Her home wasn't unattractive, but she didn't think it was lovely. Tamara hadn't bothered with decorating. There were no paintings on the walls, no vases or houseplants. Just utilitarian furniture. "Thank you," she said. The compliment seemed sincere, if misplaced. "Would you like something to drink?" She checked the time. They had to wrap this up in ten minutes. Her plan was to ease Cindy out once Brian arrived home.

"No, thank you. It's late. I won't keep you long."

Good, Tamara thought. This might go smoother than she'd anticipated. She led her to the living room and motioned for Cindy to sit on the couch. Cindy did, placing her purse on the seat beside her. Tamara sat in the plush chair.

"I keep thinking about the name you mentioned," Cindy said. "Jason Blakely. It sounds familiar, but I don't know. I wonder if you might have any information to jog my memory."

"I really don't know anything about him," Tamara said. "Let's start at the beginning, and maybe something will spark a memory for you. How did you know Sam?"

"I lived with the People of the Torch when his parents brought him there. My mother brought me there when I was a teenager, so I knew how that was. We ended up running away together."

"Why did you run away?" Tamara asked.

Cindy shifted, clearly uncomfortable. "I had to leave. I was facing certain . . . demands. I didn't want to go alone, so I took Sam with me."

It sounded a lot like Sam's novel. *Were you lovers?* Tamara wanted to ask. "Are the People of the Torch dangerous?" she asked instead.

"They murdered a friend of mine," Cindy answered. "Their leader is in prison, probably for the rest of his life. My best friend, a great swimmer, drowned while she was a member. I don't think her death was nefarious, unless you consider being driven to suicide nefarious."

"Suicide?" Tamara whispered, almost to herself. Was that a pattern with this group?

Cindy regarded her as if waiting for a proper question.

"For a long time, I thought Sam committed suicide."

"And you don't believe that anymore?"

"It's not a matter of what I believe. A man confessed to killing Sam for money."

Cindy's mouth opened, and a change came over her face, almost as if she'd been wearing a mask that had slipped off. She seemed to recover as she asked, "You think someone from the People of the Torch paid to have him killed?"

Tamara nodded. "What do you think?"

"Who else would do it?" Cindy asked.

"That question has been on an endless loop in my head."

"This all must be very difficult for you," Cindy said.

Empathy from this stranger made Tamara tear up. She'd built Cindy up as a rival, a woman Sam might never have stopped loving. But sitting here, talking to her, she realized that Cindy was just a person. Whatever happened between Sam and her was long in the past. And it might have been nothing. As autobiographical as the novel might have been, it was also fiction, likely filled with exaggeration for the sake of entertainment. The deadly hit-and-run was proof of that.

"Where does Jason Blakely fit in?" Cindy asked.

"He paid to have Sam killed. Six weeks before he died himself."

"How do you know this?"

"The FBI."

Cindy was thoughtful for a long while. Tamara wished she knew what the woman was thinking. "How did you find me?" Cindy finally asked. "Did Sam mention me when he was alive?"

The conversation had just veered into awkward territory, but Tamara pushed through. Time was short, and she wanted to keep this moving. "No. I did a little digging and learned that you were arrested with Sam. After he escaped from the cult."

Cindy nodded. "What else did you learn?" She didn't seem to take offense at what might have been considered an invasion of her privacy. She just seemed curious.

"Sam tried to write a book." She hadn't intended to reveal that, but there it was. "I think you were in the book as a fictional character."

"Who's read the book?" she asked, and Tamara wondered why Cindy wasn't surprised that she'd been a character in Sam's book.

"Just me. After Sam died. He never showed me anything while he was working on it."

"Wow."

They locked eyes, as if connecting over that one word. There was nothing else to say about it really.

"Sam was a dear friend," Cindy said. "May I see the book?"

Tamara smiled uncomfortably. "Maybe another time. It really is getting late."

Cindy reached into her purse and pulled out a yellow gun.

Chapter 33

COOPER

Cooper awoke to panic, the feeling that he couldn't get enough oxygen. He was having a coughing fit, and his lungs felt too weak to inhale between coughs. He'd gone to sleep with a sore throat the night before, his typical harbinger of a cold, and now he wondered if he might die.

He didn't fear death, not anymore, but he had more paintings to do.

He'd been dreaming that he was jogging, and he was surprised to realize that, after his family, running was the thing he would miss most in this world. As miserable as it had been at times, his lungs had always felt trustworthy. Was there anything better than running in the dark and watching the sun rise, the pastel colors of the sky, the chirps of awakening birds?

He forced himself from the cot, wobbling before finding his footing, and settled at the easel. He had four more paintings to complete. Even on the stool, he felt unsteady and feared he would keel over. He labeled the canvas: *Grim Reaper Takes Chase*.

～

Cooper hadn't wanted to take the job. It was a Tuesday, and his master's dissertation was due on Friday. The job was in Nashville and had to be done by Saturday. Cooper had considered declining, but he hadn't worked in a while and needed the cash. At forty-eight, he was feeling pressure to build his retirement savings. According to a website Lisa had found, he would have to work until he was sixty-eight at their current savings rate. Did he really want to be doing this two years shy of seventy? And, he'd reasoned, he could work on his dissertation anywhere. His motel room in Nashville would have less distractions than home.

He tailed the cherry-red Mustang in his rental, a black Honda Accord—common, nondescript. He'd arrived that morning and was still observing for windows of opportunity. He had no special instructions. The client was the target's business partner, and there were papers the client didn't want signed, hence the deadline. Cooper knew nothing else.

He was stoked about finishing his master's program. He was the first in his family to finish college and now graduate school. But no one seemed to think it was a big deal. His mother didn't understand philosophy or why he studied it. Lisa was proud of him, if slightly perplexed.

The Mustang merged onto I-40 East and exited at signs for the airport. Cooper didn't think much of it until the Mustang made a slight right onto Terminal Drive. Maybe he's picking someone up, Cooper thought. That hope was dashed when the man turned into the economy parking lot. Cooper swore and turned in behind him. He called Willie.

"I think our man is getting on a flight."

"A flight to where?" Willie asked.

"How would I know?"

The target parked the Mustang, and Cooper pulled into a spot a few spaces away.

"Yep," Cooper said. "He just pulled a suitcase from the trunk."

"Can you do it now?" Willie asked.

"A family with two children is walking toward us. Can you find out where he's going? When he'll be back?"

~

Cooper managed to book a direct flight to Los Angeles. He was annoyed at the complication and wondered how—if—he should explain it to Lisa. He'd told her he was attending an art show in Nashville. He took comfort in the length of the flight, plenty of time to work on his dissertation. He was also glad that he hadn't checked into his motel in Nashville.

The flight to Los Angeles was smooth, uneventful, and productive for Cooper. When he stood to disembark from the plane, his right leg nearly buckled with pain, a cramp in his calf. He tried to walk it off, but it only got worse as he made his way to the car rental counter. He sat to inspect his leg. His calf and ankle were swollen and painful to the touch.

He thought about skipping the rental and catching a cab to the motel. But he heard Lisa's voice, telling him to go to the emergency room. He thought back over the last few days. Had he done anything that could explain this? He'd worked out at the gym the day before, nothing out of the ordinary—treadmill, weights.

He caught a cab and told the driver to take him to the nearest emergency room.

Chapter 34

CINDY

M y son. He's on the—"

Tamara's words didn't register until after Cindy had fired the Taser. She would've given Tamara a second to finish the sentence, but Cindy was operating on adrenaline. Firing the Taser had been easy, but the violence of it made Cindy want to look away. Tamara's body stiffened, and she groaned as the darts became embedded in her stomach and thigh. Cindy had thirty seconds, no time to look away. She dropped the Taser, and as it continued to emit a current that caused Tamara's muscles to involuntarily contract, she pulled a roll of electrical tape from her purse. As if she'd done this before—she hadn't—she had Tamara's wrists bound in seconds, with no time to spare. Tamara recovered almost as quickly as the Taser had exhausted its charge.

"What are you doing?" she screamed, struggling against the tape.

"I won't hurt you," Cindy said.

"You've already hurt me."

That was probably true, but Cindy ignored it. "I just need that book. Every copy. Tell me where to find it, and I'll be on my way."

"It's on Sam's laptop," Tamara said. Her eyes darted around the room, and Cindy knew she was looking for opportunity.

"Stand up," Cindy said. "Show me."

Tamara continued to struggle. Maybe she was trying to stand. Cindy couldn't tell. Cognizant of Tamara's head and feet—potential weapons—she bent over to remove the darts from Tamara's chest. "Stay still," she said as she worked the darts from the fabric of Tamara's clothes. She stepped back, loaded the laser with a fresh cartridge, and returned it to her bag. "Relax," she said to Tamara. "Get up and show me to the laptop. The quicker we do this, the quicker I'll be out of here."

Tamara did as she was told. Cindy pulled a small flashlight from her purse to light their path up the darkened stairs. Since entering the house, she'd avoided touching anything. She wasn't going to start turning on lights.

"The laptop is on the dresser." Tamara's breathing was labored, but she seemed relatively calm, given the circumstances. Cindy located the laptop with her flashlight beam. She picked it up and stepped quickly away from Tamara.

"There are no paper copies?"

"No."

"Have you emailed a copy to anyone?"

"No."

"Lie on the bed."

"Why?"

"If you want me to leave, do as I say."

Tamara complied.

Cindy pulled a thick plastic bag from her purse. She'd been dreading this moment.

"What is that?" Tamara asked.

"You're going to be okay," Cindy said. She just had to get the bag over Tamara's head and then secure it around her neck with electrical tape. Cindy had spent hours considering how to do this deed. A knife wasn't an option. The idea of blood, warm but cooling on her hands, was repulsive. A blunt object would be worse. Ideally, she would've employed poison, something deliverable through a syringe. But she had no idea what that would be or where she would get it. Suffocation was the second-best option she'd come up with. She moved toward Tamara.

"No," Tamara whispered, horror in her eyes.

"Mom."

Cindy froze. The voice had come from downstairs. "Who is that?" she asked Tamara, her voice hushed.

"My son. Don't hurt him."

"Stop him from coming up here. Tell him to watch TV or something."

"Brian," Tamara called. "Leave the house now. Knock on a neighbor's—"

Cindy swore and tried to force the bag over Tamara's head. Tamara thrashed wildly.

"Mom." The voice again, close now. Cindy turned to see a miniature version of Sam standing in the doorway. She could almost see Sam now, the sad, infatuated teen she'd met years ago. She'd felt sorry for him then, and she'd wondered later if she could have loved him. It was a question she'd never answered. And now, in the midst of committing murder, she decided that she could have. Had things been different.

Tamara was thrashing wildly now, trying to turn her body enough to kick Cindy. Cindy reached into her purse for the Taser. She pointed it at Brian, and Tamara screamed, feral, the sound Cindy imagined any helpless mother would make. She thought of her own children, but it wasn't enough to steel her resolve. Brian stood frozen, his eyes moving between the Taser and his mother, her wrists bound, on the bed. Cindy motioned with the Taser, and Brian complied, moving to the left, clearing a path to the doorway. Cindy walked by him and didn't stop until she was back at her car.

Chapter 35

COOPER

~

Because of Cooper's cancer, the man he'd followed to Los Angeles was alive, a murder prevented. Twenty-one arrests had been made, nine confessions obtained, and seven persons of interest had been identified. FBI and local police were still following up on leads. Two convicted murderers were well on their way to exoneration.

His diagnosis didn't have as much impact as his bad decisions had, but his illness was making a difference. It was all part of his story. He took his seat at the easel and labeled the canvas: *Mortality*.

~

Cooper had rarely considered his mortality. An ironic oversight, he reflected, given his profession. On the other hand, like every other living human, he'd had to make it through each minute of each day. He'd had to brush his teeth, and mow the lawn, and pick the kids up from soccer practice. Dwelling on the inevitability of his demise was not conducive to enduring the monotony of living.

Alone in the hotel room, Cooper remembered something his ailing grandfather had said back when Cooper was in high school: *You go to the doctor for one thing, and they find a whole other thing that's way more serious than the first thing.*

Cooper had understood what his grandfather was saying, but his youth had been a buffer against feeling it.

Stage IV pancreatic cancer.

He'd gone from a cramp in his calf to the doctor asking how long his eyes had been tinged yellow—not long because Cooper hadn't noticed it—to CT scans and endoscopic ultrasounds and blood tests, to cursory overviews of pancreatic cancer. It was rarely caught early because of its tendency to be asymptomatic. Cooper wasn't the exception. The cancer had spread to his stomach and liver and probably elsewhere, but they hadn't done enough tests to be certain.

Cooper typically stayed in inexpensive motels when he traveled for work, but he wasn't working. He wasn't on vacation, either, but he'd booked himself into a nice room at a first-rate hotel. He wanted the comfort of room service. He wanted the luxury of uninterrupted thought.

He would need to call Lisa soon and tell her something. She still thought he was at an art show in Nashville.

He had a stack of pamphlets from the hospital, and he trashed them all, save one on palliative care. From the moment he'd heard his options—chemo or radiation, chemo and radiation—he'd known that he wouldn't accept treatment. He had a prognosis of six months, and he intended to die the way he'd killed: dispassionately.

Chapter 36

TAMARA

Tamara would never forget the look on Brian's face in those brief moments after Cindy left and before he ran for scissors to cut the tape binding her wrists. She was probably projecting, but she thought she'd seen a realization in his face that she couldn't protect him.

Every mother understood the painful truth of her limitations to protect her child. The reality was just starker now for Tamara. She'd watched helplessly as Cindy aimed the Taser at Brian. That moment, this night, would haunt her forever.

She hugged her son for a long while, both of them crying. And then she retrieved the card the FBI agents had left for her. Their visit felt like a lifetime ago. She dialed the number.

Chapter 37

COOPER

Why choose to confess?

Cooper had been asked the question many times in many ways. The answer seemed malleable, or maybe it was more like water in his hands, tangible but difficult to hold.

As he lay on the cot in his cell, the connection between his spirit and his body palpably tenuous, he wondered if he'd confessed to make his death a little more bearable. He was alone, a prisoner, but he didn't dread leaving the world behind. He might feel differently if he were with his family. What would it be like to lie down beside Lisa each night, not knowing if he would wake up? His children—as much as he missed them—would be reminders of what he was losing, what he would never see: their college graduations, their weddings, the births of their children. Dying alone, in prison, Cooper believed, was easier than dying in his living room, surrounded by family. But it wasn't easy. To ease his mind, he moved to his easel to paint.

~

Many people died sudden deaths: strokes, cardiac arrest, car accidents, gunshot wounds. A day after his diagnosis, Cooper oscillated between feeling more and less fortunate than those souls, depending on his mood. But Cooper wouldn't be ruled by his emotions, not at the end. He wanted to end life clear eyed, with his rational mind intact.

He sat on his room's private balcony, sixteen floors up, the air breezy and cool. He sipped hot coffee and considered the end of life. In a sense, he was already dead, unshackled from the burden of long-term planning, the requisite pragmatism for building a future. He could make different choices now. He could take an honest look at his life, how he'd lived, and he could decide how he wanted to die.

He'd been the best husband and father he could be. He loved Lisa and the twins, and more importantly, they knew it. They would never doubt his love for them. He was at peace with the family man he'd been. Sure, he could've done better, been more attentive, but he would not spend the next six months rewriting the past nineteen years.

When he thought of the murders, the way he'd made his living, he felt shame. He'd always felt shame, when he'd allowed himself to dwell on it, but he'd been trapped. It was all he'd had to take care of his family, and he'd made peace with that. Until now.

Now, he needed to find a way to atone for that shame. He had no idea what came after life, but if he met his maker, Cooper couldn't present himself empty handed. And if there was nothing, as the atheists insisted, then he couldn't leave this life an unrepentant killer.

These were big thoughts, and as Cooper grappled with them, he realized that he wasn't completely free of the burden of long-term planning. He had life insurance, but it wouldn't be enough. The twins had three more years of college and then possibly graduate school, and there was the rest of Lisa's life to think about. He still had to worry about money.

Money.

Even in death, it was a powerful force.

Chapter 38

CINDY

How was girls' night out?" Ross asked. He and her mother were sitting at the kitchen table, finishing a pie. Cindy had hoped he'd be in his study. She was home just for a few moments to retrieve something, and she didn't want to see anyone.

"Fine," she said and forced a smile. "Are the kids doing homework?"

"Purportedly," Ross answered. "They're in their room."

Cindy could barely look at him.

He stood and started to gather the pie plates.

"Don't," Annalise said. "I'll get it."

"You sure?"

She nodded, and he pecked Cindy on the lips. "I think I'll turn in early."

"Good idea," Cindy said. She started to follow him.

"Cindy, wait," said Annalise.

"Go on up," Cindy told Ross.

"Sit." Her mother motioned to the chair across from her, recently vacated by Ross.

"I don't have time," Cindy said, agitated. Honestly, she didn't know how much time she had. Tamara knew her address, and certainly she'd called the police by now.

"Please."

"Say what you need to say quickly," Cindy snapped, glancing at her watch. She didn't sit.

"Your husband doesn't know you like I do. Something is seriously wrong. What is it?"

Cindy felt an inexplicable rush of affection for her mother. She wanted to cry. But she didn't have time, even for that. "Take a ride with me. Be ready in three minutes. Bring your purse."

~

They didn't speak as Cindy backed out of the driveway. She was on edge, fearing the sight of flashing lights, the sound of a police siren. She was turning onto the expressway when her mother said, "What was so important back there?"

"A key. To a safe-deposit box."

"Are you going to tell me why you're so upset?"

"How do you know I'm upset?"

"I don't know how. But I do. Talk to me."

Cindy inhaled deeply. "Why did you come here, Mom? The FBI talked to you about a father I didn't know. Why come to me?"

Her mother was silent for a long while. "The man they suspected your father of having killed . . . ," she said slowly, hesitantly. "I didn't recognize his name. But they showed me a picture. It was the boy you left with."

Cindy nodded. "What do you want to know?"

"I want to know you're okay."

"I'm not okay. I have to disappear now."

"What does that mean?"

"I've known for a long time this could happen. It's harder than I thought it would be."

"Can Ross help? He's a brilliant attorney, right?"

"I don't know. Maybe. I can't take the risk. I was arrested after I left the People of the Torch. I spent two weeks in pretrial detention before the public defender pleaded me out. It was horrible. I can't go to prison. I don't want to leave Ross and the kids, but . . ." Cindy wanted to pull the car over. She wanted to sob in her mother's arms. But she had to keep it together. She couldn't make any mistakes. "I want you to be their grandmother." Cindy hadn't planned to say that. She hadn't planned this ride with her mother. She'd intended to retrieve the safe-deposit box key and disappear.

"How can I help?" her mother asked.

"You can't."

"Where are you going?"

"It's better if you don't know."

"I can buy you time. Give me a credit card. Tell me which way to drive, and I'll do it. I'll make charges with your card. Throw them off."

Cleverness had never been something Cindy associated with her mother. Perhaps she'd been too quick to judge. "You could go to prison for that."

"I don't care. I'll rent a car for you in my name. You can take that. I'll rent a second car and lead them in the wrong direction."

"I want you to be a grandmother to Amy and Cy. You'll be good."

"I will, but right now, I'm going to be a mother to you."

A tear rolled down Cindy's cheek.

"What will you do for money?" her mother asked.

"I have cash and diamonds in the safe-deposit box. There's also an offshore account that will keep me going for a while."

"Does Ross know?"

Cindy shook her head. "He doesn't know anything. I want you to look after him too."

"I'll never see you again?" Her mother began to cry now.

"You went nineteen years without seeing me." There was no bitterness in Cindy's voice, but she couldn't quite force a smile. "I want you to be a grandmother to my children. Maybe you can help them to understand why I've done what I've done. Why I'm leaving now."

"There's no other way?" her mother asked.

Cindy shook her head. "I tried the other way."

~

They rented a room that night at the extended-stay where Cindy's mother had once lived. The place was a dump, but the clerk welcomed cash and didn't ask for ID. When they entered their shared room with double beds, Cindy noticed the clock on the nightstand glowing red: *10:30.*

She shuddered.

~

Cindy was waiting at the bank when they opened the following morning. She didn't anticipate problems. She was almost certainly a fugitive by now, but she wasn't one of the FBI's most wanted. Not yet. It would take some time for the pieces to come together.

She retrieved the cash and diamonds from the safe-deposit box without incident. She returned to the motel and waited while her mother took a portion of the cash to open a checking account. Her mother had spent the morning calling banks until she found one that could issue a debit card on the spot.

Cindy drove them to the airport and parked in long-term parking. She gave her mother credit cards in the name of Cindy Fremont, and her mother handed her the debit card. She felt a pang at seeing the name: Jessica Taylor, the mother she'd grown up with and loved. Her mother rented a car, and they hugged before Cindy climbed behind the wheel. "Tell Amy and Cy they're survivors," she said before she drove away. Her mother would rent a second car from a different agency. Cindy had directed her to drive north toward the Canadian border. Cindy drove south.

Chapter 39

COOPER

Cooper wasn't a war hero or a politician, but one night, long ago, unable to sleep, he'd watched a documentary about Ulysses S. Grant. Indigent and ailing with throat cancer, Grant spent his last days writing his memoir, completing it five days before his death. If Cooper remembered correctly, the memoir netted Grant's widow the equivalent of what would be $12 million today.

Cooper, barely able to sit upright for the pain in his abdomen, thought of Grant as he settled at his easel. He was down to his last painting, which was just as well. He didn't have much left in him.

This painting would be the most difficult yet, the memory the hardest to bear. He labeled it *Saying Goodbye* and began with dark colors and broad strokes.

~

The day Cooper turned himself in at the Los Angeles field office, Special Agents Morris and Clark interrogated him for three hours before he asked to make a phone call. He was taken to a private room, but he had no illusions of privacy. If they hadn't wanted to record his call, they would've let him use his cell phone. He called Lisa.

"Cooper? I thought I would hear from you last night," she said, and he was taken aback by the nonchalance in her voice. He was going to change everything for her, and she had no idea.

He began with his cancer diagnosis.

"Why are you telling me this over the phone?" she asked, her voice shaky.

He didn't want to go on, but he did. He told her about his other life, the murders. She screamed and cried. She didn't believe him. She demanded that he get on a plane immediately to come home.

And then, he told her why they were having this conversation by phone. He would be taken into custody soon. He would spend the rest of his life as a prisoner of the federal government.

Chapter 40

TAMARA

Tamara and Brian looked at each other when the doorbell rang. It was shortly after noon on a Saturday. She answered Brian's unspoken question with a shrug.

"Maybe we shouldn't answer," he whispered. His anxiety was painful to Tamara, but she understood. She was anxious too. Cindy Fremont had disappeared, leaving a host of uncertainties behind. The biggest: Would she come back to finish the job?

Tamara hadn't opened Sam's laptop, but she thought about his manuscript often. Cindy's incursion into their lives had transformed her interpretation of it. Cindy had been nervous about who'd read the manuscript, but she hadn't asked what was in it. Tamara concluded that Cindy had already known and was willing to kill to conceal it. Thus, the hit-and-run had been real. And Tamara's world had been rocked again. She'd known Sam for nine years, had been married to him for seven, and there was so much she hadn't known about him. She could probably spend the next nine years reconciling the Sam she knew with the events he'd recorded, but she wouldn't do that. She didn't want to forget Sam, but she needed for him to live in her past. He wasn't her future.

And Sam's fate wasn't Brian's future. To her surprise, Sam's manu-script had turned out to be a gift to them both. The Sam she'd known had emotional issues but nothing indicative of the traumas he'd endured. The Sam she'd known had been a good husband, a loving father, and a hardworking quant in spite of the bouts of depression he'd struggled against. The Sam she'd known and the boy she'd read about made her realize that Brian's psyche wasn't a glass ornament waiting to be shat-tered. Brian was born of tough stock, on both sides, and he would be okay. Better than okay, because she was there to assure that he would have a stable and happy childhood. If she could look to the future and not give up on her own happiness, she could teach him everything he needed to know.

And when he was older and ready, he could learn about his father and Cindy and all the things that had happened to them and between them. One day, Sam's manuscript would belong to Brian. He could read it and draw his own conclusions.

For now, her priority was restoring Brian's sense of security. "Let's do this," she said, projecting confidence she didn't feel. "I'll ask who it is. If I know the person, I'll open the door. If anything bad happens, which it won't, use my phone to call 911." She handed him her cell.

He agreed and followed her to the door. She was surprised when Leonard Williams's voice answered hers. She opened the door for him.

"I have news," he said by way of hello. "I think it warrants a visit."

She invited him in and introduced him to Brian. "Head up to your room for a few minutes while we talk." Brian hesitated but did as he was told. He took her phone with him, ready, no doubt, to call 911.

"I don't want him to hear bad news," she whispered to Leonard.

Leonard responded by silently passing his phone to Tamara.

She gasped.

She was staring at Malik's face, an aged, older version.

"I've never stopped thinking about Malik," Leonard said. "When you hired me to research your late husband's past, I decided to give it one more shot."

Tamara stared at him. When Leonard didn't continue, she asked, "Are you going to tell me where he is?"

"Living in a commune in Southern California. He seems to be doing well."

Chapter 41

COOPER

Cooper was nervous as the corrections officer led him to the waiting room. He hadn't spoken to Heather Walker since the day after his confessions. He'd called her at the art gallery, and he'd been succinct, except for his apologies, which were effusive. He told her that he'd been arrested, and that the gallery would be closing. Other than that, there hadn't been much to say. Heather had become collateral damage, and there was nothing he could do about it. Now, he needed her help.

She stood as he approached the table. They might've hugged had the circumstances been different, but inmates and visitors weren't allowed physical contact.

"You look good," she said with an awkward smile.

He laughed. "I don't. But thank you." He barely recognized the gaunt man who peered out from mirrors. "You look good," he said as they took their seats.

"I am good," she told him. "I started a business with my severance." Lisa had given her a generous sum when the gallery closed. "Event planning. It's going well."

"I'm not surprised," he said.

She talked for a few minutes about the business before silence descended.

"So, Gary has been in touch," Cooper said, referring to his lawyer. Heather nodded.

"I wanted to sit down with you before you make a decision. Give you an opportunity . . . Is there anything you want to ask me, anything you want to know?"

"Why did you confess?" she asked.

Cooper nodded. He'd been asked the question more than once, and though he was always honest, his answer changed each time. "I can't undo the things I've done," he told her. "I can't prevent others from doing them. But, maybe, there is someone out there, somewhere, and I will give that person pause."

Heather nodded. "I'll do it," she said, and Cooper felt relief. Since his confessions, he'd created thirteen paintings. Heather would sell them when the time was right on the murderabilia market. She would earn a generous commission—as had been outlined for her via Cooper's lawyer—and the remainder of the money would go to Lisa and the twins. Cooper trusted Heather. She knew his family well. Over the sixteen years she'd managed his art gallery, she'd eaten many dinners at the Franklins' table.

She told Cooper goodbye, and it was painful. Goodbyes carried a permanence now that left him feeling empty and lonely. He carried those feelings back to his cell and lay down with them on his cot. He considered her question: *Why did you confess?* He'd answered her as truthfully as he could. But lately, he'd come to suspect something about himself, another truth. Had he confessed because he was looking for a final shot to succeed as an artist?

As he drifted to sleep, he hoped, for the first time, that he wouldn't wake up. He was ready. He'd done everything he could do. His story was complete.

Chapter 42

TAMARA

Tamara and Malik exchanged emails for three weeks before he agreed to her visit. Melinda and Brian accompanied her to the airport, where she boarded a flight to Los Angeles. It was the strangest thing she'd ever done, flying across the country to visit the brother she hadn't seen in four years, whom, in her darker moments, she'd assumed was dead.

His girlfriend, June—a bubbly woman in her early forties—met Tamara at baggage claim. She wore jeans and cowgirl boots and had long silver hair pulled into a single braid. Tamara was starving but declined June's offer to stop for food. They had a two-hour drive ahead, and Tamara didn't want to waste a moment.

The two women made small talk about the weather, politics, and their astonishment at the passage of time. Open fields had given way to expanses of apple orchards when Tamara broached the subject of Malik. June was open and explained that Malik had found tranquility at their commune four years before. He still had symptoms from his illness, but he'd learned how to manage them. He and June had fallen in love, and when she'd asked about his family, he'd told her they were part of an old life he'd had to leave behind.

"Why did Malik agree to see me?" Tamara asked. It had only happened on the condition that she would come alone.

"He's worried about you. What you learned about your late husband's murder shook him up. He wants to make sure you're okay."

If he worried about me, she wondered, if he cared at all, why did he leave?

The commune owned a fifty-acre vegetable farm. Malik had shared via email that he worked the fields and built custom furniture. He'd told Tamara that the physical labor and days spent outdoors were good for him.

When they pulled up to an old farmhouse, a tall man stepped out onto the porch. Tamara's stomach did flip-flops when she realized it was Malik. She bolted from the car and ran to him. She didn't know she was crying until he pulled away from her embrace to wipe her tears.

"Goodness," he said. "It must be like this in heaven when your loved ones come home."

~

It was surreal, walking the land with him, eating fresh figs and talking. The only evidence of time's passage was the years etched into his face. Occasionally, they passed someone, and Malik would stop to introduce her.

"How did you come to be here?" Tamara asked him.

"Meteor showers."

When he didn't say more, she said simply: "Explain."

"I traveled here in 2012 to watch the meteor shower. I didn't leave."

Tamara never would have anticipated that answer, and yet, she wasn't surprised. Without telling anyone, Malik had run off to chase meteor showers and, somehow, had ended up where he needed to be. "Why didn't you come back?" she asked.

"I fit in here. Everything just seemed right. A psychiatrist lives here, the first one I've ever clicked with. What are the odds? I feel better here than I ever have, and I was afraid to come back. I didn't want to fall into old ways."

"You should let the family visit," Tamara told him. "Mom, Dad, and Melinda would love to see you."

He seemed to consider her words and then shook his head. "Maybe one day. I'm still afraid of falling into old ways."

On the flight home, Tamara felt the ache of a distinct loss. She'd told Malik she would visit again, but she doubted he would allow it. And whatever happened, she would respect his wishes. If he wouldn't let her return, she would content herself with knowing he was okay. She would forever remember him in the sunlight, eating fresh figs. The image hurt now, but she could already sense that, one day soon, it would bring her peace unlike she'd felt in a long time.

～

It wasn't like Tamara to show up at a man's house unannounced. This occasion, however, warranted a big gesture. Kenneth had left several messages over the past few weeks until, finally, he'd given up.

"I'm sorry I haven't been in touch," she said, resisting the urge to squirm beneath his gaze.

He stood in the threshold of his front door, handsome as ever and watching her warily. "I assume you had your reasons," he said coolly.

Tamara nodded. "None of them had anything to do with you," she said. "How I feel about you."

"Okay."

"Okay." She thought about walking away. Suddenly, showing up here felt like a bad idea. "I've missed you," she said, "and I'm not sure what that means."

Kenneth smiled. "I think it means you like me."

"I do." Tamara fidgeted. "Like you. I just don't know how far I can go with that. I don't think I'm ready for a relationship. I may never be."

"I've never asked you for a relationship," Kenneth said. And Tamara felt confused. He'd asked her on dates. Wasn't that asking for a relationship? She had no idea anymore, which was why she hated the thought of dating. "I just asked to get to know you."

Tamara smiled. "I'd like that. I just . . ."

"Can't make any promises," he finished for her.

"Right."

He stepped onto the porch and took her hand. "We aren't teenagers," he said. "Although I've managed to retain my youthful charm." She smiled at him, and he smiled back. "We both understand that life doesn't hand out guarantees. We get to know each other, and we see what happens. We'll do what feels right. Whatever comes, I can handle it."

"Hugging you feels right," she said.

He opened his arms, and they embraced.

~

Tamara wasn't the only one who rested easier knowing that Malik was alive. Her parents were lighter somehow, younger, as if they'd discovered the fountain of youth. Perhaps they had. Melinda, the one who had been shielded (or so everyone assumed) from the worst of Malik's illness, was perhaps the most profoundly impacted.

"Did the FBI confirm the hit-and-run?" Melinda asked. She and Tamara were cleaning the carpet in Melinda's empty living room, the final chore in the house.

Tamara shook her head. "They found an unsolved hit-and-run that matches the timing and location, but they don't have evidence linking it to Cindy and Sam. Cindy might be the only living person who knows for sure."

"They'll catch her," Melinda said. "Where can you hide these days?"

Tamara shrugged. Even with mass media, criminal databases, and the digital records everyone inevitably generated, people still figured out how to hide.

The two sisters inspected the carpet for blemishes before they had to admit they were finished. There was nothing for Melinda to do now but leave. She was moving to Austin, and while Tamara was happy for her and Jeff, she didn't know what she would do without her sister. She felt her conviction not to cry slipping away.

"Don't you dare," Melinda said, her own smile tinged with melancholy. Melinda had broached the idea of Tamara relocating to Austin, but that wouldn't be possible until after Tamara finished her doctorate, at least a few years. "We cried enough last night."

They had. Over wine.

Tamara had spent the past week helping Melinda pack for the move.

Melinda's change of heart had felt as sudden to Tamara as every other crazy event of the past few months. Melinda herself didn't know how to explain it, but she'd hazarded a guess.

I didn't realize how everything with Malik has affected me. Knowing that he's alive has freed me to really think about what I've been through, what we've all been through. I was terrified of a future with Jeff, specifically starting a family, so terrified that I couldn't even face the existence of my fear.

So, you're over the fear, Tamara had asked, hopeful that they were all healing.

I'm not over it, Melinda had said. *I'm aware of it. I'm able to face it. That makes all the difference.*

Tamara couldn't say why, but at this moment, so close to Melinda's departure, she felt something similar. She was scared and she was sad, and yet, for the first time ever maybe, she felt fully prepared to embrace the future. She was a good mother, and Brian was a good kid, and they had a lot of good things ahead of them. Even if Cindy was never captured, at least Tamara knew what had happened.

She didn't know what would come next. But she was ready.

Epilogue

CINDY

Cindy listened to the phone ring, the strange quality of the tone she'd come to associate with international calls. Or maybe the strangeness was in her mind, a fabrication of her inner turbulence. She clenched the phone, braced against the rush of emotions she'd feel at the sound of his voice.

"Hello."

She'd expected the ache of longing, but that foreknowledge did nothing to prepare her for the agony of it. She nearly cried out, but she caught herself. As always, she stayed silent.

"Hello?" he repeated, a question this time. She always called in the middle of the night, and he always answered with a clear, strong voice as if he'd been awake just for her call. It was 3:30 a.m. his time, 2:30 p.m. hers.

There were a few beats of silence before he said, "Cindy?"

She didn't reply. She never did.

"I miss you. We all do."

She missed him too.

"It's not easy for the kids, but they're doing their best. We have good days. They aren't all good, but we have them."

She missed the kids more than she'd known she could miss anything.

"Your mother has been a big help. She tells the kids stories from your childhood." He chuckled softly. "The stories help me too."

She even missed her mother.

"We all know who you are. Whatever you've done, your family knows you." His voice cracked, and that brought tears to Cindy's eyes. "We love you."

She loved them too. She'd once thought that, bolstered by that love, she could do anything. She was learning about herself, her limitations. She'd thought she could kill with her own hands to protect the life she'd built. She'd been wrong. And then she'd thought she could walk away from that life.

"Ross." Her voice was weak, but she'd spoken his name clearly.

"Cindy," he said. "Cindy." He spoke her name as if it were an invocation.

"I'm coming home, Ross. I don't care what happens to me. I never should have left, and I'm coming home."

Acknowledgments

I would like to thank my top-flight literary agent Sarah Bedingfield for all she does and especially for keeping me focused on what's important. Working with you is always a pleasure. I am fortunate to have Selena James as an editor. Her uncommon acumen and gift for teaching not only improved this book but also made me a better writer. Thank you for always being generous with your time and wisdom. Wendy Muruli and her incredible insights made this story much better than it could have been otherwise. Bill Siever has an amazing eye. I hope to one day write a manuscript that will spare your red ink. Thank you, Elsa Klingensmith-Parnell, for helping me to ensure that I say what I want to say in the way I want to say it. Elyse Lyon is a whiz at catching my mistakes, and, because of that, I can rest easy. Thank you, Kyra Wojdyla, for steering this book and its author through production. And, of course, the entire team at Little A is wonderful and deserves a shout-out.

I enjoyed talks about astronomy with my colleague and friend Michael Roybal, a true Renaissance man. Thank you for sending me the cool astronomical toys. For support and generosity, I want to thank Tanya White, Tracee Washington, Sally Stieghan, Isaac Terry, Vanessa Hsu, Reem Fareed, Sita Romero, and Suzanne Brockmann.

Thank you, Ashley, my inquisitive daughter, for asking what this novel is about. Explaining anything at all about this book to a six-year-old required me to think deeply about what I was writing. And thanks to Melissa, my wife, for helping me with the adventures of Cooper and his cat, the one thing from the book I could share with our daughter.

About the Author

C. J. Washington is a data scientist and writer. He has a master's degree in computer science from the Georgia Institute of Technology and lives in Atlanta, Georgia, with his wife and daughter.